Last Chance

Fortress Security, Volume 19

Rebecca Deel

Published by Rebecca Deel, 2024.

To my amazing husband. I love you.

rebec
Your address

Your phone number   88,200 words.
Your e-mail address
(Your agent's name)
(Your agent's address)

REBECCA DEEL

SAWYER AND JANIE
by

Chapter One

Janie Moran woke, unsure what yanked her from an exhausted sleep on board the plane. The jet wasn't moving. They had landed already?

She frowned. Surely not. Janie knew she hadn't been asleep long enough to have already reached the United States. Her body felt as though she'd just closed her eyes.

She sat up and looked at the man seated next to her. His expression was grim, his gaze fixed on the front of the plane.

Across the aisle, two older women occupying the seats across the aisle were pale, eyes wide and filled with fear.

Janie twisted in her seat to look around the cabin. Everyone's expressions were grim and filled with fear.

"Turn around," a man shouted in Spanish from the front of the plane.

She jerked around and discovered two men stood by the cockpit door brandishing multiple weapons each. Both of them glared at her with contempt and arrogance.

"No one may speak or leave their seats."

The second man spoke. "If you disobey, everyone on the plane will suffer."

Disbelief settled like a rock in her gut. These two men had hijacked the plane?

Another male voice from the back of the plane chimed in next. "If you cooperate, we will release you unharmed." Left unsaid was what would happen if they didn't cooperate.

Janie gripped the arms of her seat. Holy smoke. Her plane had been hijacked. Why? What did these men want?

This plane was loaded with people. Three armed men controlling over 200 people was a recipe for disaster. Eventually, someone would try something heroic, challenging the hijackers for control of the plane.

Her brother and his wife would be horrified that her flight from Talca, Chile to Nashville, Tennessee had been hijacked. Her brother's wife, Maria, had begged Janie to take a vacation from Natural Bliss, her natural soap shop, and come to Chile for a visit.

Watching the men sporting guns, she wished she'd delayed her departure. Janie had enjoyed meeting David's wife of three months in person, and now they were making Janie an aunt. Weighing the danger she faced, Janie wished she'd opted for a different flight or just stayed home altogether.

Janie sighed. She'd longed for a little excitement in her life. This definitely wasn't what she had in mind. An attractive man with an interesting job was more in line with her dreams.

She looked out the window to see if she could figure out where they were. Nothing identified their location. Across the tarmac, other planes moved away from the hijacked plane. Police vehicles waited a distance away. She saw the tower but no name on the building. This place reminded her of Talca's airport and countryside. The hijackers had probably taken over the plane and forced the pilot to land somewhere in Central America or Mexico.

Two armed men strode up the aisle to the front to confer with the other two hijackers. So, the hijackers totaled four, all heavily armed with guns and knives. Their voices were too low for Janie to hear the words. Something had upset the four men. Their plans didn't appear to be working out. When did they ever?

She tried to concentrate on the words spoken between the men, but it was impossible with crying women scattered around the cabin.

After several minutes of heated discussion, the kidnappers faced the crowd. "Listen carefully. If you have small kids on this plane, you and your kids go to the back to leave the plane. If you're over 50, leave. Everyone else stays."

A surge of movement from people in the designated categories led to a crowded aisle. By the time the exodus ended, the number of passengers remaining had dwindled to about 50. Definitely more manageable for the hijackers.

A quick glance told Janie that she was one of only five women left on the plane. That made her uneasy.

The man with a scar running from the corner of his eye to the corner of his mouth surveyed the people left in the cabin. Dissatisfaction filled his expression. He barked out orders to his compatriots in Spanish too fast for Janie to understand. She grimaced, wishing she'd paid more attention to her Spanish language lessons from Maria.

The other three, however, had no problems understanding the orders. Two of them hustled to the back of the plane.

Scar Face said, "No one move."

Right. Like she and the rest of the hostages had anywhere to go. If they made a run for it, Scar Face and his buddies would shoot them down in cold blood.

Fifteen minutes later, the other two hijackers returned to the front and had another whispered conversation with Scar Face. He gave a curt nod and turned his attention to the remaining passengers. "Stand up. Empty your pockets and leave everything behind. You will follow orders in silence. If you fight or try to run, you will be shot." He gave an evil grin. "It's pointless to try. No one is coming to your rescue. If you want to live, you will obey."

Janie stood along with the rest of the hostages, looking with longing at her cell phone and purse still in her seat, and moved into the aisle. They shuffled their way to the back of the plane. At the back exit, she noticed movable stairs had been positioned for them to exit the plane.

"Are we being released?" one man dared to ask.

The nearest hijackers clubbed him on the side of the head with the butt of his weapon. "Silence!"

The hostage dropped to the floor, clutching the side of his head.

"Up." The hijacker kicked the hostage in the side and pointed his gun at the fallen man. "On your feet or I'll shoot you."

Two other male hostages reached down and hauled the injured man to his feet and held him steady as they moved toward the exit.

Shaken, Janie edged away from the hijackers as she passed them. Near the exit, she still felt their gazes burning into her back.

She fell in behind the other hostages and descended the stairs. Once on the tarmac, two more armed men herded them toward a delivery van.

Janie stared at the vehicle in disbelief. Fifty people wouldn't fit inside that van.

One hijacker near the van motioned with his gun for the women to climb into the back. One by one, Janie and the others complied. Soon, ten men joined them, including the man who had been seated beside her. Guess the hostages had figured out controlling 50 people would be a problem long term. Because the van had no windows in the back, Janie and the others sat in darkness and heat.

Definitely a tropical climate. Hot and humid. Despite the uncomfortable temperature, Janie shivered. How would anyone find them? As far as she knew, neither she nor her fellow hostages had anything with them. No cell phones or other devices with the capability of contacting authorities and asking for help. If they escaped, where would they go? How would they reach help?

She wished she had a map stuffed in a pocket. Not that it would do her much good. Janie couldn't find her way out of a wet paper bag with neon signs lit up, pointing her in the right direction.

"What do these creeps want?" one woman asked in a shaky voice. "I have money. I can pay ransom."

"If you're smart, you won't mention that," snapped one man. "They might take the money and dump your body in the jungle."

Several of the women gasped. Janie flinched. The guy was probably right, but saying as much to an already terrified woman wouldn't help matters.

A woman near Janie sobbed. "I just want to go home to my husband and children, but we don't have any money. I used up all our savings to be by my mother's bedside in the hospital."

Janie reached to her right and wrapped her hand around the other woman's. "All we can do is wait to find out what they want and remain calm. Don't antagonize them."

"They have to let us go," another woman chimed in. "This isn't fair."

A man to Janie's left said, "Some terrorists make a living by taking hostages and demanding ransom for them. They don't care about the hostages at all, just the money."

The hostages fell silent for a while. A woman finally said, "It's getting hot back here. Why don't they turn on the air conditioning?"

Another man grunted. "This old van probably doesn't have it."

"Be grateful we're not walking to wherever they're taking us," another said.

"Don't give them any ideas," a woman said, bitterness in her voice.

More silence as the road on which they traveled grew bumpier, jarring each of them. Several hard turns tossed them around the back of the van like pinballs in a machine.

On and on they traveled. No way to tell where they were going or how far they had traveled. Janie hated traveling blind. Then again, maybe not being able to see was better. What if the kidnappers were taking them somewhere with horrid conditions?

No point in speculating. She'd find out when they reached their destination. Why scare herself even more before she knew the facts?

The woman to Janie's right whispered, "Do you think they're going to kill us?"

"If they want money, a dead hostage won't do them any good."

That seemed to satisfy her. The information was a poor comfort under the circumstances.

"I hope you're right."

Janie squeezed her hand. So did she.

A long time later, the van slowed and came to a stop.

The atmosphere inside the van became tense. "Everybody keep your mouths shut," one man said, voice low. "We'll get through this if we cooperate."

The doors at the back of the van opened. Two men with large guns waited for them. "Out," snapped a man the size of a linebacker. "Form a line."

One by one, Janie and the others climbed out of the vehicle. She blinked against the waning sunlight, which seemed as bright as a spotlight after being enclosed in total darkness.

When her eyes adjusted, she glanced around. The jungle crowded in on an encampment of sorts. Scattered buildings littered the clearing. Most of them were small. One, however, was the size of a large, sprawling one-story house.

Scar Face climbed down from a Jeep to survey them. He sneered. After another rapid set of orders, two of the terrorists separated the men from the women and took them into one of the smaller buildings.

Linebacker waved his enormous gun at the women. "Follow me. If you run, we'll shoot."

Gritting her teeth, Janie trailed after the other women to the extensive building.

Another man opened the door for them and stood aside as they entered. Linebacker led them to the left along a corridor with rooms on either side of the hall.

Each room had an iron door with bars across a small window. Behind several doors on the left, she could hear women crying or screaming and men laughing or groaning.

Janie swallowed hard. Were these men human traffickers? If so, why take men from the plane and the women?

A hard hand grabbed her arm and jerked Janie to a halt. She gasped and glanced up at her captor, who had a head full of wavy black hair.

He smirked. "This is your cage," he said in heavily accented English as he pushed the iron door open and shoved her inside. "You stay."

Like she had a choice.

Wavy Hair grinned as he slammed the door and locked it, leaving Janie in semi darkness.

She went to the bed and sat on the side, her legs suddenly weak. Trembling, she prayed for a miracle.

Chapter Two

Sawyer Chapman dropped into a seat on the Fortress Security jet assigned to their team and heaved a deep sigh. Days of little to no sleep and little food while on the run had taken their toll on him and his teammates. A band of brothers, that was the Texas Team. A group of former cops who now worked for an elite private security company in Nashville, Tennessee were finally helping those who needed it most without having to worry about following a formal set of rules.

After so many days on the run and delivering the Argentina hostages to their families, he and his teammates were ready to go home. Sawyer had been dreaming of a long soak in his garden tub to rid himself of the grit and grime after the hard week abroad. His teammates wanted to be home with their wives or, in the case of their medic, girlfriend.

He was the last single man on their team. Sawyer shrugged. Of all the men, he could choose to eat dinner standing up, drink milk from the carton, or pick any action movie he wanted without having to cater to his woman's preferences. A great thing.

Right. So, why was he reluctant to go home to an empty house despite the draw of the garden tub with pulsing jets to soothe his aching body?

Brody's phone signaled an incoming call. Their team leader frowned and answered the call. "You're on speaker with Texas Team."

"Conference call with Brent in five minutes," Zane Murphy, their tech and communication guru, said and ended the call.

Logan growled. "The last time we had a call like this at the end of an op, Poppy was missing."

"Relax," Max said. "If one of our women was in trouble, Z would have called the husband or boyfriend directly."

"I don't like it either," Jesse muttered. "Simone is just back on her feet. What if she had a relapse?"

"Speculation won't solve the mystery." Sawyer stood. "Let's go to the conference table and find out what's going on."

His teammates followed in his wake. They settled around the conference table as Brody booted up the computer and set up the video conference.

A minute later, Brent Maddox, CEO of Fortress Security, appeared on the wall screen. "I've instructed your pilot to make a detour."

Detour? Sawyer's heart skipped a beat. That was the signal for a new mission. They were being deployed again after a grueling week? This new mission must be time sensitive.

"Hostage situation in Mexico."

Sawyer and his teammates groaned.

"Save it," Brent snapped. "A plane out of Talca, Chile was hijacked yesterday and forced to land in Pozo Rico, Mexico. From there, the hijackers took fifteen passengers out of 225 from the plane, stuffed them in a panel van, and disappeared."

"Do we have any information to point us in the right direction?" Brody asked. "Mexico is a large country. Lots of places to disappear, including the jungles."

"Not yet. Z and Simone are chasing down rumors on the Net. By the time the jet lands near Pozo Rico, they should have something for you."

"Do we know who's responsible for the hijacking?" Logan asked.

"Nothing concrete. The Pozo Rico airport officials think Vatos Locos is to blame."

Sawyer's hands fisted. "They're known for human trafficking." High-risk move, hijacking a plane. So many things could have gone wrong. Why hadn't the op blown up in their faces?

Brent inclined his head in silent agreement. "They've been branching out in the past two years as well. Trafficking people for the sex trade isn't enough money for them. They've begun holding people for ransom."

But to risk reprisal from American officials and the Federales made little sense.

"Who requested we rescue the hostages?" Max asked.

"Rowan and I are asking you to mount a rescue. David Moran and his sister Janie are long-time friends of my wife's. I know you're exhausted, but Rowan is begging you to rescue Janie. I'm asking for a favor. You're the closest team and time is running out before the hijackers decide to cut their losses."

"Transportation when we land?" Brody asked.

"Two SUVs will be waiting for you. I'll send you the coordinates of an extraction point as soon as we have a probable location of the hostages. Based on the area where Vatos Locos lives, the trek out of their territory will be long and arduous."

Terrific. Sawyer bet they'd be walking through the jungle before they reached an evacuation point. Should be a fun journey with fifteen hostages in various states of shock and injuries. Not.

"Restock from the jet's storage. I know it won't be enough, but it's all you have access to at the moment. I'll arrange an airdrop of supplies if you need them. Also, the friend who's loaning you his vehicles will provide as many supplies as he can put together for your use."

"Have ransom demands been received?" Logan asked.

"Negative."

Sawyer and his teammates exchanged grim glances. That wasn't a good sign.

"Send the information when you get it," Brody said. "We'll need as much time as possible to plan, boss."

"I'm on it. I've already sent you a map with the Vatos Locos's territory marked. We're working as fast as we can to get you more." He dragged a hand down his face. "I owe you big for this."

"No, sir," Brody said. "We're glad to help. Tell Rowan we've got this. We'll get her friend out and bring her home."

After a curt nod, Brent ended the transmission.

Brody checked his email. "Got it. I'll put this up on screen and we'll see what we're facing."

The map appeared on the wall a minute later. Sawyer grimaced. Most of the Vatos Locos's territory included sizeable areas of jungle. Of course it did. Holy cow. If they didn't get a hint on what direction to take, finding Janie Moran and the other hostages could take weeks. By then, it would be too late to save any of the victims. None of them wanted to face Rowan Maddox and tell her they'd failed to rescue her friend.

Max sighed. "I hate jungles. Are we ever going to rescue hostages from a cushy resort by the beach?"

Logan snorted. "Don't think Willow would approve of you ogling beach babes in bikinis."

His teammate grinned at the mention of his wife. "Probably not. By the way, I wouldn't be ogling beach bunnies. Not interested in any woman except Willow."

"How long is the Vatos Locos reach?" Jesse asked.

"All the way into the United States and Canada," Brody said as he scanned something on his phone. "Zane is feeding us information, and so is Simone. At last count, thirty gangs in our country and Canada are affiliated with the original group in Mexico. Law enforcement estimates the membership numbers near 10,000 now."

"No way the hijackers remained around Pozo Rico," Sawyer murmured as he studied the map. "The city is on the far edge of their territory. They'll want the hostages in an area where they won't be spotted by nosy neighbors. If I kidnapped fifteen people, I'd run for the jungle and disappear."

"Unfortunately, I agree with you." Brody shook his head. "We need a likely direction to be effective. Vatos Locos could have taken the hostage anywhere within hundreds of square miles, including the interior of a sizable jungle."

"Staring at the map of their territory isn't doing us any good," Logan said. "You heard the boss. Time to restock our supplies and see what we lack. We may have to procure supplies before we set off on this op."

Sawyer's lips curved. Procure was a fancy word for steal. He was okay with that. Whatever they needed to do to save those hostages was allowed in his book.

"We need an arsenal to take on Vatos Locos," Max said. "I don't think the jet has enough ammunition and weapons to win a war."

"We'll make do or get more," Brody said. "Let's get to it. We need to be ready to move out as soon as we're wheels down."

Over the following four hours, Zane and Simone funneled information into their email. If the information they dug up on the dark web was accurate, the team had a general location where Vatos Locos had set up their camp for holding human trafficking victims before selling them and delivering them to the buyers. Since no one had located the camp yet, it made a secure place to hold hostages.

Like Sawyer had expected, the area most likely for them to look was in the middle of a jungle. Terrific. He looked at his team leader. "We'll have to rappel from a helicopter to save time and allow us to reach the hostages faster."

"Although you're right, I'm concerned the chopper noise will draw too much attention. I'll talk to the boss and see what he can work out. We'll take the SUVs as far as we can. I don't want word leaking to Vatos Locos that a group of foreign mercenaries packing heavy landed at the Pozo Rico airport. Too great a chance we'll spook the terrorists or give them an opportunity to set a trap. Neither option will help us or the hostages."

He looked at his teammates. "Gear ready?"

"Yes, sir."

"Excellent. Back to the conference table. We have a likely target area. Let's create a plan of attack. We have little time before we're wheels down."

The team sat around the table and hashed out a plan of action. Sawyer shook his head as the discussion wound down. "This isn't good enough. We don't have enough information."

"We've gone into ops with less," Max said.

"It will have to do." Brody shut down the computer. "We don't have a choice, Sawyer. Janie and the other hostages are counting on us to rescue them. If we fail, the likelihood that the women will be sold into sex trafficking is high, as is the sure bet that the men will die, especially if a ransom demand isn't met."

"Even if it's met," Logan said. "We all know how this works. Why not make money twice? Once for ransom and once for a sale. Based on the information Simone sent us a few minutes ago, none of the hijackers were wearing masks. That makes the hostages witnesses."

"Why didn't law enforcement stop them?" Jesse frowned. "They know who these guys are. Why didn't they prevent them from leaving the area?"

"Fear," Brody said. "This gang is large and holds a great deal of power, mostly through threats and intimidation. They've also greased the right palms to convince politicians and many law enforcement officers to look the other way. Like always, we don't have friends in this part of the world on an official basis. Any help we might receive will be on the down low, but I wouldn't count on anyone having our backs. We operate as though we're on our own."

Wonderful. The team was on its own again in hostile territory. Using the name Fortress wasn't an option in this part of Mexico.

They'd end up lost in the prison system and dead within days. "Do we have a photo of Janie Moran?" Sawyer asked. He hadn't seen one in his email from either computer tech.

"Just came through. It should be in your email now."

Sawyer opened the latest email and stared at the photo of the woman who was Rowan's friend. Holy smoke. Ms. Moran was drop-dead gorgeous. He whistled. "She's beautiful."

"Did you look at the photos of the other hostages?" Brody asked, amusement in his voice.

Sawyer's face burned. "I was getting to it."

His teammates chuckled.

Whatever. A man could look, right? He ignored his teammates and returned to the email with the photos of the other hostages.

For the next few minutes, he studied the photos, memorizing each face. When he'd finished, Sawyer returned to the picture of Janie Moran. The sweetness in her eyes, the pure joy in her expression as the photo was taken caught at his heart. He couldn't stand the thought of terrorists selling her to the highest bidder. If she survived the life for long, she'd never be the same. The joy would be snuffed out like a candle, and that would truly be a tragedy.

Ten minutes later, he was still staring at her photo when the pilot announced they were approaching the private air strip Brent had secured permission to use. After a last lingering look, Sawyer slid the phone into his pocket and buckled his seatbelt.

If all went according to plan, he'd see Janic Moran in person in a matter of hours. For her sake, he hoped their plans could be followed to the letter.

Chapter Three

Janie sank to the floor and scooted into the corner. The sounds of women screaming and men moaning or laughing had gone on for hours. When would it stop?

Without a window, Janie did not know how much time had passed since she and the other hostages had arrived, but she thought it was late in the night. How she longed for noise-canceling headphones to block out the sounds that would plague her nightmares for years to come. She paused. If she lived that long.

Janie frowned. No. She wouldn't give in to despair. She would get out of here somehow. These men couldn't be vigilant all the time. Escape was possible, and she'd get away from the hijackers.

Escape. A beautiful word. Janie had to be prepared to take advantage of any opportunity to run.

And just like that, her happiness dimmed. She'd been locked in the back of a panel van without windows to watch the twists and turns of the road. No street signs and no sense of where she and the others had been taken.

If she escaped, where would she go? How far was it to the nearest city or town? And if she found a town within walking distance, who could she ask for help?

The hijackers must have connections because no one prevented them from leaving the airport where they'd landed. No one stopped them on the road, either, because they had used no evasive maneuvers to get away from law enforcement.

Janie frowned. Did that mean they were part of a cartel? She swallowed hard. If they were, those men had serious connections and power. Money talked, and people were afraid to stand up to a powerful cartel.

A high-pitched scream broke into Janie's thoughts. She stared at the steel door with bars over the window.

"No," a woman sobbed. "Please, don't."

"Shut your mouth," a man snapped. "The buyer's here. Do as you're told, and you might survive. You're not our problem anymore."

"But you promised...."

A slap, then, "I didn't promise you nothing. Now, shut your trap."

Heavy footsteps and stumbling lighter ones echoed in the hall as the man and woman passed Janie's cell.

Scar Face and a woman Janie didn't recognize. Must be one woman who was already in residence when the hijackers brought her and the rest of her fellow travelers to this place.

The woman's begging brought tears to Janie's eyes. She couldn't imagine what this woman was going to face or what she'd already survived. Soon, the woman's pleas faded to silence as Scar Face propelled her from the building.

He returned several minutes later and unlocked another cell. This one was on Janie's side of the hallway. Before long, screams and laughter from that cell filled the hall.

Janie pressed her hands over her ears, but nothing drowned out the sound of misery and fear emanating from the woman in the cell next to hers. She didn't know how long the sounds went on, but they stopped suddenly to be replaced by vicious cursing from Scar Face followed by a shout at one of his men.

More heavy footsteps passed her door. Scar Face and one of his henchmen shared a low-voiced conversation. Following that, several muffled grunts accompanied shuffling. The henchman stumbled by Janie's cell, carrying something wrapped in a blanket.

Her eyes widened. Not something. Someone. One woman on her flight had just left the building in a cheap equivalent of a body bag.

She swallowed the bile gathering in her mouth. Was death in store for all of them? If so, why had Scar Face and his friends bothered taking them from the plane?

What would happen to her brother if she died in this cell? Would he ever know what happened to her? Janie would miss out on holding her niece or nephew and helping Maria while she healed from childbirth. Yes, Maria had family who lived nearby, but Janie wanted to help as well. Would she have that chance? Only if she escaped these men and any nefarious plans they had in mind for her.

But what could she do to help herself? They had locked her in this small cell. She had nothing on her. No handy metal nail file or a lock pick set. Three clean tissues in her pocket wouldn't unlock a heavy metal door.

Janie despised being helpless. She was a capable woman who owned her own business. But this? How could she have prepared herself for being kidnapped from a plane?

Worse, she didn't know what these men wanted. Money? Something else? The people transported here with her didn't know each other. So what was the common denominator?

She thought more about that, fighting to keep panic at bay. If the hijackers wanted money from her or demanded a ransom from her family, the only person left to pay was her brother, David, and he didn't have an extra cent to his name.

Even if her brother forked over money, which she doubted, Janie wouldn't allow him to sacrifice money for her. Yes, he had insurance, but what if something went wrong during the birth and the baby or Maria needed extra care? No, she couldn't allow him to give the hijackers money.

With their parents gone, that left Janie to pay ransom for herself. She grimaced. As a new business owner, she didn't have extra money, either. Supplies and employees were expensive. Although Natural Bliss was making a profit, the profit margin was razor thin. Definitely not as much money as the hijackers would consider a profitable ransom payment. Good thing they didn't know about the trust fund Granny Irene had left her.

Somewhere in the distance, she heard several rounds of gunfire. A man screamed, followed by more gunfire and screaming. Inside the building, men ran down the hallway toward the front, shouting at each other. The women on either side of the hall were silent.

What was going on? Were they under attack or were the hijackers cutting their losses by killing the plane's male passengers?

Scar Face raced down the hall and unlocked a door. A woman screamed. Her captor shouted and cursed as he forced the woman outside.

More gunfire and the screaming abruptly stopped.

In less than a minute, the gunfire resumed, this time farther away from the building.

Janie wrapped her arms around her upturned knees. What was going on? Was she minutes away from a bullet ending her life?

Her heart rate skyrocketed as Scar Face raced past her cell again, unlocked another door, and dragged a screaming and crying woman outside.

The gunfire ramped up outside for several minutes and followed by engines cranking up, more shouts, then an eerie silence.

Janie didn't know which was worse. All the panicked activity or the sudden silence.

For long minutes, she heard absolutely nothing. No signs of life, no activity. Nothing. She frowned. Had Scar Face and his buddies abandoned the place?

Her stomach tightened into a knot. If they had left, Janie and her fellow travelers were in deep trouble unless someone found them in time to save them from starvation or dehydration. The quick glimpse she'd had around the area before the hijackers propelled her into the building didn't give Janie hope that they'd be found soon.

Jungle. That's all she'd seen. No neighbors, cars, or sounds of vehicles driving down a road. Nothing but trees.

What she wouldn't give for her cell phone. Of course, out here in the middle of nowhere, what was the chance of a cell tower being close? Next to nil. Satellite phones would be the way to communicate this far away from civilization.

Janie tightened her grip around her legs and watched the barred window of her door. Was anyone still left in the building?

Listening to the screams and moans over the past several hours had driven her crazy. Silence was unnerving. She lost track of time as she waited, seated on the floor and curled up in the corner.

When she'd almost given in to resignation, the silence was broken. A brush of fabric against a solid surface told her the building was no longer empty. Did her fellow travelers sense the same thing?

With no light in her cell, Janie's sight was limited to the barred window. She watched and waited for what came next. Was a competing group responsible for the attack on the hijackers? If so, what fate awaited her? Would this group accept she didn't have ransom money or would they too cut their losses and end her life?

One by one, the doors in the hallway were unlocked. "Clear," low masculine voices repeated over and over.

English, she realized. These men spoke English. Cautious hope reared its head. Military? Mercenaries, perhaps?

Finally, a face shrouded in shadows appeared at Janie's barred window. Seconds later, the cell door opened, and a man stepped into the room.

Chapter Four

Sawyer unlocked the cell door and stepped inside. On the floor sat a woman huddled in a corner with her back to the wall. She stared in his direction without making a sound, but he recognized her from the photo he'd memorized on the flight to Mexico.

Thank God. Janie Moran was still alive. How she was treated in her time as a hostage was anyone's guess. Sawyer feared she'd been raped and prepped for sex slavery. Hoping he was wrong, he said, "Janie?"

She blinked. "Yes."

"We're here to take you home."

Janie breathed deep and gave a brief nod. "Do you have room for the other hostages, too?"

He hesitated. How did he tell her the truth, that the hijackers had shot and killed the others in their haste to escape danger? "You're the only one here."

She frowned. "Fifteen of us were taken from the plane. Ten men and five women, including me. Where are the others?"

"I'll tell you everything you want to know after you're safe on the jet, all right?"

She swallowed hard. "Who are you?"

"We're with Fortress Security. Brent Maddox and his wife Rowan sent us."

Janie's eyes closed for a moment, then she said, "Promise you'll tell me what you're reluctant to say when we're safe."

"You have my word." He'd want to know the truth if he were in her place. Wouldn't be right to lie to her or to put the burden of telling the truth to her on someone else. Didn't sit right with him. "I'll tell you as much as I can once we're wheels up."

She smiled. "Military term."

He chuckled. "Comes from being trained by elite military soldiers." Sawyer stepped further into the room and crouched in front of Janie. "Will you allow me to help you to your feet, Janie?"

She hesitated. "What's your name?"

"Sawyer." He held out his hands. After a moment's pause, she placed both of her hands in his. Admiring her courage, he stood and tugged Janie to her feet.

She groaned and stumbled.

He caught her against him. "Are you all right?" Was she injured?

"Sorry. I sat on the floor too long."

"We need to go, Janie. Otherwise, I'd give you as much time as you needed. Will you allow me to carry you?"

Janie looked horrified. "I'm too heavy."

He smiled. "No, ma'am, you're not. My pack weighs more than you do."

"Do you think the hijackers will come back?"

Here, at least, he could offer the truth. "It's possible. We'd like to vacate the premises as soon as we can. If we're followed into the jungle, we want as much distance between us and the hijackers as we can get. May I carry you?" he asked again.

She nodded.

He didn't waste any time scooping Janie into his arms. Astonishment filled him. She felt perfect in his arms. He could so get used to this.

Sawyer angled her through the doorway and met his teammates in the hallway. "We're ready."

"Personal belongings?" Brody asked.

"None," Janie said. "They wouldn't let us take anything off the plane."

A nod, then his team leader looked at Sawyer. He gave a slight nod. Brody didn't have to say anything about keeping Janie from seeing the bodies outside in the clearing. He'd already planned to take care of that.

"Logan, take point," Brody murmured. "Jesse, take the rear. Max and I will take positions on both sides of Sawyer and Janie."

Logan led the way into the main lobby area of the building and tugged the front door open wide enough to see the clearing. After a moment, he said, "We're clear."

"Hold," Brody ordered and looked at Sawyer.

He looked down at the woman in his arms. "Janie, I need you to do something for me."

She looked up at him. "Anything."

"Close your eyes."

The woman in his arms frowned. "Why?"

"We faced resistance when we arrived," he said simply. "Bodies are on the ground. You don't need to add more nightmares to your dreams."

She huffed out a laugh. "I have a feeling it's too late for that, but I see your point." She closed her eyes.

"Thank you. I'll tell you when it's safe to open your eyes."

Janie nodded and rested her head against his shoulder. "Do you mind?"

He squeezed her for a second. "Nope. Take a nap if you like. We'll get you out of here. Before you know it, you'll be back in the states."

"I'd like to talk to my brother," she said as he carried her from the building.

Bodies were everywhere, some he knew were fellow passengers on her plane. Off in the distance, they heard the engine of a vehicle approaching.

"Move," Brody snapped.

They jogged from the clearing. Once in the trees, they disappeared from the view of anyone watching within a few steps.

The jungle in this part of the Vatos Locos territory was dense, dark, and dank.

"You can open your eyes now," Sawyer murmured as they hurried through the jungle. Thank goodness for his night-vision goggles. With almost no moon out tonight and a dense jungle, his NVGs lit up the world in green. Otherwise, he'd be stumbling around instead of running through the area.

"Doesn't do me a bit of good," Janie said. "I can't see a thing except slivers of moonlight once in a while. You're wearing night-vision goggles, aren't you?"

"That's right."

"Brent talked about using them when he was on night missions as a SEAL. I imagine they come in very useful in pitch black terrain."

His heart squeezed at her stress and fear. The pitch of Janie's voice gave her away. "They do."

Logan held up a fist, and the rest of the team froze in place. Although Sawyer thought he might have to warn Janie to remain silent until the danger passed, she said nothing as they stood deep in the shadows of the jungle, waiting for the all-clear or for the team to take out a threat to her safety.

Logan looked back at Brody and signaled that he was going hunting.

Sawyer's gut clenched. He shouldn't go alone, but he wanted heavy protection around Janie. So did Sawyer. This wasn't good, though. They shouldn't split up. Who knew how many bogeys were in this jungle tracking them.

Brody signaled Max to go with Logan. Despite the scowl from Logan, Brody wouldn't back down and gave a head shake in a silent order to suck it up and deal with having a partner.

Sawyer breathed easier. Good. The two of them had a better chance of dealing with whatever problem arose. Logan was tough, but could be injured as easily as the rest of them.

Janie put her mouth close to Sawyer's ear. "What's happening?"

He shivered at the feel of her warm breath against his ear. *Get a grip, Chapman.* "Logan heard something. He and Max are checking it out."

She nodded and rested her head against his shoulder again.

Brent and Jesse kept watch, as did Sawyer. Minutes later, they heard a muffled shout, then silence. Through his earpiece, Logan said, "One down. Three to go."

"Two down," Max murmured in seconds.

A minute later, Logan said, "Three down."

Ten minutes later, Max said, "Four down. We're clear for now."

"Copy," Brody replied softly.

"Danger is gone for now," Sawyer told Janie. "We'll start moving again in a couple of minutes."

"What happened?"

"Four men were tracking us. My teammates took care of them."

"But we still need to put distance between us and the hijackers, right?"

He squeezed her again. "We'll be fine. Trust me." But how could she? Janie didn't know any of them.

Logan and Max returned. Sawyer adjusted his hold on Janie and nodded at Logan, who turned and set off again toward their rendezvous point with the chopper. Two miles of hard slog through the jungle before they reached the landing zone. Would the hard-won distance Logan and Max gained for them be enough before more terrorists zeroed in on their location?

The last thing Sawyer wanted was a firefight with Janie caught in the crossfire. If it came down to that, though, he'd protect her with his life if necessary.

Shouts sounded in the distance. Brody's expression grew grim. "Pick it up," he murmured into the comm system. "Sounds like the men you and Max took care of have been discovered."

Logan broke into a run with the rest following suit.

"You can put me down," Janie said. "I can hold my own for a while, at least."

"Have you eaten or drunk anything since the hijacking?"

She shook her head.

"You won't last more than a couple of minutes."

"To haul your pack and me through this jungle is too much," she protested.

"If I need help, one of my teammates will carry you for a while. Right now, I'm fine." In fact, he was better than fine. He felt as though he could carry Janie for many miles.

She fell silent, but squeezed his neck a little tighter for a few seconds.

He smiled. He'd take a quick hug that like any day of the week. Perhaps she was trusting him a little.

On and on Sawyer ran with his teammates, dodging live trees and hopping over fallen ones while following in Logan's footsteps to reduce the possibility of Janie being injured by branches and bushes smacking her in the face. The team didn't want to cut a path through the jungle unless it was necessary. The fresh path would lead the enemy right to their landing zone.

Even at this early hour of the morning, the heat and humidity made Sawyer sweat as he ran. Dragging in air felt as though he was sucking pea soup through a straw. Nope, he wasn't a fan of the jungle. The beach was more his speed.

Again, Logan held up a fist and paused. Sawyer and the others froze in place. One minute passed, then two. Another signal from Logan sent Sawyer into a crouch. He set Janie on the ground with a finger pressed to his lips to remind her to remain silent. He palmed his weapon and waited.

Five minutes. Ten. A stick cracked to Sawyer's right. He hovered over Janie, his body barely brushing hers, as moved between her and the potential threat.

Without turning around, Brody signaled Max to circle around and get behind the approaching threat.

They were being stalked. Whether by man or beast, he didn't know. Either way, they needed to get the tracker off their backs and resume the journey to the LZ. If they didn't move soon, they risked a daylight pick up, and that was too dangerous for everyone, including the chopper and pilot.

Max disappeared into the shadows.

Still, they waited. To her credit, Janie didn't move or ask questions. She lay perfectly still, watching Sawyer for a sign that all was well or danger was imminent.

Absently, he reached over with his free hand and squeezed her fingers. After he released her, Janie wrapped her small hand around Sawyer's calf, gently massaging muscles beginning to cramp. How had she known exactly where to massage?

When the muscles relaxed, she switched her attention to his other calf and went to work on those knotted muscles.

Sawyer shuddered with relief as the pain subsided. Good grief. Janie Moran had serious massage skills. Where had she learned such a great technique?

He crouched lower until his mouth was close to her ear. "Thanks," he whispered.

That earned him a pat on the back of a calf.

Sawyer smiled. He didn't know where this woman lived, but he'd love a chance to get to know her better if she was open to the possibility of dating him.

Another stick cracked, followed by a muttered curse.

Brody looked at Logan, who melted into the shadows. Two minutes later, a muffled grunt told the story. Either Max or Logan, perhaps both, had taken down the threat.

"Clear," Max murmured. "Heading back."

Both men reappeared a minute later. Their uniform shirts appeared wet. Good thing their uniforms were black. Harder to spot blood on the fabric or bullet-resistant vest.

At a signal from Brody, Sawyer scooped Janie into his arms again and set off at a faster pace than before. They needed to get out of this jungle. No telling how many terrorists had been sent into the interior to find them and either retrieve Janie or kill her.

Texas Team ran for a mile before Logan once again signaled.

Sawyer scowled. How many terrorists were in this Vatos Locos group? How could they track the team through the dense jungle in the dead of night?

Didn't matter how they were doing it. The fact was, they were tracking the team with deadly accuracy.

He considered that for a moment. Was it possible the terrorists had planted a tracker on Janie without her being aware of it?

Logan tilted his head, concentrating hard. Finally, he gave the all clear, and the group resumed their run toward the landing zone.

At the edge of another large clearing, Brody pulled out his satellite phone and made a call. "It's Brody. We're ready." A pause, then, "Copy that." He looked at the others. "Two minutes. Be ready."

Janie looked at each man before settling her gaze on Sawyer. "Ready for what?"

"Choppers are noisy. It will attract attention all over the jungle. If the terrorists are close enough, they'll zero in on this location. We may be in for a firefight before we're on board the helicopter."

"Sawyer, put me down. You need both hands free. I can run the few feet to the helicopter. I promise."

Reluctantly, he set Janie on her feet, hovering close while she got her balance. "You good?"

She nodded. "Thanks for the lift."

"Any time."

A minute later, they heard the chopper in the distance. As one, Sawyer and his teammates readied their weapons, remaining in a loose circle with Janie in the middle.

Thirty seconds before the chopper appeared in the sky, Sawyer threaded the fingers of his free hand through Janie's. "You and I are going to the clearing first. The rest of my teammates will cover us. The goal is to get you inside before the terrorists open fire. No matter what happens, you run as fast as you can and climb into the helicopter. I'll be right behind you." Covering her in case of enemy gunfire.

"What about your friends? They're getting on board, too, right?"

"As soon as you're clear, we'll pile into the chopper," Brody assured her. "You focus on the goal. Sawyer will give you instructions. Do exactly what he tells you to do, and you'll be all right. We've got your back, Ms. Moran."

"Janie." She smiled. "After all this danger, I feel like we're best friends."

Brody smiled. "Janie, then. I'm Brody." One by one, he introduced the rest of the Texas Team. He glanced at Sawyer. "Ready in ten seconds."

"Copy." He squeezed Janie's hand. "Hold on to me and run as fast as you can. Got it?"

She nodded. "Tell me when."

Sawyer drew in a breath and said, "Now." He easily kept pace with Janie as she raced into the clearing. When she paused as the helicopter descended, Sawyer released her hand, wrapped his arm around her waist and caught her against his side as he urged her to quicken her pace.

Janie ducked her head against the grit and leaves whipped up by the force of the helicopter blades. When she stumbled, Sawyer scooped her into his arms and raced over the last few feet to the open side door of the chopper. He dumped her inside, then hauled himself into the belly of the beast. "Get in the farthest seat and strap in," he ordered Janie.

Bullets pinged off the side of the chopper.

In a crouch, Sawyer spun, aimed, and fired his MP5 over the heads of his teammates. One by one, Max, Jesse, Logan, and finally Brody leaped into the helicopter.

"Go, go, go," Brody shouted and joined Sawyer in firing off his weapon to protect the helicopter while it lifted into the air.

When the helicopter banked to the left, Sawyer and Brody strapped into their seats, removed their comm devices, and slipped on headphones with microphones attached.

"Any injuries?" Jesse asked.

Sawyer held up his hand, forestalling any genuine conversation until he helped Janie don a pair of headphones so she could hear what was being said. "Repeat the question, Jesse."

"Any injuries to report?"

Each one of Sawyer's teammates reported no injuries. Although he'd hoped no one had noticed that he hadn't responded, Jesse zeroed in on him.

"Let's hear it, Sawyer."

Janie gasped and twisted in her seat. Worry filled her eyes. "Were you injured?"

He shrugged.

"You never said or gave any sign."

"Details," Jesse snapped.

"Bullet nicked my shoulder. It's not a big deal."

"In the jungle, it is." Jesse unhooked his seatbelt, grabbed his mike bag, and knelt next to Sawyer. "Let's see it."

"It's not that bad," he protested. "I swear. It can wait."

"My call. Show me."

With a sigh, Sawyer ripped off his sleeve and shoved the remaining material high so their team medic could exam the wound.

Jesse studied Sawyer's shoulder and whistled. "It's nothing, huh?"

He scowled at his friend. "My arm isn't falling off."

Jesse shook his head as he dug into the mike bag. "I'll patch it until we're on board the jet. You'll be getting my full attention, buddy."

Sawyer grimaced. "Yeah, yeah."

"Are you sure he'll be all right?" Janie asked.

"I'm sure," Sawyer insisted. "A few stitches and I'll be good to go. Promise."

Jesse rolled his eyes. "Although he's not a medic, Sawyer is right. The injury isn't serious except he's been in a tropical environment and will need antibiotics along with stitches to make sure he heals properly. He's had worse, Janie. This is just another scar to add to his storytelling hour."

"I still hate it." Tears glistened in her eyes. "If you hadn't been here to rescue me, you wouldn't be injured, Sawyer."

He shrugged, hiding the pain the movement caused. "I'm glad I was here to help. I'll take a few stitches for that any time."

Jesse pulled out his alcohol wipes and a pressure bandage and made quick work of cleaning and patching the wound for Sawyer.

"Thanks, Jesse."

"Yep. I'll finish the job when we're wheels up." The medic returned to his seat.

To Sawyer's surprise, Janie wrapped her hand around his and held on tight. "I'll be fine," he said softly, even though his teammates could hear every word he and Janie spoke to each other. "I've had worse injuries on missions." And on the job as a cop.

"But I wasn't to blame for those injuries."

"You aren't responsible for it this time, either. It's the risk of the job, Janie." But he admitted to himself that it was nice to have someone care about him.

Chapter Five

Janie inched closer to Sawyer as the helicopter flew over the tops of trees toward an unknown destination. She decided she wasn't a fan of flying in a helicopter. Give her a large plane any day and she'd be fine. Flying this way was too open for her liking. She preferred a small window to see the tops of clouds rather than the tops of trees.

Sawyer glanced at her, then squeezed her hand again. "You're doing great, Janie. Just hang in there. We'll be landing in five minutes."

Surprised, her eyes widened. "So soon?"

He chuckled. "You get where you're going in a hurry, traveling like this."

"I still don't like it," she muttered.

All the men chuckled at that.

Just as Sawyer had said, five minutes later, the helicopter set down on a grassy knoll. The team from Fortress bailed from the vehicle and grabbed their gear. Four of them formed a wall of muscle near the side door, creating a ring of protection for her. Only Sawyer remained beside her in the helicopter.

"Ready?" he asked. When she nodded, Sawyer stood, tugged Janie to her feet, and helped her to the ground. After grabbing his pack, he touched Brody's shoulder.

The team leader signaled the others, and they set off at a fast pace. When Janie lagged behind, Sawyer scooped her into his arms again and picked up the pace.

"Why are we hurrying?" she asked. Was there some danger she was missing?

"We aren't far from the Vatos Locos compound, and we're still in the middle of their territory. Some of their soldiers are probably close by."

She tensed. Oh, man. She thought after escaping the compound that her problems were over. Apparently not.

"It's all right, Janie. I've got you."

"You're not safe. None of you are safe." She didn't want these kind and brave men to be targets on her account.

"Janie, look at me." When she did, Sawyer squeezed her gently. "We chose to come, and I'm glad we did. Freeing you from Vatos Locos is worth every risk we're taking. This is what we're trained to do, and we're good at it."

She smiled. "Such modesty," she teased.

"It's a simple truth. We'll get you out of here. You have my word. Trust me a little longer."

Brent Maddox was no fool. He didn't skimp on training. Brent trusted them with her life. She either accepted his judgment or she'd make the rescue underway even more difficult and dangerous for the men risking all to save her. The more she cooperated, the easier things would go for everyone.

Slowly, Janie relaxed against Sawyer. "I'm sorry."

"Don't be. You just left a terrifying situation, and you're still not in a safe place. Plus, we're strangers to you. Brent knows us, but you don't. What you're feeling is understandable."

Tears burned her eyes. A terrifying situation was an inadequate description for feeling as though she would die any minute for hours on end. She'd never forget the experience and prayed she never had to repeat it.

The team ran along an unseen path from Janie's perspective. Good thing these men were wearing NVGs. Perhaps later, Sawyer would have time to show her how they worked.

Soon, they emerged from the jungle into another clearing. Parked in the shadows of the trees were two SUVs.

"Logan, Max, check the vehicles and let's get out of here."

Fascinated, Janie watched as the two men circled the vehicles while looking at black gadgets. Curiosity got the best of her. "What are they doing?"

"Checking for trackers and explosives."

Her blood ran cold. "Explosives? Seriously?"

"We're in enemy territory. Anything is possible."

Janie wrapped her arms around her middle. This was insane. Explosives? Trackers? If she'd escaped from Scar Face and his buddies, she wouldn't have thought to check for hidden dangers.

Logan and Max gave a hand signal, and the rest of the team left the safety of the jungle to climb into the vehicles. Sawyer set Janie on the backseat of an SUV and climbed in beside her. Jesse, the medic, handed Sawyer a backpack, then took the shotgun seat while Brody climbed behind the wheel.

In seconds, the caravan drove through the clearing and onto a dirt path leading away from the area.

As they drove, the sun lightened the sky to a steel gray. "We may be in for a rough ride," Brody said.

Jesse and Sawyer checked their weapons.

Janie's stomach knotted. That couldn't be good. Was 'rough ride' a euphemism for more danger? "What's happening?" she whispered to Sawyer.

"Hoping for the best and preparing for the worst." He smiled. "Standard operating procedure, Janie. Don't worry."

"Easy for you to say."

He chuckled. "We'll handle whatever the Vatos Locos dish out."

"I don't suppose you carry a bazooka in that backpack of yours."

"Oh, you might be surprised what I carry in my bag of tricks."

"One day, when we aren't in a life and death situation, you'll have to show me what you carry."

"Deal." He stiffened. "Brody."

"I see them. Get ready."

"Yes, sir." Sawyer turned to Janie. "Get on the floor and lay as flat as you can."

"They found us?"

"Looks like it."

"More likely that they staked out the obvious escape routes," Brody said. "The road is a natural choice."

"What road?" Janie slid to the floor and curled up on her side. "It looks like a cow path to me."

"You're not wrong," Brody said. "Sawyer, in the back."

"Yes, sir." He rested his hand on the top of Janie's head for a few seconds. "It will be noisy in here. Stay on the floor. We'll be fine. You'll see."

She gave him a small smile and tried to curl into a tighter ball.

After a last stroke of his fingers over her hair, Sawyer grabbed his rifle and climbed over the backseat to the cargo area. He rolled onto his back and kicked out the back window.

Janie flinched. Someone wouldn't be happy when the vehicle was returned. She paused. Unless they stole the vehicles. Surely not. Did she care? She considered that a moment and decided she didn't care since they might have committed a crime while rescuing a hostage from terrorists.

Where were the other passengers? Did the terrorists take them away when they fled from Sawyer and his team? Something told her the answers she wanted weren't as simple as they seemed and likely ones that she didn't want to hear. Janie feared her fellow passengers were dead, not merely moved to another location.

If that was true, why was she alive? Did the hijackers run out of time to deal with her or had the decision to leave her alive at the compound been deliberate? If so, what reason could they have? She made soap and bath bombs for a living. What could Scar Face and his buddies want with a small town soap maker? None of this made any sense.

"Two bogeys moving up fast," Sawyer said.

"I see them." Brody made a call. "Max, keep watch up ahead. We have bogeys closing in on us." Seconds later, he said to Sawyer, "We need breathing room to get Janie into the jet."

"Copy that. Restrictions?"

"None. Just get it done. Our principal is the priority. Period."

"Yes, sir. Janie?"

She jerked. "Yes?"

"Cover your ears."

When she complied, Sawyer aimed and fired his rifle three times. "One down. Second one is gaining ground and moving into position to attack us from behind."

Her blood ran cold. Two vehicles were chasing them. Were the hijackers after her or the team that rescued her?

Someone's phone signaled an incoming message. Seconds later, Jesse said, "Two more vehicles coming toward Max and Logan at a high-rate of speed."

"Pincer move," Sawyer said as he aimed at another target. Two shots later, he said, "Two down."

"How's the shoulder?" Jesse asked.

"I'll live."

"How bad is it?"

"Let's just say I think you're right about me needing stitches."

"You good enough to take on another vehicle?" Brody asked. "And don't lie to me. I won't be happy if I find out you did."

"Would I do that?"

A snort. "In a heartbeat if you thought you were likely to be sidelined. Climb back into the middle and be ready to help Logan with the terrorists in front of them if he needs the assist."

"Yes, sir." Sawyer slid over the seat into the middle section. "Doing okay, Janie?" he asked as he settled near the door. He lowered the window.

"You weren't kidding about the noise level. I never realized guns were so noisy."

"To protect our hearing on the practice range, we use headphones to muffle the sound. In combat situations like ours, we frequently fire weapons from a moving vehicle."

"I heard Brody mention two more vehicles. Are you going to stop them, too?"

He studied her for a moment. "I could, but I probably won't need to take care of them. Logan is an excellent shot."

"We all are," Brody said. "Law enforcement training and Fortress Security training."

Her heart skipped a beat, then all of her tension melted away. "All of you were in law enforcement?" A team of former cops? Who could ask for more protection than that?

"That's right," Sawyer said. "We're called Texas Team because we were in various branches of law enforcement in Texas."

In the distance, Janie heard gunfire. She waited, listening for any other sounds like a car crashing or glass breaking. Amazing how many things she heard when two windows were down. More shots were fired.

Then silence.

Another signal of an incoming message. A moment later, Jesse said, "Bogeys one and two are down. Logan says we're clear."

"Excellent. Tell Max to step on it. I want no more delays."

"Yes, sir." After a short, low-voiced conversation, Jesse said, "Message delivered."

Brody made a call. "Jordan, we're five minutes out and coming in hot. The jet needs to be wheels up as soon as we board."

Sawyer raised the window. "I know you're not comfortable, Janie, but can you wait for five more minutes? The floor is the most protected place in this vehicle."

Uncomfortable was an understatement. Janie's ribs were killing her. "I'll deal with it. How's your shoulder?"

"Not good," he admitted.

"Can you wait?" Jesse asked.

"I'll survive five more minutes. I'm more concerned about getting Janie to safety than a temporary patch job on my shoulder."

Suddenly, Brody make a sharp right turn and floored the accelerator. "Sawyer, when we reach the jet, your only job is to transport Janie to safety. Jesse and I will grab your gear and provide cover fire if needed."

"Copy that."

"Wait," Janie protested. "I can walk."

"As soon as we stop, we'll be running to the jet," Sawyer said. "Unless we're very lucky, we'll have company on the tarmac. We need you inside the jet, where you'll be the safest."

But what about them? Sawyer and his friends would be in the middle of a firefight yet again because of her. To protest, though, would delay them and put these men in even more danger. She couldn't have that. Better to keep quiet and cooperate. It was the best way to protect this amazing team.

Brody slammed on the brakes. The SUV went into a skid and stopped seconds later. Immediately, the three men bailed from the vehicle. Two beats later, Sawyer scooped her into his arms again and ran for the jet parked nearby. He took the stairs two at a time, hurried into the cabin and set her on a seat partway down the aisle. "Stay here."

Sawyer ran back to the doorway, accepted a rifle from one of his teammates, and aimed the weapon at a target outside. He began firing on an enemy Janie couldn't see from her vantage point.

Soon, the rest of his teammates hustled into the cabin of the jet. Brody and Max raised the stairs and secured the door. Brody pressed an intercom button and said, "Go, go, go."

He and Max dropped into the closest seats and strapped in as the jet taxied faster and faster down the runway. In seconds, the jet was airborne.

For the first time in hours, Janie could take a full breath. The jitters were still a real thing, but at least she could breathe now.

"Sawyer, let's go," Jesse said as soon as the jet had leveled out. "You, too, Janie."

She frowned. "I'm not injured."

"You're shivering. If nothing else, you have a large case of adrenaline dump. You can lie down for a while on a bed while you watch me work on Sawyer." He winked. "Cheap entertainment. My friend hates needles with a passion."

"Who doesn't?" Janie looked at Sawyer. "Do you mind? If you do, I'll stay here and wrap up with a blanket."

He held out a hand to her. "Come with me."

That settled, Sawyer tugged Janie to her feet and led her to the back of the jet. He opened a door to a small bedroom with a bathroom. As Jesse laid out the supplies he needed to work on Sawyer's shoulder, Sawyer nudged Janie to the bed and went to a supply cabinet to get a blanket for her.

When she settled back against the headboard, Sawyer draped the blanket over her, then brought her a bottle of water. "How long has it been since you ate anything?"

"Breakfast of the morning we were taken hostage."

Sawyer and Jesse exchanged grim glances. "We'll find something for you to eat while the lidocaine works on Sawyer's shoulder," Jesse said.

"Anything is fine. I'm not picky. More than anything, I'm thirsty." But she wouldn't complain about a sandwich or even crackers. Anything to dull this gnawing ache in her gut.

"Drink as much water as you want. We have plenty on board."

Janie took him at his word and sipped the water in earnest. No guzzling, she reminded herself. No matter how tempting, drinking too much at once would make her sick.

"Take off what's left of your shirt," Jesse told Sawyer.

He reached back, tugged his shirt off, and tossed it aside. He sat on the edge of the bed near Janie. "Do your worst."

Janie couldn't help staring at his muscular chest and back. Good grief. How long did he work out every day?

"Oh, I intend to." Jesse's voice was mild. "One of these days, I'll teach the rest of you I would rather not ply my trade."

"Yeah, yeah. Just get it done, all right? I need to feed Janie."

Jesse grabbed alcohol wipes and went to work. "Tell Janie about your life before you joined the police force."

Sawyer stared at him. "Really? This is the way you plan to distract me from what you're doing?"

"Got any better ideas? It's a good story."

He snorted. "It's an old story, and I'd prefer to keep my checkered past to myself."

"You're chicken?"

"No, but it's not a pretty story, all right? Janie's been through enough trauma to last a lifetime without adding my baggage to keep her awake at night."

Shivering, Janie wrapped the blanket tighter around herself. "Will you tell me later?" she asked. "I love good stories."

"This one isn't good, but if you want to hear it, I'll tell you." Sawyer glared at Jesse. "When we're alone. I don't want to provide a sob story for the entertainment of my teammates."

Now she was really curious. What was so horrid that he felt the need to hide it from his best friends, and why was he willing to share the information with her? Good questions that she'd have answered if she listened to his tale. "Deal. Jesse, how can I help Sawyer?"

"Talk to him while I stitch him up." After injecting lidocaine under Sawyer's skin, Jesse tugged off his gloves and stood. "Now's the time to prepare Janie's meal, Sawyer. We have about fifteen minutes before I can work on your wound."

"Perfect." Sawyer rose. "Do you need another blanket, Janie?" he asked.

"I could use one," she admitted. "I can't stop shivering."

"The shakes will pass soon," Jesse said as he walked to a cabinet and pulled out another blanket. "We all have different methods for dealing with an adrenaline dump."

Sawyer took the blanket from Jesse and draped it over Janie. "I'll be back in a couple of minutes." When Sawyer returned, he brought a plate with a sandwich, chips, and a banana. "This is a chicken salad sandwich. If you don't like it, I'll get you something else. We have several options in the galley."

Janie took a bite of the sandwich and moaned. "This is wonderful."

He smiled. "I didn't know how much food to bring. If this isn't enough, I'll bring more."

"Sit," Jesse ordered Sawyer. When he did, the medic grilled him with questions about other injuries.

Sawyer shook his head. "My shoulder is the only place you need to check. The rest of my injuries are bruises and scrapes. I'll deal with them after we land in the states."

Jesse scowled. "We'll deal with the scrapes now, and I'll give you cold packs to apply to your bruises. You have to stay mobile, Sawyer."

"Yeah, you're right. Stitch me up, Jesse. I'll take care of the rest after you finish with me."

"We have a few more minutes," the medic said. "Janie, do you have any injuries? A scrape, bruises, anything. Even a minor scrape or cut could get infected."

"Some of both." She wrinkled her nose. "We were thrown around the back of the van when the hijackers transported us from the plane to the compound where you found me."

"Take a minute to settle, then consciously do an internal assessment of how your body feels. Start at the top with your head and work your way down to your feet. As you do, catalog every ache, burn, and pain."

She did as he suggested. When she opened her eyes, Janie said, "My legs and hips ache from being tossed around in the back of the van. My wrists are bruised from rough handling. I have scratches on my arms and back."

Jesse studied her, then said, "Is that all?"

"You expected more?"

"Jesse," Sawyer murmured.

The medic held up his hand to forestall Sawyer before he answered Janie's question. "Frankly, yes. Vatos Locos has a reputation as human traffickers. Look, Janie, I understand you don't know or trust me. However, if the members of Vatos Locos assaulted you, you must see a doctor for the sake of your health."

Janie stared. Human traffickers? Now everything she'd heard in that building made sense and confirmed her worst fears. Tears burned her eyes. Scar Face had assaulted and killed the woman imprisoned in the cell next to her.

Tears escaped and trailed down her cheeks. Oh, man. Now it all made horrid sense. What about the other passengers? Had the other women been assaulted and killed? What had happened to the men, including the man who sat next to her on the plane?

"Janie?" Sawyer sat beside her again and reached for her hand. He froze before he actually touched her skin. "May I hold your hand?"

She nodded and swiped at her tears. "I'm okay, Jesse. They didn't rape me."

Sawyer's hand gripped hers. "Why are you crying?"

Jesse set up his stitch tray.

Janie focused on Sawyer. His touch and focused attention gave her the courage to answer his question. "That building was filled with women before I arrived with my fellow passengers. The men were sent somewhere else. The rest of us were forced into cells in the building where you found me." Her cheeks burned. "Several men visited the women."

"No one visited you?" Sawyer asked softly.

She shook her head. "Scar Face visited the woman in the cell next to mine. He hurt her, Sawyer."

"I'm sorry."

"No. You don't understand. He and one of his men carried something wrapped in a blanket from that cell. Scar Face killed Emily." More tears slipped down her cheeks. "I think he murdered everyone except me."

Chapter Six

Sawyer squeezed Janie's hand. So close to dying and yet her life was spared. Although he was grateful, the question was why had Janie was left alive when the hijackers killed all the others? "I'm sorry, Janie."

She swiped at her tears. "The other passengers. What happened to them, Sawyer? You promised to tell me the truth when we were safe. Please tell me now."

Man, he hated this. He'd give anything to share good news instead of bad. This situation reminded him of some of his undercover operations as a cop. Sometimes when the gangs felt threatened, they murdered innocents, and as a law enforcement officer, he'd had to deliver the bad news to family and friends. "The only hostage we found alive in the compound was you."

Sorrow filled Janie's eyes. "Why would they do that? Why take us hostage if they planned to kill us, anyway?"

"I don't know, but I will find out. You have my word." He'd promise and do anything as long as she stopped crying. Her tears gutted him.

When Jesse pinched Sawyer's shoulder in various places to check the progress of the lidocaine, Janie's tears slowed as her attention shifted to Sawyer. If that's what it took to distract Janie, he'd gladly submit to Jesse's less than tender loving care.

Jesse grunted as he poked and prodded Sawyer's shoulder. "This is more than a scratch, buddy. The injury is deep."

Sawyer shrugged his uninjured shoulder. "Fix it so I'm operational."

Janie's gaze shifted to Sawyer's face. "You sound as though you expect more trouble."

"I do."

She blinked. "Why?"

"You said it yourself. The hijackers kept you alive for a reason. They'll try to put their hands on you again."

"I hope you're wrong."

"So do I." He paused. "I'm not. Scar Face and his buddies will come for you or send someone else to finish the job."

Jesse murmured, "You'll feel tugs. If you feel pain, don't tough it out. Tell me."

Sawyer nodded, his gaze locked on Janie. "Finish eating. In a few minutes, you'll be sound asleep."

She looked skeptical. "How do you know that?"

"Adrenaline dump plus an emotional shock means you'll probably need a good nap," Jesse said. "Some of us pace or run a few miles. One of my teammates lifts weights to handle an adrenaline dump. It's common for people to cry or sleep. I'm betting you're a sleeper."

Sawyer squeezed her fingers again. "Based on what you said, I doubt you slept at all. Am I right?"

Janie nodded.

"After you eat, settle back and sleep. When you wake, we'll be that much closer to the states."

Jesse finished the stitches as Janie swallowed the last bite of her food. He handed Sawyer two packets of capsules. "The red and white capsules are an antibiotic, and the white capsules are for pain." He handed Sawyer a bottle of water. "Take one pill from each bag and finish the water. I'll want to check you again tomorrow, unless Sorenson keeps you two at the clinic for a day or two."

Sawyer shuddered. Doc Sorenson was the best trauma surgeon around, but his bedside manner wasn't anything to write home about. "No way."

"You don't have a choice. The boss will decide, along with the doctor."

He scowled. "You know how Sorenson is. He'll gripe at me the whole time, telling me the dogs and cats he treats are sicker than I am."

"In this case, he'd be right. However, he might want to monitor you for a few hours. Janie, too."

She set aside her plate. "Why would he want to watch over me? I'm not injured."

Silence met her question. Finally, Sawyer said, "It's a precaution. You've been through a lot in the past two days." Then he played his ace card. "Brent will want Dr. Sorenson's assessment of your health before he transports you to Nashville."

Janie narrowed her eyes. "We'll see how long he keeps me. I want to go home."

There was the spark Sawyer wanted to see. "We'll do our best to get you out of the clinic in record time."

She settled deeper into the pillows. "You mentioned something about dogs and cats. Does Dr. Sorenson have pets?"

Sawyer smiled. "You could say that. Not only is the doc a world-class trauma surgeon, he's an excellent veterinarian too."

"Oh, I see. I guess he must have furry patients, too."

"If you show any interest at all in a dog or cat from the shelter, you'll go home with a new pet."

Janie laughed. "Got it. I'll be careful."

Jesse finished bandaging Sawyer's shoulder. "All right, my friend. You're all set until we reach the clinic."

"Thanks, Jesse."

"Yep. Janie, you're next. Show me the scrapes and cuts. I'll treat them, then give you cold packs for the bruises."

Fifteen minutes later, Janie's injuries were treated, and Jesse handed her three cold packs for the worst of the bruises.

When he left the room, Janie said, "He didn't have to do all this for me. My injuries are slight."

"No injury is minor when we're in a tropical climate. Infections set up quickly. Jesse's being cautious." Sawyer rose and dug in his Go bag for a clean shirt. After tugging it on, he grabbed a chair and set it beside the bed. He dropped into it. "How do you feel, Janie?"

"Washed out," she admitted. "I think I could sleep for a week."

"I understand. Can I get you anything before I leave you alone to sleep?"

"Can you stay? Only if you won't be in trouble, that is."

His heart skipped a beat. "You want me to stay with you?"

"Please. I feel safe when you're near."

One barrier he'd erected around his heart crumpled to the ground with a whoosh. Oh, boy. He might be in for a tough time. Janie Moran was his principal, not his girlfriend. He couldn't lose sight of that fact. "I can stay. I'll let Brody know. Otherwise, my team leader will track me down to see what's going on."

Sawyer grabbed his phone and sent a text to Brody, then settled back in his chair. "We're set. Do you have enough blankets?"

Janie nodded.

"Rest, Janie. I've got you. You're safe with me." He meant every word. No one would harm this woman. They'd have to go through him first.

She sighed, tugged the blankets up to her shoulders, and went motionless.

Sawyer watched her for several minutes until his own fatigue caught up with him. He found another blanket and settled deeper into the chair for a quick nap.

He woke two hours later, his internal alarm rousing him from a light doze. Sawyer checked on Janie, who appeared to be resting peacefully. Excellent. Now that his own adrenaline dump had dissipated, he needed food.

Slipping from the room, Sawyer laid a hand on Max's shoulder. "Monitor Janie until I get back."

His teammate rose and stood in the bedroom's doorway, his back to the room.

Satisfied that Janie would have someone near in case she woke up disoriented, Sawyer made his way to the galley. He slapped together two sandwiches and picked up two bananas. Hopefully, the scent of food wouldn't wake the woman he was guarding.

On his way back to the bedroom, Brody stopped him. "How is she?"

"Considering what she's been through, Janie's doing great."

"Was she…." He didn't finish the question.

Unnecessary. Sawyer got his meaning without the words. "Janie said the women from her plane were assaulted. She was the only one spared."

Brody frowned. "Why?"

"Question of the day, isn't it? I told her I'd find out."

His leader's eyebrows rose. "Taking this on personally, Sawyer?"

"She needed the promise, and I have to do this."

"Watch yourself."

Sawyer gave a mock salute.

"How's the shoulder?"

"Hurts," he admitted. "The bullet did some damage."

"So, more than a scratch?" Brody teased.

"A little."

The other man snorted. "Get some rest, my friend. We'll be landing in Texas in a few hours. Hopefully, the terrorists will be too busy trying to figure out who hit the compound to track us to Texas." He sobered. "Someone will come after Janie again."

"I know. I told Janie, but I don't think she believes me."

"She'll find out soon enough." Brody inclined his head toward the bedroom and returned to his seat.

"Thanks," Sawyer murmured to Max.

"No problem. She hasn't moved." Max returned to his seat.

Sawyer sat in his chair and wolfed down his meal. When he finished, he set the plate aside and settled back to watch over Janie.

Four hours later, the jet's altitude changed. They must be getting ready to land.

Before he could wake Janie, she stirred. After a luxuriant stretch, she opened her eyes and stared at Sawyer. "Hi. Have a nice nap?"

"I feel better. What's happening?"

"We'll land soon." He stood. "There's a bathroom behind you. I'll meet you in the cabin." Sawyer closed the door behind him.

Five minutes later, Janie opened the door. He straightened from the wall and took her arm to escort her to their seats. Once she strapped in, he took his seat beside her.

Soon, the pilot announced they were on approach to the airport. Within minutes, the jet rolled along the runway and came to a stop near two black SUVs.

As soon as Brody and Logan lowered the stairs, two burley men stepped into the cabin. "Injured personnel?" Blondie asked.

"Two," Brody said. "Both mobile."

A nod. "How can we help?"

"Grab gear bags. The sooner the doc gets a look at Sawyer and Janie, the better."

Blondie signaled his partner, and the two men helped the team take gear to the vehicles.

At last, Brody returned. "We're clear."

Sawyer helped Janie to her feet. "Can you walk?"

"Watch me."

He chuckled as she walked ahead of him toward Brody. His team leader stayed in front of Janie as she exited the jet, keeping her behind his taller, broader body.

Sawyer caught up with her on the first step and cupped her elbow to provide support when she wobbled. "Just a few more feet," he murmured.

Once on the tarmac, he escorted her quickly to the closest SUV, helped her into the backseat, and slid in beside her. Brody climbed into the shotgun seat while Jesse sat on the other side of Janie. If anything happened on the short drive to Sorenson's clinic, Janie would have plenty of protection.

Minutes later, the SUVs parked at the back of the clinic. The drivers got out first and scanned the area, then signaled the others. Sawyer opened the door and helped Janie from the vehicle. He guided her into the clinic while the others dealt with the Go bags and gear.

She paused halfway to the exam room, her eyes sparkling. "I hear dogs and cats." Janie turned to Sawyer with a smile.

"Dr. Sorenson's four-footed patients. Sounds like he has a full house today." He nudged her toward the exam room. "We should have time to visit the animals before we leave again."

"Where are we going to next?"

"Nashville, Tennessee."

Janie beamed.

Sawyer's breath caught. Janie Moran was absolutely gorgeous, especially when she smiled like that.

"You're taking me home. Thank you, Sawyer."

Home? He blinked. "You live in Nashville?"

"Close. I live in Hartman."

How could that be? He'd never seen her in his hometown, which wasn't that large. "So do I."

A middle-aged man strode into the room and frowned at Sawyer. "Back again, Chapman?"

He flinched. "Yes, sir." How he wished he could say they were in the clinic for Janie only. Couldn't do that, though. Brody and Jesse would have his hide if he didn't allow Sorenson to check his wound. "This is Janie. A gang took her hostage in Mexico."

Sorenson eyed her. "Injuries?"

"A few scratches and bruises, which Jesse treated. Otherwise, I'm fine."

The doc shifted his attention back to Sawyer. "You better not have pulled me away from my favorite patients to examine a scratch or bruise on you, Chapman."

"Bullet kissed my shoulder."

"Lose the shirt."

Maybe one day a beautiful woman like Janie would give Sawyer the same order. After he complied with the doctor's order, he sat on the side of the exam bed and waited in silence while Sorenson examined the injury and Jesse's repair job.

The doc grunted. "Good work by your medic. I'm not seeing signs of infection. How does your shoulder feel?"

"Like a bullet kissed me." He smiled. A long stare from the doctor had his smile fading into oblivion. Tough crowd.

"Out, Chapman. I have patients who need my attention." When Janie started for the door, Sorenson held up his hand. "Not so fast, young lady. I want to see the scratches Phelps treated, then you and I need to talk." He slid his narrowed gaze toward Sawyer. "Without an audience. You can wait outside the room."

Sawyer tugged on his shirt and stared at the doctor.

Sorenson rolled his eyes. "Yes, yes. I've got her, now get out."

He squeezed Janie's hand. "I'll be right outside the door. Call out if you need me." Sawyer forced himself to leave.

Fifteen minutes later, Sorenson opened the door. "Go home, Chapman. You're taking up valuable space and time. See one of the Fortress doctors on staff in a week. If you notice any redness, streaks, swelling, or heat, go to the headquarters clinic immediately."

"How's Janie?"

A slight pause. "Physically, she's fine. You'll need to watch her. She's already dealing with survivor's guilt."

He nodded. "Thanks, Doc."

"I don't want to see you again for a long time. Hear me?"

"Yes, sir."

"Out." He turned back to Janie, who was behind him. "You are welcome back anytime. Hopefully not for injuries. Take care, Janie."

"Thank you, sir."

Taking a chance that Janie wouldn't mind, Sawyer held out his hand to her. He breathed easier when she took his hand without hesitation, and he led her to the kitchen where his teammates waited. "We're cleared to leave."

"Excellent." Brody stood. "I'll let the pilot know we're returning to the airport." He walked from the room.

"Do you need anything, Janie?" Jesse asked. "Water, a snack?"

"Water. I can't seem to drink enough to satisfy my thirst."

"You're probably a little dehydrated." He dug into his mike bag and pulled out a familiar packet. Jesse grabbed a bottle of water and added the contents of the packet to the liquid. After he shook it, the medic handed the bottle to Janie. "I added a mix with electrolytes to help. We all drink this when we're on missions, especially in hot, humid climates."

Janie sipped the mix. Her eyebrows lifted. "It's not bad."

Brody returned. "The ground crew is servicing the jet. Grab your gear."

The Texas Team and two of Sorenson's helpers loaded the SUVs with the gear bags and they boarded the jet minutes later.

After storing their gear and strapping into their seats, Brody signaled the pilot to take off. Once in the air, the operatives settled back to take a nap.

Sawyer glanced at Janie. "You have time to take a nap like my teammates. Do you want to try sleeping?"

She shook her head. "I don't suppose you have books on board, do you?"

"We always carry books. What genre do you like?"

"Romance, historical romance, mystery, suspense, and fantasy."

He stood. "I'll be back in a minute." Sawyer made his way to the galley. Books filled one cabinet for operatives to pass the time as they flew back and forth on missions.

He scanned the titles. Hmm. No romance or historical romance. He'd have to mention that to Zane, their tech guru. Although they'd be in the air for a few hours, Sawyer thought Janie could use something totally different to read. He selected a thick book and returned to his seat. "Try this one. If you don't like it, I'll find you another book or take you to our stash so you can choose one."

Janie studied the cover. "The Eye of the World by Robert Jordan." She glanced up. "Have you read this?"

"I'm the one who put the book in the library. I love this series. Bonus that it's a long series. Each of the books is the size of a good doorstop. It should keep you busy for a while."

"This looks fabulous. Thanks for sharing your book with me, Sawyer. What will you read?"

He smiled and held up a copy of The Great Hunt, also by Robert Jordan. "Book two in the series."

They settled back to read. Before long, Janie became so absorbed in the book she didn't notice when Sawyer got up and returned with two bottles of water and placed one in her hand. "Thanks," she murmured and immediately dove into the book again.

When they landed at John C. Tune Airport, Janie frowned. "We're home already?"

Sawyer laughed. "Sorry, sweetheart. Want me to tell the pilot to take us up again?"

Janie wrinkled her nose. "I guess not."

"Do you like the book?"

"It's wonderful. I'll have to buy a copy so I can finish the book."

"Take it with you, with my compliments. I'll get another copy for the jet."

"Are you sure?"

"Positive. Everybody brings their favorite books to share with the others. This will be the sixth copy I've bought. Several of my friends have gotten hooked on the series. If you like the series, there's also an ongoing television series based on the books."

"Sold." She held the book close. "I can't wait to see what happens next. Thank you, Sawyer."

"Sure." He stood and held out his hand. "Come on. I have a feeling you have at least one person waiting to see you."

#

Chapter Seven

Janie stared in wonder at Fortress Security's headquarters building. Concrete posts and barriers were everywhere. Over twenty lined up like immovable barriers guarding the building entrance. Key card access plus retinal scans and long strings of security codes. Brent Maddox and his employees didn't mess around with security.

Good thing for her. She knew without a doubt that if anything happened while she was in this building, the surrounding people would take care of the problem before it ever became a genuine threat to her safety.

Sawyer drove his SUV into the underground garage and parked near an elevator. His teammates parked their vehicles close by.

One by one, Sawyer's teammates exited their vehicles and headed for the elevator. He came around the front of his SUV and opened her door. "Ready?"

Janie hesitated. Why was she nervous? She had been friends with Brent for several years and was even better friends with his wife. Talking to Brent should be good.

She swallowed hard, admitting the truth to herself. It wouldn't be good at all. She dreaded recounting her experiences in the hijackers' compound. But she knew Brent. He would dig for every single detail, looking for any clue why the hijackers took her and the others, yet kept only her alive.

Janie built up her courage and straightened her spine. Dithering wouldn't prevent the experience and might, in fact, cause Brent to dig harder to ferret out everything. Didn't matter how horrific or embarrassing the memories, she had to give Sawyer and the others every scrap of information. Perhaps they could locate the hijackers and bring them to justice.

She placed her hand in Sawyer's outstretched one. "Brent's waiting?"

Sawyer squeezed her hand. "He is. If you need more time, I'll take you to a conference room where you can take a minute for yourself." His lips curved. "I doubt the boss will allow you more than a minute or two before he tracks you down to demand answers."

She sighed. "That's the thing, Sawyer. I don't have any answers. I don't know why the hijackers took fifteen people from the plane, transported us to that compound, and killed all the passengers except me."

"We'll investigate and learn the truth. In the meantime, try to relax and answer Brent's questions with whatever comes out of your mouth first. Don't censor your words. Your subconscious may have the answers, but your conscious mind is blocking information."

"And if my first instinct is totally wrong?"

He shrugged his uninjured shoulder. "Won't take us long to discover what's false and what's true." Sawyer nudged her toward the elevator. "If you need a break during the questioning, let me know. I'll make sure you get a breather."

"I appreciate that." Would it be too early to take that breather five minutes after the session started?

They arrived on the sixth floor, which housed Brent's office suite, the comm center, a clinic, and several conference rooms. He guided her to Brent's office, where his assistant walked them to the boss's door.

Brent came around the desk, relief flooding his features as he hugged Janie. Those familiar arms and hard chest told Janie more than anything else that she was finally safe and close to home.

To her embarrassment, tears streamed down her cheeks. Brent held her for a while without saying a word, simply waiting. Finally, Janie stepped back and accepted the wad of tissues Sawyer handed her with a small smile of gratitude. "Sorry, Brent. I don't know where that came from."

"You're safe now, Janie, thanks to Sawyer and his teammates."

"I can't thank you enough for sending them to save me. I don't think I would have survived much longer."

"You would have found a way. You're made of steel. The Janie Moran I know doesn't give up."

"I'm glad you think so. I'm not convinced you're correct."

He waved toward the chairs in front of his desk. "Have a seat. Sawyer, sit rep."

Sawyer spent several minutes recounting events from the time he and his teammates diverted to Mexico to the harrowing escape from the hijackers.

"How many did you take out?"

Sawyer glanced at Janie, unease clear to read in his eyes. "Twenty-five, sir."

"You were the only one injured?"

"Yes, sir."

"How bad is the injury? And don't lie to me, Chapman. I'll find out and make you pay for lying."

"Twenty stitches in my shoulder. Sorenson kicked me out of the clinic." He smiled. "Guess I don't rate as a seriously injured patient."

"How long did he say you'll be off duty?"

Sawyer flinched. "A week, maybe more, depending on how the wound heals."

Brent turned his attention to Janie. "Your turn. Tell me everything from the beginning. Leave nothing out, no matter how trivial you think it is."

And there it was. The one thing she dreaded. Details. If she left anything out, Brent would know and call her hand on it.

To her surprise, Sawyer threaded his fingers through hers, lending her silent support. Such a good man. She couldn't let either of them down.

Janie drew in a deep breath and did as Brent ordered. She started from the beginning. Although she tried to report the facts just like

Sawyer had, Janie couldn't do it. Her emotions kept creeping into her recitation of events.

When she reached the point where she and her fellow passengers were shoved into the back of the van, her voice broke and tears formed in her eyes.

Sawyer said, "Janie needs a break, Brent."

Her friend's eyebrows rose. "You speak for her now?"

Sawyer's cheeks flushed. "You taught us to pay attention to our principals. Janie needs a break. Sir."

A principal? Disappointment twisted through Janie. That's all she was to Sawyer? A job? She wanted to slap herself. They'd just met hours ago. She was simply a job. Sawyer Chapman didn't know her. But inside, she felt like he should know her. Ridiculous. He didn't. End of story.

"Janie?" Brent straightened from his desk. "Do you need a break?"

She had to be honest with herself. Trembling hands weren't normal for her. "Ten minutes to walk around and get a drink would help."

A small nod. "Go. Take your time." Brent stared at Sawyer, who gave a curt nod in response.

Sawyer held out his hand to Janie. "Come on. Let's walk."

Janie clasped his hand and allowed Sawyer to escort her from the office.

"Finished already?" Brent's assistant asked with a smile.

"Not yet," Sawyer said. "Break time."

They walked down the hall. Sawyer opened a door and led her inside a small conference room. Once he seated her, the operative crouched in front of her. "What do you need?"

"Water is fine."

He studied Janie a moment. "Would you like some hot tea?"

Her breath caught. "Do you have some? I don't want to put anyone out, but I'd love a cup of tea."

"No problem." He stood. "I'll be back in a minute."

After he left the conference room, Janie settled back in the comfortable chair and closed her eyes. She had known talking about her experience in Mexico would be difficult, but hadn't expected the gut-wrenching emotions. She'd never been a sob sister. Janie wrinkled her nose. Definitely not true today. How embarrassing.

She sighed. Hopefully, Brent would forget her weepy moments and not hold them against her. She didn't want him to worry about her. She'd be fine. Falling apart all the time wasn't acceptable. She had a life to resume, a business to grow.

Sawyer returned a moment later with a to-go cup and a banana. "The tea is from me. Jesse sent the banana."

"Thanks, Sawyer." She inhaled the scent of mint tea. "Mint tea is my favorite, and I love bananas."

He smiled. "Do I get brownie points for personal delivery service?"

As Janie laughed, a few of the knots in her stomach loosened. "Definitely."

While she sipped the tea and ate the banana, Sawyer regaled her with funny incidents from his training and work as a cop in Texas. Before she knew it, she had finished her tea and banana and their break time was more than over. "We should go back to Brent's office."

"Depends on whether you're ready. We can take a few more minutes if you need them."

Janie shook her head. "I'll never be ready. I should get this over with as soon as possible." And find a place to fall apart in private.

He helped Janie to her feet. "Same rules apply. If you need to stop, we'll take a break. Brent can wait. You are my priority, Janie, not Brent."

"I know. I'm your principal. You have to take care of me."

"Hey." He stopped her before she could grasp the doorknob and turned her to face him. "It's true you're my principal, but that's not all. I care about you, Janie. I want to take care of you, and it's not only because of my job."

She stared. "You're not just saying that to be nice?"

Sawyer slowly lifted his hand and cupped her cheek. "I don't lie unless it's necessary on a mission. Never to people I care about. Not to you. Ever. If I can't answer a question because of security reasons, I'll tell you why I can't give you an answer."

Janie took a few seconds to lean into his touch, storing up the feeling of comfort and safety to get her through the next interview session. "Thank you."

"No comment about me caring for you so soon after we met?"

What could she say to that? Janie was as guilty as Sawyer. "I'm glad you do," she murmured. That was the most neutral comment she could think of without giving her own growing feelings away. Janie nuzzled his hand, hoping to convey some of what she felt.

Was she just feeling grateful to Sawyer for rescuing her? She considered that as they headed toward Brent's office, Sawyer's hand resting on her lower back. No, she knew her own mind and heart. Janie didn't feel only gratitude. This was something more, something special. Did he feel the same?

Janie pushed the emotions aside to ponder later. For all she knew, Sawyer might be involved with someone. That thought depressed her. But what did she really know about him? Only that he was handsome, fearless, hard-working, considerate, caring, and could make her feel like she was the only person in his life who mattered.

She sighed. Toast. That's what she was. Toast.

Sawyer knocked on Brent's door and opened it. He escorted Janie inside.

Brent came around his desk again and this time motioned for her to sit on the sofa in the sitting area of his office.

Sawyer sat beside Janie and wrapped his hand around hers in silent support.

Brent sat in one armchair and studied Janie's face. Finally, he said, "Ready to continue?"

No. She might never be ready. Janie nodded. "Time to finish this before I lose my courage."

He smiled faintly. "Never going to happen, my friend. Tell me the rest."

So she did. Janie might have cried silent tears the whole time, but she told Brent and Sawyer about the women and the men who visited them, often for hours at a time. She relayed the horror of listening to the assault on the woman from her plane and the men carrying her body wrapped in a blanket from the building.

At the end, Janie admitted to losing hope of a rescue before Scar Face or one of his friends raped and killed her, too. Then Sawyer and his teammates arrived in time to save her.

When the tears subsided, Brent watched her in silence for a moment. "I'm sorry you went through that experience, Janie. No one should have to wonder if they're going to die at the hands of men who are more interested in their own agenda than preserving human life. Despite the circumstances, you survived."

Right. A miracle. Or was it? She glanced at Sawyer, then shifted her gaze to Brent. "Why?"

"That's the question of the hour, isn't it? Do you have any idea why you were spared when everyone else taken from the plane was murdered?"

Janie shook her head. "It makes little sense. Why kill the other four women and ten men, but leave me alive when they could have easily killed me too in a matter of seconds?"

Beside her, Sawyer stiffened. "Ten men? Are you sure about the number?"

"I'm positive. Why?"

"If we showed you some pictures, would you recognize your fellow passengers?" Brent asked.

"Of course. I've always had an excellent memory for faces."

He stood. "Wait here. I'll be back in a minute." Before he left the office, Brent looked at Sawyer. Although no words passed between them, an unspoken message passed from one man to the other. After Sawyer gave a curt nod, Brent left his office.

"What's going on, Sawyer?"

"Be specific."

"Why did Brent give you The Look?"

Amusement lit his eyes. "The Look?"

Her cheeks burned. "You know what I'm talking about. What does it mean?"

"He passed responsibility for your safety to me while he's out of the office."

Stunned, she sat back, eyes wide. "Why? I'm safe in this building, aren't I?"

"We take nothing for granted, especially safety. While the chance of someone slipping past all our security is negligible, it's not zero."

Janie shuddered. She thought she'd left the danger behind her in Mexico. Had danger followed her home?

Sawyer squeezed her hand. "Don't worry. If something happens, we'll take care of it."

"I believe you. I'm more concerned that danger followed me home."

"Until we're sure you're safe, at least one of us will be with you."

"But you have a job to do. You can't follow me around my soap shop all day when there are other people who need saving like I did."

"Fortress has more than one team of operatives. Right now, we have a job. You."

Brent returned to the office with a file folder in his hand. He sat on the other side of Janie and handed her the folder. "Look at these pictures and tell me if you recognize the people taken from the plane with you."

She swallowed hard as she stared at the closed folder. Steeling herself for the unpleasant task of identifying her fellow passengers, Janie opened the folder. Relief swept over her. Brent had printed pictures from sources other than photos from the carnage at the compound.

Janie tapped the first photo. "This guy was about fifteen rows back from me on the plane." She moved from passenger to passenger, identifying their location in the cabin in relation to her.

When Janie turned over the last photo, she frowned. "Where's the last one?"

Brent stared at her. "There are no others, sugar."

"There's a man missing. He sat in the seat beside mine."

Brent exchanged a long look with Sawyer. "Is it possible you missed him in all the chaos?"

"No, sir." He flicked a glance at Janie, then refocused on Brent. "The bodies of the passengers were close together. We didn't miss anyone. We took pictures of all the bodies as we searched for Janie. There weren't any others except for women who had the gang's brand on their ankles and members of Vatos Locos. We took pictures of them as well and sent them to Zane."

"Is it possible the tenth man was among the dead gang members?" Janie asked. "Perhaps he wore clothes similar to the ones the gang wore."

Brent rose. "I'll have Z set up the conference room so we can examine the photos of the gang members. Perhaps your missing passenger is a gang member."

Sawyer stood and held out his hand to Janie. "Come with me. Would you like a drink or a snack?"

"Water, please."

"Feeling okay?"

She shrugged. What could she say, that she'd never feel normal again? That wasn't acceptable. Janie wouldn't let Scar Face and his pals win this terror game. She would reclaim her life and again enjoy the feeling of security in her hometown of Hartman. Somehow.

Sawyer rested his hand on her lower back as they walked from the office and down the hall to a large conference room. Once he seated her, the operative left and returned a minute later with two bottles of water. He set both in front of her. "There are plenty more in the break room. Drink as much as you want, Janie."

Soon, Brent entered the room accompanied by a dark-haired man in a wheelchair who rolled toward her.

He held out his hand. "Zane Murphy."

"Janie Moran."

"It's good to meet you, Janie. Brent and Rowan have told me a lot about you. Rowan raves about your soap shop so much that my wife, Claire, is planning a trip soon to your store."

She grinned. "That's great. Tell her to introduce herself when she comes. I will give her the friends and family discount."

Zane chuckled. "Although it's unnecessary, my wallet thanks you."

"Zane is our tech and communication guru," Brent said. "He worked as tech and comm support for the Texas Team during your rescue mission."

Janie sobered. "Then I owe you for helping Sawyer and his teammates."

"It was my pleasure, Janie. I'm glad you're here safe." Zane squeezed her hand, then headed for the computer center at the back of the room.

"As soon as you're ready, Z," Brent said as he sat on the other side of Janie.

"One minute." Several clicks of the keys later, he said, "Ready." A photo flashed on the screen.

Janie gasped.

"Recognize him?" Brent asked.

"It's the man I dubbed Scar Face. He raped and killed the woman in the cell next to mine." She shuddered, feeling as though she'd been out in a blizzard for so long the cold had seeped into her bones.

Sawyer squeezed her hand. "I'll return in a minute," he murmured and left the room.

Seeing him leave made her feel abandoned. Stupid. She barely knew the man. Janie motioned to the screen. "Who is he?"

"His name is Jorge Zapatos. He's second in command of Vatos Locos."

"Was he killed by the Texas Team?"

Brent shook his head. "He slipped away in the chaos."

Her heart sank. "That's not good, is it?"

"No, it's not."

Great. Just great. "Keep going."

Zane put up another picture, and another, followed by more.

Janie could only identify a handful of the men by their faces. "Are there any more photos?"

Sawyer returned with a blanket that he draped over her.

Brent looked at Zane. "More photos?"

"That's all we have."

"Are you sure?" Janie asked.

"There is one more member of Vatos Locos in that area, but I can't put up a photo of him."

"Why not?"

"He's the leader of Vatos Locos, and no one knows what he looks like. As far as we know, no one has a picture of him."

That couldn't be right. "In this age of photo crazy cell phone owners, how can that be?"

"It's a puzzle," Brent admitted.

She sighed. Weird, but whatever. "That still doesn't help us identify the man who sat next to me on the plane."

"He's not listed on the passenger manifest," Zane said.

"We need to identify this man," Sawyer said. "Doing so may hold the key to why Janie is still alive."

Brent turned to Janie. "You said you're good with faces."

She nodded.

"Are you willing to work with our sketch artist?"

"Of course, if you think it will help."

"What are you thinking, Brent?" Sawyer asked.

A grim expression settled on the CEO of Fortress Security's face. "I think Janie sat next to the head of Vatos Locos."

Chapter Eight

Sawyer's gut twisted into a knot. If Janie could identify the head of the gang, she had a huge target on her back. The gang was notorious for eliminating all loose ends. No exceptions. "Janie, can you think of any reason someone would want to kidnap you?"

Janie shook her head. "I make and sell soap and bath salt for a living. My customers let me know quickly if something isn't to their liking. They certainly don't create an elaborate plot to kidnap and kill me because they don't like the scent of their bath salts."

"What about in your personal life? Do you have a boyfriend or husband, current or ex, with a grudge against you?" He hated to ask these questions, but they were necessary. As a homicide cop, he'd asked similar questions of spouses, loved ones, and friends. The answers varied. The resentment didn't. Would Janie resent his probing into her private life?

"Sawyer." Brent's voice held an unspoken warning to tread carefully.

He held up a hand to prevent his boss from protesting further. "Janie?"

"Not a boyfriend or husband."

Sawyer considered Janie's response, her careful choice of words. "But someone else." Who had something against her and what caused the division?

"Yes," she murmured.

"Who?" Brent asked.

Janie remained silent.

"We want to protect you," he continued. "We can't do the job properly if we don't have all the facts."

Sawyer squeezed her fingers. "My team will protect you regardless, but we'll do a better job if we know who to look for."

Her eyes glittered. "He would never hurt me."

Brent pounced on that. "He? Give us a name, Janie."

"Why? He's not to blame for what happened to me or the other passengers on the plane. He was at home with his wife."

After a moment, Sawyer said, "Your brother?"

Brent scowled. "David threatened you?"

"It's not what you think." Janie huddled deeper into the blanket.

"Then why are you afraid?" Sawyer asked. He wrapped his arm around Janie's shoulders.

To his dismay, she shivered continuously. A reaction to reliving the events from the hijacking, or was it something else? Whatever was causing her response triggered a massive protective reaction in him. What was up with that? He'd literally just met the woman a few hours prior.

Sawyer shoved the consternation behind a steel wall to deal with when he was alone. "Talk to me, sweetheart. Tell me who scares you."

"My brother."

Brent shoved up from the couch to pace.

Not a good sign. Sawyer watched his agitated boss. Brent never paced. "Brent?"

"Not yet," he snapped.

He flinched at the sharp-edged response and turned to Janie. "Talk to me. Help me understand what's happening here."

"When our parents died in a plane crash, our grandmother took us in and raised us." She smiled. "Raising teenagers isn't for the faint of heart, but Granny Irene loved a challenge. She loved us fiercely."

Her smile faded. "Then she was diagnosed with an aggressive form of cancer. Granny Irene was gone in three months. I was a senior in college. David was already working for the engineering firm that employs him now. He was packing his belongings, preparing to move to the Chilean office where he's located now."

"What happened?"

"Because he was two years older, David expected to be named as executor of Granny Irene's estate." She looked at Brent, who had returned to his seat and now rested his forearms on his thighs. "Granny Irene made me the executor instead."

"Why?" Sawyer asked. What was she so reluctant to share?

"David is hardworking and great at his job. His employer sings his praise all the time."

"But?" he prompted.

"He's not so great at managing money."

And there it was. The secret Janie hadn't wanted to share. "He contested the will?"

She nodded. "The court rejected the challenge."

"David objected to the terms of the will?"

"He wanted control of the money from the estate."

"Your grandmother left everything to you?"

Another nod. "I was supposed to give David the amount she wanted him to have. Granny Irene gave the rest of the estate to me."

Brent whistled. "No wonder your brother was angry."

"Furious is a better description. He needed more money, although he never told me why when he pressured me to sell everything and split the proceeds evenly with him."

Sawyer and Brent exchanged glances. "Does your brother have addictions, Janie?" Sawyer asked.

She stared. "Addictions?"

"Drugs or alcohol?"

"No, of course not." Despite her vehement denial, she dropped her gaze.

"Are you sure?" Brent asked softly.

Her cheeks colored. "He left for Chile the day after his challenge was rejected. We talk little and certainly nothing about his habits."

Sawyer frowned. "Although you're not close, you visited him in Chile."

Janie gave a small shrug. "He married a sweet woman three months ago. She's been begging me to come visit them. I thought David knew she'd invited me. Turns out she didn't tell him until I was on the doorstep. He wasn't pleased. My brother spent the two weeks I was there at the office or trying to convince me to do what was right."

Jerk. "How long has it been since your grandmother passed away?"

"Almost four years."

"And he still needs money?"

"That's what he told me." Janie sighed. "He cranked up the pressure to boiling while I was there. It turns out that Maria, his wife, is pregnant. He says he needs money to prepare for the baby's arrival."

Brent hissed out a breath. "So David is using guilt to get you to change your mind about your grandmother's property. Why didn't you tell me, sugar? I would have talked to David."

And forced him to back off, too. Sawyer's boss didn't put up with anything from his employees or anyone else. If something was wrong, he called attention to it, and this had warning signs stamped all over it.

"Brent, you have enough problems to deal with daily. This is nothing compared to the life-threatening emergencies you handle. I've held firm for the past three years. I'll do as my grandmother wanted. Besides, David will receive more money in two years."

"But not as much as he wants or says he deserves," Sawyer murmured. "Right?"

Janie nodded.

"How much is he asking for?" Brent asked.

"Two million dollars."

Sawyer's head whipped toward hers. "Holy smoke, Janie."

"I know babies are expensive, but no one should need that much money to decorate a room and buy clothes and diapers." Brent scowled. "So, what does David really want the money for?"

"I don't know." She grimaced. "He never told me."

"You went to Chile to repair the relationship with your brother?"

"And failed in spectacular fashion," she said, her tone dry. "All he wanted was the money which I can't give him according to the terms of Granny Irene's will."

"Will you go back to Chile?" Sawyer asked.

"I want to see my niece or nephew. This time, though, I'm going to stay in a nearby hotel. I don't want to be in the way, and I need a place to retreat to when David continues to plead his case."

He couldn't help but admire her grit and courage. Most people would have thrown up their hands and walked away. Not Janie, though.

"Let me know when you plan to go back," Brent said. "One of us will go with you."

"Oh, but...."

"David's not as likely to corner you when someone else is with you."

Janie gave a slight smile. "Thanks, Brent."

"We could have a problem," Zane said, his voice grim.

"Sit rep." Brent turned toward his communications and tech guru.

"I'm picking up chatter on the dark web. The Vatos Locos are stirred up about someone important coming to the states soon."

His eyes narrowed. "And?"

"The visitor is bringing two heavy hitters with him to take care of a problem." Zane looked at Janie.

Chapter Nine

A ball of ice formed in Sawyer's gut. This wasn't good. Two hit men coming after Janie? Was this related to her brother or something else? Despite her detailed journey through the events of the hijacking, was it possible that Janie saw or heard something that was a threat to someone in the gang? Was Brent correct in wondering if the missing passenger was the head of the Vatos Locos?

Brent rose. "I'll return in a minute. Sit tight." He looked at Sawyer. "Take care of her."

"Yes, sir."

After he left the conference room, Janie said, "You don't have to do that, Sawyer. I'm fine. Really."

"You won't disobey your grandmother's directives in her will. I won't disobey my boss. So, do you need anything?"

"I'm still cold," she admitted. "Would the break room have more tea packets?"

He walked toward the door. "It does. I'll be right back. If anything happens while I'm gone, do exactly what Zane tells you to do. He'll keep you safe." Although Sawyer hated to hand responsibility for her safety to anyone else, he trusted Zane as much as he trusted Brent. Both of the SEALs had saved his life more than once since Fortress had employed him.

He hurried to the break room, found another packet of mint tea, and nuked the water in a to-go cup. When the brewing cycle finished, Sawyer added the lid and carried the drink to the conference room.

In his absence, the rest of his team had assembled around the conference table. Brent motioned Sawyer to take a seat.

"Has there been a development?" Brody asked.

"Two things. Z is picking up chatter from the dark web about a Vatos Locos bigwig bringing two hit men to deal with a problem in the states."

"And you think the problem is Janie?"

A nod from the CEO of Fortress Security.

Brody blew out a breath. "Nice. We're taking on a gang whose membership is 10,000 strong, plus two guest assassins."

"You said two developments," Logan said. "What's the second one?"

"Sawyer and I showed Janie pictures of all those hostages we believed were passengers aboard the hijacked plane. One man is missing. We also showed her pictures of the known Vatos Locos gang members from that compound in Mexico. The missing man's picture wasn't in the array we showed her."

Two beats later, Logan said, "Janie saw Diego Hernandez?"

Max's eyebrows soared. "Good for us. Not for our principal."

Jesse whistled.

"The danger level just increased by a thousand percent," Brody said.

"If your guess is correct." Janie looked at each man. "This is pure speculation."

"Zane doesn't raise the alarm unless he's sure." Brent shook his head. "I'm sorry, sugar."

"This makes little sense. I was just on a plane, minding my own business. Now, I'm a wanted woman just because I saw some random guy that I'll probably never see again in my life?"

"Remember what we mentioned earlier." Sawyer pressed the warm cup of tea into Janie's shaking hands. "No one knows what Diego Hernandez looks like. It's what has kept him out of prison for so long. No one knows who to look for. Now, that may change."

"What about a sketch artist?" Brody asked. "Think a session with Ian would help?"

Ian McGregor was a top-notch sketch artist who worked for Fortress but also contracted with police departments around the country is they needed an artist of his caliber. The suggestion was a good one.

Sawyer said, "You'd like him, Janie. He's very good at what he does. Ian can pull more information out of you than you realize you have inside your brain. Would you be willing to work with him?"

"Of course."

Brent looked at Zane. "Find him. Let's do this as quickly as possible so the team can take Janie into seclusion."

"Wait a minute," Janie protested. "No one said anything about going into hiding. I have a business to run, Brent. I can't disappear without an explanation and plans."

He eyed her. "Would you rather risk your life and those of your employees?"

"We don't know if I'm in danger. No offense to Zane, but the warning from the Internet could be about anything. The rumors didn't mention the name of the target."

"Of course not. Rumors leak. The Vatos Locos wouldn't want their prey to escape."

She shuddered. "You must be wrong."

"What if I'm not? Do you want to gamble on the lives of your people, Janie?"

"That's not fair. You know I wouldn't. But I'm not convinced you're right. Why would anyone consider me a threat?"

"The gang kept you alive for a reason, Janie." Sawyer wrapped his arm around her shoulders. "Until we uncover that reason, you and everyone around you are in danger."

She was silent a moment. "How long do we have before the bigwig shows up in the US?"

"Tomorrow, possibly the day after," Zane answered. "It's a guess at this point. There's not enough information on the dark web to come up with an exact time."

"Do I have enough time to check on my shop and my people? I can do it fast, but I need to check in."

"We'll work it out," Sawyer said. "Can you ask your employees to come in early? The fewer people around, the better."

"No problem. We always get started on the stock early, before the shop opens."

"You make everything from scratch, right?" Max asked.

Janie nodded. "We make stock early to bring our supplies up to full level. After that, we make stock to order or to fill out the shelves during the day. We also offer classes."

"My wife would like that."

"All our women would like it," Brody said. "Once this problem with Vatos Locos is settled, we'll book a class for the women."

Janie beamed. "I'd love to do a class with them. It will be fun."

"My wallet already hurts," Logan said, although his eyes twinkled.

The rest of the men laughed.

"Back to business," Brent said. "Create a security plan, Brody."

"Yes, sir. Location?"

"Sawyer?"

"Hartman, so she can check in on her shop," he said. Janie was having enough trouble accepting the need for protection instead of returning to her normal life. If she was in her hometown, at least she would be more accepting of the precautions.

Soon, though, Sawyer figured the hometown solution would give way to something more drastic. Vatos Locos wouldn't have difficulty locating Janie if she returned home. When they did, he and his teammates would move Janie to a more remote location unless he found out she was being targeted by someone else.

Janie smiled at him. "Thanks, Sawyer."

"We can't stay long. I know you'll want to help with the stock. It's not safe for you or them to stay for more than an hour or two. We'll work as fast as we can to solve this problem and bring you back home."

Brent glanced at his watch. "I have another meeting in ten minutes. Brody, you need a place in Hartman to protect Janie. Figure out where is safest for her. Zane can help with safe house arrangements if you need the assist. Let me know if I can help." He looked at Janie. "We've got you covered, sugar. Do what your bodyguards tell you to do." Brent pointed at her. "Don't make their jobs more difficult."

"Yes, sir."

He stood and looked at Sawyer.

Yeah, he got the unspoken message. He gave a slight nod. He would take care of Janie no matter the cost to himself.

"Zane, report to me when you and the team finish."

"Yes, sir."

With that, Brent left the conference room.

"I've never seen this side of him. Is he always like this?" Janie asked.

"At work, yeah, he is." Brody turned to Zane. "What options do we have, Z?"

"Hotel near Interstate 40, one house inside Hartman town limits, and two outside of town."

"Not the hotel," Janie said. "Too many people around."

"Agreed," Sawyer said. "Let's try a house outside Hartman first. How many of us can it house at one time?"

"All of you. However, I thought since you were in your hometown, the five of you would switch off on watch shifts."

"Not me." Sawyer glanced at Brody and received a nod of approval. "I'm permanent until the danger is gone. Everyone else can rotate in and out. How close are our houses to the safe house?"

"Farthest is fifteen minutes."

Brody nodded. "We can work with that. Who wants the first shift with Sawyer?"

"I'll take it," Jesse said. "I'll be able to keep tabs on my patient that way."

"That's settled. Has everyone restocked their Go bags?" When each man indicated they were stocked and ready, Brody stood. "Let's go. Traffic is picking up as we speak. Sawyer, you stay in the middle of our caravan. We'll separate when we reach Hartman. Move out."

"Wait," Janie said. "What about my shop? When can I go to my shop?"

"Tomorrow morning. I know you want to go sooner, but we need time to evaluate the security risks and make plans to deal with problems that might come up. Also, by going tomorrow, we'll give Sawyer a little more time to heal before he steps into full bodyguard mode." He smiled. "And as much as you won't want to admit it, you probably have jet lag. Call your shop. Meet your employees tomorrow morning, and we'll go from there."

"What will you do in the meantime?"

"Arrange an appointment with Ian McGregor and hunt for the people who have a target on your back." He glanced at Z. "Access to the safe house and address?"

"Stop by the comm center and I'll get you everything you need."

They followed Zane down the hall to his domain filled with computer screens and keyboards and a high-tech communications setup. This was the place where Z kept the teams out in the field connected and informed. Sawyer knew for a fact that his friend had a similar setup in his home office. He'd wondered more than once when Z slept. He seemed to always be on duty.

In the comm center, Zane zoomed to a set of cabinets and drawers. He opened one and pulled out a small packet, which he tossed to Sawyer. "Codes and keys, plus an address. The house is fifteen minutes outside of Hartman. Security system is top of the line. You won't have any close neighbors, so no nosy questions."

"Clothes?" Sawyer knew Janie didn't have her luggage, and he didn't want to take her by her own home in case someone was watching the place.

"We have the basics in almost every size. It should take care of you for a few days. If you're still in the safe house by then, we'll provide more clothes."

"I don't want Fortress to go to that expense. Wouldn't it be simpler to stop by our homes to get what we need?" Janie asked.

"Too dangerous." Sawyer gave Zane a chin lift and guided Janie into the hall toward the elevator. "It won't be hard for anyone to find you, Janie. A simple Internet search would do the trick."

She stopped and swung around to face him. "We left Mexico less than 24 hours ago. How could they get out of Mexico, find my house, and set up an ambush this fast?"

"We didn't wipe out the Vatos Locos gang in that compound." Taking the gang out would have meant Janie was safe. Probably. He didn't believe the gang had targeted Janie at random, not with her brother pressuring her for money. When they settled into the safe house and she'd rested, he and Jesse would question her about other potential enemies who might want to harm her. One thing he knew. Janie was definitely a target. The hijacking wasn't a random event. Now he had to find out why she'd been singled out. He wouldn't rest until he had.

She paled. "You're telling me there could be more members of the gang?"

"Yes, ma'am. They're 10,000 strong in Mexico, Central America, the US, and Canada. The men we killed have colleagues who will be glad to run you to ground and kill you if that's their orders."

"You're serious?"

"I never joke about things like this. You'll know when I'm teasing you, Janie. Your life being at stake is no laughing matter to any of us."

She sighed. "And you have no way of knowing how long it will take to handle the problem, do you?"

"I wish."

"You weren't kidding about my employees being at risk?"

He shook his head, then jabbed the elevator call button. "I'll ask Brent to assign someone to monitor the place, but I don't know if he'll be able to protect each person after business hours. We're shorthanded." Familiar story at Fortress. The boss was constantly recruiting new talent, but training them to Fortress standards took time.

"I wish I could shut down the store to protect everyone, but I haven't been open long enough to survive financially if I do." She stepped into the elevator with him. "Perhaps I should tell everyone to stay home and run the store myself."

"No."

"But Sawyer...."

"It's not safe for you to be in the same place day after day with a set schedule. You'd be begging the gang to take you out along with your bodyguards."

Her head whipped his direction. "You're talking about yourself."

"I'm not leaving your side until this is resolved or unless I know you're in a secure place with no chance of the gang attacking you."

"Surely Brent will deploy you and your team soon."

"You're our mission, Janie. We won't deploy until you're safe."

"That could take a long time."

"It's possible."

The elevator car came to a stop. They stepped into the garage to see the Texas Team waiting for them.

"All set?" Brody asked.

Sawyer gave a curt nod. "The safe house is fifteen minutes from my place. If we're compromised, we'll take Janie to my house."

"Works for me," Logan said. "Your place isn't far from all our homes. We'll be minutes away if you need backup. Brody?"

"It's a good plan. I'm sure Brent and Zane thought about that when they suggested this safe house." He straightened. "Let's move. My wife is waiting for me."

"Same," the others said, except for Jesse.

"What about you, Jesse?" Janie asked. "Will you wife be upset with you for staying to protect me?"

"Simone and I are engaged, but she'll be fine with a phone call or video chat with me and our dog, Goose."

"Goose?" She smiled.

"He's a toy poodle. His name is almost bigger than he is."

"Smart, though," Sawyer said. "I'm training him to be a watchdog."

Janie's eyebrows rose. "Seriously?"

"Don't underestimate him. He's a smart little dog. Goose has great instincts."

Jesse chuckled. "We'll introduce you to him, Janie."

"I'm looking forward to it."

"Let's go." Brody turned toward his SUV. "I'll follow you to the safe house, Sawyer. The rest of you go on home and get some rest. Sawyer will send the watch rotation in a few hours."

"Copy that."

In less than a minute, the rest of the team had driven away from the garage while Sawyer was helping Janie into his vehicle. He circled the hood and climbed behind the wheel. Soon, he turned onto

Harding Place and headed for the Interstate. Time to get Janie behind closed doors and let her regroup.

While she rested, Sawyer had some Internet searching to do.

Chapter Ten

Janie opened her eyes and stared at the unfamiliar room. Where was she? A beat later, she relaxed. Of course. The safe house. She felt as though the precaution was overkill. What if it wasn't, though? She still didn't believe this Vatos Locos gang wanted her bad enough to come after her in Hartman.

That reminded her of David. She didn't believe her own brother was responsible for her experience with the hijackers. Something else was going on here, but what?

Janie shoved aside the sheet and quilt. No matter what was happening, she wouldn't solve the problem by staying in bed. Besides, she had employees to check on, stock to make, and an appointment with Ian McGregor to create a picture of her missing fellow traveler. If he was an innocent victim, she hoped nothing bad had happened to him.

After a quick shower, Janie dressed and went downstairs to the kitchen. Sawyer was reading something on his phone and sipping coffee.

He glanced up and smiled. "Morning, beautiful. How do you feel?"

Beautiful? Wow. This guy was a charmer. "Better than yesterday. I'm ready to go back to work and help. If you feel it's too dangerous for me to be at the shop during working hours, maybe I can make some of the stock at the shop early in the morning or perhaps at the safe house. I always have extra ingredients in case I want to experiment with scents and textures at home."

"That's an excellent idea. You can still help but not be in public sight. Can your employees handle the shop if you help supply stock?"

"It will certainly make things easier for them."

"It's an excellent compromise, Janie. Thanks for working with me."

"I don't want you or your teammates at risk, Sawyer."

"No way around that. We're well trained. For your safety and protection, do exactly what we say, and we'll all have a better chance of escaping a dangerous situation with a minimum of injuries."

"You can count on it. I owe you for saving my life in Mexico."

"This isn't about balancing the scales. I want you safe. That's my priority."

And she wanted the same for him. Over the past day or so, Sawyer meant something to her. Perhaps the feeling was gratitude. She didn't think so, though. "Thank you."

He inclined his head, then handed her a mug. "Chamomile and honey tea."

Janie breathed deep and sighed. "This smells wonderful." She sipped. "The tea tastes as good as it smells."

"Hungry?"

"Not really, but I need to eat." Even if the sun wasn't up yet. She'd never been a morning person. Running her own retail business meant she'd learned to adapt. The business world didn't run on her preferred schedule.

"Something light, then?"

"Please."

He turned toward the refrigerator.

"I can cook."

"Excellent. Tomorrow morning is your turn."

Jesse strode into the kitchen to pour coffee into a mug. "You're up early, Janie. Feeling okay?"

"Fine."

He folded his arms across his chest, staring at her.

Janie's cheeks burned. So, it was a slight exaggeration. Did he have to call her on it? "I'm exhausted and achy, but I have to help my workers make stock for the store before we open for business."

Jesse looked at Sawyer, who held up his hands. The medic shook his head. "Don't push yourself," he said to Janie. "You're still dealing with jet lag and the stress of the hijacking. I know you need to help your employees, but don't push."

"I hear you."

The man snorted. "And you're going to do what you want, right?"

She smiled.

"You are as stubborn as the woman I'm going to marry soon. So, what's for breakfast, Sawyer?"

"Scrambled eggs, bagels, and fruit."

"Sounds like a winner to me."

Dismay filled Janie. "That's what you call a light breakfast?"

"Normally, I have bacon and potatoes along with this," Sawyer countered. "This is light. Besides, you decide how much you want to eat. I will not fill your plate with heaping portions. Remember, we train hard every day when we're not on missions. That includes five to ten-mile runs. If we didn't eat like this, we'd lose weight and muscle. We can't afford to do either."

Hmm. Well, she couldn't argue with the results of their regimen. Every member of their team was ripped, especially Sawyer.

After breakfast, Jesse joined them in Sawyer's SUV. He insisted on riding in the backseat and giving the shotgun seat to Janie.

Fifteen minutes later, Sawyer parked his vehicle behind Natural Bliss. Janie reached for the door handle.

"Wait," Sawyer said. "Let me check the area first to be sure there aren't any visible threats."

Oops. Fifteen minutes into their day, and she'd already forgotten his rules. "Sorry."

He squeezed her hand, then exited the SUV and scanned the area. After a moment, he must have been satisfied because he came around to open her door.

Sawyer held out his hand. "Keys to your shop?"

Of course. He'd want to check the premises before he allowed her to step foot inside the building. The problem was, she had nothing. The hijackers had forced her to leave everything behind on the plane. How could she have forgotten? "They're still in Mexico."

"No problem. Do you have an alarm?"

No problem? Was he going to break down the steel door? Good luck with that. Janie rattled off the code and watched as Sawyer pulled something from his pocket, crouched in front of the door, and seconds later turned the knob and stepped inside. "Did you see that?" she asked Jesse. "It took Sawyer about ten seconds to unlock my door."

"Slow for him. He's usually faster than that."

"You're kidding, right?"

"No, ma'am. We're trained in everything imaginable, including picking locks."

Of course they were. Who knew when you might need to break into a place to save a victim of a crime? After all, Sawyer had already picked the lock on her cell in seconds.

Sawyer reappeared two minutes later and opened her door. "Clear." He helped her from the vehicle and hustled Janie into her shop while scanning the area for trouble. Thankfully, they didn't encounter any.

Once the three of them were inside Natural Bliss, Sawyer reset the alarm. "Do you have a spare key to the shop? I could keep picking the lock, but eventually one of the Hartman police officers will catch me at it and ask some hard questions."

Janie smiled, amused. "I do. It's locked in my desk drawer inside my locked office. Do you have a stopwatch, Jesse? I'd like to see how fast Sawyer really is."

The medic chuckled.

Sawyer's eyes twinkled. "Enjoying this, are you?"

"Immensely. Jesse tells me that ten seconds was slow for you. Is he telling the truth?"

"Maybe."

"Fortress training taught you how to break into places?"

He hesitated.

Ah ha. A story. Janie pointed at him. "The truth, Chapman."

Jesse folded his arms. "Yeah, buddy. Let's hear it."

"Fortress honed my B & E skills."

Sawyer had a history of B & E? Seriously? "Wait. Weren't you a cop?"

"My entire team was in law enforcement in Texas."

"So, where did you learn to break and enter?"

"My misspent youth."

She stared. "You learned the skill when you were a kid? How?"

"We were dirt poor. My dad died in prison, leaving my mom with five kids to raise by herself. She did her best, but Mom had to work two jobs to put food on the table and keep a roof over our heads. Unfortunately, she never finished high school, so her jobs were low paying. My brothers and I raised ourselves on the streets. My oldest brother, Hugh, made sure we went to school every day. We didn't always have enough food for lunch, but he made us go every day, anyway.

"People in our neighborhood called us street rats. They weren't wrong. It's amazing none of us got into serious trouble with the gangs or the law."

"Who taught you how to pick locks?"

"Charlie, the jewel thief who lived a mile and a world away from us." Sawyer chuckled. "He caught me trying to break into his house. Instead of calling the cops, he found out my story and taught me everything he knew."

"Including breaking into safes," Jesse added.

Good grief! Picking locks and cracking safes? "Did you ever get caught, Sawyer?"

"Only by Charlie. Never by the police or anyone else."

"What did you steal?"

"Cash and jewelry. Charlie introduced me to his fence, who disposed of any jewelry and paid me a decent cut of the money."

"What did you do with the money?"

"Gave it to Hugh to buy food. Once I started lifting jewels and cash, we never went hungry again. We bought nothing to raise suspicion. If we went on a spending spree, people would talk. That would lead to disaster. So any extra money left after buying food and paying bills, Hugh managed for us."

"You were good at stealing?"

"Very."

She led the operatives into the workroom where she made stock. "What did Hugh do with the extra money?"

"He split the money six ways and dumped an equal portion into bank accounts he set up for each of us. When we turned eighteen and graduated from high school, we could take the money accumulated in our personal account and go to college or trade school. Hugh put himself through trade school to be a welder. Once he finished and landed a job, he started adding money into each account, too.

"One by one, my older brothers either went to college or joined the military. Each of us contributed money to a house fund and eventually bought Mom a home of her own, a nice condominium with neighbors her age. She's having the time of her life and no longer having to work two jobs to make ends meet. In fact, she stopped working when I went to the police academy."

Janie motioned to the stools on the other side of her working island. "Have a seat and tell me more."

Jesse headed toward the front of the shop. "I want to look around for a bit."

She started gathering ingredients and tugged on her favorite baseball hat and rubber gloves and handed a pair of gloves to Sawyer. "I'm sure the police conduct background checks on their applicants. They didn't know about your questionable skills?"

Sawyer shook his head. "Told you. I didn't get caught. Charlie taught me how to bypass alarm systems and look for surveillance cameras."

"He must have done a great job training you. What did he say about you becoming a police officer?"

He chuckled. "He was horrified."

"I can imagine. Why did you choose law enforcement as a career? Why not the military like your brothers?"

"Oh, they encouraged me to think about it, but as a street rat, I saw a lot of injustice. One street walker shared food with me almost every day when she found out who I was and what a tough time we were having keeping ourselves fed. Shana said she grew up in that kind of poverty and didn't want to see us boys come to a terrible end. She knew about my dad and what a hard time Mom was having. Mom was always kind to her, even when other people treated Shana as though she was beneath them.

"One day, Shana wasn't on her corner and no one knew where she was. A few days later, I heard that a customer beat her to death. The police never found out who killed her. I decided I wanted to right that wrong. I wanted to carry a badge and solve Shana's murder."

"Did you?"

He smiled a little. "I did. He's still in prison."

"Good for you. Does your mother know why you joined the police?"

"Of course. Mom is a sharp lady. Although I didn't tell her my reasons, she knew. I guess word got around the neighborhood about Shana sharing food with me and my brothers."

"Do you and your brothers keep in touch with each other and your mother?"

He snorted. "Oh, yeah. We're in each other's business all the time. I'm the only one not married, so I'm getting dating advice from all of them." Sawyer shook his head. "It's embarrassing."

"I think it's sweet."

He flinched. "Don't spread that around, okay? I'll never hear the end of it from my teammates or my brothers."

Janie laughed. Oh, this was a fun conversation. She could see him running wild in the streets and stealing to provide for his family. Sawyer Chapman had that knight-in-shining-armor thing going, although he would be horrified to know she thought that about him. "I'd love to meet your family one day."

He was silent a moment.

She glanced up, her smile fading. "That's not allowed?" Would she never see him again after she was finally safe? The possibility hurt her heart.

"When this is over, if you still want to meet them, I'll take you to meet my mother and Hugh along with his family. My other brothers are scattered around at different Army bases."

"It's not against Fortress rules? I don't want to get you into trouble with Brent."

"Once you're safe, the choice will be mine. I'd like to introduce you to my family. They'll enjoy meeting you."

"How do you know?"

"Because I enjoy being with you."

That brought a smile to her face. "Feeling's mutual. That's why I'm looking forward to an introduction to your mom and brothers."

He gave her a long stare before saying, "If you change your mind when you're safe again, let me know. I won't hold you to it."

"I won't change my mind." What woman in her right mind would give up a chance to meet such an extraordinary family like Sawyer's?

He seemed surprised by her quick response. "Still, I will ask before I make plans."

"Fair enough."

For the next two hours, Sawyer and Jesse rotated in and out of the prep room. Each man asked Janie to teach him how to help. The prep went much faster than normal. Together, they created enough product to fill the shelves out front and the supply stock in the back.

Pleased with the early morning work, she finished the last of the bath salt batch just as the back door opened.

Sawyer's weapon was in his hand in less than a second.

Janie laid her hand on his forearm. "It's one of my clerks," she murmured. "Good morning, Jada."

Jada Michaels squealed and stumbled back against the closed door. "Janie, you scared me to death. I thought you would sleep in this morning after all the fun in Chile, plus a long flight back to the states." She stared at Sawyer. "Who's your friend?"

He slid his weapon back into his holster and stepped forward with his hand out. "Nice to meet you, Jada. I'm Sawyer, Janie's boyfriend."

Janie's cheeks burned. She hadn't given a second's thought to how she would explain Sawyer's presence in her shop. Apparently, Sawyer had.

"My friend Jesse and I convinced Janie to teach us how to make soap and bath salt. She agreed to teach us if we helped her prepare stock for the day."

Jesse returned to the prep room, his hand resting on his weapon. "I'm Jesse."

Jada's gaze shifted from Sawyer to Jesse and back again. "Um, hi. Janie, is everything all right?"

If she wanted to protect her staff, Janie had to tell them some of the truth. No need to scare them to death, though. "Not really. I had some trouble on the plane."

Her employee stashed her purse and jacket in her locker. "What happened?"

She gave a sanitized version of events, ending with, "Sawyer and his friends are going to monitor me for a few days in case trouble followed me back to Hartman."

"Are you serious?"

"Afraid so. Look, these guys used to be police officers. Now they work for a private security firm. I'm lucky they were in the area when I was kidnapped from the plane, along with several other hostages."

Jada gasped. "Wait. Are you talking about the fourteen hostages killed in Mexico? That was your group?"

Janie nodded. "I don't want to worry you. The heightened security is a precaution."

"This makes little sense," her friend said. "Why would anyone come after you here?"

"We don't know that they will," Sawyer said. "Would you want me to let security slide and potentially risk Janie's life if the hijackers tracked her down to finish the job?"

"Oh, no." Jada sat on the nearest stool. "No way. I don't care if you and a hundred other guys camp out in the shop as long as Janie is safe."

"I feel the same way."

"When did you two start dating?" she asked. "You've been keeping secrets, Janie. I did not know you were involved with someone."

She hated to lie to her friend. Blowing a hole through Sawyer's story was no good either. "It's recent." Janie couldn't think of a better compromise.

Jada turned to Sawyer. "You better treat her like a princess, buddy. If you don't, you'll answer to all of her employees. Trust me when I say we won't be kind if you screw up."

His lips curved. "Noted. I'll do my best not to hurt Janie."

"We'll see." Jada glanced around the prep room and stared at the stockpile of stock on the refill shelves. "Do I need to do anything?"

Janie laughed. "No. Sawyer and Jesse work fast. We've prepared the normal amount of stock for the day in less than three hours."

"Wow. Want a job, guys? We can use employees who work that fast."

The men chuckled. "Sorry, ma'am," Jesse said. "We have jobs already."

"Too bad. Keep us in mind, all right?"

"Yes, ma'am."

"Any special orders, Janie?" Jada asked.

"Because of the security issue, I won't be in the shop today. Can you and the others handle the store without me?"

"Of course. Although it's easier with you, we were fine while you were gone. Now that you and your friends have made the stock, we won't have to scramble so much to finish everything."

"My boss is sending someone to stay in the shop with you and the rest of the employees today," Sawyer said. "Her name is Molly. She'll look like a customer browsing the store shelves. You'll like her."

"Will she be armed to the teeth like you and Jesse? Because if she is, she won't look like any customers we cater to."

"She'll be armed, but Molly will be discreet with her weapons."

"She's also a professional chef," Jesse added.

The back door opened again and another one of Janie's employees walked into the preparation room. She paused at the sight of Sawyer and Jesse. "Welcome back, Janie. Is everything okay?"

"I had a little trouble on the flight home. My boyfriend Sawyer and his friends are monitoring me for a few days until we're sure trouble didn't follow me back to Hartman."

"Is that why they're carrying guns?"

She nodded. "They're good men, Chelsea. You don't have to worry about them."

"If you say so." Chelsea didn't sound convinced. "Are we expecting an extra shipment of supplies?"

Janie frowned. "I ordered nothing out of the ordinary. Jada?"

"Same. We won't get another shipment of supplies until Friday. Why?"

"There's a box at the front door. I would have brought it in if my hands weren't full."

"Awfully early for a delivery," Sawyer said. He glanced at Jesse, who left by the back door. "Did you notice the name of the sender?"

"That's another odd thing. There wasn't one."

Janie looked at Sawyer. His expression was grim. "What should we do?"

"Stay here." He headed for the back door. "Be ready in case we have to leave in a hurry."

Chapter Eleven

Sawyer circled to the front of the building and stopped near his friend. "What do we have?" he asked Jesse.

"Trouble. No shipping label on the box. I hear nothing ticking, but I'm not willing to shake it to find out if I'm wrong."

Didn't blame him. Sawyer wouldn't either. "Does Hartman have a bomb squad?"

"They do. Don't know how good they are. We could call Logan." Logan was their team's explosive ordinance expert and would step in to examine and disarm a bomb if necessary.

Sawyer considered that option a moment, then shook his head. "Call the Hartman PD. We'll let them look first. If there's an explosive device inside the box that they can't handle, we'll call Logan."

A nod from Jesse. "I know the head of the bomb squad. I'll call him and report a suspicious package."

"Do we need to lock our weapons in the SUVs?"

"I'll tell Harmon we're on the job and armed. If he has a problem with it, he won't be shy about telling me. He'll pass the word to his team so they're prepared."

"Good enough. I'll escort Janie and her workers to my SUV and drive them farther away from the building."

"Good idea. They're too close if a bomb detonates at the front of the shop." Jesse grabbed his phone and made the call. When he ended it a moment later, he said, "Harmon will be here in ten minutes with his crew."

"Let's clear out and make sure no civilians get close to the building while we wait for the bomb squad."

Jesse snorted. "At this time of morning? Most people are rushing to work, not waiting to get into their favorite soap store."

"We'll have looky-loos soon. Any time they see first-responder lights, they slow down or stop to see what's going on." He jogged around the side of the building to the back, where Janie and the other two women waited. "Come with me."

"Where are we going?" Janie asked.

"To the SUV. I'm going to move the vehicle away from the building, just in case."

"Is it a bomb?" Chelsea asked, her eyes wide.

"We don't know. The bomb squad is on the way to examine it. If anything threatening is inside, they'll take care of it."

"This is terrifying," Jada said as the women followed Sawyer to the vehicle.

"We're taking every precaution. This may be a box of supplies for all we know, but we want you to be safe in case this is a threat."

"Who would want to hurt us or put the store out of business?"

Janie sighed. "The people who hijacked my plane from Chile come to mind."

Chelsea shivered. "I hope you're wrong, and this is all an embarrassing incident the bomb squad will chalk up to overly anxious people."

Sawyer hoped so, too, but he didn't like the timing. Once the women settled in the vehicle, he drove around the building to the front of the shop and parked a suitable distance away. He opened the driver's side door. "Stay inside the SUV. You'll be safe in here."

"What about you?" Janie asked.

"I'll be close."

She blew out a breath. "I don't like you being exposed to danger, Sawyer."

That made him pause for a moment. "I'll be careful. Don't worry." He closed the door and whistled, motioning for Jesse to join them.

The medic jogged toward him. Less than a minute later, he was beside Sawyer and stood watch with him. "Bomb squad is one minute out. They're running lights without sirens. Don't want to attract a lot of attention."

The bomb squad arrived right on schedule and parked a short distance from the operatives. The leader of the squad approached Jesse. "What can you tell me?"

"Not much," Jesse said. "This is my teammate, Sawyer. We're protecting Janie Moran, the owner of Natural Bliss. One of her employees arrived for work about fifteen minutes ago, discovered the box at the front of the shop and reported it to us. We checked the outside of the box without disturbing it. No labels. Moran isn't expecting any deliveries today."

"Why do you suspect a threat?"

"Ms. Moran was the only survivor of the Chilean plane hijacking two days ago," Sawyer said.

Harmon whistled. "Ugly situation."

"We're afraid Janie may still be a target."

His eyebrows winged upward. "Keep us updated. We'll be glad to help."

Sawyer shook Harmon's hand. "Appreciate it."

With that, the bomb squad approached the box at the front of the shop with their equipment. After a few moments, one of the team members, dressed in full protective gear, slowly approached the box and stopped several feet away.

Sawyer and Jesse watched as the bomb tech scanned the box with a portable machine to X-ray the contents. After a few moments, the tech gave a thumbs up to his team leader. Immediately, the team relaxed.

"The box must not have an explosive device inside," Jesse murmured.

"No way to know without opening the package. I'm curious about the contents. Who delivers packages this early in the morning? The sun's not even up yet."

"If I had to guess, I'd say Janie's deliveries aren't left at the front door, either."

"Invitation to thieves, and Hartman isn't immune to crime."

Two members of the bomb squad unwrapped the brown paper surrounding the box and peered inside. They stared at each other for a moment, then the leader motioned to Sawyer and Jesse.

After asking Janie and the other two women to stay inside for a while longer, they crossed the parking lot to join Harmon. "What do we have?" Sawyer asked.

"Take a look."

He peered inside the box and fisted his hands as he stared at the contents. A doll lay inside the box, dressed like Janie had been when the plane was hijacked. The hair was the same color and style as Janie's. The person who packed the doll had plunged a knife into the chest of the toy, an obvious threat to Janie.

The question now was who left the box for her? One member of Vatos Locos or someone here in the states who had a grudge against Janie?

Sawyer and Jesse both took pictures of the box and its contents with their phones. "You'll process the box and its contents?" Sawyer asked.

"Yeah. Want a report on our findings?"

"We'd appreciate it. Thanks for the quick response."

"Sure."

"Any chance you'll be out of here before Natural Bliss is ready to open for business this morning?"

"Don't see why not. We'll take the box with us when we leave and hand it over to the lab. We need to have a chat with your principal, though."

"Not out here." Sawyer didn't want Janie out in the open where she'd be an easy target.

"Where?"

"Janie has a workroom in the back of the shop. Should be plenty of room for an interview. You'll also want to chat with Chelsea, one of Janie's shop assistants. She's the one who first saw the box at the front of the shop. Come to the back door of the shop when you're finished. We'll be waiting for you."

"Copy that."

Sawyer returned to the SUV and opened the passenger door as Jesse walked toward the shop.

"What happened?" Janie demanded. "Was it a bomb? Supplies? What?"

"Not a bomb or supplies."

She blinked. "I want to see."

"No, baby, you don't."

Janie looked surprised. "Is it bad?"

"It's disturbing. Let's go back to the shop, and I'll talk to you about the box. In a few minutes, the leader of the bomb squad will talk to you and your employees."

"Perhaps the box was delivered to my shop by mistake."

Sawyer couldn't help himself. He cupped her nape. "I don't think so." After brushing her cheek with his thumb, Sawyer shut her door and circled the hood to climb behind the wheel. He drove to the back of the shop and parked beside Jesse.

Sawyer exited the vehicle and scanned the area along with Jesse before helping the women to the pavement and inside the shop.

As soon as they were inside with the door closed, Janie rounded on Sawyer. "Tell me what's going on."

He clasped her hand and led her to one stool, keeping possession of her hand. "The box contained a doll."

"A doll?"

"It's dressed exactly like you were on the day of the hijacking. Same color hair and hairstyle. No question that it's supposed to represent you."

"Maybe it's a gift from a customer or a friend," Jada suggested.

"No." Sawyer squeezed Janie's hand. "It's not." Putting off telling her wouldn't soften the blow. Just needed to tell it straight out and deal with the fallout. "The doll has a knife plunged to the hilt in its chest."

Blood drained from her face. "I need to see it."

"Janie...."

"Please, Sawyer. Not seeing the doll makes my imagination fill in the gaps, and it's not pretty."

"The real thing isn't, either," he warned.

"Please," she murmured.

Sawyer didn't blame her. He'd want to see the evidence himself if he was in her place. Grabbing his phone, he brought up the picture and showed it to her.

Janie gasped and clamped a hand over her mouth as she paled even further.

Jesse was on his feet in an instant. "Head down. Do you have a refrigerator in here, Jada?"

The woman pointed to a room next to the prep room.

The medic left only to return in seconds with a cold pack that he laid on the back of Janie's neck. "Deep breaths, Janie. In through your nose and out through your mouth."

She did as he ordered. Soon, her color had returned and Sawyer helped her sit up again. "Okay now?" he asked.

She nodded. "Sorry. I didn't expect to react like that. I feel like a wuss."

"You're not. That isn't a common sight, especially when the doll is meant as a threat."

"Still, I feel stupid. I'm sorry, Sawyer. I should have trusted you and not insisted on seeing the doll for myself."

He cupped her chin with his palm. "Stop," he murmured. "If I was the target, I'd insist on seeing the evidence for myself."

"Bet you wouldn't have almost passed out," she muttered.

"You'd be wrong. There have been plenty of times when I've reacted much the same while on the job." The sight of his first dead body came to mind. He'd barely made it outside before he'd upchucked. They had all been green once. Now, he and his teammates were jaded. They'd seen and dealt with too much to remain innocent of the worst mankind could do to fellow members of humanity.

A quick, hard knock sounded on the door. Jesse palmed his weapon as Sawyer moved to stand in front of Janie, his own weapon in hand.

Jesse opened the door a crack, then swung it wide to admit Harmon and one of his team members.

The bomb squad leader focused on Sawyer, who stepped to Janie's side and holstered his weapon. The teammate looked hard at him. Let him look. His job was to protect Janie. End of story.

"This is Janie Moran, Jada, and Chelsea." Sawyer said. "Janie, this is Drake Harmon and Liam Kennedy of the Hartman PD. They need to ask you some questions."

"Of course. I can't guarantee I'll have much useful information to share."

"You might be surprised." Harmon turned to the other women. "Nice to meet you, ladies. We'd also like to interview each of you."

"Of course," Jada said.

"No problem." This from Chelsea.

"Would you like some coffee, Mr. Harmon, Mr. Kennedy?" Janie asked.

"Please call us Drake and Liam, and we'd love a cup. This rollout was so early, I didn't drink my first cup of the day."

"Same," Kennedy said.

"I've got it," Jada said.

Janie smiled. "Thanks."

"Ms. Moran, tell me everything that happened this morning from the beginning," Harmon said.

"It's Janie." She gave him a detailed accounting of the events of the morning, starting from when she woke and ending with Sawyer hustling her and her employees from the shop to wait for the bomb squad to arrive.

He took her through the events twice more, pulling more details from her each time, before turning his attention to Jada, who handed him a mug of steaming coffee.

The policemen nodded their thanks and took Jada through her morning and anything she'd noticed upon her arrival, then repeated the process with Chelsea.

Once he finished, he looked at his teammate and inclined his head toward the other room. "Take the two women in there and run them through events again."

After Kennedy, Jada, and Chelsea left the room, Harmon returned his attention to Janie. "I understand you're the only survivor of the Chilean airliner hijacking."

"Yes, sir."

"Any reason to believe someone from the hijackers' crew is out to finish the job?"

"That's what Sawyer and Jesse believe."

"But you don't?"

She shrugged. "I don't know why the hijackers would come after me again. I also don't know why they spared my life, but murdered the other hostages."

"Let's assume the hijacking was intentional with you as the target. Why would anyone want to hurt you or take you as a hostage?"

"I do not know. I make soap for a living. This trip to Chile was my first time out of the country, and it might well be my last. I definitely don't want a repeat in this lifetime. In short, I'm no one important."

"Do you have an enemy, Janie?"

She hesitated.

"Say it," he ordered. "Don't think. Just say it."

Janie smiled a little. "That's what Sawyer and Brent told me."

"Wise words. So, who wants to hurt you?"

"Probably no one."

"But?" Harmon prompted.

She glanced at Sawyer, who gave her a nod, encouraging her to speak the truth. "My brother is angry with me."

"What is his name, and where does he live?"

"David Moran. He lives in Chile. I was there visiting him at the invitation of his wife." She grimaced. "I thought David knew and had invited me to his home to mend fences and meet his new bride. It turned out that his wife had issued the invitation on her own, hoping David and I would heal our relationship."

"Did it work?"

"No."

"What's the problem?"

"Money. My brother is irresponsible with money, and our grandmother stipulated in her will that David was not to be given money from the estate aside from the cash bequest she'd left him. David objects to the terms of the will."

"The estate is substantial?"

Her cheeks flushed. "Yes, sir."

"So, it's possible the hijackers realized you are a wealthy woman and wanted to cash in on the ransom, is that it?"

She laughed. "If that was their goal, they were out of luck. I'm wealthy, yes, but I don't have pots of money stashed in the bank, waiting to be taken out for a spending spree or a ransom demand. Besides, David doesn't have access to my accounts. I can't trust him with access to the funds."

"That desperate for cash?"

"Yes, sir."

"What happens to your accounts if you're in a serious accident or die? Who has access to your funds?"

That question caught Sawyer's attention. He'd yet to get around to that question himself.

"My friends, Rowan and Brent Maddox. They are my beneficiaries. If something happens to me, they'll get everything."

"Does your brother know that?" Sawyer asked.

"No."

"You should tell him," Harmon suggested.

She flinched. "I don't believe my brother wishes me harm."

"You mean you don't want to believe it, but people have killed others for a few dollars, let alone a substantial amount of money."

"The estate still is worth a good bit. I only took enough money from the estate to set up Natural Bliss. I've been living on the profits from the store."

"Why does your brother need money?"

"I'm not sure. He insinuated he needed cash to get ready for their baby. Maria is due in six months." She sighed. "I don't understand his desperation. David works for an engineering firm. He makes good money and the cost of living is less in Chile than it is here. He should be fine."

"Does he have any vices?"

Janie hesitated.

Sawyer wrapped his hand around her. "Sweetheart, you need to tell us everything. The danger won't stop unless we track down the source and shut it down. Help us do that."

"I don't want to get my brother in trouble. He's the only family I have left, Sawyer."

"He's a grown man, Janie," Harmon said. "Protecting him could cost you your life. Don't give him that kind of power over you. Besides, he may not be responsible for what happened on the plane or the doll. If he's not responsible, how can answering a few questions hurt him?"

"He'll see it as a betrayal. David already hates me."

"Then what do you have to lose?"

After delaying a few more seconds, Janie sighed. "When he lived in the US, David got caught up in gambling."

And there it was. The weakness Sawyer was looking for. Now the question was how deep was David in debt and to whom did he owe money?

Chapter Twelve

Sawyer closed the door behind the two policemen, locked it, and leaned his back against the door. He studied Janie's dejected expression. "It's not your fault," he murmured.

"Maybe I should just give David half the estate and be done with it. Granny Irene won't know I disobeyed her wishes."

"You would know. If your brother is still struggling with his gambling addiction, giving him money will feed the problem. I guarantee your niece or nephew won't see a penny."

He straightened from the door and went to her. Sawyer wrapped his arms around her and eased her against his chest.

She melted in his arms, pressing her face against his neck. "I hate this," she whispered.

Sawyer froze. He started to release her and step back, but Janie snuggled closer.

"I don't want my brother angry with me, but you're right, Sawyer. If I give him money, he'll blow the cash, then come back for more."

He rested his cheek against her temple. "It's not on you. The problem is your brother's."

"If he's responsible for me being kidnapped and this box, then it is my problem."

"No, baby. It's mine."

"Aww. You two look so sweet together," Chelsea gushed as she and Jada returned to the prep room with Jesse in their wake. "I'm so glad you found someone, Janie. You deserve a good man."

Janie glanced at her employees. "Sawyer is a keeper. Do you two need anything?"

Jada eyed her. "We're good. Aren't you staying?"

"No," Sawyer said. "Remember, Molly will be here by nine and will stay for your working hours. After this morning's special delivery, another person we trust might also join her in the shop."

"You'll be safe," Jesse assured the women. "We won't hand over your safety to anyone except those we've vetted ourselves."

Chelsea brightened. "Anyone as cute as you and Sawyer?"

The medic chuckled. "I don't know about that, but whoever it is will keep you safe."

"Good enough for me," Jada said, rubbing her hands together. "We have just enough time for a cup of coffee and possibly a muffin from the coffee shop on the other side of the parking lot."

"I'll get breakfast for you," Jesse said. "Any preferences?"

"Anything," Chelsea said. "We're not picky."

After a nod, he left the shop.

"Along with Molly and our other coworker, I'll be sending someone to beef up shop security and to change the locks. Janie had to leave everything behind in the plane, including her shop and house keys."

Jada sucked in a breath. "No wonder you're being so cautious."

"You're taking such good care of Janie, Sawyer," Chelsea said. "We can't thank you enough."

"She's special."

Jada nudged Chelsea with her elbow. "Come on. Let's go out front and check our stock supplies."

Sawyer loosened his hold on Janie. "I hope you don't mind me claiming to be your boyfriend. I couldn't think of another explanation for my presence in your life."

"I don't mind."

"If I do anything that makes you uncomfortable, tell me."

"You won't."

"Janie."

"All right. I promise. But you won't."

Jesse returned a few minutes later, laden with bags and a to-go carrier. "I bought enough for all of us, if you're interested."

"Coffee for me." Sawyer took the drink carrier from his friend and took one cup for himself. He noticed that one cup was filled with hot tea. That one he handed to Janie. "Tea for the lady."

"Jada and Chelsea are out front?" Jesse asked.

"They are," Janie said. She lifted her cup in a salute to Jesse. "Thanks for the tea. It's perfect."

The medic grinned. "Thought you could use a cup." He carried one bag and the drink carrier into the front of the shop.

Sawyer's phone signaled an incoming text. He glanced at the screen. "Molly and Jeremy will be here in ten minutes."

"I thought Molly wouldn't be coming until an hour before opening."

"After the box delivery, I didn't want to leave Jada and Chelsea here alone. I asked Molly to come early."

"I appreciate you looking after my employees."

"They're also your friends. I want nothing to happen to people you care about."

"Does that include David?"

"If he's innocent, yes."

"And if he's guilty?"

"I'll do my best, Janie. The ultimate ending is up to him." He could see she was dissatisfied. That was the best answer he could give. Whatever the price, he would stop the person responsible for terrorizing Janie, blood relation or not. "Do you think Brent would do any less?"

She gave a huff of laughter. "Are you kidding? He'd rip apart anyone he considered a threat to my safety." Janie sobered. "I can't expect less of a response from you, can I?"

"What do you think?"

She sipped her tea. "I think it's time for me to get with the program and trust my security detail. I'll try to be more cooperative, Sawyer."

"You're doing fine."

Jesse returned sans breakfast for the ladies. "I bought extra food and coffee for Molly and Jeremy. I sent her a text a few minutes ago to ask what she wanted."

"They should be here in a few minutes. We'll go as soon as Molly and Jeremy are set up in here. I need to take Janie to Fortress headquarters to meet with Ian McGregor to do the sketch of the missing hostage."

"Want me to go with you?"

He shook his head. "You're off duty as soon as Molly and Jeremy arrive. We'll drop you off at home so you can rest."

Jesse's eyebrow rose. "You forget where my woman is at the moment."

Fortress Security headquarters. "So, I guess you want to see Simone before you get a little sleep."

"Oh, yeah. Goose, too. In fact, I might take him home until his mistress is off work. He's a great napping buddy."

Sawyer chuckled. "Can't forget Goose. Want to follow us to headquarters, then?"

"If you'll stop by the safe house for my vehicle, I'll be right behind you."

Minutes later, Sawyer introduced Molly and Jeremy to Janie, Jada, and Chelsea. "You can trust my friends to take care of you and see to your safety," he said. "If anything happens, do exactly what they tell you to do. They're well trained."

"What about you, Janie?" Chelsea asked. "Will you be okay, too?"

"You forget that I've seen Sawyer at work. I'll be absolutely safe with him and his teammates."

The other women looked relieved. Jada pointed at Sawyer. "If anything happens to her, we're coming after you. Doesn't matter how well armed you are. You get me?"

Sawyer gave her a mock salute. "Got it. I won't forget."

Molly and Jeremy followed them outside and waited until Sawyer had enclosed Janie inside the safety of the SUV along with Jesse. "Orders, sir?" Jeremy asked.

"Keep an eye out. We've already had trouble this morning. I have a feeling it won't be the last time. I'm hoping by keeping Janie away from the shop as much as possible that her employees will be less likely targets. No guarantees, though."

"Understood, sir. We'll stay alert."

"I also have someone from Fortress coming to upgrade Janie's security and change her locks. I need you to drop the keys by Brody's home. He's expecting you later this afternoon."

"Yes, sir."

Once the operatives were back in the shop, Sawyer circled the hood and climbed behind the wheel. He drove toward the interstate. "You nervous about working with the artist?"

Janie looked at him. "How did you know?"

"Logical. You've never worked with a sketch artist before, so it's an unknown amid several other unknowns in your life right now."

"You're one of those unknowns."

He inclined his head. Couldn't argue with her logic. It was true. He was her biggest unknown at the moment. "Not for long." He smiled. "After all, we're dating now."

She laughed. "Of course. During your assignment. After that, I'll just be one of your crowd of admirers, soon forgotten, I'm sure."

Jesse snorted.

Sawyer wasn't so sure about Janie's statement. He had a feeling he'd never forget her, no matter how many assignments he had. She was one in a million. "Don't sell yourself short, sweetheart. You'll always have a special place in my life."

The more he thought about that, the further convinced he was that he'd spoken the truth. So, the question became, what was he going to do about it? Something to consider over the next few days.

"We'll see if you still say that after we break up," she teased. "You may be glad to get rid of me."

He didn't think so.

They stopped by the safe house for Jesse to pick up his SUV. Halfway to Fortress headquarters, Sawyer noticed a white panel van shifting lanes frequently and inching ever closer to their SUVs. Since Janie seemed unaware of the problematic vehicle, he simply monitored the van and its maneuvering.

Five minutes later, the van's driver had positioned his vehicle three cars behind Jesse. Before long, he darted into the next lane and nosed back into the lane, this time two cars behind Jesse.

He scowled. Not what he wanted to see. No question that they'd picked up a tail. He wasn't surprised, but he didn't like it. Too much was at stake to let this slide.

Sawyer used his Bluetooth to call Jesse.

"I see him," was the reply instead of a greeting.

"We're fifteen minutes from Fortress."

"A lot can happen in fifteen minutes. Want to make a run for it?"

"Not yet," he said, watching the rearview mirror. "Watch him. If he moves up again, we'll go. I'll alert Fortress. We may have someone in the area who can run interference."

"Copy that." Jesse ended the call.

"What's going on?" Janie asked.

"We picked up a tail."

"Are you sure?"

"Ninety percent. I might be wrong." But he didn't think so.

Sawyer called the Fortress comm center.

"Yeah, Murphy."

"It's Sawyer. We've got a problem."

"Talk to me."

"Jesse and I are bringing Janie into headquarters to work with Ian. We've picked up a tail."

"Location?" The sound of Zane's fingers clicking on the keyboard filled the cabin of the SUV.

Sawyer gave their position. "Do we have anyone close who can run interference?"

"Hold." Seconds later, Zane said, "No operatives are close enough to give you a hand."

"Copy. We'll take care of it ourselves if the driver becomes too aggressive."

"Description of the tailing vehicle?"

"Late model panel van, white. Two occupants. No license plate to report. They've been behind us the whole time."

A pause, then, "When did you pick up the tail?"

"I noticed the van five minutes ago. The driver has been leapfrogging to maneuver closer. They're two cars back now. One more maneuver will put them behind Jesse unless they decide to make their move on us."

"I'm surprised you didn't pick them up sooner."

Sawyer's cheeks burned. Yeah, he should have. Just showed how distracted he was. He needed to focus on his job, not on his growing personal connection to Janie. "Alert the security staff at headquarters. We might come in hot."

"Copy that." Zane ended the call just as the driver of the white van shifted into position behind Jesse.

Sawyer's phone rang a moment later. "I see them, Jesse."

"Orders?"

"We need some distance between us and them. Fortress doesn't have anyone close. We're on our own."

"No problem. Go when you're ready."

"Keep the call open."

"Copy that."

Sawyer glanced at Janie, making sure she had her seatbelt fastened. "You ready, sweetheart?"

She nodded. "Let's do it."

He chuckled and pressed the accelerator. Their SUV shot forward. Jesse stayed close. Together, they cut through traffic like two sharks swimming through a school of fish, threading their way through congestion and putting more and more distance between them and their tail.

Jesse laughed as horns honked at the driver of the van, who tried to keep up with them and get back into position or to cut them off. "Guess our friends in the van haven't taken combat driving lessons. They're ticking off everyone around them."

"Don't care, as long as they can't run us off the road."

Sawyer constantly scanned the traffic ahead and to the sides of them as well as the van still fighting to gain ground.

He tried to see the driver and passenger, but they were too far back for him to see their faces. "Did you recognize the men in the van, Jesse?"

"No, but I got a good look at them. I might do a session with Ian after Janie and see if he can get their ugly mugs in a sketch. They're Hispanic."

Ice water ran through Sawyer's veins.

Chapter Thirteen

Janie gripped the sides of her seat as Sawyer weaved through heavy Davidson County traffic with ease. She envied the skill with which he drove. Whenever she drove in Nashville, her hands gripped the wheel as though gearing up for war. That's what driving around the area seemed like to her.

She'd been so glad to move to Wilson County last year to open her business. Sure, Hartman had traffic, but nothing like this test of courage.

Another quick dash to the next lane made her heart jump into her throat. Janie squeezed her eyes shut and decided that was even worse than seeing what was coming and preparing for it.

"Still with me?" Sawyer asked.

"Oh, yeah. Do you drive like this all the time?"

He chuckled. "When I was on the job, I did. We do it if we're in the field. Around town on a normal day, we focus on driving defensively. Too many people are distracted, sleepy, or in too much of a hurry to watch out for everyone else on the road."

Spoken like a true cop. "Where did you learn to drive?"

"Police academy plus Fortress teaches its operatives and bodyguards combat driving skills."

"Well, you're certainly putting the training to good use."

He reached over and squeezed her hand briefly. "Sorry to scare you."

"Don't worry about it. You're keeping me safe. I have no right to complain." Although she wished the speed was unnecessary. "Good thing you're driving. I drive like Granny Irene. Slow and steady."

Sawyer grinned. "Good for you."

"Ha. You say that now. Let's see if you feel the same when I'm driving you around town one day."

"Looking forward to it."

She eyed him, suspicion growing in her gut. "You wouldn't be laughing at me, would you, Sawyer?"

"Who me? Never."

"Heads up," Jesse said.

Sawyer glanced into the rearview mirror in time to see the van swerve into the left lane and surge past Jesse and pull even with Sawyer.

Seconds later, the driver jerked the steering wheel to the right, slamming into Sawyer's SUV.

He scowled. "Great. Now, I'll have to explain to Bear why his handiwork is messed up. Someone is going to pay for the hardship I will suffer at the hands of the former Delta soldier."

Janie stared at Sawyer, astonished. "You're worried about the paint job when the people in the van are doing their best to run us off the road?"

"You don't know Bear. He takes any damage to our vehicles personally since he did the work to retrofit them with extra safety features."

"You sound afraid of him."

Jesse chimed in. "You bet. Anybody with half a brain is terrified of him and his crew. They're all former Deltas."

Incredible. "Your team is plenty tough from what I saw in Mexico."

"Trust me, sugar. Bear is in a class all by himself."

Hmm. This guy must eat barbed wire for breakfast.

Sawyer surged into the right-hand lane, just barely missing another sideswipe by the van.

Janie turned in her seat in time to see Jesse fall in line behind Sawyer, and the two SUVs sprinted ahead of the speeding van. She wasn't sure what was under the hood of the Fortress vehicles, but she suspected it wasn't factory issued.

Half a mile later, the SUVs exited the Interstate and raced down Harding Place toward Fortress Security's compound.

"Ending our call," Sawyer said to Jesse as he sped through a yellow light, with Jesse right behind him.

"Copy."

Sawyer immediately made another call.

"Murphy."

"We're two minutes out. Coming in hot."

"Copy that. We're ready."

"Somebody needs to catch these clowns. The van sideswiped us."

A soft whistle. "Sorry, man. I'll pass the word to Bear and company."

"Make sure you tell him it wasn't my fault, and that I was protecting a principal."

"Will do. Good luck." Zane ended the call.

Janie twisted in her seat. "They're still on us."

"I see them." Disgust crossed his features. "Where's a cop when you need one?"

"Be grateful we haven't run across one. Otherwise, you and Jesse might have gotten a ticket for reckless driving."

"Maybe." Sawyer glanced to the right, shot into a gap in traffic and hung a fast right onto a street that led to a warehouse section. "Face forward, baby. If the van hits us again, you're less likely to suffer a lasting injury if you have the seat against your back."

She faced forward again. "What about Jesse? Will he be okay?"

"He has the same training I do. Not only that, we have reinforced steel in the doors and bullet-resistant glass in every window. You're as safe as we can keep you under the circumstances. Stay with me a few more minutes, okay?"

Janie said nothing. She couldn't. Her mouth was desert dry, as was her throat. It took every ounce of control she had not to scream and distract Sawyer when he raced through four-way stops at well over 80 miles per hour. Thankfully, no cars were in the area so far. That could change in an instant.

In the distance, she saw the Fortress compound masquerading as an office complex. Armed men lined up along the security fence with many SUVs parked at odd angles.

Instead of slowing down, Sawyer pressed the accelerator to the floor. The vehicle leaped forward, closing the distance to the front gate at an incredible rate of speed.

The gates parted seconds before Sawyer and Jesse sailed through and closed immediately afterward.

Instead of skidding to a stop, they continued to race to the underground garage. As they drove underground, Janie saw the white van skidding to a stop, backing up, and racing away. Two of the Fortress SUVs at the gate went after the fleeing vehicle.

Sawyer's SUV slid to a stop seconds later, and he parked near the elevator. He exited the vehicle and circled the hood to open her door.

Janie attempted to unlatch her seatbelt and failed royally because she was shaking too hard.

"I'll get it." Sawyer freed Janie from the seatbelt, helped her to the concrete, and tugged her into his arms. "It's all right now. You're safe." He continued to hold her as she trembled, rubbing her back with one hand and securing her to him with the other arm.

"I'm sorry," she murmured.

"Don't be. It's normal to be frightened in a situation like that."

"You aren't."

"I'm trained to handle things like this."

"I still feel like a wuss," she muttered.

"You didn't scream bloody murder while Jesse and I played in heavy traffic, going over 100 miles per hour. You have courage, Janie."

She swallowed hard. "We went that fast?"

"You couldn't tell?"

"I was afraid to look at the speedometer."

"Don't blame you." He kissed her temple and continued to hold her in silence until the shakes subsided. "Better now?"

Janie nodded. "Thanks, Sawyer. Sorry if I held things up too much."

"No one will say a word. If they do, they'll answer to me." He loosened his hold on her. "Feeling steady enough to walk?"

She hesitated, assessing how she felt. Maybe in another ten minutes. Right now, no. She shook her head.

Sawyer scooped Janie into his arms and strode toward the elevator. "You'll feel better soon," he murmured.

"I think I can walk." Probably.

"I'm more than capable of carrying you, sweetheart. Let me play the hero for a few minutes."

"Where's Jesse?"

"Gone to see his girlfriend. Simone works here, too. She's a whiz with computers. We're lucky to have her on staff here." He pressed the call button with his elbow.

"Will the security people catch up to the van?"

"I hope so. Brent will let us know the result of the chase. If the team catches up with them, you won't have to worry about seeing the men in the van. You won't be anywhere near them."

"Won't do much good, though, will it?" How could it? Sawyer's coworkers couldn't force the men to talk. If these men really were from Vatos Locos, they weren't likely to talk for fear of retaliation from other gang members. "You can't torture them into giving up information."

Sawyer remained silent.

Janie studied his face. "Sawyer?"

"Don't ask if you can't handle the answer."

Her breath caught. "Brent condones torture?"

"Do you want to know?"

She considered that for a moment and shook her head. "No. I'm assuming the interrogators will get answers by whatever means are necessary."

"To protect you, Brent will remove the restraints on his interrogation team."

Feeling sick to her stomach at the thought of other people, even evil ones, being hurt on her account, Janie nuzzled his cheek with hers. Seconds later, she froze, realizing she'd crossed a line. This relationship wasn't real. The pretense was only for her employees and others outside her circle of friends who might be curious about the strange man who suddenly seemed to be everywhere with her. She and Sawyer weren't in public.

She eased away. "I'm sorry. I shouldn't have done that."

"I don't mind, Janie. Do it again whenever you want."

The elevator doors opened, sparing her from coming up with a comment. Although she wanted to fan her flaming face, the action would be a dead giveaway. Nope, she'd remain silent unless Sawyer brought up the comment again.

She should tell the operative the action couldn't happen again, but she'd be lying to herself and to him. Janie wanted to do it again, pleased to have permission to indulge herself when she wanted. Wouldn't be fair, though, unless he had reciprocal privileges. Janie supposed the most important question was whether he'd want the same right.

Sawyer carried her down the hall on the third floor to a small conference room where a tall, slender bald man sat at the large table.

He jumped up from his chair, alarm on his face. "Everything all right, Chapman?"

"She's fine. Janie, this is Ian McGregor, our resident sketch artist. Ian, meet Janie Moran."

"I'm glad to meet you, Janie. Brent told me a lot about you," Ian said.

Great. What had her friend's husband blurted to his employee? "All good things, I hope."

He chuckled. "Of course. I'm sure you'll be seeing my wife, Kim, in Natural Bliss before long."

"Tell Kim to introduce herself, and I'll give her the grand tour. She can sit in on one of our classes if she's interested in learning to make soap or bath salts."

He groaned. "You shouldn't have said that. I can already feel my wallet hurting."

She laughed.

"Do you need anything before we start? Coffee, tea, soft drinks? We have everything in the break room down the hall."

Sawyer set her on a chair near Ian. "Would you like tea?"

"Thank you, Sawyer."

He squeezed her hand. "I'll be back in a minute."

After Sawyer left, Ian studied her face a moment. "Want to tell me what upset you?"

Janie grimaced. "It's that obvious?"

"Only to someone who sketches faces for a living. Talk to me while we wait for Sawyer to return."

So the observant sketch artist knew she wasn't comfortable without her bodyguard. She sighed. Yeah, she'd officially become a card-carrying wuss.

She talked freely to Ian, telling him everything that had happened since she and the operatives had left the safe house early this morning. "Not that a big deal," she said. "I don't know why I'm having such a hard time with what happened."

"It's not every day someone tries to run you off the road and possibly kidnap you again. You have a right to feel afraid."

"The SUV was damaged, not me."

"Doesn't matter. Having absolute proof that someone wants to hurt you is traumatic, and truthfully, anything could have happened during the race to get here."

"I'm here and perfectly safe because of Sawyer and Jesse."

"Texas Team is one of the best we have at Fortress. You're lucky they were available and in the area so they could rescue you."

"Believe me. I'll never forget it."

Sawyer returned with three to-go cups. Two coffees and one tea, which he handed to Janie. "Mint tea for the lady. Straight black liquid gold for us," he said to Ian. "What did I miss?"

"I asked Janie to tell me about this morning. Now that she has, let's give her a chance to sip some tea while you fill me in on what's been going on. When she's ready, we'll get started."

Sawyer gave Ian a version of events that Janie barely recognized. Military or cop rapid-fire report style.

"What about the mission you completed before rescuing Janie? Was it successful?"

He sobered. "I suppose you can call it successful. We freed the hostages and wiped out the human traffickers, but there's a lot of trauma for the victims to work through. Five of the hostages were kids."

"You and your team spared them from a life of sex slavery and got rid of those who hurt them. What more could you do, Sawyer?"

"It's not enough."

"Never is. All you can do is your best." Ian glanced at Janie. "Are you feeling better now?"

She kept her gaze on Sawyer for a moment before she answered the artist. "I'm ready to get started. Thanks for giving me a few minutes."

"Of course." Ian glanced at Sawyer. "Are you staying or going?"

"Staying. I won't leave Janie alone, even here."

"Understood. You can stay as long as you keep quiet and don't distract Janie."

Sawyer saluted him. "Yes, sir."

Ian focused on Janie as he flipped to a clean page in his sketch pad and grabbed one of the many pencils lined up beside him. "The first thing I need is for you to give me a general description of the man we're going to sketch."

Little by little, Ian pulled details from Janie while sketching the man's face. After more than an hour, Ian turned the pad around and showed her the portrait.

Janie gasped. "That's him. That's the man who sat beside me on the plane. You're amazing, Ian."

"If we're passing compliments around, I'll just say you have the best recall of anyone I've worked with. You made my work easy." Ian turned to Sawyer. "You want the sketch?"

"I do. I'll pass it along to Zane to see if we can identify this man."

The artist frowned. "Weird that he disappeared when all the other hostages were killed, except for Janie. Why separate him from the rest?"

"That's what we're hoping to find out." He stood and helped Janie to her feet. "Thanks, man. I owe you one."

Ian chuckled. "I'll collect."

Sawyer escorted Janie to the elevator. A minute later, they exited on the sixth floor and walked to the comm center, where Zane was working. His computer console had six full-size screens spread across it, all filled with different things.

The tech guru's fingers flew over the keyboard, and data scrolled over four of the screens. The other two had maps with flashing red lights on them. Janie was amazed that Zane could keep track of all the information and carry on a conversation with someone over his headset.

"Copy that, Nico. The jet is ready. You'll be wheels up within a minute of boarding. Injuries?" Zane listened a moment, then scowled. "Sorenson won't be happy to see Joe back in the clinic this soon."

He glanced over his shoulder and pointed at two chairs nearby. "Two minutes," he murmured. When Nico and his team boarded the jet, Zane gathered a little more information, then signed off. He spun his chair around to face Sawyer and Janie. "How are you, Janie?"

"Better now. I was pretty shaken up," she admitted. Couldn't exactly hide it, not after the way she'd behaved once Sawyer parked the SUV. "No injuries, though. Did the security team find the van?"

"They did. We have the driver and passenger in interrogation. The team will get answers if the two men have any."

"What does that mean?"

"They could be hired help with no knowledge of the reason for the job."

Oh, man. She'd never thought about that possibility. If Zane was right, that would mean the interrogation team would learn nothing to help her figure out who wanted her so badly they would kill to get their hands on her. "That's not what I wanted to hear, Zane."

"Sorry. I'm only laying out the possibility so you won't get your hopes up."

She glanced at Sawyer. "Is he always this full of good news?"

"Would you rather have it straight or for him to lie to you?"

"Always the truth." She'd had enough lies to last her a lifetime.

"Good." Zane looked at her with approval in his eyes. "How did the session with McGregor go?"

Sawyer handed the tech guru the sketch. "This is the man on the plane who disappeared in the Vatos Locos compound."

Zane's eyebrows rose. "This is excellent. If this guy is in the system, we should be able to identify him."

"Janie has an excellent memory of faces."

"I can see that. McGregor must have found this job to be easy."

"He was pleased."

"I'll run the photo through our databases and send copies to the operatives' emails. Hopefully, we'll get some information soon. Make a detour by Brent's office. He's expecting you."

Beside Janie, Sawyer tensed. "Did he say what he wanted?"

Zane shook his head as his switchboard lit up. He glanced at the readout. "Later, Sawyer." The other man swung around to his keyboard and touched his headset. "Yeah, Murphy."

Sawyer led Janie from the comm room and steered her toward Brent's suite of offices. "Come on. Time to face the music."

#

Chapter Fourteen

"Get your head back in the game, Sawyer, or you'll be sitting on the sidelines," Brent snapped.

Sawyer's ears burned with fury and embarrassment. Couldn't fault his boss for the dressing down. No question he deserved it, but Brent didn't have to do it in front of his principal. "It won't happen again, sir."

Brent's ice-blue eyes glittered with his fury. "That wasn't what you wanted to say to me."

The man could read minds now? A truly scary thought. "No, sir."

"Say it."

"I don't want to get fired."

His boss snorted. "You've never worried about that before. Spit it out before you choke on it, Chapman."

"I deserved the dressing down."

"No, you didn't," Janie protested. "You're being unfair, Brent."

The man in question held up his hand. "Let him finish, Janie. Go on, Chapman."

"You usually do it one-on-one, not with the principal present."

Brent inclined his head. "Fair enough. You're right. But this isn't a normal case. This is personal." His voice rose. "You screwed up protecting a woman Rowan and I care for a great deal. I trusted you with Janie's safety, and you let me down. I won't let that slide."

"I didn't ask you to. I should have caught the van sooner, and I was distracted. That's on me."

"You bet it is," Brent snapped. "You're lucky you, Janie, and Jesse came through that situation without a scratch. As it is, you still have to explain to Bear why his vehicle needs body work. Again."

He winced. "Believe me, I haven't forgotten."

"Oh, trust me, Chapman. When he gets through with you, you'll wish you'd paid more attention to your surroundings."

"Yes, sir."

"You said you were distracted. What was so interesting that you let down your guard?"

He remained silent. If he admitted the truth, Sawyer feared Brent would remove him from Janie's security detail. He didn't want to step away from the job.

Brent narrowed his eyes. "I don't hear an answer from you. Do we have a problem here?"

Oh, man. The quiet, icy voice told Sawyer he was skating on thin ice and almost ready to break through to freezing water. "No, sir."

"Then what was the problem?"

"I was the problem," Janie said.

Sawyer froze. She knew he was struggling to remain objective where she was concerned?

Brent's eyes flicked to Janie. "Explain."

"I was nervous about working with Ian, which in retrospect was stupid. Sawyer was trying to help me get ready for the sketching session."

Close but not one hundred percent accurate. Brent was sharp. Sawyer doubted he'd buy that explanation.

The boss grunted. "Rowan wants to talk to you. My assistant will show you to an empty office so you can call her."

"Are you trying to get rid of me, Brent?"

"Caught me." He smiled. "Go. Rowan is eager to catch up with you."

"What about Sawyer?"

"He stays. He'll find you in a few minutes."

He sighed. Yep. Didn't figure his boss had bought Janie's explanation.

Janie stood. "I want my bodyguard back in one piece."

"Yes, ma'am." Brent waited until Janie closed the office door behind her before he rounded on Sawyer. "I want a straight answer, Chapman. Now."

"Janie."

"What about her?"

"She distracted me. It's not her fault. It's mine."

His boss stared for a moment, then groaned. "You're kidding, right?"

"No, sir."

"We'll develop a reputation as a matchmaker if this trend continues," Brent groused. "So, I'll ask you what I've asked every other operative in this situation, and that includes your teammates. Are you sure you can do your job?" He held up a hand before Sawyer could answer. "Think hard before you answer me. If you tell me you can handle it and you're wrong, Janie will pay the price. I guarantee if anything happens to her, you'll answer to me and Rowan."

He didn't know which was worse. They were both fierce. Sawyer thought about his growing feelings for Janie. They would be a problem, he admitted. Not enough of one to stop him from protecting her with his life. "I can handle it, sir."

"If you can't, I need to know immediately. Shove your ego aside and do what's best for her. Hear me?"

"Yes, sir. You have my word."

"I'll hold you to it, Sawyer. Dismissed."

Sawyer got out while he could, not breathing until he closed the door behind himself. The knot in his gut relaxed slightly now that he was out of Brent's office with his head still attached.

"That bad, huh?" Brent's assistant smiled at him.

"I'm lucky to survive relatively unscathed."

"Caught him on a good day."

He chuckled. "Where's Janie?"

"I took her to the small conference room where she wouldn't be disturbed." Her eyes twinkled. "And where she wouldn't hear your conversation with Brent."

"I appreciate you sparing my reputation with the client." He walked down the hall to the conference room and paused in the doorway when he heard Janie laughing.

"Everything all right?" Brody asked as he exited the elevator.

"Barely."

"What happened?"

Sawyer recounted events since he and Janie left the safe house early this morning.

His team leader flinched. "You're lucky."

"I heard that from Brent a few minutes ago, along with several other things."

Brody moved closer. "Got something to tell me, Sawyer?"

"It's Janie."

"What about her?"

"She's getting under my skin without even trying," he muttered.

"That's usually the way it works, my friend. Will Brent allow you to stay on Janie's security detail?"

"He better," Janie said. She stood in the doorway, her gaze locked on Sawyer. "I'll insist that he stay on as my personal bodyguard. I don't trust many people in this situation, but I trust Sawyer and the rest of your team."

"Good to know," Brody said. He squeezed Sawyer's shoulder. "Let me know when you're ready to go. I'm taking the next watch shift."

"Copy that."

As his team leader passed, he whispered, "Good luck."

He might need it. Maybe he really was losing his situational awareness when Janie was around. He did not know that she was standing in the doorway behind him. "Should I apologize?"

She held out her hand. When he clasped it with his own, Janie drew him into the conference room with her and closed the door. "I don't want an apology, Sawyer. In fact, I'm relieved."

"Why?"

"It's good to know I'm not in this boat by myself."

Stunned, Sawyer stared at her. "You're serious?"

"Oh, yes. I've been trying to figure out where the lines between reality and fantasy were drawn. Everything seemed real to me. I know you said the only time you lie is in the course of your work, but I'm your mission right now. I didn't know if what I was feeling for you was one sided or if perhaps the interest went both ways."

Thank God. "Definitely both ways. I shouldn't, though."

"Why not?"

"Sweetheart, as you heard in Brent's office, any distraction could be fatal. Are you willing to take that risk?"

"One hundred percent ready. I trust you, Sawyer."

"Even after what happened a little while ago?"

"You protected me. That's what happened. So, yes, I'm good with you doing more of the same."

He cupped her cheek with his palm, reveling in his right to touch her. "You're a special woman, Janie. I'm honored to be part of your life."

"Even if I come with a guarantee of trouble?"

"So do I. Will you reject me because of it?"

"Absolutely not."

"Then we'll be fine. You might want to hold off on committing to a relationship with me."

"Why?"

"My team is on deployment rotation every other month. That means I will be gone much of the month that we're on duty. The month that we're here, we train hard. When Brent is shorthanded, he might have to activate us for a short-term assignment."

"All right."

He stilled. "You're okay with that?"

"Why wouldn't I be?"

"I may be out of the country for holidays, birthdays, anniversaries, weddings, and funerals."

"I'll stay busy while you're gone. Will I have a way to speak to you during those deployments?"

"I can arrange that."

"Good. Do it."

Sawyer eased closer. "Are you sure? I'll understand if you want time to think about it."

"I'm sure. Sawyer, I'm a grown woman. I can call a home repair professional if something breaks that I can't handle alone while you're gone."

"I'll leave you a list of people Fortress uses for home emergencies like that. If anything else comes up that's not covered by the people on the list, call Brent or Zane. Both of them have a complete list of vetted repair people we trust inside our homes."

"Problem solved, then."

He couldn't believe how accepting Janie was of the challenges that came with a relationship with an operative. Of course, she hadn't dealt with the long absences yet. "My teammates' wives and Jesse's girlfriend spend a lot of time together when we're deployed. They'll invite you to join them. The loneliness can be difficult to handle."

"I'm looking forward to meeting and spending time with them." She nuzzled his palm. "Stop worrying. I have a business to run. If I have a problem with the separation from you, I'll spend time with your teammates' women and work more in the shop so I can spend time with you when you return."

He couldn't help himself. Sawyer slid his arms around her and hugged her. "You are such a gift."

"You're an unexpected blessing," she murmured. "I never expected to survive the hijacking in Mexico, much less meet someone who wanted to start a relationship with me. I have dated little recently."

"Lucky for me. I'll make it worth your while."

She squeezed his middle.

A sharp knock sounded on the door, and Brody peered inside the room. His eyebrows soared when he saw Janie in Sawyer's arms. "Breaking news for the class, buddy?"

"We're officially dating." He could make of it what he wanted. Sawyer knew this was the right woman for him. Whether Janie felt the same about him was anyone's guess.

A soft whistle from his team leader. "Does Brent know?"

"Not in so many words."

"He's aware we're attracted to each other," Janie added. "If he balks, I'll sit him down and have a talk with him."

Sawyer and Brody stared. "You're kidding, right?" Brody asked.

"No, I'm not. If I can't get through to him, I'll enlist Rowan's help. Between us, we'll make him back off."

Whew. From Sawyer's experience, no one argued with the boss and won. "You might get by with that. If we did it, Brent would suspend us."

"I don't work for him. He can't suspend or fire me."

"Don't get on Brent's bad side on our account," Brody warned. "Not worth it."

Her gaze locked on Sawyer's. "It definitely is."

Brody turned his attention to Sawyer. "Ready to go?"

"Any word from the interrogation team?"

"Not yet. They'll let us know when they have something."

"It needs to be soon."

"I hear you. They know the stakes, Sawyer. They'll move it along as fast as they can." He led the way from the small conference room. "Zane is running the sketch through the databases. No results yet."

They rode the elevator to the garage level and walked to two SUVs parked side by side.

Brody tossed him a key fob for the loaner SUV. "You lead. I'll bring up the rear." He pointed at Sawyer. "Stay focused."

"Yes, sir." Man, he would never live down his mistake. His teammates wouldn't allow him to mess up again. He glanced at Janie. Now that she was his, Sawyer had even more reason than ever to stay focused.

He opened the passenger door for Janie, scooped her into his arms, and set her on the seat. After handing her the seatbelt, he bent and brushed his mouth over hers, a light, barely there caress. Hopefully, she would give him permission to share an actual kiss with her soon. Trust had to be built between them first. He didn't want to push past boundaries she wasn't willing to move.

Sawyer climbed behind the wheel and drove from the garage. In the time they'd been with Ian and Brent, the security had remained heightened but not at the same level as when they raced through the gates.

Grateful for security's help, he made a mental note to communicate with the head of ground security to express his appreciation for their help.

He joined the traffic flow on Harding Place and headed for the Interstate. Sawyer threaded his fingers through Janie's, caressing her soft skin.

While driving, he constantly scanned the mirrors and the traffic ahead of him. They arrived in Hartman without incident.

In town, Sawyer drove squares for a while to be sure he hadn't missed a tail. The last thing he wanted to do was lead the enemy right to their doorstep.

Janie glanced at him. "I assume we're not lost."

He chuckled. "I'm making sure we didn't pick up a tail."

She lapsed into silence, content to hold his hand while they drove.

Sawyer purposely stayed away from Natural Bliss in case the enemy lurked nearby.

When he was satisfied Janie was safe, Sawyer turned toward the safe house outside of Hartman. Fifteen minutes later, he drove around to the back and parked the SUV. "We'll wait while Brody checks the house."

"Should you go with him?"

"Clearing the house would go faster," he admitted.

"Go on. I'll be fine out here."

"Stay inside the vehicle. Don't open it for anyone. You'll be safe, but if anything frightens you, honk the horn."

Sawyer leaned over and brushed his mouth over hers, then exited the vehicle and locked it. He met Brody at the nose of the vehicle. "Let's get this done so I can get Janie inside."

The two men entered the safe house, and each took one floor. Within five minutes, they'd cleared the house. No signs of intrusion. Excellent.

Sawyer returned to the vehicle and opened the passenger door for Janie after he grabbed his Go bag from the cargo area. He escorted her inside and reset the alarm.

"Any problems?"

She shook her head. "What about in here?"

"No signs of an unwanted visitor. We'll check every time we return to the house, in case our location has been compromised."

"What's next?"

"Lunch. After that, Brody and I will see what we can learn from the interrogation team and get an update from Zane. Do you have work you need to do for your shop?"

"I need to place another order for supplies. I noticed that we're running low on several items."

"You can work on one of our laptops. No one will trace your location with our laptops. We have built-in protections."

"Nice. I never would have thought about that danger. I'm glad to know that you and your team are aware of it."

"We have items to make good sandwiches."

Brody nodded. "Sawyer can grill and put killer sandwiches together."

"And breakfast," Sawyer added. "Don't forget that."

"Right. Breakfast, too. If you want anything fancy, though, you're on your own. Neither one of us is any good in the kitchen."

"Sandwiches are fine. If we want something else, I can handle kitchen duties."

"Thank God," Brody muttered. "I'd prefer not to gain fifty pounds on this assignment."

Sawyer snorted. "You'd have to put yourself on a diet and up your own workout regimen to lose the weight."

"Since I'd rather not run over five or ten miles a day, I'm glad to have other options than your food, buddy."

"Wuss," Sawyer teased.

His team leader rolled his eyes. "I'll leave the lunch portion of the program to you while I check the perimeter."

"Go. We've got this."

Brody turned off the alarm and went outside.

"We just got here. Why is Brody checking outside?"

"First, Brody isn't that familiar with the property. We each memorize the terrain and check the perimeter every 20 to 30 minutes. If anything changes, we'll recognize it immediately."

She sighed. "So much goes into protecting me every minute, doesn't it?"

"We want you safe, Janie. We go through the same procedures every time we're on a protection detail."

"I did not know you do so much work."

He took her hand and drew her into the kitchen. "Stick with me, kid. I'll teach you everything I know."

"Deal."

Together, they threw together stacks of sandwiches. Janie goggled at the pile of food on the platter. "That's enough to feed an army, Sawyer."

He shrugged. "High metabolisms plus a high-powered training regimen. We train hard to be prepared for anything at a moment's notice. The terrorists don't let us stop to catch our breaths. We have to be in better shape than they are to beat them in a fight."

"Are you?"

"Oh, yeah. Brody doesn't let us slack off. Even if he did, the trainers at Personal Security International, the training arm of Fortress, would catch it and take us off deployment rotation until we were back in shape." He grimaced. "Brody would get the worst of it. The trainers don't mess around. Most of those men and women were Special Forces. They don't put up with less than one hundred percent effort from every operative. We don't want to get on their bad list. They have devious minds with inventive and painful training sessions. None of us wants to spend extra time with them. As it is, we have to go in for retraining every six months. It's a brutal two weeks. We all hate it, but the training works. We're in better shape than most active Special Forces units."

She sat down abruptly. "You really could have carried me for miles, couldn't you?"

He nodded.

"I did not know, Sawyer."

"No reason you should."

"I'm impressed and in awe of what you've accomplished."

He was silent a moment. "Does the amount of training we have to go through bother you?"

"No. In fact, I'm grateful. It means you're more likely to come home to me in one piece. Next time you go to PSI, thank the trainers for me."

Man, wouldn't that give Durango, the primary trainers for Texas Team, a real laugh? "I'll do that."

They just sat down together at the kitchen table when Brody returned. He looked at Janie. "Call your brother."

"I'd planned to ask soon if that was permissible. Why?"

"He's at your store, demanding to speak to you."

Chapter Fifteen

Janie stared at Brody. "David is here?" What was her brother doing in the country? She'd only been back about 24 hours herself. Why had David flown in from Chile? "Why would he come here?"

Brody watched her. "If what we suspect is true, you know why."

No. She shook her head, unable to believe her brother was involved in what had been happening to her for the past few days. But why else would he show up out of the blue since he was still angry with her and wanted an angle to force her to share Granny Irene's estate?

Granted, he couldn't pick up the phone to call Janie since her cell phone was still in Mexico, but he could have called the store. David had the number. Although he had never used it, she included it in all her emails to him.

"Did he say what he wanted?" Sawyer asked, his hand covering Janie's.

"Not according to Jeremy. He showed up, demanded to see his sister, and refused to tell the operatives or employees why he flew in. The operatives explained Janie was out for the day and wouldn't be back in the store. Apparently, he became belligerent with the employees and threatened them plus the operatives if he wasn't able to contact Janie. He's using the worried brother card to gain sympathy, but it's not working. Jeremy and Molly are skeptical of his good intentions."

She groaned. Of course he would demand to be in her life now. As much as she didn't want to do it, Janie knew she had to see him. The Texas Team wouldn't be happy with her. "I need to see him, Sawyer."

"Are you sure you want to do that? He could be responsible for the hijacking, as well as the attempts on your life since you've been back."

"And he might not be responsible." She held up a hand, already knowing what he would say. "I know. I'm not facing reality. What if we're wrong and he's not responsible for what's happening? Besides that, if I don't see him face to face, he'll keep after my employees and your friends until he gets what he wants. You want to talk to him, right?"

"You bet we do. We have several questions for him."

"This is your chance to do it without having to catch a flight to Chile to find out if he's responsible for the hijacking."

"I still don't like it," Sawyer said. "I feel like I'm throwing you to the lions. If he is responsible for the hijacking, this might be a trap. I don't want you caught in another one."

"This is the only way. We have to try. I can't stay in hiding forever."

"It hasn't been more than a day, sweetheart."

"And already we've had two attempts to either kill or reacquire me." She shook her head. "Let's find out if David is responsible or if he's tangled up in something and can't get out on his own."

Sawyer sighed. "Your heart is too soft, Janie. This is risky."

"Please? You can make it safe for me. I'm asking you to work something out so I can have some answers and my employees will be safe."

He glanced at his team leader, eyebrow raised.

"Wuss," Brody muttered.

Sawyer punched his friend on the shoulder. "We'll make it work, Janie. All of us will talk to him."

"He'll want to talk to me alone." She knew David. He wouldn't pass up a chance to press his case one more time.

"Not happening. Where you go, I go. Period."

"He won't be happy about it," she warned. Her brother would be quite vocal in his displeasure.

"Tough. Your safety is my priority, not his happiness. If he loves you as much as he'll claim, David will understand my precaution."

Not likely. "You don't know him like I do."

He inclined his head. "He doesn't know me, either. Yet."

Well, this would be fun. Unless she missed her guess, David had met his match. "All right. I'll follow any rules you lay down so I can see him. Maybe we'll mend our broken relationship."

Sawyer brushed his mouth over hers. "For your sake, I hope so." His voice gave away his skepticism.

She felt the same way. Still, Janie wouldn't give up on David. Despite everything, she still loved him. "Thanks, Sawyer."

"I just hope we don't regret this plan." He grabbed his phone and called Jeremy. "It's Sawyer. Brody and I are bringing Janie into Hartman. Send Moran to Main Street Coffee Shop in ten minutes. We'll meet him there." After answering a few cryptic questions, Sawyer ended the call and slid the phone back into his cargo pocket. "Let's go. We don't have much of a head start."

"I'm riding with you." Brody opened the back door and stepped outside to scan the area. He glanced over his shoulder. "Clear."

Sawyer wrapped his arm around Janie's shoulders and tucked her close to his side. After resetting the alarm, he escorted Janie to the SUV and helped her into the shotgun seat. He drove into the town of Hartman and headed for the coffee shop.

"Why aren't we meeting David at my shop?"

"Too great a chance that the person who left the box at the front of the store will be lying in wait for you to return."

Of course. She should have realized his logic. The precaution of staying away from the shop wouldn't change just because her brother showed up unexpectedly. In fact, his appearance in town was even more reason to go somewhere out of her normal routine. Since Janie didn't drink coffee, she didn't go to coffee shops in town.

Sawyer and Brody remained vigilant during the drive. Thankfully, the journey was uneventful. Just the way she liked them. After what happened earlier this morning, she would never take a peaceful drive anywhere for granted.

When Sawyer parked in the lot beside the coffee shop, Brody climbed out and went inside the establishment. Two minutes later, Sawyer received a text. He circled the hood of the SUV and opened Janie's door. "Straight inside," he murmured. "We'll sit at the back of the shop in the corner. Brody's waiting for us."

Janie glanced around as they hurried to the door of the shop and Sawyer ushered her inside.

Brody lifted a hand, and they joined him at the back corner table. Sawyer seated Janie, then the two men sat with their backs to the wall.

"Want tea or something else?" Brody asked her.

She shook her head. "I don't think I could keep anything down."

"We don't have to do this," Sawyer said. "We can leave right now."

"I wish. I can't."

"Your choice for now. If you decide at any point that you want to end the meeting with David, tell me, and we'll be out of here."

"Heads up," Brody murmured, gaze on the man who walked into the coffee shop.

The stranger spotted the group in the corner, and headed in their direction, his gaze fixed on Janie. He strode to her chair, yanked her to her feet, and wrapped her in a bear hug. "Janie! Thank God you're all right. Why didn't you call me as soon as you were free?"

Stunned at David's enthusiastic hug, Janie wrapped her arms around her brother. "I'm sorry, David. I didn't have my phone. The hijackers forced us to leave everything on the plane."

"That's no excuse. You have my number. You should have called me from the shop at least. I was worried sick about you."

Janie freed herself and stepped back. Sawyer had stood and was behind her. "We didn't exactly part on good terms, bro."

"That doesn't mean I don't care about you, sis. You should know that by now. It's us against the world, right?"

Maybe. The problem was David said all the right things for an audience. As soon as they were alone, however, all bets were off.

"Who are your friends?" her brother asked.

Sawyer held out his hand. "I'm Sawyer, Janie's boyfriend. This is Brody, my teammate. Please, join us. Would you like coffee?"

David's eyes narrowed. "Boyfriend? You didn't mention you were dating anyone, Janie. When did this happen?"

"It's recent."

"I'm going to order coffee for us and tea for Janie. I'll be back," Brody said and rose. He went to the counter to place an order.

"How recent?" David demanded, ignoring Brody's absence. "I should have heard about this."

Since when? He'd shown no interest in her dating life. "It doesn't matter," Janie countered. "I'm a grown woman. My relationships are my business."

"What do you know about this guy? He could be after your money."

"Like you?" Sawyer asked, his voice mild.

David scowled. "What do you mean by that?"

"Exactly what it sounds like. I know how much pressure you've been putting on Janie to divvy up Granny Irene's estate against the wishes expressed in her will."

"So? It's only fair. Janie and I are Granny Irene's only remaining relatives. I deserve half of the estate."

"Your grandmother disagreed, Moran."

"You know nothing about our family," Janie's brother snapped. "Keep your nose out of our business."

"Anything that concerns Janie is my business."

"He's right, David." Janie eyed her brother. "Sawyer knows about the will and why Granny Irene set the terms as she did."

"She was wrong," he insisted. "I'm fine. I don't have a problem. If you won't believe me, ask Maria. She doesn't lie. She'll tell you that Granny Irene was dead wrong."

What was the point of arguing? David wouldn't be satisfied unless Janie gave him exactly what he wanted. "Why are you here, David?"

His jaw tightened. "Really? A bunch of deranged hijackers kidnapped you and you ask me that? I was worried about you. When I didn't hear from you, I was afraid you'd been seriously injured in the hijacking. No one could tell me anything. It's like you vanished off the face of the earth."

Janie stared. Seriously? Her brother hadn't even bothered to take her to the airport the morning she left Chile. "I still could have been in Mexico. You took a risk coming to Hartman. Why would you do that?"

"Where else would I find you if you were rescued? You wouldn't have come back to Chile where Maria and I could care for you properly. I had to come to you." He sounded bitter about the matter.

Temper lit a fire in Janie's blood. How dare he put this on her? He was the one who had frozen her out unless he was trying to wear her down and sway her to his way of thinking.

Brody returned carrying a tray with four drinks. He handed the first one to Janie. "Tea for the lady." Then he handed Sawyer and David cups of coffee before taking the last one for himself. He set two bowls filled with creamer and sweetener in the center of the table.

Brody and Sawyer ignored the bowls. David doctored up his drink with a lot of creamer and sugar.

"You need to come back to Chile with me," her brother said after a long sip of his coffee. "Maria is worried sick about you, and I'll never hear the end of it if I don't bring you back home."

She heard what he didn't say. David wasn't worried about her. "I'll call her tonight."

"That's not good enough. I'm not letting you upset my wife. She's pregnant. Maria can't have shocks to her system. It's not good for her or the baby."

"Really, Moran?" Sawyer watched him much as a cat did a mouse. "Not above using blackmail to get your way, are you?"

"Shut up. This is none of your business. It's between me and my sister, so butt out."

"Not happening," he said, voice soft. "The danger to your sister still exists. She's not safe, especially anywhere in South or Central America."

David stared. "What are you talking about? Of course, she's safe." He rounded on Janie. "What is this clown filling your head with, sis? This is ridiculous. The hijackers aren't in the US. No one is after you now."

"You're wrong."

He snorted. "Prove it. You can't, can you? Your boyfriend just doesn't want you out of his sight and out of his influence." David stabbed a finger in her direction. "I told you this guy was after our money."

"That's enough, David." She'd had enough. The accusations were uncalled for. "I'm not going back to Chile. I have a business to run."

"You have employees. They can take care of your little store for a few days."

"They've already been carrying the load for over two weeks. I'm not asking them to do it again this soon. It's not fair to them."

"You have that little control over your own workers?" He shook his head. "Fine. I'll take care of it for you." He stood and wrapped his hand around her wrist and tugged. "Let's get it over with, then we'll swing by your house to pack a few things before we go to the airport."

She gasped at the sharp pain in her wrist.

In less than a beat, Sawyer gripped David's wrist. Her brother hissed and released her, shaking his hand.

"What are you doing? I should sue you for bodily harm."

"First, Janie said she wasn't going to Chile. You weren't listening. Second, you don't put your hands on her without her permission. Period. Third, no one hurts Janie and gets by with it. Fourth, she doesn't have her passport. She can't travel internationally without that passport."

"Oh, yeah? How did she get back into the country?" he demanded.

"Private arrangements."

"This is ridiculous," David snapped. "I want to take her home."

"Forget it."

"I can't go, bro," Janie said. "Even if I wanted to leave, I won't bring danger to your wife and baby."

"That makes little sense. You're safe now."

"She's not," Brody said.

"What do you mean?"

"Since Janie's been back in the US, she's been a target."

"All the more reason to get her out of here." He swung his gaze back to Janie. "Come on, sis. You shouldn't be hanging out with losers. I can protect you."

Janie couldn't help it. She laughed. "Trust me, David. You don't know what you're talking about."

He looked offended. "Why do you say that?"

"We're in black ops," Sawyer said.

Her brother's eyes widened. "Are you serious? Janie, are you crazy? These guys are mercenaries. You shouldn't have anything to do with them. They're dangerous."

"You bet they are. The best kind of dangerous. They protect innocents like me in dangerous situations."

"For money," he snapped. "They charge people for this noble service of theirs."

"Believe me. I'm grateful for what they do."

David stared at her with speculation in his eyes, then shifted his attention to Sawyer. "You rescued my sister from the hijackers, didn't you?"

Sawyer inclined his head.

"I knew it." He rounded on Janie again. "How much did these jerks charge you?"

"Nothing." It was true. Although she'd offered to pay, Brent had refused her offer. "They work for Brent's company, so no money exchanged hands."

David's jaw tightened. "I should have known. When did you start dating this guy?" he asked with a glare at Sawyer.

"It's recent."

"How recent?"

"None of your business, David. I'm a grown woman. I don't answer to you."

"I'm just looking out for you."

"I'm lucky Sawyer and his team were close enough to rescue me."

"Wait a minute." David's eyes narrowed. "The news said a group attacked the hijackers and killed dozens of people. You're trying to tell me these two guys did all that damage?"

"There are five of us," Brody murmured. "I won't apologize for doing what was necessary to rescue Janie."

His face flushed. "I didn't ask for an apology. But the facts prove my point. You and your buddies are mercenaries. You kill people for money."

"They did their jobs, David," Janie insisted. "Because of it, I'm still alive. Now, back off."

He held up his hands. "Fine. Have it your own way. I have things to do." He stalked from the coffee shop.

Janie closed her eyes for a moment, then sighed. She looked at Sawyer and Brody. "I apologize for my brother. He shouldn't have insulted you."

"It's not your fault, baby," Sawyer said. He squeezed her hand. "His attitude isn't on you."

"It's not fair, you know. David doesn't know you at all, yet he's judging you by your job title. He doesn't see the honor and integrity you and your teammates have."

The two men exchanged glances, then Sawyer said to her, "Thanks for saying that."

"You don't know how many people have accused us of being baby killers," Brody said grimly.

Her eyes widened. "Should I not have mentioned to David what you do for a living?"

"He knows Brent and what Fortress does. As soon as he found out who we work for, your brother would have known." Sawyer shrugged. "We usually tell the public that we work for a private security company without giving too many details. It's a protection for ourselves and our families."

"I didn't even consider that, Sawyer. I'm so sorry. I didn't mean to compromise anyone's safety."

"You didn't. Like I said, David knows about Fortress. No way to hide the truth from him, anyway. Besides, if he is involved in the attacks on you, I want him to know you have people watching over you who have your best interests at heart. For me, the stakes are a lot higher and more personal."

Brody finished his coffee. "Ready to get out of here now? We're too exposed with this many windows in the coffee shop."

Janie stood and picked up her tea. "I'm ready."

Brody and Sawyer tossed their empty to-go cups of coffee and escorted Janie outside the shop.

She glanced at the other side of the parking lot and froze. Her brother was arguing with two men. Both of them appeared to be of Hispanic descent.

Chapter Sixteen

Sawyer's eyes narrowed as he watched Janie's brother argue with the two men. That David knew anyone well enough to argue with them was puzzling and made Sawyer reconsider how long the man had been in Hartman.

He grabbed his phone and took several pictures of the trio before tucking Janie into the passenger seat of his SUV and circling the hood to climb behind the wheel.

"Did you get them?" Brody asked.

"Yep."

"We need to run the photos through our databases to see if we get a hit."

"I'll take care of it as soon as we return to the safe house."

"Drive down the block and park behind a building," Brody instructed. "I want to check the vehicle for trackers."

Excellent idea. He'd planned to do that before his team leader mentioned it. Sawyer drove to one of the local banks and parked behind the building.

Brody hopped out with his electronic signal detector in hand and circled the vehicle. He paused at the rear of the SUV, dropped below Sawyer's line of vision only to reappear a moment later. He walked to a car four spaces over and pressed his hand to the wheel well, then returned to the SUV.

"One tracker."

"How did they know which vehicle we arrived in?" Janie asked.

"We were the only customers inside the coffee shop," Sawyer said. "The rest of the customers were in the drive-through lane."

He drove to Main Street and turned in the opposite direction that he'd been heading, taking detours through neighborhoods and doubling back on himself, turning squares to see if he could spot a tail.

After 30 minutes, Sawyer headed for the safe house. He glanced at Janie. She was staring out the side window, her hands fisted. "You okay, sweetheart?"

She shook her head. "This is so wrong," she muttered. "I don't understand why this is happening."

"We'll figure it out and when we do, everything will make sense."

"What can you do to help with your shop, Janie?" Brody asked.

Sawyer's friend was trying to distract Janie. At the moment, there was nothing anyone could do. They needed more information.

"I need to place another order for supplies. I'd planned to do that after lunch, but my brother's sudden appearance distracted me."

"We have laptops with encryption at the safe house. You'll be able to place your order without fear of anyone seeing what you're doing."

Didn't mean the enemy wasn't monitoring her business's suppliers. Still, Sawyer knew the chances of that were remote. If they tried to get a lock on her location, they'd fail. Zane's safeguards on the laptops were too good to break without several alerts on Fortress's end to warn of hacking.

"What about dinner?" Brody asked. "Do you and Sawyer have a meal in mind?"

Sawyer glanced at his team leader in the rearview mirror. "We haven't had lunch yet. The sandwiches we put together are in the refrigerator, waiting for us."

The other man glared. "I'm a growing boy. I have to plan ahead."

Janie laughed. "What did you have in mind? I don't know what ingredients we have in the kitchen."

"I think lasagna would be perfect after the day you've had."

"Are you making it?"

Sawyer groaned. "Trust me, Janie. You don't want Brody attempting it. We'd have the fire department at our door in minutes."

"Hey," Brody protested. "I'm not that bad."

"You're worse."

Together, he and Brody regaled Janie with tales of their cooking disasters and kept Janie rolling with laughter.

She wiped tears from her face as she glanced over her shoulder at Brody. "You have to be pulling my leg. No one as intelligent as you two could be that bad at cooking."

"A lot you know," Brody groused. "I think Sawyer's gene pool is missing the cooking gene."

"I must be kin to you," Sawyer tossed back.

"How does your team survive when you're in the field if all of you are so bad at cooking?"

"MREs," they said at the same time.

"What are those?"

"Meals ready to eat." Brody shook his head. "They have plenty of nutrition but taste like cardboard."

"They're in packets," Sawyer added. "Sometimes, they include dessert."

"Does that make up for the lack of taste in the rest of the meal?"

"Not really, but when you need fuel and you're out in the field or on the run, you eat what you have."

"What happens if you run out of MREs?"

"We scrounge. We know what plants and fruits are safe to eat."

"No meat?"

Sawyer shook his head. "No time to hunt something and prepare it. Besides, the jet also carries food for us. Once we're wheels up, we can eat as much as we want."

"And drink real coffee," Brody said. "I think I miss that the most when we're in the field. We don't have time to sit down and enjoy coffee."

"I thought you would have said you missed Sage above all else," Sawyer said.

"That goes without saying." A sly smile curved his mouth. "I guess you'll be joining the rest of us in missing our significant others."

He smiled. "Yeah, I will." He planned to complain as much as his teammates.

Sawyer turned left onto the country road where the safe house was located and soon parked behind their temporary quarters. He and Brody went through the same routine of checking the house for unwanted intrusion while leaving Janie locked in the SUV.

Within two minutes, Sawyer returned for Janie and escorted her inside the house. After he reset the alarm, he and Brody set the platter of sandwiches in the center of the table and glasses of cold water, along with empty plates. They also set a bag of potato chips next to the platter.

"Choose the sandwich you want," Sawyer said. "Brody and I will eat anything that doesn't eat us first."

"I'm not hungry."

"Your body needs fuel, Janie."

She sighed. "All right. I'll try." Janie studied the pile of sandwiches and chose one filled with chicken and cheese.

Although she ignored the chips, Sawyer didn't push. If she ate the sandwich, he'd be happy.

When they finished lunch, Sawyer retrieved his laptop, logged on, and handed the computer to Janie. "Take your time. Brody and I have work of our own to do."

"I can wait. I don't want to interfere with your job."

"I'll use the safe house laptop. Brody has his own computer with him."

"Thanks for letting me use your computer."

He squeezed her shoulder and left her to work. Sawyer retrieved the safe house laptop, logged in, and transferred the photos he took to the computer and loaded them into the databases to see if the faces of the strangers were in the database system.

While the search ran, he researched Janie's brother. The deeper he dug, the less he liked what he was seeing. David Moran had a long history of making bad choices. While he'd never been in trouble with law enforcement, he was heavily in debt, despite drawing a good salary from the engineering company employing him.

He'd fared marginally better since he moved to Chile and married Maria. However, his debt load was growing at a rapid rate again. From what Sawyer had dug up, David was borrowing heavily against his house and didn't have enough equity to borrow against it again.

Lately, he'd started taking advances on his credit cards to fund his expenses. Sawyer frowned. No sign of where he spent the money. Ferreting out that information might require someone with more computer expertise than he had.

Immediately, he thought of Simone, Jesse's girlfriend. She was a computer whiz. Since his team already had Zane running checks for them, Sawyer sent Jesse a text message. He received a reply less than a minute later.

Excellent. Sawyer messaged Simone and thanked her for taking the time to see what she could find out about Janie's brother.

That done, he shifted his attention to researching Vatos Locos. A very organized and regimented group from what he could tell. Hard to believe the group at large was 10,000 strong, the members stretching from Chile all the way up into Canada. Of course, they didn't have a formal roster for him to see. The leader's lieutenants had been photographed frequently. The leader? Nowhere to be seen. Like the tech team at Fortress had said, no identity on the leader.

So how did the group keep the members accountable? They must have divided the membership among the lieutenants. The leader's underlings kept their assigned members in line. This was a slick operation, more like a military campaign than a group of thugs bullying their way to the top of the food chain.

He frowned. Was it possible some of the gang's top lieutenants were former military? That would explain the ruthless organization. It would also mean these guys were more dangerous than he originally thought. Former military meant an actual plan instead of a fly-by-night operation.

Why had these men targeted Janie? Had she seen or heard something that she shouldn't have? If so, what could it be? Was Brent right about her missing fellow hostage?

His laptop signaled a result on the search for identification of the two men arguing with Moran. He clicked on the tab and scanned the results.

Sawyer's jaw tightened. Not good.

"Sawyer?"

He glanced up at Janie. "Yes?"

"Is something wrong?"

Did he hold back the information that was sure to upset and disillusion her? Less than a second later, he answered his own question. No way was he starting a relationship based on lies with this woman. She was too important to him.

He wouldn't be able to tell her everything because of mission security. However, this wasn't a case of protecting information for the sake of mission security. He simply didn't want to bring more pain into her life. Since there was no way to prevent it, he'd rather not bring her wrath down on his head. Let David deal with his sister's anger and disappointment.

He pushed back from the table and set his laptop in front of Janie. The two men appeared on the screen side by side.

"Who are they?"

"The two men arguing with your brother. They're known members of Vatos Locos."

Janie stared for a moment, then she sighed. "That's not what I wanted to hear."

"I know. I'm sorry."

"We'll have to talk to him again, won't we?"

"You okay with that?"

"No, but what choice do I have?"

"You could let me and one of my teammates talk to him."

"We don't know where he's staying."

"It won't take long to find him. Our tech people are excellent, especially Jesse's girlfriend." He cupped her face between his palms. "Are you sure I can't take care of this for you?"

Janie shook her head. "Thanks for wanting to protect me. I can't lay this responsibility on you because it's hard. Besides, you don't know my brother as well as I do. I'll know if he's lying."

So would he. However, Sawyer wouldn't insist. Janie Moran was a strong woman who knew her own mind. If she felt she needed to do this herself, he had to step back and walk beside her instead of in front of her. "All right. Finish your order for the shop. I'll contact Fortress and have them locate where your brother is staying."

Sawyer grabbed his phone and stepped outside the back door. Walking the perimeter while he talked to the Fortress tech sounded like a great idea. He needed to walk off his frustration.

Zane answered his call. "Miss me already?" his friend teased.

"Ha. Only your wife misses you that quickly, my friend."

Zane chuckled. "Ouch, man. That hurts. What do you need?"

"A location on David Moran." He summarized the conversation with Moran and the suspicious exchange between Moran and two Vatos Locos soldiers.

A soft whistle broke the silence. "That's not good."

"Tell me about it. Janie's having a hard time accepting her brother might be responsible for the attacks she's endured for the past few days."

"What's your gut say?"

"He's involved in this somehow. I don't know how deep he's in, but he's not as innocent as Janie wants to believe."

The sound of Zane's fingers clicking his keyboard at a rapid pace drifted through the speaker. "Got him. He's at Kingsbridge Inn, Room 217."

"Next question. How long has Moran been registered there?"

More keys clicking, then, "Three days."

Sawyer stopped walking. "Are you sure?"

"No question."

David Moran had been in Hartman before Janie had returned to the states.

Chapter Seventeen

Sawyer ended his call and slid the phone into his cargo pocket. As he continued his circuit around the property, he considered how best to tell Janie that her brother was holding back information.

By the time he finished the circuit, he'd still not come up with a good way to pass on the information to Janie. Sawyer grimaced. There wasn't one. Perhaps her brother had an explanation for his presence in Hartman. He already had a pretty good idea what Moran would say. Whether or not it was the truth was anyone's guess.

He entered the safe house to find Janie sipping tea while she stared at the screen in front of her.

"Everything all right outside?" she asked without glancing up.

"No signs of incursion."

She flashed him a quick grin. "I'll take that as a yes. Brody made a fresh pot of coffee since you took his perimeter check."

He made a beeline for the coffeepot and poured himself a mug of the steaming brew. A sip of the liquid had him sighing in satisfaction.

"That good, huh?"

"It's excellent. Still working?"

She nodded. "I need a few more minutes."

"Take your time." His news could wait.

Sawyer walked to the security room, where Brody monitored the cameras set up around the house and property.

"Feeling restless?" Brody asked when Sawyer dropped into the seat beside him.

"I called Zane and asked him to find out where Moran is staying. He's at the Kingsbridge Inn on Highway 231, Room 217."

His friend studied his face for a moment. "What else?"

"Janie's brother has been in town for three days, longer than Janie has been back in the US."

"He insinuated he'd only been in town for a few hours."

"I know. I also ran the photos of the two men he was arguing with through our databases and got a hit."

"Who are they?"

"Juan Delgado and Esteban Varga. They're lieutenants in the Vatos Locos."

Brody growled. "I was afraid of something like that. We need to have a talk with him soon."

"I'm waiting for Janie to finish working on her shop order."

"You shouldn't take her with you, Sawyer. Moran could be dangerous. For certain, his friends are."

"I'm not hiding the truth from her. No matter how difficult the news is , you wouldn't hide the truth from Sage."

Brody froze. "Like that, is it?"

"Time will tell, but I think so."

"Be careful, my friend. I only had to deal with Sage's parents. You have Janie plus Brent and Rowan to handle. I'd rather deal with the vice president and his wife than our boss and Rowan. They'll chew you up and spit you out if you hurt that woman in there."

"Trust me, I haven't forgotten." Talk about a nightmare scenario. If things didn't work out between him and Janie, he'd better have an excellent reason to end things with her and not hurt her heart. Yeah, piece of cake. For a saint, maybe. Sawyer was anything but a saint.

Grabbing his phone, Brody sent a text message and received a response seconds later. "Max will be here in ten minutes to go with us. He was already on his way to keep watch."

Sawyer relaxed a little more. Excellent. If Moran was still dealing with the lieutenants from the gang, Sawyer and Brody wouldn't be outnumbered. While the two of them could handle three opponents, Janie would be too close to the action for Sawyer's comfort. In such a close space, anything could happen.

Minutes later, Janie walked into the security room and glanced around. Her eyes widened. "Look at all the screens," she murmured.

"We have several security cameras around the house and property," Sawyer said. "During a watch shift, we monitor the cameras and walk the perimeter in case the cameras failed to pick up an intruder." Not likely, but they didn't take chances.

"I did not know this much security was in place. No wonder you wanted to stay here."

"What kind of security do you have at your home?" Brody asked.

Her face flushed. "Not much."

Sawyer straightened. "How much is that?"

"No security system." She held up a hand. "Look, I know I should have looked into it. I've been focused on getting Natural Bliss up and going. I have good security at my shop."

"Baby, you need protection at home, too. Especially now that you're involved with me. I'll talk to Brent and have him set up a security team to install a system at your home." Brent should have insisted Janie have a security system. Sawyer was surprised he hadn't.

She flinched.

Understanding dawned on him. "He doesn't know."

"I didn't want to worry him."

"It's necessary for your safety, Janie. Although we try not to bring our work home with us, nothing is one hundred percent secure. I want to schedule the installation team to come to your home tomorrow and install a top-of-the-line security system."

"Sounds expensive."

"It's better than losing your life because you don't have the protection."

Janie blew out a breath. "You're right. I'm just being tight-fisted with Granny Irene's estate money, and that's ridiculous. She wouldn't want me to risk my safety to save a few dollars."

"You're more important than your business," he murmured. "Brent will cut you a deal. We have deep discounts for friends and family. You definitely qualify."

"All right. Thanks for setting that up for me, Sawyer."

"Of course. I'm glad to help. Besides, you having a security system will give me peace of mind when we're deployed."

She watched him long enough that Sawyer had to resist the urge to squirm. "I should have thought of that. Brent always makes a big deal about Rowan using their security system when he goes out with a team. Naturally, you would want the same safety precautions for anyone you care about as well. Do you tell your mother and brothers to be more watchful when you deploy?"

He smiled. "Caught me. I warn them without words. I don't want to send a text in case it's intercepted, so I send a picture of a backpack. When I return, I send a picture of an open suitcase. Like you said, it's a precaution. I want my family to be extra vigilant when I'm on a mission. The Fortress tech team also keeps close watch on the Internet. If there's a breach, they contact my family. We have enemies, Janie. Not everyone appreciates the work we do in the shadows."

"I do. I wouldn't be alive if you hadn't arrived when you did."

He brushed his mouth over hers. "I'm glad we were close." Sawyer turned to Brody. "We're going to see Moran."

Janie's head whipped toward Sawyer. "You found my brother?"

"Zane located him in two minutes."

"So he's not trying to hide."

Brody stood. "Even if he was, he can't hide from our tech team for long. Very few people can live off the grid. Too easy to make mistakes and give yourself away."

She shrugged. "Cash and carry."

"Security cameras are everywhere," he countered. "Zane already knew David was in Hartman. Wouldn't take long to find him via security feeds and traffic cams. He'd start with the coffee shop and follow him from there."

"However Zane came by the information, I'm glad to know where to find David. I don't like how we left things between us."

Brody sent Sawyer a pointed look. "I'll check the perimeter one more time, then make certain the SUV is ready."

Right. Not subtle at all.

Janie stared at Brody as he left the room, then shifted her gaze to him. "Something is wrong. What is it?"

Janie Moran was one sharp lady. "When Zane located your brother, he also told me David had been in town for three days."

Her brows knitted. "How is that possible? I haven't been home for three days."

"That's right."

"But what does it mean?"

"Your brother lied."

"Why? What good would it do?"

"Keeps you from suspecting him and his motives. Janie, he arrived in Hartman before you did. What does that say to you?"

"That he cared enough about me to come to the only place where he knew I would eventually return."

And perhaps he came to Hartman to finish the job the hijackers could not complete.

"Don't." Tears filled her eyes. "Please, Sawyer. Don't say it."

Heart breaking for her, Sawyer wrapped his arms around her and held her close for a moment. "I'll uncover the truth, no matter what it is or where it leads, Janie. When I do, we'll handle the fallout together."

She sniffed. "I don't want David to be responsible for the attacks."

"If he is?"

"He'll be responsible for the deaths of more than a dozen people who were innocent." Her voice broke. "I can't handle that."

"Yes, you can." He eased her closer to his body. "You're strong, Janie, and you're wise enough to know you were an innocent victim as well. If David is responsible, you'll deal and live a vibrant life because to do otherwise would give him more power over you than he deserves."

Janie was quiet a moment, then murmured, "You're right." After a few more beats, she loosened her hold on him and stepped out of the circle of his arms. "Come on. Let's get this over with. If I'm wrong about David, I'd rather know the truth than live in a fantasy world that could lead to harm for you and your teammates."

Sawyer's respect for Janie and her strength grew. A tough lady, indeed. He led her from the security room. They stopped by his room to grab his Go bag, then proceeded to the back door.

After they reset the alarm and stepped outside, Sawyer escorted Janie to the SUV where Brody and Max were engaged in a quiet discussion.

"Ready?" Brody asked, his gaze shifting to Janie.

"Yes. Thanks for coming, Max."

"No problem, Janie." He opened the back door for her and Sawyer, then sat on the shotgun seat while Brody climbed behind the wheel.

During the drive into Hartman, Sawyer and his teammates remained vigilant. Fortunately, no trouble interrupted the journey to Kingsbridge Inn.

Brody parked at the side of the hotel. He and Max stepped out and scanned the area. A signal from Brody had Max slipping around the corner of the building.

"What's he doing?" Janie asked.

"Checking to see if he spots a threat to you."

"And if he does?"

"We'll deal with it. Don't worry yet. Let's wait and see if Max notices anything worth worrying about first."

She lapsed into silence, although Sawyer knew she was still concerned about the upcoming confrontation with her brother. Couldn't miss the clenched fists and shallow breathing as she looked out the window at the nearly empty parking lot.

"Janie."

She turned. "Yes?"

"Trust me?"

"Always."

"Then you know I will stand for you and with you. David's decisions are his own, and he'll have to live with the consequences of his actions. If he's innocent, you and he have nothing to worry about. Unlike what your brother thinks, our skills aren't for sale to the highest bidder. I care about you, Janie. No one is going to hurt you on my watch. No one." Including her brother.

A nod. "I believe you. Thanks for watching out for me."

His vow was a slight comfort, he knew. His gut said David Moran was up to his neck in trouble. Whether he was responsible for the danger to his sister was another matter. He just hadn't figured out what trouble dogged Janie's brother and if that trouble had spilled over onto her.

Max returned a moment later and signaled the area was clear. Brody turned and gave a slight nod to Sawyer.

He glanced at Janie. "Ready to do this?"

A ghost of a smile curved her lips. "Not really, but I don't want to wait either. The delay will only make things worse."

Good call. "Wait for me to come around." He circled around the front of the vehicle and opened Janie's door. "If the confrontation becomes too much for you, let me know. I'll get you out of there while Max and Brody learn the answers we need."

"I'm not a coward," she said shortly, and went to walk ahead of him.

"Hold it." Sawyer caught her upper arm and turned her back toward him. "That's not what I meant. You are a tower of strength. That doesn't mean I want you to endure verbal abuse from anyone, including your brother."

"He wouldn't do that," she protested. Her eyes told a different story, that she wasn't as sure about David as she projected.

"Yeah, he would. He already has." He cupped her chin and raised her face to his. "I won't let him get by with it," he warned. No one could abuse Janie. Ever. She was his to protect, and no one would hurt her if he could prevent it.

"I understand."

He brushed her mouth with his and straightened. Sawyer glanced at Brody. "Ready."

"Max." Brody inclined his head toward the front entrance. "Sawyer, you and Janie follow him. I'll bring up the rear. Let's get this done and get out of here. My skin is crawling."

Sawyer wrapped his arm around Janie's shoulders and stayed alert in case trouble lurked inside the hotel. Brody wasn't prone to exaggeration. If his team leader felt trouble was near, you could bank on it.

He sighed. Great. Taking Janie into the lion's den wasn't on Sawyer's list of priorities. In fact, that was the last place he wanted her.

Resolved to place himself between Janie and any threat, Sawyer drew her closer to his side as they entered the inn's lobby and walked to the elevator.

Less than a minute later, they approached room 217. Max held up a fist, then pointed to the door. It was ajar.

Sawyer's gut tightened as he nudged Janie against the wall beside the door. Moran might have left the door like that if he was getting ice. However, Sawyer had a clear view of the alcove from here. Janie's brother wasn't there.

Brody moved up beside Max. Both men drew their weapons and Max nudged the door open further with his elbow. They entered the room noiselessly.

"What's going on?" Janie whispered.

"Trouble."

Brody stepped into the doorway, his expression grim. "Max is calling for an ambulance. Moran is down."

Chapter Eighteen

Janie gasped and pushed at the immovable wall of Sawyer's back. "Sawyer, I have to see him."

"Janie, it's not pretty," Brody warned. "Be prepared."

Her heart sank. "What happened to him?"

"Someone worked him over. He's alive but unconscious."

She shoved at Sawyer again. This time, the man reached back to grasp her hand and walked into the hotel room with her.

On the floor by the wall, her brother lay sprawled on his back. His clothes were ripped and bloody in several places, and his face was bruised, swollen, and mostly covered with blood. His nose was definitely broken, as were several fingers.

Janie tugged free of Sawyer's hold and dropped to the floor beside her brother. Oh, man. He looked terrible. What happened to him? More importantly, who did this to David? For goodness' sake, he'd only been in town a few days. How could he have made enemies so quickly? "David, it's Janie. Can you hear me?"

No response.

"Come on, bro. Wake up for me. I want to hear a few more bad-tempered remarks from you. Don't let me down."

Still nothing.

With trembling fingers, she stroked the hair away from his forehead. "Oh, David. Come on. Wake up."

Max ended the call to the dispatcher. "Ambulance is five minutes out. Cops will be right behind them."

Tears burned Janie's eyes. "I don't understand. Why did they hurt him? Wouldn't it be simpler to take what they wanted and get out as fast as possible?" She looked at Sawyer. "Burglars don't waste time beating people. This took a lot of time, didn't it?"

He knelt beside her and wrapped his arm around her shoulders. "They took their time working him over methodically." Sawyer pointed to David's swollen and bloody mouth. "If you look closely, you'll see finger marks. They didn't want David to attract attention when they broke his fingers. One of them clamped a hand over his mouth so his screams wouldn't carry."

"They? You're saying more than one person did this to my brother?"

He nodded. "At least two men worked him over."

Bile surged into Janie's mouth as she contemplated the pain her brother must have endured while she'd eaten lunch and placed an order for the shop. If they'd come sooner, Sawyer and his friends could have prevented the worst of the injuries.

How many internal injuries did he have? He hadn't roused to consciousness. Did he have a concussion, or a fractured skull? Janie wished Jesse had come with them. He must be exhausted after staying awake all night to watch over her, but his medical expertise would be invaluable right now.

Nearby, sirens cut off abruptly.

"Come on." Sawyer stood and drew Janie to her feet. "We need to move out of the way so the EMTs can help David."

"Why doesn't he wake up?" she whispered.

"I don't know, baby." He drew her into the circle of his arms as Brody went to the door to direct the EMTs inside the room. "The county hospital is good, and the facility is only minutes away. He'll receive the best care."

"They'll let me see him, right?"

"They should. You're his only relative in the area."

Janie groaned. "Oh, no. I'll have to call Maria and tell her what happened."

"Let the police handle the notification. His wife will want details you can't provide."

"Right here," Brody said to someone in the hall. "We have a victim, David Moran, who has been beaten and is unconscious."

Two EMTs rushed into the room and assessed Janie's brother, taking his vitals and contacting the hospital.

At one point in the conversation, one of the EMTs asked, "Does anyone know if Mr. Moran has any allergies?"

"None," Janie said.

As the medics resumed their assessments, two policemen arrived. Immediately, they pulled their weapons and pointed them at Sawyer and his friends. "Drop your weapons," the taller cop commanded the Fortress operatives.

"Take it easy," Brody said. "We're licensed to carry, and we're on duty."

"What kind of duty?"

"Bodyguards. The victim's sister has been threatened several times over the past few days," Max said. "We also used to be on the job in Texas."

"We're going to reach for our identifications and carry permits," Brody added.

"Slow," the shorter man snapped. "Keep your hands where we can see them."

As Sawyer reached for his identification, he placed his body between the twitchy cops and Janie. When he and his teammates handed over their credential wallets, Janie waited to see if they'd end up in handcuffs and stuffed in patrol cars. That would be unfair. They had done nothing wrong.

Finally, the cops handed back the cred wallets and introduced themselves. "What happened here?" Officer Wallace asked.

"The victim, David Moran, is the brother of our principal, Janie Moran. Janie is also Sawyer's girlfriend," Brody said.

Although Max glanced at Sawyer, he didn't question Brody's statement. Good thing. If he had, the cops would have separated Sawyer from Janie and taken him in for more intensive questioning. Since he was responsible for her safety, he wouldn't allow that to happen. The idea of Sawyer being stuck in an interrogation room for hours while the cops grilled him caused Janie's stomach to tighten into a knot.

Wallace and Reese studied Janie for a moment before turning their attention to David. "What have we got, Blue?" Reese asked the older EMT.

"Mr. Moran has a head wound, broken nose, and broken fingers, along with contusions all over his body. He hasn't regained consciousness. Probably has internal injuries. We need to transport him to the hospital as soon as possible."

A nod from Reese. "A detective will be at the hospital later to talk to him."

"If he's awake," muttered the other EMT.

Janie shuddered. She would gladly put up with his verbal tirades just to hear his voice again. Her brother had to get better. He was her only living relative.

After a glance at the cops, Sawyer gathered Janie into his arms again and held her while the medics prepared her brother for transport. Within minutes, they left the room.

"I need to go with them. David shouldn't be alone," Janie said.

"We have questions before you go," Officer Wallace said. "We'll get you out of here as soon as possible, Ms. Moran."

"Get on with the questions," Sawyer said. "She's David's only relative, aside from his wife."

Both officers straightened. "Wife's name and address?"

"Maria Moran," Janie answered and rattled off David's address and Maria's cell number.

"They live in Chile?" Reese asked.

She nodded. "David works for Horizon Engineering. They have an office in Talca, Chile. David has lived in Talca for three years. That's where he met Maria. They haven't been married long."

"All right. We'll notify Mrs. Moran in a few minutes. What happened here?"

Sawyer told of their arrival at the inn and discovery of David unconscious on the floor. "We called for an ambulance. You arrived within a minute of the EMTs."

"Any idea who might want to harm Mr. Moran?"

He shook his head.

"You sure?" Reese pressed. "Seems unusual for the vic to suffer such a dramatic beating for no reason."

"Can't help you with that."

"Sawyer," Brody murmured. "Tell them."

"No proof," he countered.

"It might help them look in the right direction."

"And it might not."

"Let us be the judge of that." Reese looked from one person to the next until his gaze returned to Sawyer. "You used to be on the job, Chapman. Talk to us. Help us do our jobs."

He blew out a breath. "Look, this might have absolutely nothing to do with what happened to Moran. I think it does, but I have no proof." He explained about the hijacking and the subsequent attacks and threats. "We came to the inn to ask David why he lied about when he arrived in town."

Wallace frowned. "When did he arrive in Hartman?"

"Three days ago. He came to town before Janie returned to the states."

Reese whistled. "The detectives are going to have a field day with this one."

"Wonder if Vatos Locos are involved in this mess." Wallace shook his head. "Those boys are bad news. They're dangerous and don't care if innocents are caught in the crossfire."

"Trust me, we know," Max said grimly.

"How?"

Sawyer glanced at Brody, who gave a slight nod. "Our team rescued Janie in Mexico. When Vatos Locos didn't want to release her, we cleaned house."

"Does the vic have a connection to the gang?"

"Possibly." He summarized meeting David at the coffee shop and the confrontation they'd seen in progress as they left.

"You recognized the men as members of the gang?"

"Not at the time. I took pictures of them with my phone and ran their faces through our database systems at Fortress Security."

Both cops straightened. "You work for Brent Maddox?" Reese asked.

"That's right."

"Tough outfit," Wallace muttered. "How did you get on with them?"

"Maddox asked us to come in for an interview after we were recommended to him as another potential black ops unit."

Reese's eyebrows soared. "Black ops, huh?"

"He only interviews by recommendation," Max added.

Enough already. Janie wanted to get out of here. "Do you need to ask anything else? I really need to go to the hospital. David doesn't have anyone else here. The doctors may have questions about his medical history no one else can answer."

"Go," Reese said. "Don't leave town without letting us or the detectives know."

"Yes, sir." Janie headed for the door with the operatives falling into step with her.

Max passed her in the hall and headed for the stairs. Sawyer nudged her in that direction.

"Why aren't we taking the elevator?" she asked.

"Stairs are faster and safer."

She blinked. An unexpected answer.

Max led the way across the lobby to the front doors.

Sawyer drew her to a stop several feet from the door and waited until Max signaled everything was clear. He and Brody escorted her to the SUV.

When they arrived at the hospital, Sawyer gave her name to one clerk who motioned for her to come forward and answer a host of questions. Minutes later, she and Sawyer were taken to the exam room where David lay unconscious.

The medical team worked quickly to assess his injuries and form a plan of action to treat David. The doctor turned to her. "You're Mr. Moran's sister?"

"That's right. How is he?"

"The EMTs gave you the general rundown on his condition. What they didn't tell you is your brother is in a coma."

Chapter Nineteen

Sawyer drew Janie against him, his arm circling her waist. "What kind of internal injuries?"

"The kind that requires surgery to repair." He turned to Janie. "Is he married?"

"Yes, sir. His wife is in Chile."

He blew out a breath. "Do you know his medical history?"

She nodded.

"Good." He pointed at the nurse hovering nearby. "Answer her questions while the others prep your brother for surgery. We don't know what we'll find when we get in there, so the operation could take a while."

"Of course. Whatever information you need."

The doctor headed for the exam room door. "Candy, get what we need while I talk to the surgeon and reserve an operating room." He didn't wait for a response.

"Sorry about that," Candy said with a sympathetic smile at Janie. "Dr. Fentress can be abrupt, but he's a skilled physician."

"As long as he can help my brother, I'll put up with a terrible bedside manner."

"Come out into the hall. We'll give the medical team more room to work on your brother." Candy took them to a row of chairs and motioned for Janie to sit beside her. "Now, let's go through Mr. Moran's medical history first."

The next few minutes were filled with question after question. Thankfully, Janie knew most of the answers. Candy finished the last question as the medical team rolled Moran out of the exam room and headed toward an operating room. She stood. "Go to the family waiting room down the hall and to your right. The surgeon will find you when the operation is complete."

"Thank you, Candy."

"Of course. If you need anything, let me know. I'm working until 7:00 tonight. When I leave, I'll introduce you to my replacement."

Sawyer escorted Janie to the family waiting room, grateful they were the only occupants. He seated her on the couch, then crouched in front of her, his hands cradling her trembling ones. "Can I get you anything? A soft drink, water, tea?"

Janie shook her head. "I don't think I could swallow anything and keep it down."

"I'll let you get by with that for now. Soon, though, you need to hydrate. If the surgery takes a long time, you need to eat as well." Sawyer held up a hand. "You won't want anything, but you must keep up your strength. David needs you, and you can't help him if you're weak and woozy from neglecting yourself."

She breathed deep, then nodded. "You're right. I have to take care of myself so I can help with his care if Maria will let me."

"You worried she'll blame you for David's condition?"

"Who else is to blame?"

"The people who beat him, Janie. Not you. You aren't responsible for what David got involved in. If this is a burglary, you had nothing to do with it. If the attack is connected to Vatos Locos, you were a victim yourself. You certainly didn't bring them to your brother's hotel room. No matter what your heart might tell you, you aren't responsible for David's condition. Lay the blame at the feet of the ones who beat your brother."

"My brain knows you're right. My heart insists I could have prevented this. I know it makes little sense because I couldn't have prevented what I didn't know was going to happen."

"You care about your brother. I would feel guilty if my enemy attacked my family, despite taking every precaution to prevent them from being targets."

Tears trickled down her cheeks, breaking Sawyer's heart. He sat beside her on the couch. "Come here." Gathering her against his side, Sawyer held her while she cried.

After a long time, she fell into a fitful sleep against his shoulder. He kissed the top of her head and sent a message to Zane. If his friend could get the inn's security cam footage from the time they left David in the coffee shop parking lot, they might see who attacked Janie's brother.

He received a response seconds later. Excellent. Perhaps they could find something to give them a direction. The sooner they located the perps, the better. He wanted Janie free from threats as soon as possible.

While Janie slept, Sawyer multitasked by digging deeper into the backgrounds of the two men who had been arguing with Moran in the coffee shop parking lot. The more he read, the less he liked what he was seeing. Those men were straight-up killers. If they were the ones who worked over Janie's brother, David was lucky to be alive.

If they didn't want him dead, what did they want? He frowned. The logical answer was Janie. But why? What made her such an attractive target? Was it the money or something else? If he could figure out the motive for the hijacking and kidnapping of the hostages, the puzzle pieces would fall into place.

Janie sighed and snuggled closer. "What's wrong?" she murmured.

"Thinking."

She opened her eyes. "And that makes you unhappy?"

"In this case, yes. I can't figure out the motive for the hijacking. If we nail that down, we'll know who gave the order to take over the plane."

"Whoever gave the order planned in advance."

"Yes, they did. No one has claimed responsibility for the hijacking."

"We already know Vatos Locos were the hijackers."

"Appears that way."

"But you're not convinced?"

"Nope. Makes little sense for them to pull off the hijacking without a hitch and leave with hostages yet still not claim credit for it. Why didn't they send ransom demands? They could have made a bundle of money on each hostage. Instead, they killed all the hostages except you."

"Texas Team arrived before they could make ransom demands."

"Maybe." He still didn't buy it, though. "Why not send ransom demands, wait until the money was paid, then kill the hostages?"

"Perhaps they never planned to demand ransom. It's risky. Wouldn't it make more sense to sell the hostages into sex slavery?"

Sawyer stiffened. "Did they threaten to sell you?"

"Not directly." Her face flushed. "The few hours I stayed in that cell made it obvious the women across the hall were being trafficked to local men and gang members. Scar Face visited the women from the plane when he accidentally killed one of my fellow passengers. Then you and your team arrived, and the gang killed hostages as fast as possible." She shuddered in his arms. "I thought I was going to die, Sawyer. My cell was the last one."

"Shh. You're safe now," he murmured. "I won't let anyone hurt you again, sweetheart."

"I wish you had arrived ten minutes sooner," she whispered. "Maybe the other men and women would still be alive."

He circled back to something she'd said a minute earlier. "The hijackers killed the trafficked women first?"

She nodded. "I don't know why."

They were likely in rough shape and would have been eliminated soon, anyway. None of the trafficking victims last long in the trade. "I'm sorry you had to go through that, Janie. But I'm so grateful Scar Face and his buddies hadn't visited you."

"So am I."

His phone signaled an incoming text. Sawyer glanced at the screen, satisfaction filling him. "Zane sent the security footage from the inn for us to watch. He says he doesn't have time to dig through it himself."

"I didn't think about security footage. That's great, Sawyer. Perhaps we'll see who hurt David."

"Let's find out." He didn't have a problem showing her hours of recordings. Janie wouldn't see anything except people coming and going from the inn. No chance of seeing her brother with the two people who worked him over. The boring video feed would also keep her mind occupied and give her something to do to help her brother.

He logged into his email and pulled up the message from Z. His friend had sent the footage in one- hour increments.

Sawyer glanced at Janie. "This will probably be as boring as watching grass grow."

She laughed. "Bring it on. At least I'll be helping. If we find anything, will we send it to the police?"

"Anything to help the boys in blue."

"Ha. Somehow, I don't believe that statement was sincere."

He chuckled. "Caught me."

Sawyer tapped the screen and started the footage from the first hour Zane had sent. Since it was likely the footage wouldn't show anything, he sped it up.

Fifteen minutes in, Janie glanced at him. "You're right. This is boring."

"Told you. A lot of police work is like this. You trace leads that often go nowhere. You kick over rocks to see what crawls out. Boring police work leads to clues, which leads to the solution to your puzzle."

"And you enjoyed it, didn't you?"

"I did. I didn't enjoy the red tape and rules I had to follow. All the work we did could be for nothing if he or she pleaded down to a lesser charge or turned state's evidence against a bigger fish. When the law worked for you, it felt great. When it didn't, we felt as though we had wasted many hours of work."

When the hour of security footage ended, he queued up the next hour.

"Wait," Janie said. "Although Zane sent five hours of footage, it looks like we have ten hours of videos to watch. Why so many?"

"He sent camera footage from the front of the inn in one set of videos and footage from the back of the inn with the other set."

"Do you think we should watch the first hour of footage from the back of the inn before we move on to the second hour?"

"Good idea. Let's see if our thugs came in the back door during the first hour."

"Do you think they arrived that early?"

"Nope. They were still at the coffee shop with David during this hour. They might have accomplices who kept watch on the inn to report in when your brother arrived."

"Will we be able to spot them?"

"Maybe. Let's get through the video feed first. We'll make note of anyone who seems suspicious and investigate later."

Sawyer found a blank sheet of paper and a pen and handed both to Janie. "Each video is time stamped. Write the time and if the footage is from the back or front door."

Ten minutes into watching the back door footage, he noticed a white panel van backing into a slot at the rear of the parking lot. The occupants remained inside.

Frowning, he paused the video and pointed at the van. "Write the time stamp. The two men stayed inside the van for a long time." When she'd made a note of the time, Sawyer backed up the feed to see if he could spot the license plate.

No such luck. The back of the van never faced the camera. He set the video in motion again, keeping watch on the suspicious van and its occupants. The footage ended with no movement from the occupants. Weird. "Time for hour two," he murmured.

"You sure know how to show a woman a good time on a date," she teased.

"It's my superpower."

Janie laughed. "Good to know. Front door first, then we'll go back and watch the van in the back."

Sawyer tapped the video clip. Halfway through the footage, an SUV parked near the front door of the inn and David Moran got out. He made his way quickly into the inn's lobby, where they lost sight of him. "Write the time David arrived."

He scowled, frustrated that Kingsbridge Inn didn't have security cameras inside the establishment.

They continued to watch to the end, then switched to the security footage from the back of the inn. Ten minutes after David arrived, the two men in the white van climbed out and headed for the back door. One of them pulled out a gadget and pointed it at the keypad. Seconds later, they opened the door and walked inside.

Sawyer paused the feed, backed it up until he focused on the faces of both men, and sent a copy to himself, his teammates, and to Zane.

"What are you doing with the photo?"

"I sent copies to my teammates and to Zane. Z will run the photo through our databases to see if we get a hit on them." He already suspected the group they were dealing with, but confirmation would be good. "If they're in the database, we'll have names to go with the faces." And if they were lucky, an address, too. He'd love a chance to get more information from these guys.

They continued to watch the security footage and saw the two men return to the van an hour after entering the establishment. They laughed as they climbed into the vehicle and drove away, their expressions ones of satisfaction.

Although they watched the rest of the footage Zane sent, nothing else happened out of the ordinary until the four of them arrived and found David Moran beaten and unconscious on the floor of his hotel room.

"The two men hurt David," Janie said.

"That's how it appears."

"The men aren't the same ones who argued with David in the coffee shop parking lot. How could he make four men angry with him in a brief space of time?" Janie scowled. "David doesn't live here, and he's only been in town a few days. This isn't about David. It's about me, isn't it?"

"Not necessarily. We'll figure it out, Janie. Give us time."

"How much time do we have? Who else has to fall victim before we stop these men?" She stopped and her eyes widened. "What if they go after Maria? She's pregnant. We can't let them hurt her. I'd never forgive myself if anything happened to her or the baby. David would never forgive me, either."

"Hold up, sweetheart." He brought her hand to his mouth and kissed her knuckles. "The Hartman police should have contacted Maria by now. She knows her husband is in the hospital. Will Maria travel to Hartman?"

"Absolutely. She adores my brother. There's no way she'd stay in Talca when David is injured. She'll be here by tomorrow at the latest."

"She'll be with David as much as possible. I'll ask Brent to assign someone from Fortress to monitor her while she's here."

"I don't think she'll enjoy having a bodyguard. Maria likes her privacy. I'm afraid she'll be even more paranoid while she's here because of what happened to her husband."

"Our people are good at what they do. They'll watch her and switch out every few hours so she doesn't see the same people all the time."

Janie leaned her head against his shoulder. "You already planned for this contingency, didn't you?"

He shrugged. Being prepared for every situation was how his team survived in the field.

"Thanks, Sawyer. I should have known you'd take care of things without me asking."

"We're still learning each other."

His phone signaled an incoming message. He glanced at the screen, then pulled up his email to see the information Zane sent.

His blood ran cold as his hand tightened around the phone.

"What's wrong?" Janie asked.

"Zane ran the faces of the men in the van through our databases."

"And?"

"He got a hit." He wrapped his hand around hers. "Both men are known members of Vatos Locos."

Chapter Twenty

Sawyer drew Janie into his arms. "Breathe, sweetheart," he murmured. Hearing that the two men who probably attacked David Moran were members of the gang targeting her had caused blood to drain from Janie's face.

"This is my fault," she whispered.

"It's the fault of the men who beat him. Your lifestyle doesn't bring you to the attention of criminals. You have done nothing wrong. We need to focus on your brother and his choices. He has a history of gambling, so let's start there." He wouldn't let her take the blame for this fiasco. No way the hijacking and attacks were Janie's fault.

A man in scrubs walked into the waiting room. "Moran family?"

Sawyer stood and helped Janie to her feet.

"I'm David's sister."

The man held out his hand. "Chris Vanderpool. I'm the surgeon who operated on your brother."

"How is he?"

"Mr. Moran came through surgery fine. I had to remove his spleen. He has several cracked ribs and bruises all over his body, seven broken fingers, and a broken wrist. All of those can and will mend. I'm most concerned about the head injury."

"How bad is it?"

"Your brother has a cerebral edema. His skull is fractured and his brain is swelling. There's a real danger of seizures as well."

"He's still in a coma?" Sawyer asked.

A curt nod from Dr. Vanderpool. "He's in the ICU where we can monitor him closely. I wouldn't be surprised if we have to go back into surgery to relieve pressure on his brain. For the moment, all we can do is watch and wait."

"May I see him?" Janie asked.

"I'll have the nurse come for you in a few minutes. Although he won't respond, he'll know you're there when you talk to him."

"What are his chances, Doc?" Sawyer asked.

Vanderpool hesitated. "Depends on Mr. Moran. The longer he's comatose, the less his chances of recovery. I'll check on him during my shift. After that, the hospitalist will check on him frequently and keep me informed as to his progress. Do the nurses have your cell phone number, Ms. Moran?"

Janie glanced at Sawyer.

"We'll make sure they have a number where Janie can be reached," Sawyer said. "David's wife may fly in from Chile."

"Make sure the nursing staff has all current contact numbers." Vanderpool turned back to Janie. "I know you want to stay with your brother. Since he's in the ICU, you can see him once an hour for a couple of minutes. Do yourself a favor. Visit your brother when the nurse comes for you, then go home to rest. If his condition changes, we'll call you immediately. The best thing you can do for him is take care of yourself." After a nod, he left the waiting room.

Sawyer wrapped his arms around Janie. "He made it through surgery. That's a good sign."

She shuddered. "I know you're right, but it doesn't feel like enough."

What he wouldn't give to have Jesse here now. His team medic, however, was getting much needed rest. Unless Sawyer had misunderstood the surgeon, the chances of David waking up overnight were slim. He'd either update Jesse when his friend woke or ask Zane to hack into hospital records and send the notes to Jesse.

He frowned. Since Zane was already doing several things for him at the moment, he'd ask Simone to hack into the hospital's computer system. She loved hacking into files to which she wasn't supposed to have access.

Sawyer was still holding Janie when a nurse came to the waiting room. "Ms. Moran?"

Janie spun. "Yes."

"Dr. Vanderpool asked me to escort you to the ICU so you can see your brother for a minute."

They fell into step behind her.

"I'm Heather, by the way. I'll be taking care of Mr. Moran tonight."

"I'm Janie. This is Sawyer."

When they arrived at the room, Heather paused before pushing open the door. "He has several lines attached to him. Some are monitoring his vitals. Others are delivering medicine to keep him comfortable and to prevent infection. You'll also notice the bruising and swelling is significantly worse since you last saw him. He's been through a traumatic experience and surgery and it shows. His body is healing and even though he can't respond to you at the moment, he'll hear you. Talk to him. Reassure him he'll be fine and that we'll take good care of him, all right?"

"Yes, ma'am."

"Ready?"

Janie nodded.

Heather pushed open the door and led them into the recovery room. Patients in various stages of recovery from surgery filled several beds. David Moran was in the last bay.

Oh, man. Sawyer flinched. Moran looked rough, almost unrecognizable with his head bandaged and his face bruised and swollen.

Janie gasped.

Heather turned. "You okay?" she whispered.

The woman who clung to Sawyer's hand like a lifeline straightened and gave a brief nod. "It's all right if I talk to him?"

"Absolutely. Just a couple of minutes. He needs as much rest as possible. His body is fighting hard to recover from his injuries." After a quick glance at Sawyer to assess his reaction to the sight of Moran, Heather left them alone with Janie's bother.

She walked to his bedside and leaned close to her brother's ear. "David, it's Janie. Can you hear me?"

No response.

"You're in the county hospital, bro. The surgeon and nurse tell me you're doing fine. You need to let your body heal, David. You've been through a hard experience, but you'll recover. Do you hear me? You'll be all right. I'll be nearby. If you need anything, tell your nurse. Her name is Heather. She's very nice. You'll like her."

Still nothing.

Janie sighed. "I wish you would wake up and tell me what happened. Sawyer and I found you unconscious on the floor of your room. I hope the other guy looks worse that you do, David."

A tear streaked down her cheek. "You scared me, bro. Get better so you can snipe at me and give me grouchy answers to all my questions." She wiped her face with her free hand. "The police will contact Maria. If she's able to come, we'll take care of her, all right? You don't have to worry. She'll be safe here. I love you, bro. Rest now. I'll come back later to check on you. Don't give Heather grief." After brushing a light kiss against her brother's ear, the only place on his face not bruised, Janie turned away from her brother and walked from the room with Sawyer on her heels.

Once in the hall, Janie turned into Sawyer's arms.

He held her close. "You did great in there," he murmured.

"That was the hardest thing I've ever done."

"I'm proud of you. Come on." He wrapped his arm around her shoulders. "Let's go back to the house."

"What about Brody and Max?"

"They're waiting in the lobby."

She smiled. "I should have realized they wouldn't leave you here alone to guard me."

"Never. We have each other's backs. Besides, they're tasked with your safety, too." He escorted her to the stairs.

They reached the first floor and walked to the lobby, where Brody and Max waited. The men turned when he and Janie approached.

"How is he?" Brody asked.

"Holding his own. Still comatose. We'll tell you more on the ride back to the house."

Soon, they were inside the SUV and heading out of town.

"Sit rep," Brody said.

Sawyer gave his teammates an update, ending with, "I want to ask Simone to hack into the hospital's computer system to get a copy of the report on Moran."

"Do it. Jesse will interpret the medical jargon and help you better understand what's really happening with Moran."

"But he's only a medic," Janie protested. "Will the information be something he'd understand?"

"Sure," Max said. "Jesse is almost as well trained as a doctor. He's the guy to ask if you don't understand something doctors and nurses are telling you. We all depend on him for medical knowledge and skills beyond patching us up on missions."

"Do you think Simone will mind if we ask her to do something illegal?"

Sawyer and his buddies burst into laughter. "Oh, no, sweetheart. Simone is all about working against the establishment. Anything to thwart the rule of law. She's the best we've ever seen, aside from Zane. This will be child's play for her."

"And she'll enjoy helping a friend," Brody said.

"What if she gets caught?"

"She won't. Simone Kent never leaves a trail."

"It's a good thing she's on our side. Tell her I appreciate her help. Anything she can find out will help."

Sawyer slid his phone from his pocket and called Simone. When the medic's girlfriend answered on the first ring, he said, "You're on speaker with Brody, Max, and Janie. Can you talk for a minute?"

"Hold." A moment later, Simone said, "Go."

"I need a favor."

"Name it."

He laid out what he needed from the hospital records.

"Piece of cake. Give me five minutes."

"Thanks, Simone. I owe you one."

"Nope. No debt between friends. Besides, I'm always happy to do some hacking for a good cause. Later, Sawyer." Simone ended the call.

Brody chuckled. "Unless she's busy with something else more important, I think she'll get back to us in less than the time allotted."

"No bet there," Max said. "She thrives on deadlines."

"Must be nice," Janie muttered. "I hate them."

"And yet you still come through," Sawyer pointed out. "Simone works better and faster while facing a deadline."

Seconds later, Sawyer's phone signaled an incoming text. He glanced at the screen and whistled. "You nailed it, Brody. Simone has already sent the information to my phone. She also sent a copy to Jesse's email. She says Jesse is at home sleeping. He took Goose with him. He'll look at the report when he wakes."

Janie shook her head. "I can't believe she hacked into the hospital records that fast. I can't wait to meet this woman."

"You'll like her," Max said. "We all do."

Her eyes widened, and she twisted in her seat to stare at Sawyer. "Is anyone monitoring David?"

Sawyer raised her hand to his mouth and kissed her knuckles. "Someone from Fortress will be close twenty-four hours a day. Brent already cleared it with hospital administrators. I wouldn't have left the hospital unless someone was there to watch over him."

Not sure it was wise to admit he suspected her brother was in deep with the gang and would sell out Janie in a heartbeat if it meant keeping himself from further harm. The problem was, though, that David was comatose. Guilty or not, Janie's brother was vulnerable to attack. Sawyer could also be wrong in his assessment of the situation.

Brody glanced in the rearview mirror and frowned. "Heads up."

Sawyer looked out the back window. "SUV?"

"Yep. For now, they're staying four car-lengths back."

"Won't last," Max said.

"What should we do?" Janie asked.

"Lose them." Sawyer squeezed her hand.

"Would you do that if I weren't with you?"

"No. We'd lose them, then slide in behind them and force them to pull over so we can get some answers."

"Do what you normally would. This is your opportunity to learn more information."

"I'm not putting you in the line of fire."

"You said the Fortress vehicles have extra safety features. Trust them and find out who hurt my brother."

"This isn't a good plan," Brody warned. "Brent will have our hides for risking your safety."

"I'll take care of Brent. Now, how can I help?"

"Sawyer?"

He wanted to put his foot down and refuse her request, but she was right. This was the best option for ferreting out information fast. Didn't matter if she intervened with Brent or not. Sawyer and his teammates were in for a major dressing down by their boss. "Do it. Janie, slide down in the seat but leave your safety belt on."

When she complied, Sawyer said to Brody, "Go."

Immediately, the SUV surged ahead, weaving in and out of traffic, taking quick turns, racing to the next corner, and taking another turn.

Suddenly, Brody whipped into a parking lot and raced to the back of a building. As soon as he stopped, he unlocked the doors and Max hopped out.

"Where's he going?" Janie asked.

"To see which direction the other SUV goes after they pass our location. We'll fall in behind them, spook them a bit, and when we're far enough out of town, force them off the road for a chat." At least, it should work that way. With their luck, the men in the SUV had friends in another vehicle, waiting to join the chase. If that happened, the Fortress operatives might have to regroup and try again another time.

Max dove back into the SUV. "They turned right on Sycamore."

As suddenly as he stopped, Brody took off again and swung a fast right followed by another right seconds later. "There they are."

"They'll rabbit," Sawyer warned. Sure enough, seconds later, the other SUV took off, and the chase was on.

Brody stayed several car lengths behind them in case the SUV's passenger fired shots to slow down the operatives. Once they exited Hartman, Brody sped up and closed the gap between the vehicles.

The other SUV tried to shake them and couldn't, the driver swerving all over the road.

Sawyer scowled. Good thing they were on a country road with little traffic.

"Need to force him off the road soon," Max muttered. "He'll cause an accident if we don't."

On a long straightaway, Brody floored the accelerator and came up on the left rear panel of the other vehicle. He swerved to the right, forcing the other SUV to go sideways. The other driver slammed on his brakes and came to a sudden stop.

"Perfect," Max said as he and Brody bailed from the SUV with weapons drawn.

In less than a minute, Sawyer's teammates had the two men face down on the ground with their hands cinched behind their backs with zip ties.

Brody glanced at Sawyer and gave a hand signal.

"Want to help?" Sawyer asked Janie.

"Absolutely. What can I do?"

"We need to get the SUVs off the road in case someone drives by. We don't want to attract the wrong attention. If we do, the cops will be on us in minutes. Follow me in this SUV. We'll park to the right behind the trees."

He helped Janie into the driver's seat, then jogged to the other SUV and drove it behind the thick stand of trees where the vehicles would be hidden from view.

Janie parked the Fortress SUV beside the tango vehicle and climbed out. "How else can I help?"

"Stay in the vehicle."

She gave him The Look.

Yeah, Sawyer didn't think that directive would fly. He sighed. "Sweetheart, the interrogation won't be pleasant. We need answers. If these men have them, we'll extract information however we have to."

"You won't kill them?"

"No, but they don't know that. We do an excellent acting job when necessary. Can you handle it?"

"I'll deal. Let's go." She exited the SUV and walked with Sawyer toward the restrained men, who glowered at Brody and Max.

"Stay at least ten feet away from them," Sawyer murmured. "If they get loose, I don't want you too close."

"Got it."

Brody glanced at Sawyer. "Call for a pick up. We need these men on ice."

He motioned for Janie to sit on a fallen log and pulled out his phone. When Zane answered, he told the communications guru what they needed and gave the location.

"Copy that. Thirty minutes long enough to learn what you need?"

It'd have to be. Sawyer didn't want Janie out here longer than necessary. "We'll make it work."

"Injuries?"

"Not yet."

"Keep it that way." Zane ended the call.

Sawyer frowned. Z wouldn't say that if his wife's life was on the line. Granted, Sawyer and Janie weren't at that point yet, but he saw them moving in that direction. Janie Moran was special.

He slid his phone away and laid his hand on her shoulder. "Doing okay?"

She nodded. "They aren't saying anything."

"They will."

Brody eyed the two men, who glared at him and the others. "Why were you following us?"

No response.

"Sir." Max showed Brody something on his phone.

After a quick glance at Sawyer, Brody turned his attention to the two men. "Oscar De La Cruz and Cristo de La Cruz. You're both members of the local Vatos Locos gang."

Not what Sawyer wanted to hear. Unfortunately, he wasn't surprised. At 10,000 members strong, the gang had many foot soldiers to call on for any job.

The thugs straightened and exchanged glances.

"Let me tell you how this is going to go. You either tell us what we want to know the easy way or you can tell us the hard way."

"The easy way is less painful," Max said. "Of course, I'd rather you choose the hard way. Nothing I like better than working over a couple of losers. Improves my day." He smiled, more a baring of his teeth, and flexed his hands as though loosening them for heavy physical labor.

"So," Brody said. "Who's going to talk first?" He waited a beat. "No takers?" Their team leader shrugged. "Too bad for you. Don't say we didn't offer."

He flicked a glance at Sawyer. "In or out?"

Sawyer hesitated.

"Go." Janie brushed her fingers over the back of his hand. "I'll be fine. I promise."

Taking Janie at her word, Sawyer said, "Stay here."

She nodded.

He strode to the strangers sitting on the ground. Sawyer knelt on one knee behind the bigger of the two men.

Max knelt behind the skinny guy.

Both men tried to turn to see what Max and Sawyer were doing.

Sawyer smacked the back of his target's head. "Eyes forward," he snapped.

"Look at me," Brody ordered in the harsh cop voice they'd used on the job in Texas. "Why were you tailing us?"

The men looked sullen.

Brody gave a slight nod.

Max and Sawyer clamped a hand over each man's mouth and pinched hard between the neck and trapezius muscle. Excruciating pain zinged through the thugs' bodies and they howled in agony, although the shouts were muted.

After a minute, Brody gave the signal to ease up.

Skinny shuddered and sobbed. Big Man glared at Brody.

Sawyer looked at his team leader. The big guy would not talk unless they used a lot more pain and pressure. If they used that kind of force, they'd likely damage the nerves. He shook his head slightly.

"All it takes to stop the pain is answering our questions. Once you do, you're free to go."

The two brothers looked at each other, clearly skeptical.

Smart. Sawyer and his teammates couldn't allow these clowns to walk away. They were too dangerous to Janie's safety. Also, others would come after Janie when these two failed to check in.

The law of averages said eventually, one team would succeed in kidnapping or killing Janie. Sawyer wouldn't let either possibility happen.

"Why were you following us?" Brody flicked a glance at Max, who immediately went to work on his target.

After two minutes, Brody signaled Max. The operative released Skinny, who shuddered and wept.

"We can keep this up all day," Brody said to Big Man. "Your brother can't. After another round of persuasion, he'll have permanent nerve damage."

Big Man sneered. "I don't believe you."

A shrug. "You won't be the one to pay the price, will you?" Texas Team's leader gave a slight nod.

Max rested his hand on Skinny, who began to wail and beg his brother to stop the torture.

Big Man held out for 30 seconds, then caved. "All right. Please, don't hurt him anymore."

"Why were you following us?" Brody asked again. "Last chance, De La Cruz."

"Not you. Her." He inclined his head toward Janie.

"What do you want with her?"

A shrug. "Just do what we're told."

"What are your orders?"

"Grab the woman and report in."

"Who were you supposed to call?"

"Carlos."

"Last name?"

A glare, then, "Noriega."

"Who is he?"

Another shrug. "Works for a lieutenant."

"His job?"

An arrogant expression settled on his face. "Fixer."

Sawyer's blood heated to boiling. And Noriega was planning to fix the problem with Janie? Yeah, he could just bet how that problem would be solved.

Not happening. Noriega would have to go through him first.

#

Chapter Twenty-One

Janie stood beside Sawyer as the team from Fortress drove away with the De La Cruz brothers. Two other men drove the brothers' SUV and followed the Fortress team.

"What happens to them now?" she asked. Honestly, she didn't care as long as they weren't turned loose to cause more trouble. Getting rid of these two or putting them on ice was the simple part. The hard part was handling the other 10,000 members who could be sent after her.

She scowled. This was ridiculous. Why were the Vatos Locos going to so much trouble to acquire her? Was it money? Her inheritance from her grandmother wouldn't hold a candle to the coffers of the gang since Sawyer said they were into everything, including human trafficking. Her money was a pittance compared to the illegal activities in which they were involved.

"The team will take the De La Cruz brothers to a black site where they'll uncover every bit of information the men have on the gang and why they're determined to take you again." Sawyer swung around to face her. "They won't get their hands on you, Janie. We won't let them take you again."

He would try, but what were the odds he would always succeed? The last thing she wanted was for Sawyer and his friends to suffer injuries while protecting her against a constant stream of opponents. As good as the Texas Team was, the odds were against them being successful in defeating every member of the gang without injuries on the side of the good guys.

Sawyer cupped her nape and drew her against him. "Trust me. Trust my team."

"I want you safe," she whispered. "I don't want to lose you or your friends."

"We're well trained, careful, and have great incentives to survive firefights." He bent his head and brushed his lips over hers. "You've added to the many reasons I have to live, sweetheart. I don't take that lightly."

Beside the SUV, Max whistled. "Let's go. Clock's ticking."

They joined Max and Brody in the SUV and resumed their journey to the safe house. This time, the drive was peaceful, although the operatives remained alert. Several detours later, Brody parked behind the safe house.

Used to the routine by now, Janie waited in the vehicle for the Max and Brody to return after clearing the house. Three minutes later, Brody appeared at the back door and signaled to Sawyer.

"We're clear." He climbed out and reached back to help Janie from the vehicle. After escorting her to the safe house, Sawyer locked the door and reset the alarm. "Are you hungry?"

She stared. Hungry? The way she felt at the moment, Janie might never eat again.

His lips curved. "I'll take that as a no."

"Just the thought of eating makes me nauseated."

"Your body needs fuel, whether or not you feel hungry. I'll prepare dinner. I think at least one item on the menu will be easy on your stomach."

She'd see. "I thought you didn't cook."

"I don't. I grill." He winked at her, then nudged her toward a stool at the breakfast bar. "Have a seat. You can be the straw boss."

"What's that?"

"The person who tells everyone else what to do on a job."

"The supervisor?"

"You're the most beautiful supervisor I've ever had." He walked to the refrigerator and pulled out three large packages of meat, set them on the counter and opened the pantry door. He perused the contents and bent to grab several large potatoes and aluminum foil.

Sawyer dumped the lot on the counter. "What do you think?"

"I think you're feeding a starving army. Good grief, Sawyer. Do you guys eat this much all the time?"

He shrugged. "Fast metabolism and intense workouts plus missions where we might not get to eat more than one fast meal a day mean we burn calories."

"Must be nice," she muttered.

"You're perfect."

"I'm carrying too much weight."

"Not from where I'm standing."

"It doesn't bother you that I'm rounder in places than I should be?"

"You're perfect," he repeated. "If anything, I think you'd look good with another pound or two."

"You're nuts."

"Nuts about you," he countered.

"Where were you when I was a teenager, anxious about my appearance?"

"Working to keep food on the table and help my mom with as much of her responsibility as possible. She was always too thin. For several months, Mom said she was too tired to eat much. When we finally caught on to the fact that she was giving us boys her food so we'd have enough, my brothers and I made it our mission to work part-time jobs wherever we could find them and make sure we had enough food in the house so Mom would eat too."

"Did it work?"

He walked to the spice cabinet, pulled out several bottles, and carried them to the counter. "Took a few months, but Mom eventually regained the weight she lost and was better able to handle the workload and stress."

"Does she still work?"

Sawyer smiled as he laid the steaks on four plates and sprinkled each with the various spices. "Her job now is a full-time grandmother, mother, and mother-in-law. She also volunteers at a few organizations that are important to her."

"You and your brothers are taking care of her financial obligations."

He inclined his head. "We owe her everything. My brothers and I bought her a car and a house. We also deposit money into her account every month for expenses and fun money. Most of the time, we have to beg her to spend money. She still has a hard time letting go of dollars for herself. Now, if you ask her to spend money for one of the grandkids or one of us boys, she's all over it. Can't get to the store fast enough."

Sawyer smiled. "We love spoiling her. Lately, though, someone else has been stepping into that role."

Oh, now, this was interesting. "Who?"

"Her new beau."

Her mouth dropped. "Your mother has a boyfriend?"

He flinched. "Please, let's not call Luke that. We prefer the term friend. Mom is the one who called him her beau."

How sweet was that? "I think that's wonderful. Good for your mom."

Sawyer flipped the steaks over and liberally applied spices to that side as well. "Yeah, she deserves every bit of happiness she can find. My brothers and I give her grief over it, but we're happy for her."

"Can I help with dinner? I feel guilty being the straw boss."

He nodded at the potatoes. "Scrub those, cut them in half, and slather butter on them before wrapping them in aluminum foil."

Perfect. Keeping herself busy occupied her mind with something other than worry for her brother.

Janie slid from the stool, gathered the potatoes, and got to work. As she finished wrapping the last potato in foil, Sawyer went outside to heat the grill.

When he returned, his expression was grim.

Janie's heart skipped a beat. "What's wrong? Is it David?" Had something happened to her brother? She should have stayed at the hospital despite the doctor's encouragement to rest.

"The surgeon is taking David to surgery. Brain bleed."

"I have to go back to the hospital." Her voice broke. What if David died? She didn't want him to die alone.

"Give me a minute to tell Brody and we'll go."

Within five minutes, Max was driving the SUV to the hospital with Janie and Sawyer in the backseat. Brody had agreed to stay at the safe house to finish dinner and wait for Logan to relieve him for a watch shift.

They drove to the hospital in silence, making the journey in less than fifteen minutes. Although Max pushed the speed limit, he didn't take detours this time.

During the drive, Sawyer kept his hand wrapped around Janie's. As soon as the SUV stopped at the entrance to the emergency room, he climbed out and reached back to help her down.

The two of them hurried to the ICU floor and the desk where a nurse told Janie that David's surgery had just begun and not to expect an update for a while on his condition. Once again, they were directed to the family waiting room.

This time when she dropped to the couch, Sawyer sat beside her and gathered her into his arms.

"He has to be all right," Janie whispered. "I don't care if we never see eye to eye on anything. I want him alive to gripe at me."

"I understand." Losing one of his brothers would devastate him. While holding Janie close, he sent Jesse a text. If his friend was awake, he'd respond.

Less than a minute later, Sawyer's phone signaled an incoming call. "Talk to me," Jesse said.

He told the team's medic what the nurse had conveyed. "We're in the family waiting room."

"I'll be there in a few minutes." Jesse ended the call.

His teammate's haste gave him an indication of how serious the situation was.

"What did Jesse say?" Janie asked.

"He's coming."

She raised her gaze to Sawyer's face. "Is that good?"

He could lie to her. He wouldn't. "The medical issue is serious enough that Jesse feels he's needed here."

"I'm glad to have someone knowledgeable about medicine to answer my questions." She smiled a little. "Medical jargon is tough to interpret." She rested her head against his chest again.

Minutes later when Jesse walked into the waiting room, Janie was still in the same position. "Updates?" the medic asked.

"Not yet. Thanks for coming, Jesse."

"We're family, Sawyer. Our family has expanded to include Janie."

"I can't repay you for this," Janie said. "I doubt you want any products from my store. However, if Simone comes in, I'll be happy to give her the family and friends discount."

"She's already planning to come into Natural Bliss with the other women."

"I'll take care of them. I know exactly what to do for them."

"How long have you been waiting for word from the doctor?"

"About an hour."

A slight nod. "So, Janie, has Sawyer told you about his encounters with spiders on our missions?"

Sawyer rolled his eyes. Yeah, figured his teammate would tell funny stories on him. Jesse and the others had plenty of stories to tell on each other. As long as the stories occupied Janie's mind with something other than worry for her brother, he'd allow himself to be the brunt of Jesse's tales.

Janie straightened. "Oh, this has to be good."

"Not nearly as good as Jesse is making it out to be," Sawyer muttered. What man wanted his girl to know his own personal kryptonite?

The team medic grinned. "Depends on who you ask." He launched into the first story about Sawyer's close encounter with a Goliath bird-eating tarantula.

Janie shuddered. "I don't blame you for being afraid of them, Sawyer."

"Not afraid exactly." Total lie. "They're creepy. When they feel threatened, they rub the hairs on their legs together to create a hissing sound."

"How big are they?"

"The size of a puppy."

"I guess you don't want one for a pet."

"No," he blurted. "Never."

She gave him a wicked grin.

Sawyer scowled. "Not nice."

The lady laughed. "Couldn't help it. I wouldn't want to be anywhere near one either."

A doctor walked into the waiting room. "Moran family?"

Sawyer helped Janie to her feet.

"I'm his sister. How is David?"

"We had to remove part of his skull to relieve the pressure on his brain and get to the bleeder. He survived the surgery, Ms. Moran, but I won't know how much damage was done before he wakes up."

"He's still comatose?" Jesse asked.

The doctor studied Jesse for a moment. "It's Jesse Phelps, right?"

"Yes, sir. I'm a friend of Janie's."

"I see. Yes, Mr. Moran is still comatose. We got him into surgery quickly, which saved his life. The question remains if he'll have lingering repercussions from the brain bleed." He pulled a phone from his pocket and scanned a message. The doctor sighed. "I'm sorry. I have to go. The nurse will give you updates and let you know when you can see Mr. Moran again." And he was gone.

Janie turned to Jesse. "What did he mean by lingering repercussions?"

"You want the truth or a cleaned-up version?"

"The truth. I'd rather know so I can prepare myself."

"Look, the doc is right. You'll have to wait until David wakes up before you know the extent of the damage. However, depending on where the bleed was located, your brother could have paralysis, vision problems, memory loss, and coordination issues, among other things."

She stared.

"The good news is he was in the hospital when the bleed occurred. That means he received immediate treatment, which gives him a better chance of recovering fully."

"But not a guarantee of full recovery," she murmured.

Jesse shook his head. "When he wakes, we'll see how he is. The doctors here are among the best in the nation. We also have some of the best rehabilitation facilities in the country. David will have many options available to help him recover as much as possible."

Janie sighed. "In other words, I won't know anything for a while."

"I'm sorry."

"At least he's alive, so I have hope. The brain bleed is the result of the beating, isn't it?"

Jesse inclined his head.

"I wish I could get my hands on those jerks," she muttered.

Sawyer held back a smile. His lady was fierce. Good for her. "You'll have to get in line behind me and the team. You can have what's left."

She pointed at him. "I don't think so. I get first crack. You and the Texas Team can mop up."

Jesse grinned. "Nice. Sawyer, she reminds me of Simone. I'm impressed."

An hour later, a nurse walked into the waiting room. "Ms. Moran, your brother is back in the ICU if you'd like to see him for a couple of minutes. He's still in a coma, but his vitals have stabilized." She glanced at Jesse and a big smile curved her mouth. "Hey, Jesse. Good to see you again."

"Thanks, Daisy. You're David Moran's nurse?"

She nodded. "I'm on duty until 7:00 tomorrow morning. I know you're a paramedic, but I'm only supposed to let two people at a time into the room. Family only."

"No problem. Janie and Sawyer will visit David. I'm here to offer moral support and jargon interpretation."

Daisy laughed. "All families should be lucky enough to have you explain medical terms." She turned to Janie. "Is Sawyer your husband?"

"I will be when I convince the lady to set a date," Sawyer said.

"Aww. Congratulations. I'm happy for you. If you'll come with me, I'll escort you into the ICU. Remember, only two minutes, all right? It's even more important for David to rest after this second surgery."

"We won't stay long," Janie promised. "I want to remind him I'm close, and he will get better soon."

"He has more bandages now," Daisy warned. "Don't let it upset you."

This was tough for anyone, much less someone who had a rocky relationship with her brother and feared he wouldn't survive. But

Janie was made of sturdy stuff. She could handle this. Sawyer had faith in her.

Daisy led them to the nurses' desk and inclined her head toward the room David was assigned.

Sawyer threaded his fingers through Janie's and escorted her to the room.

She walked to David's bedside and wrapped her free hand around her brother's. "David, it's Janie. You're going to be fine. Do you hear me? You had a setback, and the doctor took you back to surgery. You came through with flying colors, bro. I'll be close if you need me. Daisy, your nurse, will have my number, and she'll call me when you ask her to contact me. I love you, David. Rest, and I'll be back later to check on you." After squeezing his forearm gently, she turned to Sawyer with tears in her eyes.

He wrapped his arm around her shoulders and walked with her from the room. In the hall, he nodded at the Fortress bodyguard assigned by Brent to watch over Janie's brother. Thankfully, the hospital administration was cooperating because of the extreme circumstances and ongoing threat to David's safety. "Let's talk to Jesse, then we'll return to the house."

They found Max and Jesse in the waiting room. Both men rose. "How is he?" Jesse asked.

"Bandaged up like a mummy," Janie said. "He looks rough, Jesse. Worse than when I saw him earlier."

"It's normal. Bruising and swelling will increase over the next few days, then recede. He'll be colorful for a while."

"What about security?" Max asked.

"A bodyguard is on duty in the hall outside David's room," Sawyer said.

"Good." Jesse turned to Janie. "I know you want to stay. You can't help your brother that way. He'll need you at full strength when he wakes."

"If he wakes." Her voice broke.

"He's stable for now. That's a good sign. Go back to the safe house and rest, Janie. Taking care of yourself is the best thing you can do for your brother."

"Although I know you're right, I hate to leave him here alone."

"He has a good nursing staff here as well as top flight surgeons and physicians. He'll be well cared for. What the staff can't do is take care of you."

"It's our job to watch your back," Max said. "Sawyer wants to take care of your needs. Let him."

She looked at Sawyer.

"They're right."

Janie's eyes narrowed. "No one better try to convince me to leave the hospital if you're the one in ICU. I won't have it. They'll have a fight on their hands."

"Wouldn't think of it. In that case, you'd get a different support. This is what's best for both you and David. It could be hours before we know anything. The nursing staff will watch over him. When he's out of danger and awake, you'll help care for a grumpy patient."

"How do you know he'll be grumpy?"

"We would be. Men don't make the best patients."

She held up both hands. "I give up. You're right. Let's make sure Daisy has a contact number and we'll go."

Sawyer squeezed her hand. "I'll take care of it. Be back in a minute." He walked to the desk and spoke to Daisy. After confirming she had the number for Fortress, Sawyer walked a few paces away and called Zane.

"What's the latest on David Moran?" his friend asked instead of a formal greeting. After an update, he whistled. "Buddy, I hate to hear that about anyone. Look, just because David had excellent care within minutes of the bleed doesn't mean he'll recover fully. As good as they are, doctors aren't miracle workers. Sometimes, the best care in the world isn't enough to reverse the damage."

Zane knew that from personal experience. An IED had injured the Navy SEAL in the Sand Box and, despite heroic efforts of the medical personnel, he was paralyzed and rode a wheelchair from one place to another.

"This is going to be a long road to recovery, and the surgery and therapy might not be totally successful," Zane continued. "I don't want to hurt her, but Janie should be prepared for that outcome."

"She knows it's a possibility, Z. Although Jesse was careful, he was straight with her."

"Sorry," the tech guru muttered. "Sore spot."

"No apology necessary, my friend. If David has side effects from the brain bleed, Janie will need someone who's been through something similar and come out the other side to a full and successful life, though a different one."

"Keep us updated, all right? It's obvious Janie is important to you. If we can help her or her brother, we will."

"Thanks, Z. The hospital is supposed to call with updates on David's condition. Make sure the person covering the comm system knows to contact me immediately."

"I'll take care of it. Do you want a satellite phone for Janie and a set of tracking jewelry?"

"The sooner, the better."

"Done. I'll have an operative deliver both to the safe house. He or she will send you a text to let you know they're on the way."

"Good. Surprise visitors won't be greeted with kindness."

"Copy that."

Sawyer ended the call and returned to the family waiting room. "All set. Daisy has the contact information for Fortress. The tech and communication staff know to contact me if a call comes through from the hospital."

Relief flooded Janie's face. "That's great. I'll have to put together a gift bag for Zane's wife in thanks for all his extra work on my behalf."

"Unnecessary, but Claire will love it." He held out his hand to Janie. "Let's get you home so you can rest. You won't sleep in the waiting room." Neither would he nor his teammates. Too much movement and too many exits to watch while protecting Janie.

He and his teammates headed for the stairs. Minutes later, they reached the first floor exit.

Max held up his fist to signal the others to wait, then opened the door enough to see the parking lot and scan for threats. He glanced over his shoulder and nodded.

Excellent. The sooner Sawyer escorted Janie away from here, the better. His skin was crawling. Not a good sign. "Spiders," he murmured to Jesse and Max.

They both palmed their weapons. Jesse fell in behind Janie while Max led the way to the vehicles.

Somewhere nearby, a vehicle's engine idled. Sawyer scanned the parking lot. No vehicles had their lights on, so he couldn't pinpoint the location. He didn't like it.

Max's head swiveled to the right. "Dark truck," he said over his shoulder.

"Copy."

"What's wrong?" Janie whispered, pressing closer to Sawyer's side.

"We have company. Hear the engine running?"

She nodded.

"No lights on inside or out."

"Not again."

"We'll handle it," Jesse said. "You do exactly what Sawyer tells you to do. Max and I have your backs."

"Dandy. Who has yours?"

The medic chuckled. "I like her, Sawyer. Hang on to this one."

"That's the plan."

The idling engine revved.

"Move," Max snapped, shifting to stand between Janie and the truck peeling from the parking space.

The dark-colored truck raced toward them.

Chapter Twenty-Two

Sawyer rushed Janie to the space between the two Fortress vehicles as gunshots shattered the peaceful night in a hail of gunfire.

Between one beat and the next, Sawyer took Janie to the ground, flipping at the last second to take the brunt of the impact. He rolled, covering Janie's body with his own. His weapon was up and tracking in case the jerks in the truck stopped to fire more shots at Janie.

Glass shattered and car alarms blared around them in a discordant cacophony, making it impossible to hear anyone approaching.

Finally, the gunfire ceased. A moment later, Max said, "Clear."

Sawyer leaped to his feet, scooped Janie into his arms, and put her to their SUV. Max climbed behind the wheel.

Once beside Janie and buckled in, Sawyer said, "Go."

"What about the police?" Janie asked. "Do we have to stay and give a report?"

"Nothing to tell except a dark-colored, late-model truck raced from the parking lot and someone in the vehicle fired shots at us."

"No plates on the truck," Max added as he accelerated onto Main Street and drove toward the outskirts of town in the opposite direction from their safe house. "Do you know how many dark-colored trucks are registered in this county alone?"

"Too many?"

"Exactly. If we stayed to talk to the police, we'd be sitting ducks for another attack."

"We won't risk your life that way." Sawyer threaded his fingers through hers. "We'll ask the Fortress tech geeks to track the truck."

Max snorted. "Won't help."

"We might catch a shot of a face to run through our databases."

"Doubtful, but call them. We'll see what comes of it."

Sawyer called to Fortress headquarters.

"Fortress Security. Wiseman."

"Runner, it's Sawyer. What are you doing on duty? Thought you'd be out pounding the pavement."

A chuckle. "You're a fine one to talk, Chapman. You run as often as I do at night."

Truth. Nighttime was the worst for memories to haunt him.

"What do you need, buddy?"

Sawyer reported the incident in the hospital's parking lot. "Hack into the security and traffic cams in the area and get me what you can on the truck and its occupants."

"More than one occupant?"

"Driver and shooter. Couldn't see into the back. Everything happened too fast. I was more interested in protecting Janie."

"How fast do you need the footage?"

"Yesterday."

A snort. "I hear the same thing from every operative who calls requesting help."

"Not surprised. In this case, it's true. The attacks against Janie keep coming. I need to know who's behind them before she's kidnapped again or killed."

"I'm on it, Sawyer."

Now he felt bad. "Sorry. I'm concerned." Although he had a bad feeling everything tied back to Vatos Locos.

"This search will be my priority."

"I owe you one."

"Nope. I love a challenge. I'll get back to you soon." Wiseman ended the call.

"Who answered?" Max asked.

"Wiseman."

A nod. "He'll get what you need. He's almost as fast as Zane and Simone."

Sawyer would feel better if one of them did the search. Both, however, we're already deep diving for information.

Once they were safely inside the safe house, Jesse went home until time for his shift.

Max went to the security room. A moment later, Logan walked into the kitchen.

"Steaks and potatoes are in the refrigerator," he said.

"Any trouble?"

A head shake. "A stray cat set off the perimeter alarms."

Sawyer relaxed. Excellent. "When does the next watch shift start?"

"Three hours. You and Jesse have the watch. Go sleep." With that, Logan refilled his coffee mug and left the room.

Sawyer cupped Janie's nape, his thumb brushing over her jaw. "We missed dinner. Are you hungry?"

She wrinkled her nose. "Not really."

"You need fuel, sweetheart. Would you like me to heat the potato for you? It shouldn't be too heavy on your stomach."

"That sounds good."

He nudged her toward the breakfast bar. "Have a seat while I heat the food." After removing the foil and spreading the potato on a plate, Sawyer turned on the microwave. "What about a drink? We have soft drinks, water, juice, coffee, or I can make tea for you."

"Water, please."

He set her plate with the potato and a glass of water on the counter in front of Janie and heated his own meal. Soon, he sat beside her and went to work on his steak and potato.

"The steak smells great," Janie said. "I'm sorry to miss the treat."

"No worries. I'll grill for you again soon."

When Sawyer finished his meal, he rose to prepare hot tea for Janie and poked around the cabinet until he found the right combination for her.

He dumped a bag each of chamomile and mint into the water and nuked the concoction. When the heating cycle finished, he set the mug in front of Janie. "Chamomile mint tea."

"Thanks. I hope it will help me sleep." She grimaced. "For a few hours at least. I need to return to the store to prepare more stock."

Not what he wanted to hear. If the Vatos Locos members had intelligence greater than a houseplant, they'd know exactly where to find Janie tomorrow morning.

A muscle in his jaw twitched. He'd handle anything that happened at the shop. This was Janie's livelihood, and her workers needed help with the workload. That thought reminded him to confirm that two Fortress bodyguards would be available to protect Janie's workers. "All right." He brushed his mouth over hers. "Come on. I'll walk you home, Ms. Moran."

She grinned. "My room is across the hall from yours. We can walk there in under a minute."

"That's part of my cunning plan."

"To spend a minute walking me to my room?" She looked skeptical. "I'm not convinced."

"I'm walking you home at the end of our date so I can kiss my girl goodnight at her door."

Her breath caught. "Are you serious?"

"Sweetheart, I meant every word."

She slid from the stool and picked up her mug. "Let's go. I want that kiss more than I've wanted anything in my life."

He chuckled. "Same." Sawyer took the mug from her and wrapped his free arm around her shoulders as they walked.

After nudging the door open with his shoulder, Sawyer stepped back and motioned her inside. Once across the threshold, he closed the door and set the mug on her nightstand. He drew the woman of his dreams into his arms.

Slowly, he lowered his head and captured Janie's mouth with his. Immediately, fire raced through his veins, heat suffusing his body and raising his core temperature to at least a thousand degrees.

Janie just did it for him in every respect, and now he was addicted to her taste. No other woman would do for him. He was well and truly hooked on Janie Moran.

Janie wrapped her arms around his neck. After another intense kiss, she stared at him with wide eyes. "Sawyer," she whispered.

"I know. I feel it too."

"I didn't know it would be like this."

"Neither did I," he admitted. "This is special."

"If these kisses become more intense, I might melt into a puddle at your feet."

He hugged her tight for a moment, then forced himself to step back. "I have to leave while I still can."

"Do you have to go?"

His mouth curved. "My control is whisper thin. A couple more kisses like those, and I won't be able to leave." He put more distance between them. "I'll see you in a few hours. If you can't sleep, come to me. We'll curl up on the couch and watch a slow cozy mystery guaranteed to put you to sleep."

Janie grinned. "What if I like cozy mysteries?"

Sawyer gave a mock sigh. "Sorry, Janie, but that goes in the negative column. I'm afraid I can no longer say you're perfect."

That brought a laugh from his woman. He winked at her and gripped the door handle. "Need anything? Water, a snack?"

She shook her head, eyes still twinkling with amusement. "Get some sleep, Sawyer."

"Yes, ma'am." After a last heat-filled glance, Sawyer left the room, closing Janie's door behind him.

He stopped steps away from her door and leaned against the wall, fighting for more discipline. After winning the battle, he continued to his room. Logan was right. He needed to sleep for at least two or three hours.

Sawyer took a quick shower, put on fresh clothes in case they had an interrupted night, and stretched out across the bed. Between one breath and the next, he was asleep.

At the three-hour mark, Sawyer's internal alarm woke him. Slipping his feet into tactical boots, Sawyer left the room and came to an abrupt stop when he saw Janie's door standing open.

He peered into her room. The bed was empty and made. Sawyer heard her soft laugh downstairs.

He followed the sound of her voice to the kitchen. She was sitting at the breakfast bar with a mug of tea. Logan leaned against the counter, cradling a mug of coffee.

His teammate gave him a chin lift. "You look better." He picked up another mug and handed it to Sawyer. "Strong enough to cure anything that ails you."

He sipped, his brows knitting. "What did you do, double the amount of coffee?"

A slow smile from his friend. "You're tough. You can handle it."

Maybe. Wow. Had to admit, though, the caffeine would push back brain fog and fatigue for several hours.

Sawyer sat beside Janie and leaned over to kiss her. "I'm surprised you're up. Everything okay?"

"I woke a few minutes ago and couldn't go back to sleep. Do you mind if I help you keep watch until it's time to leave for the shop?"

Although concerned she'd be exhausted, he knew how it was to have worries chasing away sleep. He reached over and squeezed her hand. "I'll be glad to have your company."

His statement made her cheeks turn pink and her eyes sparkle. Score one for him. He glanced at Logan. "Who's on watch with me?"

"Jesse volunteered to take the next shift in case you need him."

Sawyer's watch vibrated. He checked the readout. "Jesse's here. Tell Poppy thanks for loaning you to us for a few hours."

A slight smile curved Logan's mouth. "Will do. Let me know if you need me." After finishing the last sip of his coffee, Logan turned off the alarm and went out the back door.

Within seconds, Jesse stepped into the kitchen. His eyebrows soared when he saw Janie at the breakfast bar. "Hey, sugar. Why are you awake at this hour?"

"Couldn't sleep. Sawyer is going to teach me how to keep watch."

"Good idea. You two can watch the monitors. I'll handle the perimeter until we leave for the shop."

"Aren't you going home to sleep?" she asked.

"Brody will take over at seven. I'll go to the coffee shop and get breakfast and drinks for everyone."

"What about Simone?"

"She'll get her treat after I'm off duty. I'll take her coffee and breakfast, and pick up Goose."

"I can't wait to meet your dog," Janie said. "He sounds like a delightful companion."

Jesse chuckled. "He thinks he's a big dog. We have to watch him like a hawk when we take him for walks. Otherwise, he'll take on neighborhood dogs ten times his size."

The medic poured coffee into a mug and headed for the back door. "I'll check the perimeter and return in a few minutes."

"Come on." Sawyer held out his hand to Janie. "Let's watch his progress on the monitors."

In the security room, he seated Janie at the console and sat beside her. He pointed to the screen. "There's Jesse. Do you recognize where he is?"

She studied the monitor a moment. Her face lit up. "The back fence."

"He'll come around the left side of the house soon."

Sawyer pointed out landmarks and matched them up with the terrain until the medic returned to the safe house.

Jesse tracked them down a minute later. "How did our operative-in-training do?"

"She did great."

Janie rolled her eyes. "After Sawyer pointed out the landmarks I should have recognized."

"Cut yourself some slack," Jesse said. "You've only been outside in the backyard for five minutes. We spend hours walking the grounds or staring at monitors where we see the same views for hours."

"Do you get bored?"

"Sure, but we recognize any change in the terrain because we spend so much time studying it."

"I'll remind myself of that when I'm falling asleep watching the unchanging picture on the screen.

That's what Sawyer wanted, a night so boring and uneventful that Janie could rest another hour or two before the trek to the shop.

"Unless you need me, I'll go back to the kitchen. Simone is sending me a few files." Jesse's intense gaze told Sawyer the files were linked to David Moran.

"We'll watch the monitors for another hour. If things are quiet, I'll teach Janie what we look for on perimeter checks."

"Works for me." Jesse patted Janie's shoulder and left.

Sawyer glanced at Janie. She was staring at him. "What?"

"You're expecting trouble."

"We always expect trouble."

"How often does it happen?"

Too often. "Enough. Do you need to work on anything for the shop?"

"Changing the subject on me?"

"Maybe. Did it work?" He didn't want to add to the worry and stress on Janie's shoulders. She had enough to handle as it was.

She laughed. "Yes, it will. I wanted to explore fresh scents for soaps and bath bombs we might offer in the shop. I didn't have a chance last night. So, Mr. Chapman, what scent reminds you of summer?"

"Strawberries and peaches."

"Good choices. I'll see what I can do about that."

"Wait." His eyes narrowed. "That's for women. Men don't want to smell like fruit after a shower."

Amusement lit her eyes. "That's disappointing. I wanted to breathe in the scent of strawberries when you kissed me. Now what will I do?"

"Not nice, lady."

More laughter. "Since strawberries and peaches aren't high on your list, what do you suggest for men?"

"Ocean breeze and mountain air. Not pine," he added quickly. "Reminds me of the household cleaner my mother used to use."

"Got it. No pine. Is there a laptop I can use?"

"Watch the monitors. I'll get mine." He took the stairs two at a time, dug his laptop from his Go bag, and carried it to the security room, where he set the computer in front of Janie. "Anything happen?"

"Does seeing a fox trot across the backyard count as an event?"

He chuckled. "Sorry I missed it."

While Janie started her search, Sawyer texted Wiseman to see if he'd come up with anything on the truck in the hospital's parking lot.

A response came seconds later. He scanned the information and scowled. No surprise to learn the truck was stolen.

Sawyer shot off another text, asking the tech to send footage of the incident. He received a notification that the footage was in his email in less than a minute.

A second message came as Sawyer scanned the incident footage. His hand clenched.

A small, soft hand wrapped around his. "What's wrong?"

"Maria will be in Hartman at noon today."

Chapter Twenty-Three

Janie smiled. "I'm so glad she could catch a flight. Maria's arrival will give David another incentive to wake up." Her brother adored his wife.

Her smile dimmed. She wouldn't be able to offer her sister-in-law a place to stay. Janie already knew without asking that Sawyer wouldn't allow anyone to know the location of the safe house, much less stay with them.

She didn't blame him. As he'd reminded her more than once, her safety was his priority. Remembering the sizzling kisses they'd shared and the care and affection he continually showed her, Janie sighed. Sawyer Chapman was an amazing man. Having him in her life was worth the stress and fear she'd experienced at the hands of the hijackers and the local affiliates of Vatos Locos.

Sawyer cupped her cheek with his palm. "Everything all right?"

She nodded.

He looked skeptical. "Talk to me."

"I feel bad that I can't offer Maria the same hospitality that she gave me in Talca. I know we can't compromise the safe house's location, but I wish I could help."

"We can make reservations for her at a hotel near the hospital and arrange for snacks, water, and soft drinks in her room. Would that work?"

Her heart melted. How had any woman let Sawyer slip through her fingers? Janie wrapped her arms around his neck. "Thank you, Sawyer. That's perfect."

He brushed her lips with his. "I'm glad to take care of it for you." After a lingering kiss, Sawyer grabbed his phone and called the hotel closest to the hospital. Following a conversation with the front desk clerk, he ended the call and said, "All set. The clerk is having snacks and drinks set up in her suite. They'll be ready for her by ten o'clock this morning."

"You didn't have to reserve a suite. I'm sure she'll be at the hospital most of the time. A room would have been just fine." She'd have to repay him for the expense. Janie knew without asking Sawyer wouldn't accept the offer of payment. Maybe a home-cooked meal would be a good way to show him how much she appreciated his help.

He shrugged. "Anything to make your life easier."

Her heart melted. "That's it. I'm keeping you."

"Promise?"

"You're not escaping now. You've spoiled me, and I'm not letting you go."

Sawyer watched her with an intense gaze. "Early days for you, Janie."

Wait a minute. She'd been teasing. Sort of. Her heart skipped a beat at his serious expression. "But not for you?"

"No."

What did that mean? Surely not what she hoped it meant. They'd only known each other for a few days. What would he think if she blurted out the truth of how she felt? Would she be the only one adrift in an ocean of overwhelming emotions?

"Ask," he murmured.

She tilted her head and gathered courage for the most terrifying thing she'd done in her life. "What do you mean by that, Sawyer?"

"You're it for me."

Her heart turned over. "Spell it out for me." Did he feel as she did? It was too soon, wasn't it?

"I love you. Is that clear enough?"

Janie stared. "Say it again."

"I love you." When she opened her mouth to blurt out that she loved him as well, Sawyer placed two fingers over her mouth to stop the words. "No. Say nothing right now. Think about it. Give me a chance to win your heart, Janie."

"But...."

"Wait. Please. I'm not rushing you for an answer. I only wanted you to know where I stand, and I'm willing to wait as long as it takes. Just don't tell me no." Vulnerability showed in the depths of his eyes.

She couldn't leave him in limbo while they figured out who wanted to kidnap or kill her.

Janie cupped his face with her hands. "Sawyer, stop."

His face drained of blood.

"Look at me, love."

He stilled, gaze locked with hers.

"I love you, Sawyer. More than I ever thought possible in such a brief span of time. But during the past few days, you've shown me your heart. It's time I showed you mine. I adore you, and I know to the depths of my being that you're the only man for me."

Relief flooded Sawyer's face, and he captured her mouth with his. Long moments later, he said, "Thank you for trusting me with your heart."

She smiled. "How could I not?"

"Any chance you'll marry me in a few weeks?"

Weeks? Whoa! Sawyer Chapman didn't waste time when he wanted something. "I want time to really get to know you and meet your family. I also want to be available to help David if he'll allow it."

"No problem."

She leaped into the unknown, praying she wasn't making the biggest mistake of her life. "In that case, yes, Sawyer. I'll marry you."

He leaped to his feet, tugged Janie to hers, wrapped her in his arms, and swung her around. "Yes!" Sawyer stopped mid-swing and set her back on her feet. An odd expression was on his face.

"What is it?"

"I messed up."

She blinked. "How?" Had he changed his mind already?

"I should have talked to the men in your family first."

Men? "David's in a coma. You can't talk to him." Hopefully soon, though. Unfortunately, David was combative when Sawyer confronted him in the coffee shop. He wasn't likely to change his mind this fast. "He wasn't your biggest fan."

"I planned to tell him, not ask his permission." He swallowed hard. "It's Brent I'm worried about."

"Brent?"

"He's the closest male family member you have. Correct?"

Sawyer was right. Brent was family. "Yes."

"I have to ask his permission."

"Are you worried he'll turn you down?"

He shook his head.

But he was worried about something, though. "What concerns you?"

"He'll remove me from your protection detail."

"Why would he do that?" She held up a hand. "Wait. Never mind. This is the same deal as what he tells the other operatives involved with their principals, isn't it? The distraction thing."

"That's right."

"I'll take care of it."

Sawyer was silent a moment, then said, "Please, let me handle it."

"But it's not right for him to separate us."

He cupped her nape. "I won't let him do that, but I may not be part of your protection detail."

"I don't understand."

"You will. Trust me, all right?"

For the moment, Janie would let Sawyer work it out on his own. If Brent tried to replace her protection detail, he'd have a fight on his hands from Sawyer and from her. "All right."

Jesse walked into the security room and stopped just inside the doorway. "Should I leave again?"

Sawyer shook his head. "Find anything?"

The medic glanced at Janie. "I did."

Her stomach knotted. "Is this about David?" What had she not known about her brother and would it come back to haunt David or her?

"Indirectly. I asked Simone to check into Maria's background."

"Why?"

"It's standard procedure to check into everyone connected to our principals," Sawyer said as he seated her at the computer console. "You'd be surprised how many problems lurk in background checks."

She sat as her knees weakened. Jesse's girlfriend must have found something. "Don't keep me in suspense, Jesse."

"Your sister-in-law, Maria, has relatives who are in the upper ranks of Vatos Locos."

Janie's breath stalled in her lungs. "Is she sure?"

"Simone traced the family line and last name of Reyes."

"That's a popular last name in Chile." Janie had lost count of the people she'd met with that last name while visiting Maria and David. "It's like Smith or Jones."

The medic's expression was sympathetic. "You're right, but Simone doesn't make that kind of mistake, Janie. She traced the family lines back several generations and hacked into databases, bank records, hospital records, and the like. She's not wrong. Your brother's wife is connected to the gang targeting you."

Stunned, she sat back in her chair. "But it makes little sense. I didn't detect any animosity from Maria, and I lived with them for two weeks. Wouldn't I have sensed something was off?"

Sawyer wrapped his hand around hers. "Maybe she wasn't involved in what's been happening to you."

"He's right," Jesse said. "Although Simone is still digging, she has yet to find evidence Maria is involved with Vatos Locos."

She appreciated their efforts to protect her and spare her feelings. However, the facts had to be faced. "But Maria's family members are part of the gang. She told me she's close to her family and is in contact with them daily."

"We'll look into it more, Janie." Sawyer raised her hand to his mouth and kissed her knuckles.

"If Maria is involved with the gang, is David safe with her?"

"He has a bodyguard outside the room."

"You were inside with me. Can the bodyguard stay inside, too?" There had to be something they could do to protect David from either Maria, her family, or other gang members.

"You weren't in ICU," Jesse said. "You were in a private clinic in Texas for a few hours. Your brother is still critical. The medical staff is already making an exception in allowing the guard to stand watch in the hall. They won't allow us to post a bodyguard inside that small room."

Sawyer frowned slightly. "I might have a solution to our problem."

"What do you suggest?" Janie asked.

"We can hide a camera and listening device in his room so the bodyguard can monitor things from the hallway."

Relief flooded her. "That's a brilliant solution. Who can set that up?" The sooner the better, as far as she was concerned.

"I'll take care of it when we visit David." He paused, then said, "We should take care of this before your sister-in-law arrives."

Right. If Maria planned to hurt David, she would never act on her plan if she knew she was under observation.

She sighed. And now she felt like a terrible person for even entertaining the notion that the sweet woman she'd spent two weeks with might be capable of something so awful.

"We need to stop by Fortress headquarters so I can pick up equipment." Sawyer cupped her cheek with his palm. "Any chance you'd be up to going to the shop extra early this morning?"

"Sure."

He glanced at Jesse. "You interested in an early morning run?"

"Of course." The medic pulled out his phone and sent a text. "Can we stop for breakfast before we head to Nashville?"

Janie grinned. "Instead of going to the coffee shop, what if I call the Sunrise Cafe and have Sunny put together three breakfast specials to go?"

"That sounds fantastic."

"Thanks, Janie." Sawyer brushed his mouth over hers. "You're an angel."

"I'll remind you of that when I'm tired and cranky."

He chuckled. "Deal."

Janie stood. "Give me five minutes, and I'll be ready."

Soon, they were on the road back to Hartman. For once, Janie wished she was a coffee drinker. She could use a heavy shot of caffeine.

As Sawyer crossed Hartman's city limits, he glanced at Janie. "Need anything before we go to the shop?"

"I imagine you and Jesse could use more coffee."

"Always. What do you need?"

"Since I doubt any store that's open this early has Irish or English Breakfast tea, I'll settle for a soft drink with caffeine."

"I'll see what I can find." Sawyer parked at a large gas station and went inside. He returned five minutes later carrying a cardboard drink holder with three to-go cups and a plastic bag.

He handed Janie one cup, then handed the second cup to Jesse. "Coffee for us," he said to Janie. "English Breakfast tea for you."

Her breath caught. "I didn't know they stocked my favorite tea."

"They carry boxes of English Breakfast and Irish Breakfast. I bought a box and dumped a tea bag in hot water."

She sipped and groaned. "It's wonderful. Thank you, Sawyer."

They parked behind Natural Bliss minutes later. Almost like magic, a figure emerged from the shadows in the alley.

"Wait here." Sawyer exited the SUV and met the man. They shook hands, and the stranger handed Sawyer something. After another minute, the man left.

Circling to the passenger side, he opened Janie's door and helped her to the asphalt. "Ready?"

"With my favorite tea and two excellent helpers, how can I not be ready?"

He smiled and guided her toward the back door.

"Didn't Fortress upgrade my locks yesterday? I don't have a key."

Sawyer showed her a shiny key on his palm. "I do."

He expected that problem and solved it. Sawyer Chapman was amazing. He entered the premises first and checked that all was secure before he allowed her into Natural Bliss.

Soon, the three of them worked quickly to create new stock for the shop. To her surprise, Janie discovered the shop had sold almost everything yesterday. Nice problem to have, but it meant they'd have to work faster today.

By the time they finished their tasks, the sun was just peeking over the horizon, changing the sky from black to steel gray with streaks of pink, red, and orange. A beautiful dawn, Janie thought as she set the last of the new stock in place and returned to the back room and the Fortress operatives. "That's the last."

They stored the supply tubs and cleaned up, then Jesse and Sawyer escorted Janie to the SUV. After a detour by Sunshine Cafe, they joined the traffic on Interstate 40 and headed toward Nashville.

Janie breathed a sigh of relief when Sawyer parked in the underground garage at Fortress Security headquarters an hour later.

Thank goodness traffic had been lighter than normal since they'd left Hartman so early this morning.

"Let me know when you're ready to leave. I'll be with Simone." Jesse exited the SUV and headed for the elevator.

Sawyer circled the hood and opened Janie's door. He lowered her to the concrete. "Do you want to meet Goose?"

Her breath caught. "I'd love to meet him. Is he here?"

"He's always with Simone or Jesse. Brent isn't sure about giving Goose the title of mascot, but the dog has special permission to be in Simone's office when she's on site."

"Perfect. Now, how can I help you?"

"I'll show you an equipment vault where I'll pick up what I need to set up surveillance in David's room."

He walked with her to the elevator and pressed the button for a subterranean level. Less than a minute later, they walked down a concrete corridor with several steel doors on each side of the hall.

She also noticed several surveillance cameras set up along the hall. "These are all equipment rooms?"

Sawyer stopped in front of one door and glanced at her. "Some are."

Janie eyed him. "Do I want to know what's behind the other doors?"

"Weapons, ammunition, C-4, blasting caps, grenades, rocket launchers, and more."

Her mouth gaped. "Good grief."

"We have to be better armed than the terrorists we go up against on missions. Fortress has two floors of equipment rooms and weapons supplies."

Oh, man. She knew his job was dangerous. This information, however, brought Janie face to face with reality. "Some of these rooms better have protective equipment for you and the other operatives." If they didn't, she would scour the Internet to find things to protect the man she adored with every fiber of her being.

Sawyer cupped the side of her neck and brushed his thumb over Janie's cheek. "Our safety comes first always. Brent pours a lot of money into training his assets." He kissed her lightly, then turned to swipe his identity card through the reader, then input two long strings of numbers, and finally allowed the security system to scan his retina. Tumblers shifted, and Sawyer opened the door.

Janie surveyed shelves filled with surveillance equipment. Most of the equipment was a mystery to her. Sawyer had no problem identifying and choosing what he wanted to use to protect her brother.

He slid the equipment into a cloth bag, led her from the equipment vault, and locked the room again. "Ready to meet Goose?"

She grinned. "I can't wait."

Sawyer chuckled and nudged her toward the elevator. Once they arrived on the fourth floor, he guided Janie to the right. They stopped in front of a door at the end of the corridor. From inside, they heard the sounds of a dog barking and a man chuckling.

After a quick knock, Sawyer opened the door. "I brought a visitor to meet Goose." He ushered Janie inside the office.

A toy poodle raced toward Sawyer, yapping in excitement. Chuckling, he picked up Goose. "Hey, Goose. How's my night watch buddy?" Several licks later, the dog noticed Janie, wiggled his tail in greeting, and gave a high-pitched bark.

Janie's heart squeezed. "He's beautiful."

A woman approached. "I agree." She held out her hand. "I'm Simone."

They shook hands. "Janie. Thanks for lending Jesse to us. His help has been invaluable."

"He's wonderful, isn't he?" Simone beamed at her future husband.

Jesse captured Simone's hand before turning to Sawyer. "Ready to go?"

"Not yet. I need to see Brent for a minute." He glanced at Janie. "Want to spend a little time with Goose? I won't be long."

And he didn't want her to go with him. That much was obvious. Hopefully, Sawyer and Brent could hash this out with the right outcome. If they couldn't, she'd pull out the big guns. She and Rowan would tackle Brent and his stubbornness. She smiled. Brent wouldn't stand a chance. "I'd like to play with Goose."

He looked relieved. "Great. I'll be back in a few minutes." He gave her a light kiss and left the office.

#

Chapter Twenty-Four

Sawyer knocked on Brent's door and flinched when he heard the growl from his boss. Maybe this wasn't the right time to talk to his boss.

Brent flung open the door. "Are you in or out? I don't have time to waste today."

"In."

"You have five minutes. Go."

In military fashion, he gave a rapid report on the latest, including the connection between Maria Moran's family and Vatos Locos.

Brent scowled. "You're telling me Janie's sister-in-law might be partly to blame for Janie being taken hostage?"

"I'm still looking into it."

"What else?"

He stiffened. "You know, don't you?"

Brent rose slowly. "Know what?"

Way to box himself in. "I love Janie, and I want your blessing to marry her."

The boss's ice-blue eyes glared at him. "What did you say?"

"You heard me."

"You've got to be kidding me. How many days have you known Janie?"

"Four."

"And you're planning to rush her down the aisle to an altar or, worse, to a justice of the peace? Or perhaps to Vegas for a quickie wedding?" Brent leaned closer. "Over my dead body, Chapman."

"I didn't say that. I'm not planning to rush her anywhere." Not for lack of desire, though. He'd give anything to place a wedding band on her finger today, but rushing Janie wasn't fair. "I'll give her time to really know me and to figure out if she can handle my job."

The boss grunted. "She can." He blew out a breath, still glaring daggers at Sawyer. "You're something else. I sent you to Mexico to rescue Janie because I trusted you, not because I expected you to sweep her off her feet."

"Yes, sir. In this business, things happen fast. Janie and I have been through more in the past four days than many couples experience in a lifetime. I know what I want, Brent. What I need. She's everything."

"And if I'm wrong and she can't handle your job with Fortress?"

"I'll ask you to assign me to a position that won't send me on missions."

"You would leave the Texas Team for Janie?"

"In a heartbeat, if that's what she needs to be happy."

"What about you? Can you live with that decision?"

"I can live without my team. I can't live without Janie."

Brent held his gaze for a long moment. "Is this one sided or does she feel the same?"

"It goes both ways."

More staring, then, "Your objectivity is shot, Chapman. I should set you down and assign another operative to cover Janie."

"You can, but I won't leave her side. Why tie up another operative when I'll be her bodyguard, regardless of what you choose to do?"

Another scowl. "Don't tempt me. I want to suspend you until this matter is resolved. I don't want to lose you to distraction at the wrong moment, and I especially don't want to lose Rowan's best friend."

A ball of ice formed in Sawyer's stomach. "Leave me on the team, Brent," he said, voice soft. "No one is more invested in protecting Janie than I am. No one will touch her on my watch. You have my word."

His boss pointed at him. "That's the only reason I'm leaving you in place."

Thank God.

"However, I'll have a word with Brody. He'll report to me every two hours. If he feels you're a danger to yourself, Janie, and your teammates, you'll be suspended for the duration of this op. Understood?"

"Yes, sir."

"Screw this up and hurt Janie, Chapman, and you'll answer to me." He bared his teeth. "And then my wife will mop the floor with you."

Sawyer flinched. "That's cruel, boss."

"It's the price you pay for ticking off my woman."

"Noted." He'd do everything humanly possible to avoid that scenario. Rowan Maddox was protective of her friends and didn't mind using a mean streak to do it.

"You have my blessing. Dismissed."

"Yes, sir." Sawyer left the office before his boss lit into him again and counted himself lucky to have survived with his skin intact. Brent Maddox was not the man to tick off. No question in Sawyer's mind that Brent would make sure he paid dearly if he did anything to hurt Janie.

Never going to happen. He'd sooner slit his own throat than hurt the woman who owned his heart.

All he had to do was keep his head in the game and protect her while he and his teammates tracked down the person giving orders to kidnap Janie and everything would be fine. Simple, right?

His stomach knotted. If the plan was so simple, why did his gut tell him he was running out of time to bring this to an end before Janie ended up paying the price?

He returned to Simone's office and paused in the doorway, watching Janie play with Goose. The worry weighing her down since they found her brother on the floor of his hotel room was nowhere in evidence as she played tug of war with the tiny poodle.

She glanced up and her smile faded. Sawyer regretted the loss. "Time to go?"

"I need a few minutes to set up the surveillance equipment in your brother's room."

Janie gave Goose a scratch between his ears and stood. "Thanks for letting me spend time with Goose, Simone. Your dog is wonderful."

Simone beamed. "Jesse and I think so, too. Come by and play with Goose anytime. The next time we have a Texas Team barbeque, I'll bring Goose along so he can see you."

"I'd love that." She crossed the room to Sawyer. "I'm ready."

"That's my signal to get back to work." Jesse bent and kissed Simone. "I'll call you when I'm off duty."

"Be safe, love."

The medic squeezed Simone's hand and left with Sawyer and Janie. In the elevator, he said, "How did it go with the boss?"

"About like I thought it would."

Janie looked up at him. "What does that mean?"

"He dressed me down and said if I messed up, I'd be answering to him first, then to Rowan." He shuddered as Jesse whistled. "Tell me about it," he muttered to his friend.

"Are you still on my security detail?" Janie asked.

"Yes, ma'am. However, I'm on probation."

She frowned. "Explain."

"Brody is to check in with Brent every two hours. If my team leader or the boss doesn't like what he's seeing or hearing, I'll be suspended until the op is over."

Janie's frown morphed into a scowl. "That's not fair. I won't accept anyone else guarding me except you and your team."

The elevator came to a stop at the garage level. Sawyer guided her to his SUV. "I told Brent I wouldn't leave your side for any reason."

"I'll talk to him. No one is separating us. End of story."

Although he appreciated her loyalty, Sawyer stopped her in the garage with a hand on her shoulder. "It's a matter of your safety and that of my team. The stakes are sky high, Janie. If I'm distracted at the wrong time, you could be hurt." He cupped her cheek. "And that would kill me, sweetheart."

"Nothing is going to happen to me. You won't allow it." She laid a hand over his heart. "Just make sure you watch out for yourself, too. If I lost you now, my heart would shatter."

Was it any wonder that he loved Janie Moran more than life itself? "We'll watch out for each other. That way, we'll both sail through this op without injuries that might delay my plans."

Her eyebrows rose. "What plans, Mr. Chapman?"

"Plans to romance you until I'm able to slide a wedding ring on your finger, Ms. Moran."

"Hey," Jesse called from the SUV. "You realize this garage echoes, right? No secrets unless you want everyone to know you're sweet talking the pretty lady into marrying you."

Sawyer chuckled. "I hear you." He nudged Janie toward the SUV. "We need to go. It may take a couple of visits to your brother to set up everything in the room."

"I'll talk to David's nurse and see if I can get an extended visit with my brother. They've been pretty accommodating."

"We'll work around it if they won't agree." He lifted her to the passenger seat of his SUV and dug into his cargo pocket.

Sawyer handed Janie a phone. "Zane had this delivered overnight. This is your satellite phone so we can communicate when I'm on missions." Then he gave her a bracelet, necklace, and a watch. "Each of these pieces has a GPS chip embedded in the design. If we're separated, I'll be able to track your location if you're wearing any of these pieces." After brushing her mouth with his, Sawyer circled the hood and slid behind the wheel.

An hour later, Sawyer parked in the lot at the hospital and escorted Janie up to her brother's room with his equipment in a lightweight backpack.

When they stopped at the ICU desk, David's nurse gave Janie a quick update. No change in her brother's condition. "Would it be possible for me to spend a few extra minutes with David?" Janie asked. "His wife is flying in from Chile this afternoon and I'm sure she'll want to spend as much time as possible with him. I don't want to interfere with her time."

"I think that will be all right. If he shows signs of distress, I'll come get you so he can rest."

"Thanks. I'm grateful to all of you for taking such good care of David."

Sawyer threaded his fingers through Janie's as they walked to David's room. He paused beside the new bodyguard on watch. "I'll be adding surveillance equipment to the room. Keep an eye out, Chris."

"You got it, Sawyer."

While Janie talked to her brother, Sawyer unzipped the backpack and pulled out his gear. As fast as possible, he set up a small surveillance camera in a place that gave them a view of the room and David. Next, he set up a listening device to catch anything being said in the room.

After testing the equipment, he sent the link to Chris and stepped outside the room to talk to the bodyguard. "Get it?" he murmured.

"Yep. Clear picture and sound."

"Make sure the guard on the next shift also has the link before you clock out."

"Copy that."

"Any change in David's condition?"

"None that I've seen."

"His wife will arrive in a few hours." Sawyer sent Chris a picture of Maria Moran. "She has family ties to Vatos Locos."

A grim expression settled on Chris's face. "I'll be on the lookout for her. Will she be traveling with family?"

"I don't know." And he should have checked. "I'll find out and let you know."

"Appreciate it."

Sawyer returned to the room. Janie was still standing by her brother's bedside, whispering to him about her store and the fresh scents she planned to incorporate into her stock of soap, body butter, and bath salts.

"You need to wake up and tell me what you think about the scents, David. I'm not sure if my male customers will appreciate them. I could use some advice from you."

No response.

Sawyer sent a message to Simone, asking for an update on Maria and the possibility of her traveling with family members.

He received a response less than two minutes later. Not the response he wanted to see.

"Sawyer?"

Janie's voice drew his attention from the screen to her face. "What is it?"

"You tell me. You look unhappy. Bad news?"

No use trying to hide the facts. Janie would find out in a few hours, anyway. "Your sister-in-law is traveling to the US with one brother and a cousin. Both are members of Vatos Locos."

Alarms went off. Jesse barreled into the room seconds ahead of the nurses.

Janie's eyes widened. "David?"

Jesse signaled Sawyer to get Janie out of the room. He followed them into the corridor.

"What's going on?" Janie demanded. "Why did David's alarms go off?"

"His blood pressure skyrocketed into the stratosphere. Did he show he had risen to consciousness?"

Janie shook her head. "I talked to my brother the entire time Sawyer was setting up the surveillance equipment. There was no change."

Jesse frowned. "What did you say just before the alarms went off?"

"Sawyer told me Maria is traveling to the US with her brother and cousin. They're members of Vatos Locos."

A soft whistle from the medic. "David might have heard what Sawyer told you. It's possible the news upset him."

"It's good that he reacted, right?"

"Could be. We'll see what the doctor says."

A man in a white coat raced into the room.

Sawyer set his pack against the wall and wrapped his arms around Janie.

In silence, she held on tight, her body trembling.

Heart hurting for Janie, he kissed her temple and glanced at Jesse. The medic looked grim. Not a good sign. Jesse knew more than he'd told Janie. Maybe he was protecting her. Perhaps he didn't have concrete answers to share. Either way, Sawyer was afraid Janie was in for more bad news.

Twenty minutes later, the doctor emerged from David's room. "Ms. Moran?"

Janie turned in Sawyer's arms to face the doctor. "Yes, sir."

He held out his hand. "I'm Jeff Carroway, the hospitalist. Your brother is stable for the moment, but he's had a stroke. We won't know how much damage has been done until he's fully conscious and we're able to run a few tests. We'll be taking Mr. Moran to surgery soon so the neurosurgeon can try to remove the clot."

Janie gasped. "Oh, no."

"Do you know what caused the stroke?" Sawyer asked.

"Not specifically. However, given the severe head trauma, a stroke wasn't unexpected." After answering a few more questions and informing them that another physician specializing in stroke care would check on David's progress throughout the day, the doctor went to his next patient as the orderlies arrived to take David to the operating room.

David's nurse exited the room. "Do you know when Mr. Moran's wife is expected to arrive?"

"Around noon," Sawyer answered.

Heather glanced at her watch. "Another three hours. The surgeon definitely won't wait. Look, I don't know how long Mr. Moran's operation will take, Janie. You can go to the waiting room or you can go to work or your home and we'll call you once the operation's complete. We'll also call if there's any change in his condition."

Janie glanced at Sawyer, her preference plain on her face.

Although he didn't want Janie in this hospital longer than necessary, he'd want to wait for word if one of his brothers was going under the knife. "Your choice," he murmured.

"Is it safe?" she whispered.

"We'll make it work, whatever you choose."

"We'll be in the waiting room," she told Heather.

"I'll let you know when I hear anything."

"Thanks, Heather."

Sawyer wrapped his hand around Janie's and escorted her to the family waiting room. After seating her on the couch, he crouched in front of her with her hand sandwiched between both of his. "Would you like some hot tea, sweetheart?"

Tears glimmered in her eyes. "How do you always know the perfect thing to help me?"

"Tea is your comfort drink."

"For future reference, hot chocolate also is a favorite."

"Noted." He rose. "I'll be back in a few minutes." Sawyer looked at Jesse, who gave a curt nod.

He headed to the cafeteria and bought coffee for himself, Chris, and Jesse, and tea and hot chocolate for Janie, along with snacks. Hopefully, he'd be able to coax Janie into a light snack until he could feed her lunch. If things didn't go well for David, though, she wouldn't feel like eating.

With the drinks in a carrier, Sawyer headed back upstairs to the ICU floor. He stopped by the room and gave Chris coffee and a snack. "Need a break?"

"I could use five minutes."

"Let me hand the rest of the drinks and snacks to Jesse and Janie, and I'll take over." He returned a minute later, sans the hot drinks and food. "Go."

Ten minutes later, Sawyer joined Janie and Jesse in the waiting room. "Anything yet?"

"They're prepping David for surgery," Jesse said.

Janie's eyes widened when she saw the cardboard carrier with multiple drinks. "What did you bring?"

"Guess." He handed her one cup and watched her breathe in the scent.

"Chocolate. Thanks."

Sawyer handed her the second cup. "Try this one."

She sipped. "Mint tea. This is wonderful. You'll spoil me."

He brushed her mouth with his. "That's the goal, sweetheart."

"What did you get yourself?"

"Coffee, hot and strong." He handed the remaining cup to Jesse.

Sawyer and Jesse took turns watching the activity in the hallway and the nurse's desk. Although Janie answered a couple of calls from her employees, she waited in silence for word on her brother's condition.

Two hours after the surgery began, the neurosurgeon strode into the waiting room. "Moran family?"

Sawyer stood and helped Janie to her feet.

"I'm David's sister, Janie. How is my brother?"

"He's stable at the moment. We're keeping a close watch on him."

"Were you able to remove the clot?" Jesse asked.

"Part of it, but not all. The clot is too far into the brain. I'm sorry, Ms. Moran."

Sawyer wrapped his arm around her shoulders. Not the news they'd been hoping for.

"What does that mean for David?" she asked. "Will he be all right?"

"Mr. Moran will need therapy. We won't know the extent of the damage he suffered from the stroke until he wakes and we're able to run tests on him. I wish I had better news to give you."

"Is he out of danger?"

"For the moment."

"When will I be able to see him?"

"Mr. Moran is still in recovery. He should be back in his room in about an hour. The nurse will come get you when he's able to receive visitors." He hesitated. "You should prepare yourself, Ms. Moran. Your brother is likely to need a lot of help when he's released from the hospital. He'll need rehab. Depending on his recovery, he may not be able to live alone."

Janie nodded. "He won't be alone. David is married. In fact, his wife is expecting their first baby in a few months."

A slight frown. "Where is his wife?"

"On her way here from Chile. She should arrive in a couple of hours."

"I see." He paused, listening to a page over the PA system. "I have to go. If you have more questions, please let the nurse know. We'll be glad to give you more information. We also have people who will help you or Mrs. Moran with the next steps after David is released." He left the waiting room.

Janie turned into Sawyer's arms and buried her face against his neck.

"We'll deal with it," he murmured. "If Maria can't provide the help David needs, we'll make sure he gets every resource available to help him recover as much of his life as possible."

"This is awful," she whispered. "How will I explain this to Maria?"

"None of this is your fault. No one holds you responsible for what happened to David."

"I wish he'd stayed home. If he had, he'd still be whole and healthy. Now, his life will be forever changed."

"Wait and see," Jesse said. "Let's not expect the worst. Once he wakes up, the doctors will have a better assessment of his condition and his chances of recovery."

Sawyer continued to hold the woman he loved for several minutes. Finally, she loosened her grip and returned to the couch, where he crouched in front of her. "I need to check in with Brody and Brent. I won't be far." After another glance at Jesse, Sawyer walked a few feet away from the entrance of the waiting room.

He called Brody first and reported the latest.

"Need more help with security at the hospital?"

"Yeah, we do." He told Brody about the connection between Vatos Locos and Maria's family members. "I'm not a big believer in coincidence."

"Neither am I. When are Maria and her escorts arriving?"

"Within the next two hours, according to Simone and Zane."

"Call the boss and update him. We'll be at the hospital in a few minutes. Watch your back and stay focused." Brody ended the call.

Sawyer's next call was to Brent.

"Talk to me."

He repeated the information he'd reported to Brody. "The rest of Texas Team will arrive at the hospital soon to help me protect Janie."

"I don't like this."

"Neither do I. The danger circling Janie is edging closer by the minute, and we still don't know why they want her."

"Must have something to do with the hijacking."

"Agreed, but is it a case of wrong place, wrong time, or did the hijackers deliberately target Janie?"

"That's the question of the year." After a few more instructions, Brent ended the call.

Sawyer returned to the waiting room and crouched in front of Janie where she sat on the couch. "You okay?" he asked.

"Not really."

"What can I do to help?"

"Walk with me. I need to get out of this room."

"Go," Jesse said. "I'll stay close in case the nurse reports a change. I'll let you know if I hear anything."

"Thanks." Sawyer helped Janie to her feet and escorted her to the elevator. He had the perfect place in mind for Janie to walk.

They rode the elevator to the first floor, and he guided her to the garden. He found a bench under a large tree. "Want to sit or keep walking?"

"Walk."

He walked along the concrete path around decorative bushes, trees, and flowers.

Janie stopped every few feet to admire a different flower or plant. She glanced up at Sawyer with a bright smile. "This garden is gorgeous."

"You're into plants?"

"Working in my garden at home helps me throw off the day's stress and worry."

He squeezed her hand. "I'm glad you found something that works for you."

"What helps you get rid of stress?"

"Running and working out with a teammate during the daytime. At night, I read."

"What do you read?"

Yeah, she would have to ask that question. His teammates knew of his obsession. None of the women he'd dated over the years cared enough to ask. More confirmation that Janie was the only woman for him. "Westerns and fantasy." His cheeks burned at the admission.

"My father loved reading them and watching any cowboy movie or television series. I enjoy watching them myself although I don't read them. Do you take a book with you on missions?" Janie asked as she continued along the path.

"I always travel with two books. So do the rest of my teammates. Sometimes we have a chance to read. Most of the time, the missions are fast and furious and my only chance to read is on the jet."

She asked more questions about the reading habits of his teammates, seeming to enjoy the variety of reading tastes among the Texas Team.

"Janie!"

Sawyer pivoted and stepped in front of Janie as a dark-haired woman and two other men came toward them at a fast clip.

"It's Maria," Janie said and stepped out from behind the shelter of Sawyer's body.

Sawyer refrained from hauling her back behind him. Barely. One glance told him the two men with Maria were armed with more than one weapon. How had they scored weapons that quickly?

David's wife hugged Janie. "What happened to David? Why is he in the hospital?"

"The doctor didn't tell you?"

Maria shook her head. "He said David was in the hospital in critical condition, but didn't give me details. Of course, I had to come immediately."

"Do you feel all right?" Janie asked as Maria swayed on her feet. "Do you need to sit down?"

"I need answers to my questions," the other woman snapped. "What happened to my husband? What did you get him involved in?"

#

Chapter Twenty-Five

Sawyer straightened at the venom in Maria's voice. Where were these accusations coming from? Janie was as much a victim as her brother. Why would Maria blame Janie for David's condition? "We should sit down somewhere more private to discuss this."

Maria rounded on him, anger snapping in her eyes. "Who are you?"

"Sawyer." He inclined his head toward Janie. "I'm hers."

David's wife snorted. "Her what? Lapdog?"

Janie gasped. "I know you're upset, Maria, but there's no reason to take your anger and fear out on Sawyer."

"Who is he to you?" the other woman insisted.

"The man I'm going to marry."

Maria stared. "You never mentioned a boyfriend, much less an engagement when you were in Chile."

"You and I were getting acquainted, and I was trying to mend the relationship between me and David. You took me sightseeing and to your favorite restaurants, as well as to meet some of your family members. Plus, we shopped for baby items. We were constantly busy. I would have told you and David about Sawyer when we talked on the phone after I was home. The hijacking and the aftermath prevented me from contacting you."

"David said you weren't involved with anyone, Janie. That's why he was so upset when you were taken hostage on the plane. He didn't think you had anyone to advocate for you."

"Really?"

"Why else would he drop everything and fly to America? He feared you'd be alone with your injuries and fear. And this is how you repay him? You withheld information that would have meant he stayed home with me where he belonged. You're the reason my husband is in critical condition. It's your fault." Maria's voice had risen to a screech by the time she finished her rant.

Sawyer had had enough. "Your accusations are unfair and untrue." He spoke calmly, although he'd like to lay into the woman and tear apart all the unfounded accusations.

This wasn't the place for a long, heated discussion. The skin at the back of his neck tingled, a sure sign they were being observed. He had to get Janie back into the safety of the hospital. Too many lines of sight out here for his comfort. "If you want to discuss this further, we'll go inside. I'm sure you'd like an update on your husband."

She glared at him. "Where is he?"

"At the moment, he's in recovery."

Maria blanched.

Fearing she might faint, Sawyer took a step toward her. Immediately, the two men with Maria moved to stand between the woman and Sawyer. Their hands hovered near their weapons.

"Back off," the taller one said in heavily accented English.

"Mrs. Moran looks as though she's ready to pass out. Take her inside the hospital where she can sit down while she talks to the nurse about David's condition."

"You speak as though you know David," the shorter man said.

"We've met." Sawyer hadn't been impressed with Janie's belligerent, arrogant brother.

"He never spoke of you to me," Maria said. "When did you speak to him?"

"Yesterday."

"You're lying. He said nothing about meeting you or seeing his sister. Why are you lying to me?"

"Your husband probably didn't have time to call you after we spoke."

"Why not?"

"He was attacked after he returned to his hotel room," Janie said. "David could not call before he was injured."

"I don't understand."

"Take Mrs. Moran inside. Now," Sawyer ordered. His skin was crawling now. Not a good sign.

The two men stared at Sawyer before Tall Man herded Maria toward the hospital entrance. "Come. You need to speak to one of the medical personnel and sit down to rest. You must do what is best for the baby, yes?"

Maria leaned her head against the man's shoulder, allowing him to lead her toward the building without protest.

After another fulminating glare, Short Man spun and followed the other two.

Although Sawyer longed to rush Janie to safety, he didn't want to make Maria's family members uncomfortable with his presence.

Janie glanced at him, unasked questions in her eyes.

"Wait," he murmured.

Instead of arguing, she snuggled into his side and watched her sister-in-law's progress toward the hospital.

Sawyer wrapped his left arm around Janie, leaving his other hand free to palm his weapon if necessary. "Thank you."

"For?"

"Trusting me." Once Maria and her family members were out of sight, Sawyer guided Janie into the hospital.

Instead of following them into the elevator where they'd be trapped in close quarters, Sawyer nudged Janie toward a deserted waiting room off the lobby.

"Tell me what's wrong," she said once they were out of sight of anyone coming or going from the building. For the moment, the lobby was empty.

"Someone was watching us outside."

"And you didn't want to have a long and drawn out argument with Maria in the open."

"Too dangerous."

"Do you think Fortress might be watching over us? Is that what you felt?"

Sawyer shook his head. "My teammates would have let me know if they were on the hospital grounds. No, the watcher wasn't one of my team, sweetheart."

She sighed. "I don't have a long list of enemies, so that leaves Vatos Locos. Is it possible they were protecting Maria from afar?"

"Maybe."

"But you're not buying it."

Another head shake.

"Sawyer." Max strode toward them. "Everything all right?"

"Maria Moran and her bodyguards are here, and Mrs. Moran is blaming Janie for David's injuries."

A soft whistle sounded from the other man. "That's cold."

"She's upset." Janie looked upset herself. "I understand. I would feel the same if Sawyer had been injured."

"I doubt you would have blamed Maria for Sawyer's condition," Max said.

Sawyer's phone vibrated. He glanced at the screen. "We need to go upstairs."

"What's wrong? Is it David?" Janie asked as she hurried to the elevator with Sawyer and Max.

"Jesse didn't say." Sawyer ushered Janie inside the elevator and pressed the button for David's floor. Was her brother out of surgery already?

Jesse met them when they stepped off the elevator. He motioned for them to follow him to the waiting room.

"What's wrong?" Sawyer asked.

"Mrs. Moran."

"Is the baby all right?" Janie asked.

"The baby isn't the problem. It's Maria. She's trying to prevent you from seeing David."

Her face went pale. "Why?"

"She told the nursing staff you were dangerous to her husband's health, and she's demanding that you be banned from his room."

"Can she do that?" Sawyer wrapped his arm around Janie's shoulders and drew her against his side.

"Maria brought a signed power of attorney in case of incapacitation with her. The hospital has no choice but to treat her wishes as David's."

"I can't see him or talk to him?" Janie asked.

"I'm sorry," Jesse said, voice soft.

"He'll think I abandoned him. How will I know his condition? Maria will forbid the nursing staff from giving me updates on the phone as well." Tears glimmered in her eyes.

Jesse rested his hand on her shoulder. "You'll know, even if we have to ask Simone to help with information retrieval."

Frustrated that he couldn't fix the problem for her, Sawyer brought Janie's hand to his mouth and kissed her fingers. "I'm sorry, Janie."

"So am I. I thought Maria and I were friends."

Sawyer's phone signaled an incoming message. Although tempted to ignore it, he checked the screen and scowled.

The medic eased closer and lowered his voice. "What?"

"Z is picking up increased chatter from the gang about a VIP in Hartman."

Jesse's brows knitted. "One of Maria's bodyguards?"

He shook his head. "I don't think so. They're muscle, not leaders." And that worried him. Who else would come to Hartman from the Vatos Locos organization and would that person escalate the danger to Janie and possibly David?

"Your services are no longer required. You're dismissed." Maria's voice drifted into the waiting room.

Sawyer, Janie, and Jesse entered the hall. Maria was speaking to the Fortress bodyguard.

"I'm sorry, ma'am. I have orders."

Her face reddened. "David is my husband. I have my own guards to watch over him. I don't know you. Leave or I'll have you removed from this hospital."

Sawyer caught Chris's eye and signaled for him to stand down.

Maria swung around to glare at the three of them. "You're not needed here."

"We reserved a suite for you and your men," Sawyer said and handed her his card with the name of the hotel near the hospital written on the back. "The staff is expecting you and promised to take good care of you."

She stared at him, eyes widening. "You made reservations for me?"

He inclined his head.

"Why would you do that?"

"You're part of Janie's family, and family is important to us both."

"I see," she murmured. "Perhaps I underestimated you, Sawyer."

His eyebrows rose at the word choice. A translation issue? English wasn't Maria's first language.

Tall Man stepped in front of Maria and folded his arms across his chest. "Go now. Mrs. Moran doesn't need you here while she sits by her husband's side."

"What if you need something, Maria?" Janie asked. "I'd like to stay to help."

"I'll be fine. Please, go." Maria motioned to Short Man. "My brother will take care of anything I need."

Tall Man moved a step closer. "Go or we'll have security remove you."

Maria rested her hand on the man's arm. "No need for threats. Janie has a successful business to run. She is busy." To Janie, she said, "I'll call if there's a change in David's condition. For now, I need to be alone. Please."

Janie gripped Sawyer's hand tighter. "I don't have my phone. I was forced to leave it behind on the plane."

Sawyer squeezed her hand tight. Although Janie now had a satellite phone, he didn't want Maria or her men to have the number.

"You must have another number where I can contact you."

"The card I gave you has my number on it," Sawyer said. "Janie will be with me."

"You didn't waste any time, Janie." Maria's smile was mocking. "You've already moved in with Sawyer. David must not know. Now, I have to wonder what else you've been hiding from him and me."

"Nothing important."

"You haven't told me about the hijacking. Your experience must have been terrible."

Sawyer squeezed Janie's hand again in silent warning. She glanced at him. "Maria wants to be alone, sweetheart. She's exhausted after traveling from Chile. We should let her rest."

"Of course." Janie turned to Maria. "Please call if I can help you or David."

After signaling Chris to follow them, Sawyer led Janie toward the elevator.

"Wait."

They paused, looking over their shoulders at Maria and her entourage.

"Are you angry with me, Janie?"

"We're family."

They walked onto the elevator, rode to the lobby, and left the building.

In the parking lot, Chris said, "I'm sorry, Sawyer. I'd hoped to be of more help to you and Janie."

"There is something you can do."

"Anything. Just name it."

"Would you mind going to a different waiting room and watching the video feed?"

The bodyguard shook his head. "Of course not. If David needs protection, I'll have to bulldoze over Mrs. Moran's bodyguards to get to him. I'll enter the hospital from another door and make my way to the family waiting room on the opposite end of David's floor. I doubt the Chilean visitors will explore the entire floor."

Sawyer shook Chris's hand. "Thanks, buddy. We appreciate the help."

As Jesse dropped back to cover them, Sawyer tucked Janie under his shoulder and Chris went to his own vehicle to move it to a different location, then reenter the hospital unobserved to watch over David.

When they reached his SUV, Sawyer unlocked the vehicle and helped Janie inside as the rest of his teammates approached. "Are you all right, sweetheart?" Sawyer murmured as he trailed the backs of his fingers down her cheek in a light motion.

"I feel like I'm abandoning David. I shouldn't have agreed to leave."

"This was for the best. We'll still have eyes on your brother, but Maria and the others don't know that. If anything happens, Chris will know in seconds."

"Is there sound?"

He smiled. "There is. However, even if I hadn't planted bugs in the room, Chris can read lips."

"You thought of everything."

"He's your brother. I know what he means to you."

"Sit rep," Brody said as soon as he and the others arrived.

Between them, Sawyer and Jesse reported the latest events to their teammates.

Logan scowled. "Janie, what is going on with Moran's wife? Was she like this when you were in Chile?"

"Maria acted like we were best friends. I don't know what happened. When I boarded the plane in Talca, she asked me to come back when the baby was born. Now, she acts as though everything that happened to David is my fault. I don't understand it."

"What about our bodyguard?" Max asked.

"Chris went back into the hospital to monitor things from a different waiting room. If something happens, we'll know within minutes."

"Anything else we need to know?" Brody asked.

"Zane sent a message a few minutes ago. There's a lot of chatter from the Vatos Locos organization about a VIP arriving in Hartman."

Logan grunted. "That's the last thing we need. Any idea who this person is?"

"Zane is still chasing down leads."

"He needs to chase them faster," Max muttered. "I want a name yesterday so we know who we're looking for."

"Same," Sawyer said. "At the moment, everyone is a suspect."

"What else is new?" Brody quartered the parking lot. "All right. Logan, follow Sawyer and Janie to the house. Make some calls. See if one of your contacts has more information. Zane and Simone have their hands full. The Phantom team is in a hot zone with Shadow unit, so the tech wizards are tied up for the next two hours at least."

"I need to take care of Goose," Jesse murmured.

"Go," Sawyer said. "Thanks for coming to the hospital."

Janie hugged the medic. "I appreciate you interpreting medical jargon for me. I'm sorry Maria didn't see the value of having you near."

He patted her back. "I'm glad I could help." Jesse glanced at Brody and Sawyer. "Keep me updated."

Forty minutes later, two Fortress SUVs parked behind the safe house. Sawyer motioned for Janie to stay inside, then exited the vehicle and met Logan.

"I'll check the perimeter." His friend moved into the shadows.

Sawyer locked his SUV and headed to the safe house. Within minutes, he returned to the SUV, where Janie and Logan waited. "We're clear." He escorted Janie inside the house.

"I'll be in the security room," Logan said and left the kitchen.

After resetting the alarm, Sawyer went to the coffeemaker to prepare another pot of coffee. "Are you hungry, Janie?"

She wrinkled her nose. "Not really, but I know I should eat. Something simple sounds good." Janie opened the refrigerator to peruse the contents. "We have the ingredients for a pasta salad topped by grilled chicken. How does that sound?"

"Like heaven." Sawyer started the brew cycle. "How can I help?"

"You up for sous chef duties?"

"Oh, yeah." He walked toward the refrigerator. "Tell me what you want, and I'll go to work."

Janie told him the list of vegetables she wanted chopped, then searched for a large cooker, filled it with water, and scoured the pantry until she found pasta. "Yes!" She did a fist pump and opened two boxes of dried noodles.

Once she poured noodles into the boiling water, Janie returned to the refrigerator, grabbed a block of cheese, and cut the cheese into bite-size chunks.

Sawyer finished chopping vegetables at the same time Janie cut the last of the cheese. "Now what?"

"As soon as the pasta is ready, we'll drain it, add the dressing I'm making, and mix in the rest of the ingredients."

Huh. This recipe didn't look too complicated. Perhaps he could learn to make something simple like this. "Show me how to make the dressing."

The next few minutes passed in a blur as he created the dressing following Janie's directions and grilled chicken breasts to slice for the pasta salad.

Soon, they plated the food, and Sawyer carried a plate plus a mug of coffee to Logan in the security room. Since his teammate was engaged in a phone conversation, Sawyer set the plate and mug on the computer desk and left the room. If Logan had anything to report, he'd let them know.

He returned to the kitchen and joined Janie at the breakfast bar. His first bite elicited a deep groan. "Janie, this is fabulous."

She grinned. "All because of my skilled sous chef."

Minutes later, Logan joined them, his plate and coffee mug empty. "Dinner was excellent. Thanks, Janie."

"I had help, but I'm glad you enjoyed it."

"Learn anything?" Sawyer asked.

Logan's expression darkened. "The VIP coming to Hartman is due to arrive any time, and he's here to lead a cleanup mission."

Sawyer's blood turned to ice water. The Vatos Locos VIP was here to lead a hit squad. His gut said the target was Janie.

Chapter Twenty-Six

Janie looked from Sawyer to Logan and back. "What is it? What's wrong, Sawyer?" Whatever was going on wasn't good. That much was plain.

"The Vatos Locos VIP is coming to Hartman to lead a hit squad."

Oh, man. "Let me guess. The target is me?"

"No confirmation of the target's identity," Logan said.

"But?"

He inclined his head.

Great. Nothing like having one of her worst nightmares roar back to life. "So we're back to the same puzzle. Why do they want me? As far as I know, I've never crossed paths with Vatos Locos."

"Maria is related to several members of the gang," Sawyer reminded her. "With 10,000 plus members, no one knows the complete roster."

She sighed. "All right. I'll give you that point. Since I don't know the members, I might have encountered more than one besides the hijackers. That still doesn't solve the mystery of why they want me."

"I might have an answer for that one," Logan said.

Sawyer folded his arms. "Let's have it."

"My contacts have heard several references to a money debt."

A frown. "That's not all, is it?"

"Two deep sources mentioned the VIP's compromised identity."

Blood drained from Janie's face. "The missing hostage."

Logan glanced at her with approval in his eyes. "Agreed."

She shoved her fingers through her hair. "I don't get it. The hostage was just another guy I saw once. Why does it matter if I might remember him? Fortress didn't get a hit on facial recognition. Why do Vatos Locos members care?"

"They'll care a great deal if the missing hostage was the leader of Vatos Locos."

"Wait a minute. Fortress has a sketch of the hostage's face. I'm not the only one who would recognize him now."

"They don't know that, sweetheart," Sawyer said. "As far as they know, you haven't realized the importance of the missing hostage."

"What does this mean long term, Sawyer?"

"There are thousands of members."

Her hands fisted. "And?"

"They won't stop coming until you're dead or we stop them."

Janie scowled. "Who cares if I saw the gang's leader? I'm not a threat to anyone. Who's going to listen to anything I have to say about someone on the hijacked plane who disappeared? Maybe I lost track of the passenger in the chaos at the compound."

Sawyer cupped her nape and drew her into his arms. "You know why."

That earned him a scowl. "Details would be nice since I have little experience with criminals."

"The leader's primary protection from attack has been his anonymity. As soon as he's outed as the gang's leader, he'll be a target of every rival gang wanting to take over his territory and businesses."

She swallowed hard, forced to face the dangerous reality of her situation. "Do we at least know this man's name?"

"Working on it," Logan said. "One of my contacts should call in the next hour with the information."

Sawyer's eyebrows rose. "Do I want to know how deep undercover your contact is?"

"No."

"Trustworthy?"

"He hasn't lied to me yet."

"Doesn't build my confidence in his loyalty to you."

A shrug. "He owes me for saving his life and that of his family. He won't risk retaliation by lying to me or setting me up."

Janie stared at the other operative. Those statements weren't a joke. Good grief. How dangerous were Sawyer's teammates? Then again, as long as they did the job, did she care what lines they pushed to protect their principals?

Since she was one of those principals who depended on their skills, the answer was a resounding no. Texas Team did what was necessary to save their principals and their loved ones. Of all people, she wouldn't fault them for it.

Janie turned to Sawyer. "Let's assume you're correct and I'm the target of the gang because I'm a threat to their leader's identity. How will we convince them to call off the hunters?"

He gave her a slow smile. "We identify him, capture him, and convince him to bring the hunters home."

Skepticism filled her. "You make it sound easy."

"Simple plans can work."

Somehow, she didn't think this situation would be resolved so easily. "If this man is the mysterious leader of the gang, I doubt having a chat with him will do the trick."

"Probably not."

"Do I want to know how you'll convince him to cooperate?"

"No."

With Sawyer watching her so carefully, Janie had to work at keeping her expression neutral. This was not the time to act squeamish about the methods used by the man she loved.

Janie gave a slight nod. "Then I won't ask for details."

His response was a soft, light brush of his lips over hers. "Do you need to do anything else to prepare for tomorrow at the shop?"

She shook her head. At least she'd had enough downtime to order supplies and pay invoices.

"Want to watch a movie with me? It might help you relax so you can sleep."

"Hmm." She tapped her chin with her forefinger. "Sit on the couch in the circle of your arms and snuggle close for a while? Granny Irene didn't raise a fool. I'd love to spend some time with you."

Logan's eyes lit with amusement. "And on that note, I'm headed back to the security room."

Sawyer chuckled as his teammate left the room with haste. "Go choose something for us to watch while I do another perimeter check. I'll return soon."

Mindful that Sawyer wouldn't be a fan of a movie with a large romance plot, Janie picked up the remote control for the television and scrolled through the stations. Spotting one of her favorite movies, she chose that station and settled back to watch and wait for Sawyer.

The movie was just beginning when the operative joined her on the couch. He wrapped his arm around Janie's shoulders and tucked her close to his side. "How did you know this movie is one of my favorites?"

She laughed. "It's my favorite movie, too."

"Nice." He kissed her temple and settled deeper into the cushions. "I'll have to do a perimeter check every half hour."

"I'll pause it when you're outside so you won't miss anything."

"Thanks, sweetheart." Another kiss from him.

They watched the movie until time for Sawyer to check outside again. He returned two minutes later.

Logan walked into the living room, his expression grim.

Sawyer stopped. "What?"

"My contact called."

"And?"

"The Vatos Locos VIP heading to Hartman is Diego Hernandez, the leader. Word is that since no one has been successful in taking care of your woman, he plans to kill Janie himself."

#

Chapter Twenty-Seven

Sawyer scowled. Diego Hernandez planned to kill Janie? Over Sawyer's dead body. No one would harm Janie and live to tell the tale. No one. "Has your contact seen Hernandez's face? Would he recognize him if we sent the sketch of the missing hostage?"

His teammate shook his head. "I sent the photo. Harry has never seen Hernandez."

Great. Just great. If they were right and the missing hostage was Diego Hernandez, the danger to Janie wouldn't stop until the Texas Team had a chat with the gang's leader.

"How else can I help?" Logan asked.

"If your source is right, Hernandez will be in a Vatos Locos stronghold. I want to know the location of every compound within driving distance."

"Copy that. Brody sent a message. He'll be taking the next bodyguard shift."

Sawyer glanced at his tactical watch. Two more hours. "All right. Need more coffee or a snack?"

"I wouldn't say no."

Janie set aside the remote and stood. "Food and coffee coming up."

Although she tried to sound upbeat, the pitch of her voice sounded off to Sawyer.

"Thanks, Janie." Logan stared at Sawyer for a beat in a silent command to fix the problem, then headed for the security room.

Right. He followed Janie into the kitchen and poured coffee into a to-go cup. Logan would appreciate the extra caffeine kick to stay alert.

After capping the cup, he turned to see Janie filling a dinner plate with fruit, cheese chunks, and rolled-up luncheon meat. Her hands trembled so hard she barely completed her task.

Enough. Sawyer couldn't stand by and watch fear overwhelm the bravest woman he knew.

When Janie reached for another slice of meat to roll and place on the plate, Sawyer took her hands in his. "Hey."

She froze, shaking.

That was more than enough. Logan could wait a few minutes. Sawyer scooped Janie into his arms, carried her to the living room, and set her on the couch where he joined her, tugging the beautiful woman into his arms.

He said nothing as he held her close until the shaking stopped. Shock. Yet something else for which Diego Hernandez had to answer. No one had the right to terrorize the woman he loved.

"Sorry," she whispered.

"Don't be. You know what it is."

"Adrenaline dump."

"Are you better now?"

She nodded. "I'll need a nap soon, won't I?"

"It's almost time to sleep, anyway."

"We have an early start tomorrow. I don't know if I'll be able to sleep much."

"Anything is better than staying awake all night." He kissed her. "Ready to take Logan his snack?"

She huffed out a breath. "He probably thinks I forgot him."

"Not a chance." He helped Janie to her feet. "Come on. We'll take him food and coffee, then I'll walk you to your room."

"Walking me home again, Mr. Chapman?"

"You bet, Ms. Moran. It's standard operating procedure to walk a date to the door and hopefully score a kiss at the end of a date."

"Some date," she murmured.

"We had dinner and watched a movie. In my book, that's a date." Janie laughed as she entered the kitchen.

Excellent. Sawyer breathed easier. Crisis averted for the moment. If they found the right information in time, Janie wouldn't be afraid anymore.

Once they delivered Logan's snack, Sawyer escorted Janie to her room. He cupped her nape and drew her body against his. "Was our date pleasant enough for me to earn a goodnight kiss?"

She twined her arms around his neck. "I enjoyed it very much, but I'd like a redo. Maybe we can finish the movie one night when all this is over."

"Deal. I'd love to watch the movie without interruption except for popcorn and soft drink refills."

"Perfect." She stood on her tiptoes and kissed Sawyer. "I'll make a note to stock up on supplies for our date."

Sawyer settled his mouth on Janie's for a deep, extended kiss. "I like that plan. Maybe we can do a double feature."

"Even better." Janie backed out of Sawyer's arms and into the doorway of her room. "I love you, Sawyer."

"I love you, too, sweetheart. Come to me if you can't sleep. I'll be close."

She flashed him a smile, retreated into her room, and closed the door.

Sawyer took a minute to bring his heart rate out of the stratosphere. Holy smoke. Janie Moran just did it for him. When he could think straight and draw in a full breath, he headed downstairs to the kitchen, where he poured himself a mug of coffee and joined Logan in the security room.

"She settled for the night?" Logan asked.

"For a while. I don't know if she'll sleep long." So far, she'd only managed three hours of sleep at a stretch. He had a feeling tonight wouldn't be any better. "Any progress on the search?"

"Already have one probable location." Logan held up his hand. "I know. You want it nailed down yesterday. I'll make more calls, but confirmation takes time."

Sawyer squeezed his friend's shoulder. "Keep hunting. I'm going to do more research on Maria Moran and her bodyguards."

Logan paused with his hands hovering above the keyboard. "Need help? I can multitask."

"Let me give it a shot first. If I can't come up with anything, I'll let you know."

After a slight nod, the other operative returned to his task.

Sawyer grabbed his laptop, then glanced at his watch again. "Time for another perimeter check." He started to stand, but Logan waved him back down.

"I've got it. I need to stretch my legs."

"I'll monitor your progress while I check in with the boss."

Logan grabbed his empty plate and coffee cup and left. A moment later, he appeared on the security cameras.

Sawyer called Brent, who answered on the first ring.

"Maddox."

"It's Sawyer."

"Sit rep."

He gave his boss the latest update, including the name of the head of Vatos Locos, who was in Hartman or would be soon.

A sigh. "Not surprised. Every mission is more complicated than we realize at the beginning. What do you need?"

"An army." Possibly two. How would he pull this off while keeping Janie safe? Janie wasn't wrong. Sawyer and his teammates must convince Diego Hernandez to call off the hunt and drain the account holding the bounty money. The Vatos Locos leader would want to distance himself from the pay-to-kill order.

"Lucky for you, Durango and Artemis are in town to train together. They're available to help for the next week."

Thank God. He'd take those ten people over an army any day. They were skilled and ruthless. Besides, while the gang numbered several thousand members, all of them weren't in this area. "You don't know how glad I am to hear that news."

"I'll put them on alert. They'll be ready to assist if you need them. In the meantime, keep a close watch on Janie. Her schedule is too predictable."

Sawyer stiffened. "You know this how?"

A snort. "Come on, Chapman. My wife and I have been friends with Janie for years. We helped her set up Natural Bliss last year. Rowan stepped in several times when Janie needed more help in the shop or when her employees were out sick. We know her routine. If we know it, anyone who pays attention will know her routine as well. Watch Janie carefully, Sawyer. Rowan doesn't want to lose her and neither do I."

"Same." The thought horrified him. He'd just found her and to lose her this soon? Not happening. The boss was right. Janie's predictable routine would make her an easy target. He'd have to make sure she was covered. "I'll take care of her, sir."

"I'm counting on it." Brent ended the call.

Logan dropped into the seat beside him. "How'd it go?"

"Brent is worried."

"He has reason to be concerned. So do you."

"I'm aware."

"Then let's find what we need to protect your woman and extract her from the mess she's in."

Logan dove back into his search for probable gang locations as Sawyer resumed his background research on Maria and her bodyguards. After scanning official records, Sawyer pushed back from the computer console and stood. "Time for another perimeter check. Need more coffee?"

"Better switch to water now."

"I'll bring water in with me when I return."

"Thanks."

After depositing his mug in the dishwasher, Sawyer disabled the alarm and walked outside. While he walked the perimeter, searching for anomalies, he considered his options to keep Janie safe from Hernandez and his cronies. Precious few, he realized. He evaluated and discarded multiple ideas until he settled on the only viable plan. Risky option but necessary.

Circuit completed, Sawyer returned to the house, reset the alarm, snagged four bottles of water, and went to the security room. He gave two bottles to Logan, then resumed his seat and tackled Maria Moran's social media accounts.

He flinched at the sheer number of posts with photos included. Sawyer could spend hours looking at everything Maria shared with the world.

What about her bodyguards? Both of them were her cousins. Would they be as apt to post their whole lives for the world to see? Probably not since they were members of Vatos Locos. The gang wasn't interested in using social media as a recruiting tool.

He checked social media accounts for the names of the two men and came up with zip.

Back to Maria's posts then. He planned to go to the very beginning of her posts, but it made more sense to scan posts beginning a year before she met David Moran.

He scanned photographs, recognizing her bodyguards in several pictures. Sawyer noticed several photos of Maria in the arms of a man with his back to the camera.

Huh. He checked the date the photo was posted. Two months ago. Sawyer studied the shot. The man Maria watched with blinding love in her eyes was not Janie's brother.

"Find something?" Logan asked.

"Trouble in paradise." He turned the laptop so his teammate could study the photo.

"That's not Moran?"

"Nope. His shoulders aren't that broad. Also, this guy is at least six inches shorter than David."

Logan grunted. "That's not a look shared between siblings or cousins."

"Makes me wonder if this man has something to do with what's happening to Janie."

"How?"

"Janie's Granny Irene left her a lot of money in her will, provided she gave nothing except a bequest to David. The grandmother was well aware of his tendency to blow money at casinos and the racetrack."

"He's in financial trouble. Makes sense that Maria might want to solve their money problems the easy way. Think it's possible Maria is tired of her husband and hoped to get rid of him when Janie wouldn't bail him out of trouble again?"

"Pretty extreme way to handle things. Why not just divorce David and start fresh with Mystery Man?"

"Perhaps David wouldn't cooperate, especially now that a baby is on the way."

Made sense. "Custody would be messy, considering the judicial system of two countries would be involved." He dragged a hand down his face. "I hate to tell Janie about this."

"We don't have proof."

"In this case, a picture is worth a thousand words. I think we're right, but I don't know if it has bearing on what's happening to Janie." Or rather, he didn't want to think Maria Moran was cold-hearted enough to kill an innocent woman and her own husband for Granny Irene's money. Then again, he'd known people to kill for a lot less than a few million dollars.

"Get rid of the husband and the sister-in-law, and start a new life with your lover and baby with the grandmother's money." Logan grimaced. "Cold."

Sawyer looked at the photo again. Not much to go on except the back of Mystery Man's head. "Wonder if Janie met him in Chile."

"Only one way to find out. Ask her when she wakes."

Brody arrived an hour later. "Sit rep."

"Found something interesting while scanning Maria Moran's social media pages." Sawyer angled his laptop so his team leader could see the photo array he'd downloaded from the social media site. "What do you see?"

The other operative studied the photos for a minute, then said, "A woman in love."

"That's not David Moran."

Brody's gaze flicked back to the photos. "How long ago were these posted?"

"Two months."

A soft whistle. "Has Janie seen these?"

"Not yet."

"I'm curious what she'll make of the pictures." He studied Sawyer's face. "You haven't slept?"

"No time."

"Make time. You'll only get about three hours as it is. Go, Chapman. That's an order."

He scowled, but shut down his laptop. Much as he hated to admit it, the short nights of sleep were catching up with him. "Won't you need help overnight?"

"Jesse will be here in an hour. Logan will stay until Jesse arrives. Go, Sawyer."

"Yes, sir."

Sawyer took the stairs two at a time, peered into Janie's room to make sure she was all right, then got ready for bed. Minutes later, he stretched out on top of the quilt on his bed and dropped into sleep.

An internal alarm woke Sawyer a few minutes before 4:00 and admitted to himself he felt more alert. Hopefully, Janie would be safe soon and the team could rest before Brent sent them out again for another mission.

He splashed cold water on his face and changed clothes. Ready for another day, Sawyer grabbed his laptop and Go bag, and walked into the hall, glancing at Janie's room. The door was closed, indicating she was awake and preparing for the early morning trek to the shop.

Wishing he could persuade her to avoid the shop wouldn't change her mind about going. Although Janie had cooperated with his requests to keep her safe, in this one thing, she was immovable. Sawyer didn't blame her. Natural Bliss was her livelihood, and her staff couldn't handle everything by themselves long term.

While he admired her work ethic, trouble was coming, and soon. Short of kidnapping Janie and spiriting her away to a deserted island, his only recourse was to hope for the best and prepare for the worst. He prayed the worst wouldn't have deadly consequences.

Sawyer walked downstairs to the kitchen.

Brody turned and studied him for a moment. He gave a brief nod. "You look better." He handed Sawyer a mug filled with coffee. "Janie sleep okay?"

"She didn't leave her room during the night." If she had, Sawyer would have awakened immediately. "Everything okay overnight?"

"No excitement unless you count a coyote stalking a cat through the neighborhood."

"Quiet is good."

"Won't last. Something's coming."

"Yeah." He booted up his laptop to bring up the picture of Maria with Mystery Man. When the photos loaded, Sawyer studied the photo array he'd cobbled together from images on Maria's social media pages.

Who was this man? He wasn't an expert on emotions, but he'd become good at reading people's expressions while on the job as a cop. Maria Moran wasn't exchanging pleasantries with a family member or a friend. She loved this man. What did that mean for David?

Nothing good. He wasn't a fan of Janie's brother, but he didn't wish him trouble in his marriage either.

Sawyer left the photos up on the screen and rose to prepare tea for his soon-to-be wife. The thought stole his breath. As soon as Janie was safe, he'd shop for her engagement ring. No way would he deploy again without a ring on her finger, so every man recognized she was taken. He wanted a spectacular engagement ring and wedding band. She deserved the best.

He filled a large mug with water, then searched the tea cabinet for a flavor Janie might enjoy. Sawyer spotted a box of chamomile honey tea. Something soothing and a little sweet to start her day right.

After dumping two bags of tea in the water, he nuked it and found a large travel mug with a lid. When the heating cycle finished, Sawyer set the tea aside to steep. Light footsteps on the stairs heralded Janie's approach.

She walked into the kitchen and straight into Sawyer's arms. "Good morning," she murmured.

"Good morning, beautiful." He kissed her, mindful of his team leader watching them. "Sleep okay?"

Janie shrugged. "I woke frequently, worrying about David. Have either of you heard how he's doing?"

"Simone hacked into hospital records an hour ago," Brody said. "He's in the security room."

She eased away from Sawyer and turned toward the hall. "I'll be back in a minute."

As soon as she was out of earshot, Brody turned to Sawyer. "What was that?"

"The kiss?"

"Don't play dumb, Chapman. Are you wanting to be kicked off her security detail?"

"We're getting married as soon as possible. Whether or not I'm on her detail, I won't leave her side. End of story."

"Does the boss know this?"

"He does. If I can't keep my head in the game, he'll replace me." He folded his arms across his chest. "Don't tell me you would have done anything different. We all saw how protective and territorial you were with Sage. You didn't give control of her security detail to someone else."

"I had a history with Sage," Brody snapped. "We had years to build a relationship. You've had days."

"Janie is mine to protect, Brody. I love her more than I thought possible in such a short time. Don't ask me to step aside. I won't do it, even if it means resigning from Fortress."

His team leader hissed out a breath. "Do not get distracted. You hear me? I don't want to make a call to your mother and brothers to tell them you're dead."

"I'll stay alert. I have a lifetime of plans with Janie."

"You have to stay alive to fulfill the plans."

Janie returned to the kitchen, her expression troubled.

"What did Jesse say?" Sawyer asked.

"They're seeing signs he's coming around. But they still don't have any idea how much damage has been done. Worse, I won't be allowed to see him. What if he thinks I've abandoned him?"

He wrapped his arms around her. "I'm sorry, Janie. Fortress has access to the best medical professionals in the business. As long as David is in the US, he'll have the best medical care we can provide."

"He has good insurance."

"Excellent. Between the insurance and Fortress, he'll have everything he needs to recover as much as possible. Hopefully, your sister-in-law will change her mind about allowing you to visit soon."

Sawyer released her and turned to pour her tea into the travel mug. Hopefully, his girl would find the taste soothing.

"Where did you get these pictures?" Janie asked, shock on her face.

He turned to see Janie staring at the computer screen. "I copied them from Maria's social media posts. Do you recognize Mystery Man?"

She turned to him, her face white. "He's the missing hostage."

Chapter Twenty-Eight

"Are you sure?" Sawyer joined Janie at the breakfast bar in front of his computer. How did she recognize her missing fellow hostage from the photos?

"Positive. Who is he?"

Brody answered the question. "Logan's contacts came through on the identification of the passenger. His name is Diego Hernandez, the leader of Vatos Locos."

A ball of ice formed in Sawyer's stomach. Not the confirmation he wanted to hear. "Sweetheart, how do you know this is the missing hostage? I couldn't find a picture of this man's face anywhere on your sister-in-law's social media posts."

Janie pointed to something on the man's hand. "The signet ring. I recognized it, as well as the scar on the back of his neck."

Sawyer took the photo Janie indicated and dumped it into a Fortress program to clean up and enhance the picture. A minute later, he turned the screen around for her to study the shot again. "Take your time. Do you recognize him from the plane?"

She did as he asked, then nodded. "I'm positive he's the missing hostage."

"Did you see Hernandez when you were visiting Maria and David?"

"No, and I didn't recognize him when he sat beside me on the plane." She looked at Sawyer. "Maria knew him before she married my brother?"

He hesitated, loathe to hurt her. Couldn't be helped. She needed to know the truth. "I don't think so. I went back over a year on Maria's social media pages. Hernandez didn't appear in her photos until two months ago."

She stared at the screen again. "She's in love with him," Janie murmured. "You can see it in her face and in the way she looks at him." She sat at the breakfast bar. "This will break David's heart. I don't know if he'll fight to recover when she leaves him for Hernandez."

"That's assuming Hernandez is looking at your sister-in-law the same way she's looking at him," Brody pointed out. "We never see his face."

"Brody's right." Sawyer sat beside Janie. "Don't assume the worst until we have all the facts." He had little doubt that David and Maria's marriage was doomed, baby or no baby. Maria loved another man and that would be a blow to a man reeling from a vicious beating and a stroke with still unknown repercussions.

Janie looked at him without saying a word.

He held up a hand. "I know, baby. I think you're right. However, we deal with one thing at a time. Do you know if David suspects his wife loves Hernandez?"

Janie shook her head. "He barely talked to me when I was in Chile, and Maria never mentioned Diego."

"All right." He leaned over and brushed her mouth with his. "We need to leave soon. Would you like to pick up breakfast on the way?"

"If it includes an apple muffin from Tabitha's Cafe, absolutely."

"You got it."

Jesse strode in. "Breakfast?" he asked, his expression hopeful.

"Stopping by Tabitha's Cafe on the way into Hartman."

"I love her food."

"Good thing since it's the only food place open at this hour." He poured the medic a to-go cup of coffee, picked up his own, gave Janie her tea, and grabbed his Go bag. "Ready?"

She nodded and glanced at Brody. "Thanks for keeping watch overnight."

"Glad to help." He turned to Sawyer. "I'll lock up. Keep me updated. Max will take over from Jesse. He'll contact you when he leaves home."

"Copy that." He ushered Janie to the SUV.

"I'll follow you in." Jesse unlocked his SUV and climbed behind the wheel.

Once Janie was set, Sawyer stored his gear in the back and settled into the driver's seat. He drove toward town, detouring ten miles out to stop by the cafe. He parked near the entrance and came around to help Janie to the asphalt. The three of them went inside and ordered breakfast to go. In less than five minutes, they resumed their journey toward Hartman.

Despite Janie's protest that she wasn't hungry, she consumed both the apple muffin and banana muffin he'd bought her. When she finished, she sat back with a sigh.

He polished off his own banana muffin. He didn't know anyone who made better muffins than Tabitha. "Need anything else?"

"I'll be fine until later in the morning. Thanks for stopping at Tabitha's, Sawyer. Her muffins are wonderful."

When he reached the parking lot of the strip mall where Janie's shop was located, Sawyer parked at the back of the shop. "Ready?"

She nodded. "Let's get this done. Maybe I can convince Maria to let me see David."

He exited the vehicle and circled the hood to open Janie's door.

Sawyer held out his hand. "I want to check the shop before you go inside." When she handed him the key, he glanced at Jesse, who gave a slight nod.

Unlocking the door, he slipped into the back room of the shop and disabled the alarm before checking every room and storage area of Natural Bliss. He breathed easier when he finished the sweep and found the shop clear.

He returned to Janie and Jesse. "We're clear. I'll grab my Go bag and join you in a minute."

Sawyer grabbed his gear and headed inside the shop. Once he closed the door behind him, he locked it, set his bag out of the way beside Jesse's, and joined Jesse and Janie at the long table. "What are we creating today?"

"More oatmeal and honey bath salts, bath bombs, soap, and body cream. We also need to create products with a tropical breeze scent."

He froze. "Tropical breeze?"

Janie smiled. "Someone said men wouldn't like girly smelling bath products. We're trying your idea today."

Sawyer grinned. "Nice."

"Hope you still think so when you're elbow deep in the ingredients. If you don't like it, we'll find out fast."

They worked fast as a team and ended up refilling stock in five different scents, plus the new one Janie created for Sawyer. When they finished, the sun was lightening the sky to a steel gray.

"I'll check the perimeter of the shop while you help Janie add stock to the shop and the stockroom," Jesse said.

After he left, Janie looked at Sawyer. "Are you sure I can't persuade you and Jesse to join my team of employees? You are fantastic assistants." She nudged him gently with her elbow. "No question that my sales and profits would go up. Can't lose with two assistants who look as handsome as the two of you."

He gave her a mock scowl. "Hey, you're not supposed to notice that other men are attractive."

Her eyebrows soared. "That restriction wasn't in the engagement contract."

Amusement had his lips curving. "I'm amending the contract. No noticing other men."

Janie laughed. "Deal. Besides, I only need you to send my profits through the roof. The women won't be able to resist buying stock you recommend."

Jesse returned. "All clear. What's next?"

"I'd like to wait for my employees to arrive unless you think it's too dangerous for them and for us," Janie said.

Sawyer didn't blame her for wanting to check in with her employees. They'd been carrying the shop load by themselves for several days. He didn't like the idea of Janie being in the shop. Something was coming, and soon. He didn't want Janie in the danger's path. "How soon will they arrive?"

"Another hour. We arrived very early today."

"To change your schedule," Jesse said. "Routine is good, unless you have someone tracking your movements. Let's not make it easy for them to find you, sugar."

She sighed. "All right. I can call my employees later to see how things are going."

A knock sounded on the back door.

Sawyer glanced at Jesse, who murmured something to Janie and urged her toward the stockroom. She hurried out of sight and closed the door.

With Janie safe for the moment, Sawyer checked the security feed in her office as the knock sounded again. His eyes narrowed. Why were Maria Moran and her bodyguards here at this hour of the morning?

He returned to Jesse. "Maria and her entourage," he murmured to Jesse and unlocked the door. "Mrs. Moran, what are you doing here?"

"We're on the way to the hospital to see my husband as soon as we're allowed. Since we were this close, I wanted to stop for a tour of Janie's shop and give her an update on David. May we come inside? We won't take much time." Maria offered a slight smile.

Although he stepped back to allow the three Chileans inside the shop, he was uneasy. He felt to his bones that something was off. Was it just his suspicions because of Maria's infidelity with Hernandez or something else?

"Maria, what's wrong? Is David all right?" Janie hurried from the stockroom.

"There you are. Everything is fine, Janie. I'm sorry to disturb. I remembered you telling me you came to the shop early every morning. I convinced my cousin to stop on the way to the hospital so I could see Natural Bliss. Do you have a few minutes to give me a tour?"

"Of course. This room is the prep room where we create salts, soaps, and lotions for the shop."

Maria wandered to the table on which sat several large bowls and plastic containers of supplies. "So this is where the magic happens."

Janie laughed. "Would you like to see the store itself? If you see anything you'd like to try, I'll be glad to give you samples."

Maria smiled. "I don't need samples. I already know exactly what I want."

"Come with me." Janie led Maria into the front of the store.

Sawyer followed them, his uneasiness growing. He glanced at Jesse and signaled him to be on alert.

The medic dropped back so he could watch the two bodyguards as they followed Sawyer and the women into the store.

As Janie and Maria walked around the store, Matias Reyes eased up beside Sawyer. He snorted. "Women," he muttered. "Always wanting more bath stuff. I don't understand it."

"Janie's products are natural, and she has a large customer base."

Maria's brother looked at Sawyer. "You don't mind your woman working?"

He frowned. "Why should I? This isn't the Dark Ages, and she loves the work."

"My woman doesn't work. She stays at home where she belongs." A careful look at Sawyer. "I make plenty of money so she doesn't have to provide for me."

Why was this guy trying to get a rise out of him? He glanced over his shoulder to see Lorenzo, Maria's cousin, had drawn Jesse into a conversation near the doorway to the workroom.

"Matias," Maria called. "Come here. See what you think of this scent."

Despite his muttered curse, the brother crossed to Janie's side to sniff the contents of a jar.

Sawyer walked closer.

Matias shoved the jar away. "No," he snapped. "Too strong for real men." He glanced at Sawyer. "Perhaps Janie's man doesn't agree." He motioned Sawyer over. "Come. Sniff this and tell us your opinion."

Something was off here. "Pass. Janie, come here, baby."

Maria reached into her purse as Janie started toward him. She pulled out a gun and pointed it at Sawyer as Matias wrapped his arm around Janie's neck and yanked her against his chest, a gun pressed against her temple.

Janie gasped and tried to pull Matias's arm away from her neck without success.

Sawyer's gun was in his hand and pointed at Matias in a split second. "Let her go," he snapped.

Matias pressed the muzzle harder against Janie's temple. Blood trickled down the side of her face. "You can shoot me. If you do, your woman will die. My weapon has a hair trigger. A bit more pressure, and I will blow a hole in her pretty head."

"Put down your gun, Sawyer," Maria ordered. "Do it now or Janie and your medic friend die."

"Jesse?"

No response.

The barrel of a gun pressed against the back of Sawyer's neck. "Drop your gun. Your friend is unconscious and can't save you. If you fight us, he dies. Choose."

"Put down your gun, Sawyer," Maria repeated.

"Maria, why are you doing this?" Janie asked. "What did I ever do to you?"

"Shut up. No one asked you to speak," Matias said. "Your man hasn't taught you how to act properly." He smirked. "Perhaps because he isn't one. No matter. I'll be glad to teach you." Matias gave a slight nod.

Sawyer started to turn, but he wasn't fast enough. Pain exploded at the back of his head, and the world went dark.

Chapter Twenty-Nine

"No!" Janie lunged away from Matias, only to have him yank her back against his body. "Sawyer!"

Maria's brother tightened his hold until his grip was excruciating and would leave bruises on her upper arms. "Stop fighting or I will kill your man. Do you want to watch him die?"

She froze, horrified. "No. Please, don't hurt him."

"We need to go," Lorenzo muttered. "The sun's coming up, and these bruisers won't be out for long." He kicked Sawyer in the ribs.

Maria rolled her eyes. "So kill them and be done with it. We won't have to worry about them if they're dead, will we?"

Fury at the situation and terror for Sawyer and Jesse exploded inside Janie. She thrashed violently enough to break free of Matias's hold and raced to Sawyer. Dropping to her knees beside him, she cupped his beloved face with her hands while scanning his body for a small weapon with which to protect him, Jesse, and herself.

When she realized none of his visible weapons were small, her heart sank. "Sawyer," she whispered. Janie released his face and ran her hands over his jacket as though checking for further injuries.

She touched a small lump in his inner pocket. What was that?

"Get her up, Lorenzo," Maria snapped. "This is pathetic. Don't you have a spine, Janie? You're a disgrace to strong women everywhere."

"Sawyer, please wake up." Her voice sounded choked as she lowered her upper body to cover his chest. Her hands roamed over his ribs until she could slip her left hand into the pocket and grip the object.

"Up." Lorenzo grabbed her right arm, yanked Janie to her feet, and toward him.

She kept the hard object in her fist and shoved her hands into her hoodie pockets. If she was lucky, they wouldn't search her before they took her away.

Before she could evade the blow, Lorenzo slapped her. "My cousin isn't the only one who knows how to tame a woman," he murmured. His gaze slid over her body. "Keep pushing me, and I'll ask the boss to give you to me first."

First? Janie's eyes watered from the pain of the blow. She didn't know what to make of Lorenzo's statement, but it couldn't be good.

"If you say another word, your man will pay the price," Lorenzo said, his voice almost a growl. "Do you understand?" His grip on her arm tightened.

She nodded.

He glanced at his cousins. "Let's go. He's waiting."

"What about Sawyer and Jesse?" Maria asked. "We can't leave them alive. They're too dangerous."

A snort from Matias. "Forget them. Let Janie's man suffer, wondering what she's enduring."

"Are you crazy? They work for a security company."

"Wannabe cops. No threat, Maria. Besides, they have no way of tracking her. She could be anywhere in the country by the time they figure out which direction to go." He smirked at Janie.

Janie remained silent. Let them think she had no hope of escaping. She would never give up trying to get away from Maria and her cronies. Sawyer and his teammates would find her.

Lorenzo shifted his hold from Janie's arm to her neck. He squeezed, his eyes lit with amusement at her struggle to breathe. When her vision started going dark, he eased the pressure. "Very good," he murmured. He stroked his thumb along the side of her throat. "You have a cell phone?"

Again, she nodded. She hated to give up her satellite phone, but if she tried to hide it, they would check her for it and might find the weapon she'd taken from Sawyer.

"Leave it here." Lorenzo watched as she complied, then said, "Now remove all your jewelry. Let your man think you've run off without him." He smiled. "Another twist of the knife to his heart."

No, no, no. No GPS trackers for Zane and the others to use to find her. But what choice did she have? Janie removed the jewelry and the watch and laid them beside the phone.

"Look at your man."

She complied. Sawyer was still out cold, his skin pale.

"That is the last time you will see him. Come." He used his hold on her throat to force Janie to the back door of her shop.

In less than a minute, Lorenzo shoved Janie into the back of a large black SUV with tinted windows. He followed her inside and closed the door. His left arm circled her neck and anchored her to his side. "If you cooperate, you may live another day." He leaned down and bit the side of her neck.

Janie cried out as pain flashed through her.

"Don't damage her too much," Matias warned. "He won't be pleased if you do."

"You worry too much, cousin."

"And you should have a care for your life." Matias started the engine and drove away from Natural Bliss. "Keep her under control. I don't want her attacking me while I drive."

Lorenzo chuckled. "Don't worry. We'll get to know each other until we arrive at our destination. She'll be too busy to cause you trouble."

"For pity's sake," Maria hissed. "At least wait until he gives you permission to do what you want with her. I'd rather not lose you because of that tramp."

Tramp? Maria had a lot of nerve calling Janie a tramp after what she'd done to David.

"Are you going to fight me?" Lorenzo whispered. "I love it when my women fight."

"I'm not your woman," she said, voice cold.

He smiled. The sight chilled Janie to the bone. "You will be soon. If you're holding onto hope that your man will find you, don't waste your time. The world is an enormous place. It's easy for one woman to disappear. No one will find you until it's too late."

She refused to answer him. What was the point? Lorenzo, Matias, and Maria didn't know the Fortress operatives, especially Sawyer, like she did. They would never give up. Sawyer would tear the world apart to find her. She knew that like she knew the sun would rise tomorrow morning. Whether she would be alive to see the new day dawn was anyone's guess.

Lorenzo laughed. "Oh, this will be fun. You're a stubborn one."

He had no idea.

Throughout the drive, the man held her pinned to his side and continually trailed his fingers through Janie's hair and along her neck, circling the bite mark he must have made. Although she showed no outward sign of the revulsion she felt, Janie's skin crawled everywhere he touched her. An intimidation tactic, one designed to make her feel helpless and hopeless. She refused to give him the satisfaction of knowing he scared her. More than once on the drive, Lorenzo bit her neck in the same place and whispered in her ear how she tasted like his favorite candy.

Ninety interminable minutes later, Matias turned off onto a side road and followed a winding gravel and dirt path deep into the countryside.

Despite Janie's attention to her surroundings, she wouldn't be able to find her way out of this area without help. Hopefully, Maria and her brother and cousin wouldn't check her for weapons. If they did, she'd lose every advantage she had to protect herself until the Texas Team found her.

Another thirty minutes passed before Matias exited a forest to stop at the gates of a large compound.

Janie stared at the dense bars of the front gate and the thick concrete walls surrounding the complex of buildings. Even if she escaped her captors, she had nowhere to go unless she found an unguarded exit.

Her resolve hardened. She wasn't giving up, no matter how bleak the circumstances seemed. Holding on was the only option. She wanted a future with Sawyer Chapman. He'd promised, and she was collecting on it.

Two guards at the gate peered into the vehicle. Satisfied, they opened the gate and allowed the vehicle to pass into the compound. Matias drove to a large building in the center of the compound and parked. He and Maria climbed out. She hurried into the building, leaving Janie on her own with the two goons.

Matias opened the back door, reached inside and hauled Janie out. Lorenzo joined his cousin. Each of the men grasped one of her arms and marched her toward the building.

Inside, they headed down a long hallway and stopped outside a closed door. From inside, Maria's laughter sounded muffled.

Lorenzo knocked on the door and turned the knob when told to enter, and pushed the door open.

Inside the room, Maria's arms were twined around a man's neck. She sneered when she saw Janie. "Look, sweetheart. Your guest has arrived." She lowered her arms.

The man turned to stare at Janie.

Her blood ran cold at the sight of Diego Hernandez.

Chapter Thirty

Sawyer groaned and batted at the hard hand shaking him. His head felt as though it weighed two tons. And the headache? Unspeakable pain that made him want to puke.

"You with me?" Jesse asked.

"Head hurts," he muttered.

"Yep. Me, too."

"What happened?"

"Based on what I saw on the security footage, we were pistol whipped by Lorenzo Reyes."

And just like that, the fog cleared. "Janie?" Sawyer struggled to sit up, his gaze taking in his teammates. Janie was nowhere to be seen. "Where is she?"

"Gone." Brody reached down and hauled Sawyer to his feet.

He swayed a few seconds, then steadied. His stomach lurched as though it planned to turn itself inside out. Luckily, his stomach stayed in place. "What do we know?"

"Not enough." Logan motioned for Sawyer to join him at the counter where he'd set up a laptop. Janie's sat phone and GPS jewelry were on the counter as well. "Watch."

The burning need to get out there and start looking for the love of his life boiled up inside Sawyer. "We need to go," he snapped. Standing here watching security footage wasn't on his agenda. He needed to find Janie. Now.

"Go where?" Max rested his hand on Sawyer's shoulder. "If we had more than a general direction, we would have hauled you into an SUV while you were still unconscious and followed Janie. We don't have enough information yet."

"Settle." Brody pointed at Sawyer. "We'll get her back. First, you need to see this." He nodded at Logan, who set the camera footage in motion.

Although he itched to get moving, he made himself watch the footage Logan had set up to run at a fast speed. His hands clenched into fists as he watched events play out, stunned at Janie's boldness in protecting him from further harm.

As he continued to watch the action unfold, he noticed her left hand. On reflex, he patted the inner pocket of his jacket and discovered it was empty. "She took one of my knives," he murmured.

Logan straightened. A slight smile curved his lips. "She armed herself. Tough lady."

"If the Reyes men don't discover the weapon," Max said.

Sawyer's eyes narrowed when on the screen, Lorenzo Reyes slapped Janie. "He's mine." Anger burned through him at the thug's treatment of her.

"If you get to him first," Logan murmured. He stopped the video feed a minute later when Maria and her family hustled Janie from the building.

"Did we get a plate number on that SUV?" Sawyer asked.

"I called it in to Zane. He's hacking into traffic cams as we speak."

"We're on a short clock. Hernandez has no reason to keep Janie alive once he has her in his hands." The thought of Janie not being in this world made Sawyer sick. He needed her.

"We know what's at stake, Sawyer, but we need a direction," Brody said. "As soon as we have one, we'll head out."

Not good enough. Janie was everything to him. He turned to Logan. "I asked you to search for Vatos Locos holdings in the area. Did you finish the search?"

His friend nodded. "There are several in the Middle Tennessee area."

"Are they close together or scattered?"

"Scattered."

Finding a direction didn't seem too hard a task. The question was how far out were the holdings and how many traffic cams would confirm the direction? Time was short. Janie's life could literally be measured in minutes if she was in Hernandez's hands now.

A chance. A slim one, but a chance. He'd take it.

Jesse handed him a capsule and a small bottle of water. "Take it. No arguments. You have to be functional, and I can all but see the pain in your head."

He swallowed the capsule and eyed the medic. "What about you?"

"Already took the meds for myself, too."

Sawyer turned to Logan. "Talk to me."

"Speculation only. It's not productive."

"Talk."

"They took your woman for a reason."

Sawyer stilled. He thought back through what they knew and what they didn't and realized his friend was correct. "If all they wanted was to snip off a loose end, they would have killed Janie, not gone to the trouble of taking her with them."

"Why do they want her?" Logan prompted. "If not to silence someone who can identify Hernandez, what do they want?"

"Why is she valuable to them?" Brody asked.

"Two reasons. One, she's a direct link to the team who killed so many of the gang members."

"And the second reason?" This from Max.

"Money."

His teammates glanced at each other, then back at him. "Explain," Brody said.

"David has a gambling problem. He owes a chunk of money to the gang."

Brody frowned. "Janie's a new small business owner. Does she have the money necessary to bail her brother out of debt?"

"Yes, and no. She has money left in trust from her Granny Irene. One stipulation, though, was that she couldn't give it to David.

Granny Irene left David a lump sum, and that's all he was to receive. If Janie tries to give more money to her brother, the will stipulates the rest of the money left in the trust goes to charity. She and her brother will both end up with nothing."

"Does David know that?" Jesse asked.

"He should."

"Doesn't mean his wife knows the truth," Logan said. "Especially if he didn't tell her everything."

"Or if David used Janie as a bargaining chip to get more time to come up with the money to pay off his debt," Max said, his expression grim.

"David is still unconscious, so we can't demand the truth from him." Sawyer dragged a hand down his face, coming up with solutions and discarding them almost as fast as they appeared. "If they took Janie for money, I'll give them every penny I have."

"You know it doesn't work that way," Brody murmured. "They'll take the money, then kill you and Janie both."

"With me by her side, Janie has a chance to survive. Alone, she has no chance at all. I don't care about the money. I love her, Brody."

"Think with your head, not your heart. Paying them won't solve the problem."

"I don't have a better solution. Do you?"

Silence descended on the group.

Logan's phone signaled an incoming message. He grabbed his phone and scanned the screen. "Zane sent the traffic cam footage."

"Put it on screen," Brody said. "Let's see where the vehicle went."

Once again, Logan set the footage to run at a higher speed.

One shot caught Janie in the backseat with Lorenzo. His arm was wrapped around her neck. Lorenzo was biting her.

Without thinking, Sawyer took a step toward the laptop, his fist clenched.

Jesse grabbed his arm. "Hold," he snapped. "We need to see it all."

"I'm going to kill Reyes." Sawyer's voice came out harsh. No one had the right to hurt Janie, especially a no-good thug like Lorenzo Reyes.

"Later. Right now, we need every bit of information we can get from the footage to save your woman."

Right. He shrugged off the medic's hold and nodded at Logan. Shoving his fury behind a concrete wall in his mind, Sawyer refocused on the screen.

He prayed his teammates could pick up clues to the destination of the Reyes family because Sawyer's attention was riveted to glimpses of Janie. Every time he saw her, good old Lorenzo was touching her. Janie's hair, face, neck, and ears were all favorite targets of the slimeball holding her so tightly against him.

Every so often, Sawyer noticed a look of smug satisfaction on Maria Moran's face. She was in full agreement with what was happening to Janie. That woman had a lot to answer for. If David was lucky, he'd live long enough to divorce Maria. Janie must be devastated at the betrayal by her sister-in-law.

He frowned. Was Maria behind the plot to kidnap Janie? If so, did David have a say in the event planning before he arrived in Hartman? For Janie's sake, Sawyer hoped that wasn't the case. Despite David's treatment of her, she loved her brother.

Something on the screen caught his attention. "Freeze that."

Logan did as ordered.

"Back up five seconds." When the picture on the screen shifted to the one he wanted, Sawyer moved closer to the screen. He pointed to the right side of the picture. "Can you enhance that, Logan?"

When his friend did as requested, Sawyer studied the screen. "Clean that image. I think it's a road sign."

A moment later, the image on the sign became clearer. Highway 31. He turned to Logan. "Does that mean anything to you?"

"Maybe. There are two compounds in that direction. Depends on where they go from here."

"How many more traffic cam clips do we have to watch?" Brody asked.

"Two."

"Let's see them. We'll decide what to do once we've seen the footage."

Logan set the first clip in motion. Another quick shot of Janie plastered up against Lorenzo, her expression one of fear. Lorenzo's mouth was against Janie's ear.

The last traffic cam footage showed Maria turned around in her seat to watch her cousin paw Janie. The clip ended seconds later.

"That's it?" Sawyer asked. "No more footage?"

"None." Logan glanced up, a smile beginning to curve his mouth.

Hope blossomed inside him. "What is it? Share with the class, Fletcher."

"I know where they took Janie."

#

Chapter Thirty-One

Diego Hernandez frowned as he stared at Janie. He glanced at the Reyes cousins. "What is she doing here?"

The two men exchanged puzzled glances. "You wanted her brought to you," Matias said.

"Who told you that?"

Matias's gaze flickered to Maria. "I thought you wanted Janie here, sir. If I misunderstood, I apologize."

Hernandez's expression hardened as he turned to Maria. "You did this?"

The other woman swallowed hard. "I thought having her here would please you."

"I don't need another woman in my life."

Anger flickered in Maria's eyes. "Of course not. This whole thing is David's fault. I thought the trust-fund money would make the trouble you've experienced worth the hassle he's put you through."

"You thought adding another layer of problems would be a good thing? You told me she has friends, specifically a boyfriend. Do you think he'll forget about her?"

"He doesn't matter, baby. Sawyer is nothing. He'll never find her. He does not know where she is. Besides, we made her leave her phone and jewelry behind as though she had changed her mind about being with him."

"Does he know who took her?"

Maria grew pale.

Hernandez cursed and backhanded Maria so hard she fell, sprawling on the floor.

"Diego." Tears poured down her cheeks. "Please, don't be angry with me. I thought you would be happy."

"Not your job, woman. Now, I'll have another mess to clean up besides the hijacking. That was also your idea, was it not?"

"To get the money David owes you."

"And the mess you made of the situation with your husband?"

"How was I to know the men wouldn't do the job right?"

Janie's heart sank. Maria had arranged to kill David. How could she betray the man she professed to love?

"Go to my room," Hernandez snapped. "I will deal with you in private."

Maria scrambled to her feet and rushed from the office.

Once the door closed behind her, Matias cleared his throat. "Sir...."

The boss cut him off with a wave of his hand. "Silence." Hernandez glared at Janie. "You've been nothing but trouble since the moment I laid eyes on you, Ms. Moran. Did my woman and her family blindfold you for the journey, at least?"

Oh, man. This definitely wasn't good for any of them. "No, sir."

He closed his eyes and sighed. "Matias, you took her phone, correct?"

"Yes, sir. I swear." Maria's brother stood straighter. "No one will find her."

"At least you did something right." He sounded disgusted as he turned his attention back to Janie. "What am I going to do with you, Ms. Moran?"

"Take me back to Hartman and turn me loose. Simple solution to your problem."

He sighed. "If only the answer was that easy, but you know I cannot do that."

"A girl can hope."

His lips curved slightly before he sobered. "I will consider options. In the meantime, you will be my guest." He glanced at the Reyes cousins. "Take her to the training building and lock her in one of the cells. I'll decide what to do with her later. Report back to me as soon as you have secured Ms. Moran."

Janie's stomach knotted. The description of the holding area sounded a lot like what she'd endured in Mexico. Man, she hoped she was wrong. Those hours before Sawyer and his teammates rescued her were horrendous. She never wanted to repeat them.

"Yes, sir." Lorenzo gripped her upper arm again and propelled her from the office with Matias on her other side.

Once they were outside, Lorenzo glanced at Matias. "We're in deep trouble, cousin."

Maria's brother scowled. "I know. I thought we were following Diego's orders. I didn't know Maria had set this whole thing in motion. I should have, the manipulative little witch."

"Wouldn't have been so bad if everything had worked out like she said it would," Lorenzo muttered. "But she lied, Matias. We'll be lucky if the boss doesn't kill us all."

"She doesn't have to worry." Matias sounded bitter. "She's carrying Diego's baby. We're the ones who will pay. He doesn't tolerate failure."

"You could let me go," Janie said.

Lorenzo snorted. "That would lead to us being dead sooner. No thanks, baby. I'd rather roll the dice on Diego's good will than know for certain I will die."

Matias slid his cousin a glance. "You could offer to take Janie off his hands."

Wait. What? No, that was a terrible idea. She needed to stay here in this compound until Sawyer and his friends arrived. If Lorenzo moved her to yet another location, Janie's chance of being found before it was too late dropped to zero.

Speculation lit Lorenzo's gaze as he thought over Matias's suggestion. "We both get what we want that way," he murmured. "It might work. We'll see what mood he's in when we return to his office. I would enjoy training this one."

Janie quelled her rising panic. She'd find a way to stay in this compound or, better yet, escape and contact Sawyer. Whatever she had to do to stay alive and get back to the man she adored was her next course of action.

When they arrived at the front door of a building on the edge of the compound, Matias unlocked the door and the two men ushered Janie inside. They escorted her upstairs to the last room on the right.

Lorenzo shoved her inside. He gave her a hard look. "Turn around."

Her stomach knotted. "Why?" Before she could draw in a breath, the man slapped her. Tears stung her eyes.

"Do as you're told. Turn around."

Afraid he would continue to hit her and cause her eyes to swell shut, Janie turned around.

Rough hands yanked her arms behind her back. Seconds later, she felt a thin plastic strip circle her wrists.

"Climb on the bed and lie down," Lorenzo ordered. "Now." After she complied, he folded his arms across his chest. "If you remain quiet, I won't gag you. If I hear anything from you at all, I will not be happy. Do you understand?"

Janie swallowed hard. His threat was hard to miss. She nodded.

"The door will be locked. You're on the second floor. There's nowhere to go. Get some rest." He smirked. "If things go like I want, you'll need it. Neither one of us will sleep much." After a long look, Lorenzo glanced at his cousin and inclined his head toward the corridor.

They left the room and locked the door behind them, leaving her trussed up like a turkey awaiting slaughter.

Janie shivered. Bad analogy. She waited a few minutes to be sure Lorenzo and Matias were gone. When she heard nothing, Janie rolled onto her side and worked her way into a sitting position.

She wiggled her wrists. The plastic flexed but didn't loosen. Too bad the Reyes men were skilled at using zip ties.

Janie felt sure Sawyer could free his hands with no problem. Unfortunately, she didn't have the same knowledge or skill.

She did, however, have the knife she'd taken from Sawyer's pocket. If she was careful, she could cut the plastic and free herself, hopefully without slicing her wrists.

Since she didn't know if she was in the building alone, Janie would have to exercise caution in getting the knife. If the weapon fell on the hardwood floor, anyone in the building would hear and investigate.

Thinking through her options, Janie scooted to the center of the bed and twisted to the side so she could grasp the edge of her zippered hoodie. She tugged and shook the fabric until Sawyer's knife dropped to the bed.

She studied the weapon for a moment. The knife required pressure on a side button before the blade would release. If she was lucky, the knife wouldn't spring back and cut her fingers or palm.

No other choice. She could either figure out a way to use Sawyer's knife or lay back down and wait for the Reyes cousins to tell Janie about her fate.

She scowled. That wasn't happening. She needed to get out of here before Diego decided what to do with her.

Janie wiggled and scooted until she grasped the knife in her right hand. Her thumb found the button to release the blade. Holding her breath, she pushed the button.

Nothing happened.

Dismayed, she tried again. Still nothing. She knew the knife must open somehow. Sawyer wouldn't carry a defective weapon.

She considered the problem for a minute. What if this wasn't a button to push but one to slide? After gripping the knife handle gingerly and positioning the weapon as far from her body as possible, Janie slid the button to the side.

The blade released, slicing through the hem of her hoodie. She breathed a sigh of relief. At least she hadn't sliced her skin.

Adjusting her grip on the knife, Janie eased the tip of the blade under the zip tie and went to work. After long minutes and a few slips ending with nicked skin, the plastic fell away from her wrists. Yes!

Relieved that she'd accomplished the first step of her goal, Janie took a moment to catch her breath. She eased her hands to the front, wincing at the pain from shifting her arms to a normal position.

That's when she saw her forearms. Multiple scratches marred the smooth surface. At least she hadn't sliced a vein in her bid for freedom. These scratches would heal in time.

Janie rubbed her shoulder joints to increase the blood flow and ease the ache, then surveyed the room. A door stood ajar to the left. Closet or bathroom?

Gripping the hilt of the knife, she rose and crossed the room to the door. Pushing it open, she peered inside a small bathroom. Janie examined the door. No lock.

She scowled. Of course not. Besides, from the looks of the aged wood, one good kick and the door would fly open.

The room had a window facing the back of the building. If she was lucky, guards assigned to the compound would focus more on the front rather than the back.

Janie wished she had Sawyer's knowledge of all things security. What if the compound had security cameras stationed around the area? Unless the cameras were blindingly obvious, she wouldn't notice them. She'd have to be fast and hope the guards were slow.

Next task. Could she escape this building? Her hand tightened around the knife hilt. No other option if she wanted a life with Sawyer.

In case a guard looked up at the bathroom window, Janie stood to the side and eased aside the curtain just enough to see outside.

She studied the options. Few. No convenient tree grew right outside the window. No ladder left against the wall.

Janie crossed to the other side of the window and looked for an escape route.

Nothing.

She could try to jimmy the lock on the door and escape downstairs, but how soon would the Reyes cousins return to the building? They might catch her.

For that matter, she didn't know if a guard had been left inside the building to make sure she didn't escape. She had to decide soon or risk having someone discover she'd escaped the zip tie with a knife.

That meant she had two choices. Try to unlock her bedroom door and take her chances of being caught inside the building or escape through a window.

Door first, she decided. If she couldn't escape that way, she'd have no choice but to go out a window despite her room being on the second floor.

Janie returned to the bedroom and walked to the door. She listened for a moment to be sure no one was standing guard right outside the door. When she heard nothing, she gently twisted the knob. It didn't give.

Sawyer's knife had been handy with the zip tie. Wonder if it would work on jimmying a locked door? Only one way to find out.

After another moment of listening for any movement outside the door, Janie slid the blade between the door and the jamb's striker plate. She drew the knife down until it bottomed out on the door latch. She swept the end of the knife and slowly pushed the latch inward, working until the bolt slid out of the jamb.

Breathing a sigh of relief, Janie pulled open the door and peered into the hallway. Clear.

Hoping she wasn't making a huge mistake, she pulled the door to her room closed. The latch caught. So, whatever happened, she couldn't retreat to the room for safety. Hopefully, the locked door would slow down the Reyes men a few more seconds and give her time to find a hiding place.

With quiet steps, Janie made her way downstairs to the first floor. So far, no sounds to indicate she had company in the building. Excellent. If her luck held, she'd escape.

And then what? The question stopped her in her tracks. She couldn't march into the compound. How would she escape into the countryside?

Not only that, Janie didn't have a clue where she was. The Reyes cousins had driven her miles off the main road to reach this compound.

One thing at a time. She'd figure it out as she cleared each hurdle. First thing to do was get out of this building before the Reyes cousins found her and locked her up again without Sawyer's knife.

Janie walked to the back of the building, trying to stay away from windows. She grasped the knob of the back door.

Gunfire erupted in the compound.

She froze.

A second later, Janie heard someone shove a key into the lock at the back door. She scrambled back and raced from the kitchen and collided with Lorenzo Reyes.

He scowled, gripping her arms in a painful hold. "How did you get out of the room?"

Behind her, Matias said, "Later. If you want to keep her, get her out of here."

Keep her? Panic exploded inside Janie. She had to get away from Reyes. Distraction. That's what she needed. "What's going on? Who's shooting?"

"Let's go." Lorenzo propelled her toward the back door. "If you fight me, you'll regret it." Without giving her a chance to do anything except comply, the man dragged her toward the compound wall.

To the left was an iron gate. Maria's cousin held up an access card in front of the scanner and the gate swung open far enough for them to slip through the opening. The gate locked behind them.

"Where are we going?" Janie slowed her pace as much as possible without being blatant about it.

"Shut up," Lorenzo snapped, voice low.

"Please, tell me what's happening."

"You're coming with me. That's all you need to know."

"I thought Diego wanted me locked up."

"Until he decided what to do with you. He gave you to me." Lorenzo forced her to move faster as he grabbed his weapon and hustled her deeper into the woods.

Her blood ran cold. "Why are we running away from the compound?"

"We have unwanted visitors." His grip tightened. "You're mine. I'm not giving you up."

"Sawyer is here, isn't he?"

Lorenzo cursed. "He shouldn't have been able to find you. It doesn't matter. He won't stop me from taking you. You belong to me now."

"Let me go, Lorenzo. You can still get away if you leave me here."

"Shut up."

"He'll never stop looking for me. When he finds me, you'll die. Is that what you want?"

Maria's cousin stopped suddenly and spun to face her. "If you don't shut your mouth, I'll knock you out and carry you out of here. I don't tolerate mouthy women. You're mine until I grow tired of you. Do you understand?"

"You have a death wish."

His expression dissolved into one of fury. He backhanded her, sending Janie sprawling on the forest floor. "Last warning, Janie. Shut your mouth. I enjoy hurting women. Give me one more reason, and I'll show you why women fear me."

She fell silent, watchful. Delay was one thing. Getting injured would seriously hamper her escape.

With a slight nod of satisfaction, Lorenzo clamped his hand around her wrist and yanked Janie to her feet and into motion again.

Before they'd gone over ten feet, a woman dressed in black emerged from behind a large tree. The gun in her hand was pointed at Lorenzo.

Chapter Thirty-Two

"Where?" Sawyer demanded, his gaze locked on Logan. The mission clock ticked in his head. If he didn't find Janie in the next few hours, she could be lost to him forever.

His jaw tightened. That would not happen. He loved her and would tear apart the world to find her.

"Maria and the Reyes cousins took Janie to Chestnut Springs."

He stared. "Chestnut Springs?" That made little sense.

Brody scowled. "That's two hours from here in the middle of nowhere. If you're wrong...."

"Janie's dead." Logan's expression was grim. "I know."

"You said the Reyes men could have taken her to two locations." Jesse folded his arms. "How do you know Chestnut Springs is the right one?"

Logan turned back to his computer and brought up a map of the area. "The last known location of the target vehicle is here." He pointed to a red dot on the map. "The next traffic cam should have picked them up here." He pointed at a green dot. "They never passed that camera. The only Vatos Locos compound near there is Chestnut Springs. The Reyes cousins and Maria must have turned off the main road between those cameras."

He tapped the section, and the map magnified. "One of the Vatos Locos compounds is here. The only way to get to the area is on this road." Logan pointed. "Since we heard about a Vatos Locos VIP coming to Hartman, I've been monitoring chatter on the dark web. Much of it is centered on the Chestnut Springs area. They took Janie to that compound, Sawyer. How long she'll remain there or remain alive is anyone's guess."

"Gear up," Brody said. "I have a call to make." He walked outside.

Max said, "I'll get your Go Bag. Save your strength and save your argument. You'll need every second of recovery time, and it still won't be enough."

Instead of wasting time arguing, he told Max where the Go bags were. His friend returned a minute later with Go bags plus Jesse's mike bag. "Pack heavy."

Sawyer donned his gear, starting with his bullet-resistant vest. Layer by layer, he added more weapons and slipped his communication device into his ear.

Brody returned. "We're set. Maddox is rerouting a helicopter to the airport. Another team is meeting us at the rendezvous coordinates."

"Who?" Sawyer asked.

"Artemis."

The knots in his gut eased slightly. Nice. Those women were lethal.

Brody took less than two minutes to suit up. "Let's roll. Max, drive Sawyer's SUV. Jesse, ride with them." He held up a hand when Sawyer opened his mouth to protest. "Save it. No one wants a concussed driver on the road."

"Fine." It wasn't, but what choice did he have? His primary goal was to reach Janie before Hernandez or one of his cronies hurt her. He tossed Max his keys.

The team loaded up in two SUVs and headed for the Hartman Airport. Ten minutes after they arrived, a helicopter landed on the pad close to their vehicles.

The rotors continued to spin as they ran to the helo and boarded. Once they were strapped in, the pilot lifted off and headed for Chestnut Springs.

"How long will we be in the air?" Sawyer asked the pilot.

"About 40 minutes." Jake Sikorsky glanced over his shoulder. "Maybe less if we have a good tailwind. The boss told me your girlfriend was kidnapped. I'm sorry, buddy."

"Me, too."

"I'll do what I can to cut down on the flight time."

Sawyer lapsed into silence, running through various scenarios in his head. None of them were good. If anything happened to Janie, he would take out as many of the gang as he could. He didn't care about the boss's orders to stay under the radar while on US soil. Nothing mattered but Janie. He didn't want to live without her.

Twenty-five minutes into the flight, Brody checked his phone and glanced at Sawyer. "Artemis is on site. Everything is quiet."

Wouldn't stay that way when they discovered the Fortress teams. "Have they seen Janie?"

A slight head shake. "They've split up and are watching every part of the compound. If Hernandez moves Janie now, Artemis will see it. They'll do what they can to protect her."

Sawyer's hands clenched around his rifle and willed the helo to fly faster.

Soon, the pilot said, "We'll reach the landing zone in two minutes."

"Copy that." Brody turned to the rest of the team. "Check your comm devices." When everyone had checked in, he called Zane. "We're one minute out. Join the loop."

A minute later, Zane said through their earpieces, "Artemis is looped in as well. Maddox also has Durango on standby in the area if you need them."

"Copy that," Brody said.

"Copy," a female voice murmured.

"Iona, have you seen the Reyes cousins?" Brody asked.

"Affirmative. No sign of either woman."

"Janie is the priority, not Maria," Sawyer said. He refused to apologize when Brody glared at him for breaking protocol. Too many people speaking on the comm loop would create confusion.

"Roger that," Iona replied, voice soft.

They maintained radio silence for the rest of the flight. As soon as the helicopter touched down, the Texas Team opened the side door and hopped out. Once they were out of danger, Jake lifted off and flew to a nearby location to wait for word from the team.

"We're on the ground, Iona," Brody murmured. "Rendezvous in ten minutes."

"Copy."

Brody motioned for the team to move out. As they jogged toward the compound, Sawyer and the others scanned the area, looking for perimeter defenses.

Logan held up a fist.

The team froze.

Brody glanced at Max and pointed to a camera secured to a tree fifteen feet away.

Max circled around to get behind the tree, shimmied up the trunk, and disabled the camera. The gang would know something was wrong, but Logan didn't have time to create a loop. Hopefully, the gang would assume the problem was some kind of technical malfunction.

When he finished, Max came down the tree trunk. "I don't think the camera caught sight of us, but I can't be sure."

A nod from Brody, then, "Let's move. The faster we reach our destination, the better. If they saw us, let's not give them time to prepare for an assault."

Although running made Sawyer's head hurt worse, he sucked it up and ran full tilt with his teammates.

Minutes later, they arrived at the rendezvous site to find Iona, leader of Artemis, waiting for them.

"Sit rep," Brody said.

"Something is going on. Not sure what yet. The rest of the team stayed in place to keep watch for your girlfriend, Sawyer."

"Still nothing?"

Sympathy filled her eyes as she shook her head. "We would have told you if we'd seen her. We know how important she is to you." Iona turned her attention to Brody. "How do you want to approach this?"

He sighed. "If it was night, I'd use infrared to find Janie. Since that's not an option, we'll have to do it the hard way."

"Breach and search?"

A nod.

Another woman broke into the comm feed. "Iona, I think I found Sawyer's woman."

Iona tapped her earpiece. "Location, Teagan?"

"A building at the back of the compound. The Reyes cousins left together a few minutes ago. I saw a curtain move on the second floor. Whoever is inside the building is being very careful not to be seen."

"We need visual confirmation before we launch the distraction."

"Copy that."

Sawyer tapped his earpiece. "Zane, can you get us a satellite image of the compound?"

"Working on it." His fingers tapped on the keyboard, then, "Coming now."

Texas Team and Iona grabbed their phones. "Where is the building?" Sawyer asked her.

She studied the photo for a minute and pointed. "Here. The wall is close to the building. Is your woman an athlete?"

He smiled. "Nope."

"She won't be climbing the wall without help. A gate's back there as well. We can disable the locking mechanism. Access is key card."

Brody studied his phone screen for a moment, then said, "All right. This is what we're going to do." After he laid out his plan, he glanced around. "Anyone see holes in the plan?" When no one voiced a concern, he said, "Iona, if you or your teammates see an imminent threat to Janie, I want to know about it. Understood?"

"Copy that."

Brody slid his phone away. "Move out."

They covered the distance between the rendezvous point and the compound in minutes. Brody gave the signal for his team to scatter, and Sawyer headed for the back of the compound.

He activated his earpiece as he skirted bushes and scanned for roaming guards and more security measures. "Teagan, heading your direction now," Sawyer murmured.

"Copy."

He'd covered two hundred feet when someone brushed up against a bush and kicked a rock, muttering curses. Sawyer slipped behind the cover of a large tree and waited. Despite his driving need to get to Janie, he couldn't let this guy continue tromping through the woods and stumble across one of the other members of the Texas Team or Artemis. He didn't have to wait long.

A man dressed in jeans, a black t-shirt, and tactical boots walked into view, scowling down at his phone. He shoved it into his pocket as he passed Sawyer's position.

Sawyer slipped out behind him and wrapped his arm around the gang member's neck, putting him in a sleeper hold. The guy was out in less than ten seconds. He made quick work of cinching his wrists and ankles with zip ties and slapping a piece of duct tape over his mouth to keep him quiet.

He activated his comm device. "One down." Sawyer resumed his journey to the back of the compound, stopping twice more to handle roving guards.

He returned to a job to cover the remaining distance between himself and Janie when Teagan broke into the comm chatter.

"Janie's in trouble. I don't have a shot. Permission to create a diversion?"

"Go," Brody said. "Sawyer, go."

"Copy." Weapon in hand, he ran. No need to work around the security cameras now. Vatos Locos would know Fortress was on the scene in seconds.

Rifle fire broke the silence of the woods. In the compound, shouts and curses peppered the air as much as return fire from handguns and rifles.

"Lorenzo Reyes has Janie," Teagan reported. "They're leaving the compound on foot."

Sawyer pushed himself harder. "Location?"

She gave the coordinates. "No shot, Sawyer. Iona?"

"Track and maintain a visual."

"She's priority," Sawyer said. "Whatever it takes, don't let him escape with her. I'm two minutes out."

"Copy."

A ball of ice formed in his stomach as Sawyer raced toward the coordinates Teagan reported as she kept pace with Reyes and Janie.

Minutes later, she hissed. "Reyes hit her. Orders?"

"Stop him now," Sawyer snapped. Seconds later, he heard Reyes curse.

"Who are you?" the thug shouted.

"Your worst nightmare," Teagan said.

"Get out of my way or I'll kill you."

"I can't let you leave, buddy."

"What are you talking about?"

"I have orders to stop you from taking the woman. The person who gave the orders will be seriously ticked off if I fail. I don't want to face his wrath. If you're smart, you won't either."

"He's not my problem, but you are. You'll be dead in two seconds if you don't get out of my way. When I shoot, I don't miss. Move."

Weapon up, Sawyer moved into sight. "I don't think so, Reyes."

Reyes dragged Janie in front of his chest as a human shield and pressed the barrel of his weapon to Janie's temple. "You. I should have known. How did you find us?"

"Drop your weapon, Reyes." He didn't dare let himself look at Janie. A distraction could be the death of them all. "Now."

"She's mine. Diego gave her to me. I leave with her now or she dies."

"I don't like those options." Janie was wheezing. Reyes was holding her too tight, choking her. "Baby, turn your head to the right."

"You talk to me," Reyes snapped. "I own her. I speak for her."

Janie turned her head, and the wheezing subsided. She slid her hand into the pocket of her hoodie. What was she doing?

Afraid to give away her movements, Sawyer kept his expression neutral as his woman pulled out the knife she'd taken from his pocket. What was she planning? Whatever it was, he needed to provide a distraction to cover her movements.

He took two steps forward. "You're not leaving here, Reyes. This is your last chance to come out of this alive. I'm not letting you leave with her. You'll have to go through me to take Janie."

An ugly smile curved the other man's mouth. Reyes did exactly what Sawyer wanted him to do. He moved the barrel of the pistol from Janie's head, pointed it at Sawyer, and fired.

The impact of the bullet sent Sawyer sprawling on the ground. He sucked in a breath. Oh, man. That was going to leave a bruise. Thank God for bullet-resistant vests.

"No!" Janie pressed the button to release the blade and slammed the steel to the hilt in Reyes's thigh.

Reyes screamed and reached down to yank the blade from his body.

Janie dropped to the ground and rolled away from her captor.

Reyes cursed, aimed his weapon at Sawyer again. "Get back here or I'll shoot him a second time."

Teagan threw her knife at the other man, her aim true. A split second later, another blade buried itself in Reyes's other thigh. He screamed again, clutching the hilt of the second knife.

Ignoring the pain in his chest, Sawyer scrambled to his feet and covered the distance between him and Reyes at a dead run and tackled him. Two rabbit punches to the gut and one right cross, and Reyes was out.

Sawyer wasn't finished punishing the man who had taken Janie from him. He continued to pummel Lorenzo Reyes until his face was a pulpy mess. He wanted to kill the man who had hurt the woman he loved.

A small hand clamped on his shoulder. "Sawyer, I've got him," Teagan said. "Ease up. He's not worth the cost you'll pay if you kill him. Go check on Janie."

Janie. Sawyer shook his head to clear the tunnel vision, leaped to his feet, and raced to Janie's side. She was still sprawled on the ground. Was she hurt worse than he thought? He couldn't look at her when Reyes used her as a human shield. Sawyer knew himself well. If he'd seen Janie's injuries, he would have lost his focus.

Gently, he moved Janie to her back and froze when he finally saw her bruised and swollen face and the split lip. "Oh, baby."

Fury boiled up inside Sawyer. He turned his head to glare over his shoulder at the culprit and started to climb to his feet. Lorenzo Reyes was a dead man.

"Sawyer!" Tears trailed from Janie's eyes. "You're alive. I thought Lorenzo had killed you."

"I'm wearing a vest." He kissed her forehead and again shifted his focus to the man who hurt Janie. "Give me a minute. I'm not finished with Reyes."

A soft hand clamped over his wrist. "No. Stay with me," Janie murmured.

His gaze swung back to the woman he needed more than his next breath. "He hurt you. No one hurts you and gets away with it."

She smiled slightly and winced as her lip bled more heavily. "I think you hurt him worse than he did me. Stay with me, love."

He settled by her side again. "I reserve the right to revisit the plan to make him pay. He's earned it."

Janie laughed. "I think he'll be in jail."

"Doesn't mean I can't get to him," he muttered, glaring again at the unconscious man.

"I don't want to visit my husband in jail. You hear me?"

Laughter from the Fortress operatives sounded over Sawyer's comm device. He brushed his mouth over hers, light as a feather. What he wouldn't give to take the kiss he wanted so badly. Soon, he consoled himself. When Janie's mouth was healed. "Yes, ma'am."

"Let's finish this business and get out of here," Brody said. "All the alphabet agencies and local cops will be here in a few minutes. Jesse, check Janie while we tie up the garbage."

"Copy," operatives from both teams replied.

Jesse emerged from the trees with his mike bag and knelt by Janie's side. "Let me check you for injuries, then we'll get out of here, all right?"

"I hope you have cold packs in your bag."

"Restocked everything after we flew in from Mexico." He winked at her. "I have you covered, sugar."

"Thank goodness."

Sawyer wrapped his hand around Janie's and waited in silence while the medic checked her for injuries.

His throat tightened and his eyes burned. What if she had internal injuries? He should have the helo pilot take them straight to a hospital. If he did, though, Sawyer bet the medical staff would report her injuries to the authorities, and he'd be the prime suspect in her assault. They'd separate him from her.

Not happening. He was never leaving her side again if he could help it.

Two minutes later, Jesse sat back on his heels. "I'm seeing multiple bruises and those scratches on your wrists. Janie, we're going to ask you a few questions and we need you to answer them with complete honesty, no matter how uncomfortable it makes you feel. Got it?"

Her hand tightened around Sawyer's. "All right. What do you want to know?"

Sawyer knew what was coming. He hadn't allowed himself to dwell on the possibility, but the time for denial was over. Whether or not the worst had happened, nothing would change how he felt about this woman. "Look at me, sweetheart."

Her gaze locked on his. "What is it, Sawyer? What's wrong?"

"I love you, Janie. No matter what you tell us, nothing will change how much I adore you. And by the way, we're getting married as soon as I can arrange it. I'm not waiting any longer. I know I promised to give you time, but I almost lost you today. No matter what you tell us about your experience at the hands of the Reyes cousins, nothing will stop me from marrying you."

Tears filled her eyes. "Sawyer."

"Want me to do this?" Jesse murmured.

Sawyer shook his head, gaze still locked with Janie's. She was his. He'd walk through anything she faced, good or bad. They'd deal with it together as a team. He would always be there for Janie. "Were you unconscious after you were kidnapped?"

She stilled. "No."

Man, he hated to ask her these questions, hated more that they were necessary. For the sake of her health, though, he had to know the truth. "Second question, and this one is harder. Were you sexually assaulted after you were kidnapped?"

Janie's eyes widened. "No, Sawyer. I promise."

He lifted her hand and turned it to examine the scratches on her wrist and forearm. "These injuries resemble those I've seen on survivors of rape who fought their bonds and their attackers. How did you get these injuries, baby?"

"Your knife. My hands were secured behind my back with a zip tie. I tried to be careful, but the knife slipped several times. I give you my word, Sawyer, that none of the men touched me." She swallowed hard. "If Lorenzo had been successful in taking me away, he would have assaulted me." Tears spilled down her cheeks again. "You saved me."

His own eyes filled with tears at the relief he felt. He'd still love her no matter what, but convincing a traumatized Janie that he loved her beyond reason would have taken a while. Sawyer brushed her lips with his.

Jesse reached over and squeezed her free hand. "You did well, sugar. We're making you an honorary member of the Texas Team."

"Really?" She beamed at the medic.

"We saw the security footage from the shop. You protected me and Sawyer from further harm, took one of Sawyer's many knives, and were strong enough to use it when, under normal circumstances, you wouldn't hurt anyone. You are one tough lady, and we're proud to call you ours."

"Enough with the mushy stuff," Max complained. "Get a move on already. If we don't leave soon, I'll be late for a date with my wife."

Laughter sounded over the comm device. Sawyer smiled. "Max is complaining that we're taking too long. He has a date with Willow."

"Not to mention the law enforcement officials about to descend on us," Brody said dryly. "I'd rather skip that part of the program. We'll have to deal with the feds eventually, but I want to do it on our turf, not here."

"Yeah, yeah. We're moving." Sawyer helped Janie to her feet and swept her into his arms.

"I can walk," she protested. "You must hurt after being shot."

Jesse stopped him. "Where were you hit?"

"Vest. Only a bruise. I'll live." Janie was hurting and there was no need for her to suffer if he could prevent it. "I need to hold you, Janie. Let me."

Her arms tightened around his neck. "I love you, Sawyer."

"I love you, too, sweetheart."

"Get a move on," Logan groused. "Save the mush for later."

First step was to get Janie out of these woods before law enforcement stopped them. Second, Sawyer needed to have her checked out by a doctor he trusted. That meant a trip to Nashville. "Brody, have the helo pilot meet us at the landing zone. I want the doc on duty at Fortress to check Janie."

"Jesse?"

"I agree. We need to make sure she doesn't have internal injuries or fractures. Reyes was rough on her."

"I'm fine," Janie protested. "But Sawyer should see a doctor."

"I'll see the doctor if you will," Sawyer said.

"Dirty pool, Chapman."

"Deal with it, Moran. Besides, we need to do as much as we can to reduce the swelling and bruising on your face before your brother sees you. Otherwise, he'll think I'm responsible for your injuries."

"David," she murmured. "How will I tell him Maria is responsible for his injuries and mine?"

"Lead off with 'you're a lucky man, David,'" he suggested. If Maria had roamed free for much longer, she would have asked someone to finish the job of making her a widow.

"Good plan." She kissed his jaw. "David will need help to recover, love."

"Let's make sure you're all right first, then we'll tackle the rest of it, one step at a time. We'll handle everything together."

#

Chapter Thirty-Three

FBI Agent Layton Saunders glared at Sawyer and the rest of the Texas Team. "You should have waited for us to arrive on scene before you left. You used to be cops and know how law enforcement works. We have to interview witnesses and victims as soon as possible or they lose details." He jabbed a finger at Sawyer. "You're lucky I don't arrest you for interfering with an investigation."

"You'd have to arrest all of us," Brody said. "We put Janie's health and safety above everything else."

"If you arrest my team, you'll make an enemy of Fortress." Brent's eyes blazed with fury. "Do you really want that?"

Saunders's partner, Heath Lowell, frowned at Saunders. "You're wasting your breath, Layton. You know as well as I do Fortress is President Martin's choice for off-the-books missions. If you want to go through all the channels to bring this to his attention, you're on your own."

"They broke the law," Saunders fumed. "They're cowboys."

"Maybe. They also gave us Diego Hernandez wrapped in a bow along with his whole inner circle, and more information and proof is coming in every hour. We have enough to shut down the entire organization."

"We don't even know how they got their information."

"Do you care? I don't." Lowell turned back to Sawyer. "Start from the top. Once we finish with you and your team, you're free to go. We'll interview Ms. Moran as soon as the doctor is finished with her."

They thought they were going to dismiss him? Not happening. "I'm staying with Janie during her interview."

"That's not how we work," Saunders shouted.

"Tough." He wouldn't back down. "It's the only way you'll talk to Janie. Keep pushing, and you'll have not only me, but also one of our lawyers in the room as well."

"Back off, Layton," Lowell snapped. "That's an order."

Hands fisted, Saunders said through clenched teeth, "Yes, sir."

"Start from the beginning, Sawyer." Lowell flipped open a small notebook. "Once you finish, we'll get information from the rest of your team."

He drew in a deep breath and began. Sawyer censored details about the mission they'd finished before diverting to Mexico to free Janie. He clarified details when requested by Lowell. Otherwise, he shared the steps they'd taken to discover the identity of the missing passenger and the source of the threat to Janie.

When he related how Janie had been taken, Saunders snorted in disgust. Sawyer understood. He'd bear the blame for that failure for the rest of his life. Because of him, Janie had suffered needless injuries.

Once he finished, the interviewers turned to Brody and the rest of his teammates. While they talked, Sawyer frequently checked his phone. The doc should be finished with Janie soon. The only reason Sawyer had agreed to leave Janie in the clinic was because Teagan volunteered to stay with her every minute.

When Lowell finally began his interview with Jesse, Sawyer's phone signaled an incoming text. He checked the screen and rose.

"Where do you think you're going?" Saunders snapped. "We aren't finished with you."

Sawyer glanced at his boss. "The doc is finished with Janie."

"Go," Brent said.

"Wait a minute!" Saunders stood.

"Sit down, Layton," Lowell ordered. "Sawyer will return with Ms. Moran." He shifted his gaze to Sawyer. "Isn't that right?" His eyes held a subtle threat.

Depended on Janie's state of mind. If she was ready to talk, he'd return with her. Without a word, he left the conference room and went to the elevator. A minute later, he stepped out and turned left. Soon, he opened the clinic door and walked inside.

Teagan met him in the reception area. "She's shaken up, but fine."

"Something happen?"

"She had to tell the doctor everything that happened. Reliving the experience brought back the fear and trauma she endured." Teagan folded her arms. "I like her, Sawyer. Don't hurt her or screw this up. You hear me?" Left unsaid was the probability that Teagan would retaliate if Sawyer hurt her new friend.

He flinched. "Yes, ma'am. No worries. She's everything to me."

She punched him in the shoulder. "Make sure you treat her like she's a priceless gift. Need me to stay?"

"I've got her. Thanks for the help."

"Anytime, my friend. See you around." Between one beat and the next, Teagan was gone.

Cherry, the doctor's receptionist, stood. "This way, Sawyer. I think your girlfriend needs a hug."

"She can have as many as she wants."

"Chocolate cures everything, you know," she whispered.

His eyebrows rose. "Is that right?"

Cherry nodded. "My husband learned the secret years ago."

"Thanks for the tip." Sawyer followed her down the hall to one of the exam rooms.

"She's waiting in here." The other woman patted his arm. "Take good care of her. She's special."

"Believe me, I know. Thanks, Cherry."

Another pat, and she returned to her desk.

Sawyer knocked on the door and stepped inside.

Janie turned from staring out the window. "Sawyer." She ran into his open arms.

He wrapped his arms around her and held her against him. For long minutes, he trailed one hand up and down her back in a soothing motion. With the other hand, he cradled the back of her head, hoping the hold would help her feel secure. When her trembling stopped, he murmured, "Ready for one more hurdle?"

She wrinkled her nose. "Not really, but what choice do I have?"

"If you need to wait, I'll make sure you have time to regroup." No doubt the delay would tick off both agents, but Janie's wellbeing was more important than their interview.

Her lips curved. "I appreciate the potential save, but I don't think the feds would be happy with us."

"I don't care. My goal is to protect you, no matter what that looks like."

She kissed him lightly. "Thank you, Sawyer. I'd rather get the interview over with as soon as possible."

"All right. If you need a break, we'll take one together. The interview questions can wait a few minutes while you take a breather."

Together, they returned to the sixth floor conference room. All the men in the room stood when Janie walked inside.

Sawyer escorted her to the empty seat next to his. Once she was settled, the men around the table returned to their seats.

The FBI agents introduced themselves to Janie. Lowell flipped to a clean page in his notebook. "Do you need anything, Ms. Moran? Water, tea, coffee? We'll be here a while, and we want you to be as comfortable as possible."

"Water, please."

Jesse left the room and returned with two bottles of water. He placed them in front of Janie. "Staying hydrated will help," he murmured.

"Ms. Moran stays," Saunders said. "The rest of you, get out."

No one moved.

Sawyer should have known his teammates would remain to protect him and Janie. "Give it up, Saunders, and get on with the questions. You have one hour. After that, you'll have to wait until tomorrow."

"You aren't in charge of this investigation," he snapped.

His supervisor stared at Saunders. The junior agent turned a bright red and closed his mouth. When his colleague lapsed into silence, Lowell shifted his attention back to Janie. He smiled. "Ready, Ms. Moran?"

She nodded.

"May I call you Janie?"

"Please."

"I'm Heath. My partner is Layton. We're sorry to meet you under these circumstances, Janie, but we're glad you're safe. Tell us what happened from the beginning, all right? Start with the hijacking and go forward from there. We need every detail. Your boyfriend and his friends have given us a thorough picture of what happened based on their observations. To keep Hernandez in prison longer, we need your eyewitness testimony."

"Will I have to testify against him?"

"I would plan on it."

"We can protect you," Saunders said. "We have safe houses. I guarantee Hernandez will never find you."

Sawyer stiffened. "You're talking about witness protection." No way. Not without him. If he had to, he'd take a leave of absence and go with her, but he'd prefer Janie wasn't dependent on the feds for safety.

Saunders scowled. "You're willing to risk her life by letting her wander around town without protection?"

"If Janie needs witness protection, we'll put her in our security protection program," Brent said. "That's nonnegotiable, gentlemen. She will not be hidden with the Marshals."

Lowell held up his hand to quell the response from his partner. "Let's get on with the interview. We'll discuss security arrangements for Janie later. That all right with you, Janie?"

Under cover of the table, her hand wrapped around Sawyer's. "Yes." Her fingers were icy.

Sawyer sandwiched her hand between both of his, hoping to instill warmth. He looked at Lowell. "Go easy."

A slight nod from the agent, then the questions. Janie told them everything, starting with her rocky relationship with her brother, and took them through her rescue outside the compound.

"Let's go through it again," Lowell said. "I'll stop you when I need clarification on details."

"Fifteen-minute break first," Sawyer said and stood. He helped Janie to her feet. "We'll be back."

"Hey," Saunders protested. "No one gave you permission to leave with our witness."

He ignored the furious agent as he led Janie from the conference room. In the hall, he guided her toward the break room.

Once inside, he grabbed a chocolate bar and seated Janie on a comfortable leather sofa. "Rest here a minute. I'll make you tea."

Paper crinkled behind him, and Janie moaned. "Oh, Sawyer. This is perfect. How did you know I needed this?"

Score one for Cherry. He smiled. "Got a tip from a lady whose husband figured out the secret to helping her feel better. Now I know it works for you, too." He planned to keep chocolate on hand for his woman from now on.

Sawyer removed the cup of tea from the microwave, secured a lid on top, and sat beside her after handing her the tea.

"Thanks, love." After finishing the tea and her chocolate bar, Janie leaned her head against Sawyer's shoulder. "How much time do we have before we have to go back?"

"Enough. Take the time you need, Janie. You'll remember more details when you're not so tense and have a little food on your stomach."

He gave her as much time as he could without ticking off the agents waiting to finish the interview. When he couldn't wait any longer, he said, "We need to return to the conference room unless you're not up to answering more questions. If you're not, I'll stop the interview and we'll resume tomorrow."

She shook her head. "I don't want to drag out the interview. Let's finish this."

An hour later, the questions were answered, and the agents were gone. "You should rest, Janie," Brent said. "Until we're sure the threat to you is over, you can't go home or stay by yourself."

She groaned. "Come on, Brent. Texas Team needs to go back to their own lives."

"No. The only other option is for you to stay at my home."

Janie frowned. "Absolutely not. I won't bring danger to your doorstep. Your family means too much to me to put a target on their backs."

"Then you'll return to the safe house. The guys will trade off keeping watch."

"We'll be fine," Brody told her. "Trust me. Our wives and Jesse's girlfriend don't mind. One shift a night is much better than being gone for weeks at a time."

"All right. Please, tell the ladies I appreciate your help and the sacrifice they're making for my safety."

Max rose when Sawyer helped Janie to her feet. "I'll drive you to the safe house and take the first watch. Both of you need rest. You've been through an ordeal."

"My head is pounding," Sawyer admitted.

Janie turned. "Do you need to see the doctor before we leave?"

"He checked me out while the tech took X-rays of your ribs. I have a slight concussion and a pretty bruise on my chest. Otherwise, I'm fine. I'll be cleared for duty in a few days."

"What about you, Max? I thought you had a date with your wife."

"We changed it to a dinner date. She said she's looking forward to meeting you."

Janie turned back to Sawyer. "I still need to check on David."

"Simone hacked into the hospital records again," Jesse said. "There's been no change. Go to the safe house, rest, and use cold packs to help with the bruises and swelling." He winked. "Doctor's orders."

She saluted and allowed Sawyer to lead her from the conference room.

Chapter Thirty-Four

Janie paused outside her brother's hospital room the next morning. She'd spoken to the doctor and learned David was awake and asking for Maria. Although her brother's prognosis was good, the road to recovery would take many long months and included a lot of physical therapy. He couldn't go back to Chile soon.

She dreaded the next few minutes. How did you tell your brother that his wife had tried to kill him in order to be free to go to her lover, who might be the father of her baby? And to cap off the bad news, she had to tell David that he wouldn't be able to live on his own for a long time.

A powerful arm circled her waist. "How can I help?" Sawyer asked, voice soft.

Tears burned her eyes as she turned into his arms and hugged him. "You're already doing exactly what I need you to do. This will be hard. He hates depending on anyone. Now, he'll be surrounded by people until he's ready to live on his own. I also don't know if his company will hold his job."

"But he will recover. It's a miracle he's still alive, Janie. The details will work themselves out."

"I'm afraid he'll blame me."

"How can he? The people who set things into motion are in jail. You're as much a victim as he is."

"I don't know if he'll see it that way." Janie brushed his mouth with hers and stepped out of his embrace. "Come on. This won't be easier if I delay."

She knocked on the door and stepped inside the room. Her brother turned his head to stare at her, no expression on his face.

She tried not to let that rattle her as she walked to his bedside, with Sawyer at her side. "I'm glad you're awake, David. I've been so worried about you."

He struggled a moment, then said, "Why are you here?" His words were halting, as though he had to think hard to speak.

"To see you."

"Want Maria."

Her smile faded. "She can't come, bro."

"Why?"

"She's in jail."

He blinked. "No."

"I'm sorry."

"Lying."

Sawyer squeezed Janie's hand. "Let me," he murmured. "David, Maria is responsible for your attack. She asked men from Vatos Locos to kill you so she could get her hands on the money from your grandmother's trust fund, then she'd be free to go live with her lover."

"No."

"She's also responsible for the gang hijacking Janie's plane."

"Lies."

"Truth," he countered. "Look, man, I'm sorry, but we have proof. Maria wanted you dead."

David remained silent for a moment. "See her. Now."

"The feds have her in custody, where she'll stay until her trial. She's dangerous to you and to Janie."

Her brother turned his face away.

"I know this is hard to hear, but she kidnapped Janie yesterday morning and intended for her cousin Lorenzo to rape her, then kill her."

David's head snapped around. He glared at Sawyer.

"He's telling you the truth," Janie said. She took a chance and rested her hand on her brother's arm. "That's why my face is so bruised. Lorenzo hit me. If Sawyer and his teammates hadn't arrived when they did, I wouldn't be here. Sawyer saved my life, David."

Her brother's gaze slid to Sawyer, an unspoken question in his eyes.

"She saved my life, too. We'll tell you the entire story later. It's complicated and long."

"Has the doctor talked to you about your prognosis?" Janie asked.

"No."

She gently squeezed his arm. "You're going to recover, but you need several months of therapy to get there."

He shook his head. "No money."

"You're covered."

"How?"

"Granny Irene. While I'm not allowed to give you money from the trust fund, I may take money out to pay for your medical needs. I checked with the family lawyer to confirm."

"Job?"

"I'll call your employer and talk to the human resources department this afternoon. The main thing you need to focus on is your health."

"No place to go."

"You'll stay with us," Sawyer said. "That's another thing we need to talk about before the nurse kicks us out of here. Janie and I are getting married tomorrow." He lifted her left hand and showed David the engagement ring he'd purchased first thing that morning. "I'd like your blessing."

Silence, then, "If I say no?"

Janie's heart sank.

"I'll still marry her, but you'll break your sister's heart. I love her, David. You have my word of honor that I'll never hurt Janie. She'll always have first place in my heart and life."

"Want the money."

"No. I don't want money from her or her trust fund. I'm well paid for what I do, and I need nothing from Janie except her love. I'll take care of her and our children when we have them. Nothing in this world matters more to me than your sister."

David studied him for a moment. Finally, he said, "Okay."

"I have your permission to marry Janie?"

A slight nod.

The tears she'd been holding back now streamed down her cheeks. Janie bent and kissed her brother on the forehead. "Thank you. I have another question for you. No pressure, all right? Would you like to be present for the wedding?"

His forehead furrowed. "How?"

"We can get married here in your room. The doctor said he would allow Sawyer's teammates and Brent and Rowan into the room as long as the ceremony was short."

"Church."

"When you're better, you can walk me down the aisle for a formal wedding. However, we don't want to wait to get married, and this will allow us to move you into our house as soon as you're released."

"Too much work for you."

"Family is never too much work," Sawyer said. "We'd be honored to have you with us until you're ready to live alone. I'll bring in private nurses until you can handle things on your own. You're strong and stubborn. You'll be back on your feet and able to care for yourself before long."

"Sure?"

"We're positive. This is what we both want, David. Will you let us help?"

Another slight nod. "Thanks."

"I'm looking forward to getting to know you better over the next few months."

The door opened, and the nurse stepped in. "It's time to go. Mr. Moran needs to rest."

Janie squeezed David's arm again. "We'll be back tomorrow. Do what the nurses tell you. They'll call me if anything changes. If you want me to come back today, tell them and they'll call me."

"Wedding plans. Go."

"I love you, David. I'll see you tomorrow."

Outside in the hall, Janie beamed up at Sawyer. "You heard him. Wedding plans. Go."

He chuckled. "We have a lot of work ahead of us today."

"Want to change the plan?"

"Not a chance. I can't wait to slide a wedding band on your finger tomorrow. I love you, Janie Moran almost Chapman."

"I love you, Sawyer Chapman." She couldn't wait to see what tomorrow held and every day thereafter.

#

About the Author

Rebecca Deel is a preacher's kid with a black belt in karate. She teaches business classes at a private four-year college in Nashville, Tennessee. She plays the piano for her church, writes freelance articles, and runs interference for the family dogs. She's married to an amazing husband and is the proud mom of two grown sons. She delivers occasional devotions to the women's group at her church and conducts seminars in personal safety, money management, and writing. Her articles have been published in *ONE Magazine*, *Contact*, and *Co-Laborer*, and she was profiled in the June 2010 Williamson edition of *Nashville Christian Family* magazine. Rebecca completed her Doctor of Arts degree in Economics and wears her favorite Dallas Cowboys sweatshirt when life turns ugly.

Read more at rebeccadeelbooks.com.